Andrew M. Greeley

Younger Than Springtime

A TOM DOHERTY ASSOCIATES BOOK
NEW YORK

This is a work of fiction. All the characters and events portrayed in this book are either products of the author's imagination or are used fictitiously.

YOUNGER THAN SPRINGTIME

Copyright © 1999 by Andrew M. Greeley Enterprises, Ltd.

A Forge Book
Published by Tom Doherty Associates, LLC
175 Fifth Avenue
New York, NY 10010

www.tor.com

Forge® is a registered trademark of Tom Doherty Associates, LLC.

ISBN: 0-812-59026-0
Library of Congress Catalog Card Number: 99-22198

First edition: September 1999
First mass market edition: September 2000

Printed in the United States of America

0 9 8 7 6 5 4 3 2 1

In memory of Kurt Keisling

Charles's Love Story

1948–1949

Prelude

❧❧

"O'Malley," Father Pius, my hall rector, shouted at me, "that picture is evil. I forbid you to display it in this hall."

"It's not evil, Father," I said firmly. "It's no more evil than the picture of Eve in Michelangelo's *Last Judgment*."

I was in no mood for another fight with Father Pius. I had other problems on my mind. I had been thinking about what was I to do to help my friends Rizzo and Boland.

Farley Hall, late February of 1949. Father Pius was staring at the print with a mixture of fascination and horror, his face twisted into caricature by perhaps an inch and a half of naked womanly breast.

Lovely, graceful womanly breast.

"You're not a great artist!"

"She's a beautiful woman, however, just as the model for Eve was."

"She's *naked*!"

"No she's not," I insisted. "Look, down here in the corner you can see a bit of her swimsuit!"

"*Swimsuit!*"

"I admit that it's a two-piece ensemble, Father Pius, but it's really quite modest. So is she."

I was deliberately making trouble, as alas for me I had always done. Just as tacking her on the wall had been a deliberate exercise in baiting both Father Pius and everyone else in the hall.

However, Rosemarie was indeed really quite modest.

"Only whores wear two-piece swimsuits," he bellowed, falling into the trap I had laid for him.

"My mother wears a two-piece swimsuit, Father."

He tore the print from the wall. "I'll not tolerate it in this hall."

"That's my property you're destroying, Father."

"Remember"—he spun on me—"that you're on probation. One more violation and you're out and I mean *out*."

I was on probation because of the charge of drinking. But you don't drink, you say?

Right. But at Notre Dame in those days you could be threatened with expulsion for drinking even if you didn't drink.

"Be that as it may, Father, you have no right to destroy my property. I'll protest to the president."

He ripped the print into little pieces and threw them on the floor.

That picture of Rosemarie sealed my fate at Notre Dame. It also sent my life in a direction I had never intended, which I thought then I did not want, and which even now, all these years later, I don't fully understand. It won me my first prize as a photographer and bound me to Rosemarie in an intimacy that I'll never understand.

I have the picture in front of me today. It brings back a mix of bitter and sweet memories that I still cannot sort out. Pornographic it certainly is not. Next to the picture is the one I snapped when we were children at Lake Geneva. Same girl, a little younger, I tell myself—beautiful, mysterious, haunting. And haunted.

But I read that into the second picture. In fact, I consider the picture of Rosemarie now, a five-by-nine enlargement like that which had offended Father Pius. Completely different from the other shots I took that morning, it is framed just under the tops of her breasts, so that her bare shoulders, and wet black hair, could be that of a naked woman on the beach in early morning. She is no longer merely a pretty but ordinary girl. She is rather the Rosemarie of my imagination in those days, save in one important respect: while she is indeed mysterious and alluring, a fresh promise of abundant life, there is really no hint of doom in her wondrously erotic pose, as there had been in some of my earlier pictures of her. Rather, fresh from the water, excited by the touch of my fingers exhilarated by her swim and flattered by the camera's eye, Rosemarie is happy. More than happy, she is indestructible. Vulnerable, yes. Fragile, yes. But also indestructible.

I whistle to myself "Younger Than Springtime," which I also associate with the picture. She does look as young as early spring (in English poetry, not in Middle Western American reality).

1

That first summer after I came home from Germany was one of the worst times in my life. At first, I could not find a summer job, not even at O'Hanlon and O'Halloran, the accounting firm that had promised me work next summer. I was no longer the sergeant who knew how to get things done at the HQ of the First Constabulary Regiment in Bamberg. Rather I was an unemployed veteran, uneasy about the prospect of college. I still felt guilt about my German lover who had introduced me to passion and then disappeared after I had saved her and her mother and sister from the fate of women ''war criminals'' turned over to the Russians. I also longed for the pleasures of our love. Or lust. Or whatever it was. She still haunted my dreams, sometimes confused with my mother and my sister Peg and Rosie, my kind of foster sister.

Moreover, I had wasted my time in Bamberg, a picture-postcard medieval city out near the Bohemian Alps, only forty kilometers from the Red Army. Bamberg had eaten up two precious years of my life. I had joined the army to earn the right to a college education under the GI Bill because I had assumed that after the war the Depression (now called the Great Depression) would return and that my parents would not be able to afford college tuition for me.

I had been spectacularly wrong. When I was discharged, honorably enough, in the spring of 1948, America was in the midst of early phases of the greatest economic boom in its history, one that, despite some fits and starts, has continued for almost a half century. My father's architectural skills had made our family wealthy again. For him and my mother, the Depression was merely an unpleasant interlude that had ended. For me it had been the matrix of my life. I had been in a rush to finish my education and find a safe and secure job before the Depression would return. Now my parents could afford to send me to college (though I would not accept their money). I had wasted two precious years and committed more mortal sins than I could count.

And everyone said that I had grown up!

Even my priest, John Raven, who should have known me better, insisted that I had been a hero in Bamberg and that women adored me.

Dad had decided to build our house in Grand Beach. I thought that the idea was the worst familial folly yet. We couldn't afford it, I was sure. And when the Depression came back?

"Oh, we can afford it all right, son," he laughed. "No doubt about that, although I can't give you the precise figures. That's your mother's department."

Which was like saying that a drug addict was responsible for controlling the flow of drugs.

"And if the Depression comes back, well, all that can happen is that we'll lose it. When you've been through that once, you don't worry about it the second time."

While the house was being built that summer, we rented a house across the street from the site to supervise construction and enjoy the beach. Dad had designed one of the first "modern" homes in that section of the Dunes, a redwood house that might have fit just as well in Marin County, with sweeping porches and vast windows letting in the sun and the wind. Many of our neighbors lived in homes that seemed to react to the beauties of summer on the lake by enclosing their inhabitants in cramped darkness.

I was quickly converted to the South End of Lake Michigan, one of the best vacation sites in all the world—though not so spectacular that I improved my swimming, that summer or subsequently.

Dad drove back and forth to Michigan City from the site of the new St. Ursula every day. Mom and Michael and the girls spent the whole summer there, looking brown and fit and happy.

Dear God, how much difference a little bit of money makes.

And yet how little real difference it made.

My children and nieces and nephews, who weren't there, regard the late forties and the fifties as "Dullsville." Ozzie and Harriet and tail fins, and "togetherness." They cannot understand the excitement of those times because they weren't there when tens of millions of American families climbed out of poverty for the first time and many millions more slowly became convinced that they would never see hard times again.

Before I got my job at the Board of Trade that summer, as I impatiently walked the beaches and the dunes, I believed the conventional wisdom still: there had to be another depression. All the cars and washing machines and dryers and dishwashers and cameras and new homes and television sets, whose screens were little bigger than the holes at peep shows, were a trick. The bottom would drop out soon. It had to. There was *always* a depression after a war. Everyone knew that.

A few people didn't know that and they amassed vast wealth because they perceived that the pent-up demand of fifteen years of depression and war combined with the money saved during the war had changed economic history. I learned to be skeptical about what everyone knew to be true.

In 1948, however, I did not share the exuberant confidence of my contemporaries that a new era was dawning, an era when the good life would be available for almost everyone.

One late afternoon as I ambled down the beach, my Leica (a present from Trudi, my former Hitler Jugend lover) in my pocket, feeling very sorry for myself, I heard women laughing on the porch in front of our rented house, no doubt at me, at poor sad Chucky Ducky. I climbed the steps wearily.

That summer all the women in the family had taken to wearing two-piece swimsuits. I hasten to add that they were not the sort of garb you might see on *Baywatch,* indeed the amount of fabric involved might exceed that of the contemporary bikini (against which I personally have no objections) by a factor of ten. They were more like the structured, padded bras and corsets that women were required to wear under their clothes. However, underneath and out in the open were two different matters; and the extra couple of inches of womanly flesh now laid bare to sunshine and male eyes were, I thought, legitimate matters for attention.

"Here comes the sergeant," warned my sister Peg (née Margaret Mary), "we'd better clean up our conversation."

Peg was a sonatina in brown, hair curled around her face, snapping brown eyes, an elegant mobile face, dark skin with a string of small freckles across her nose, a tall, elegant Irish countess whose intense affection for me had sometimes kept me out of trouble and sometimes got me into worse trouble. I returned that affection in kind. Neither of us were prevented by our mutual affection from constant verbal conflict.

"He's just out archiving the rubble," Rosie Clancy observed. "So people will know what Grand Beach was like before the Irish moved in."

"I don't think we ought to ask him to join us in Michigan City tonight," Peg replied. "We'd be accused of contributing to the delinquency of a minor."

Rosie—or Rosemarie as I now insisted on calling her—was only a foster sister. Three years younger than me and the same age as Peg, she had drifted down the street as a small child and adopted our family, because her father was a rich jerk and her mother a drunk—or so I saw it then. She and Peg had become inseparable allies, usually against me, except when someone was picking on me. I often thought that Peg was a cougar slinking through a forest while Rosie was a timber wolf charging at prey.

That wasn't exactly fair because they were both lovely young women and not forest animals. Well, not exactly.

Rosemarie was an inch or two shorter than my sister and more slender. Her skin was buttermilk white, her hair midnight black, her eyes as blue as Lake Michigan on a whitecap day. She had been a pretty child. Now she was the most beautiful young woman I had ever seen.

"He does look like he's fourteen," my sister Jane added.

Jane, two years older than I, was a graduate of Rosary College and a teacher at our parish Catholic school. She wore a diamond ring garnered from Ted McCormack, a former Navy pilot who was now in medical school. More voluptuous than Peg and Rosie, she was also more exuberant and infinitely less complicated. Or so I thought then.

"Now, my dears," my mother, April Mae Cronin O'Malley, reproved them gently. "Don't pick on poor Chuck. He's adjusting to civilian life."

My mother, one of the great Dr. Panglossas of the modern world, could see the good side of everyone, including her pint-sized son with the wire-brush red hair. She was also a stunning beauty in her very early forties and the only one of the four who was wearing a strapless two-piece swimsuit.

I finally realized when I had returned from Germany that she and my father—a once impoverished and now very successful architect—made love often. At first, that shocked me. Parents weren't supposed to engage in such dirty behavior. On reflection I was delighted. How could anyone sleep in the same bedroom with such an elegant woman and not make love to her? I had not shared this insight with Peg or Rosie and probably wouldn't.

"I am shocked," I announced solemnly, as I sank into a vacant chaise and liberated a bottle of Coke from a cooler, "at the deterioration of the morals of American women in the postwar world. Prosperity and immorality, I have always said, go hand in hand."

"What are you talking about?" Peg demanded, her nose wrinkling. "We're not immoral!"

"He means our swimsuits." Rosemarie's pale skin flushed the attractive light pink that it acquired at the slightest hint of embarrassment.

The incest taboo—or whatever—forbade erotic fantasies about the other three women. However, foster sister or not, Rosemarie was an appropriate target for such desires, especially when she blushed.

"But darling," my mother argued, "they wear these two-piece suits even at Miss America pageants."

"Ah, we're having a bathing beauty contest here at Grand Beach. Well." I put my Coke aside and rose to my feet. "It's easy to pick the winner."

I kissed my mother on the forehead.

The younger women applauded—for the good April, not for me.

"Chucky," she said with notable lack of conviction, "you are simply impossible."

"No, just improbable," Rosemarie commented. "He's even worse than before he left for Germany. . . . A little cuter maybe, but worse."

Rosemarie and I had maintained the pose of bitter foes for much of our lives. I don't think we fooled anyone, not even ourselves. However, we had begun a correspondence while I was away. I wrote her a note of sympathy for her mother's death. The letters were remarkably gentle and affectionate. We had both sworn that we would abandon our conflict style when I came home and act like adult friends instead of quarreling siblings. We were now testing the limits of our new relationship.

Rosemarie would be irresistibly appealing, I told myself often, if only she didn't drink so much. I was also not quite sure I approved of the conspiracies of everyone in my family to match the two of us permanently. Everyone except my brother Michael, who was studying to be a priest and seemed to be unaware that there was such a thing as marriage.

I ignored Rosemarie's suggestion that I was cute.

"For a moment I thought I had wandered into the foundation-garment section at Sears," I observed.

I almost said "Marshall-Field's." "Sears," however, conveyed a slightly lower social class and hence was more effective as a troublemaking statement.

"Chucky!" they all protested.

"Mind you," I continued blandly, "I wouldn't mind wandering through the foundation-garment section of Sears. I think it would be great fun. But now one can find scandalously undressed women on a porch overlooking Lake Michigan."

General outraged laughter.

"Chuck, darling," my mother insisted, taking off her prescription sunglasses and glaring at me as she giggled. "You're a prude!"

"No, ma'am, good April Mae. My whole point is that I'm not a prude. I applaud, as any healthy male would, the decline of womanly virtue. I merely observe that you would never have dared to appear in public in the costumes your daughters affect when you were their age."

"If you think we're so wonderful, Chucky," Rosemarie said with an impish grin, "why don't you take pictures of us instead of dead fish and driftwood on the beach?"

Score one for the foster sister.

"That would distract me from studying for my admission to Notre Dame," I said lamely. "Which reminds me, I must beg back to my books."

They laughed again as I rose to enter the house.

"Mind you," I added, turning at the door, "my wondrous foster sister has suggested an attractive idea."

More laughter.

Now I would have to take some pictures of them, especially of Rosemarie.

At that time I was obsessed with the notion that I had wasted my time in Germany and that I had to make up for the years I had lost. I was twenty years old and I figured that I should at least enter Notre Dame as a second-semester sophomore. That would reduce my lost time to a semester.

Early the next morning, I grabbed my Leica and started a sunrise patrol of the beach. My plans were to archive the debris washed up on the shore from the lake and left there by Friday-night parties.

I walked all the way to New Buffalo and back. As I approached our construction site I saw a swimmer cleaving the quiet waters of the lake with a tough determined crawl. I paused to admire his stroke. I did not often wish I were athletic, but that particular morning with thunderheads already rising in the sky and curtains of humidity descending on the hot sands, I thought it would be refreshing to swim that well.

The swimmer came ashore near where I was watching. He was a she, in an eye-catching black two-piece swimsuit. Still a long way from a bikini, it disclosed a good deal more of Rosemarie than the one she had worn yesterday.

"Hi." Rosemarie pulled off her swim cap. "What are you watching, watchman?"

"Venus arising from the sea."

A blush suffused her face. I could cause that pretty easily, couldn't I?

"Silly! I have a lot more clothes on . . . do you think this suit is scandalous? I'm afraid that the good April does."

Scandal is in the eye of the beholder. My eye at that moment.

"She'll probably have one of her own before the summer is over."

We laughed together, the companionship ratified and restored instantly.

My prediction was, needless to say, perfectly accurate.

"Why don't you take a picture of me with that cute little camera?" Rosemarie had noted immediately that I was not carrying her gift. "Is it German? And you never take pictures of me anymore. Why not?"

"Afraid so much beauty would shatter the lens."

"Now you're being really silly." She walked toward me as I clicked away. "Do I make a good model?"

"I think you know the answer to that question."

I look at the pictures today. Indeed she made a wonderful model—a very pretty young girl in a swimsuit from which the armor of the vast, heavy bras and extensive girdles had been removed. "Finished?" She smiled crookedly.

"Almost . . ." I thought of a pose, banished it from my head, and then said, "Would you mind slipping the straps off your shoulders?"

"Uhmm . . . glamour." She complied instantly. "For your room at the Dome, I bet. To show off the wicked girl you know who will lose her faith and her soul at the University of Chicago. Lower? All right, but no lower than this, understand?"

She was having the time of her life posing. My fingers were trembling uneasily as I fixed the telephoto attachment over the lens. In subsequent years I shot pictures of many unclad and underclad women. My fingers always tremble. You never get over some things.

"Not quite right." I walked over to her and pulled the top of her suit a little lower, exposing a hint of the tops of her breasts. She stood, quiet and passive, only the tightness in her jaw and her silence hinting that I was frightening her. I pulled the bra down a little bit more.

"Chucky . . ." she exclaimed nervously.

My fingers still trembling, I finished my arrangements with one more gentle tug.

"Chuckie!"

"Are you really afraid of me, Rosemarie?"

"Well." Her chin rested on her chest, her hands were clutched behind her back. She looked at me out of the corner of her eye. "I'm always a little afraid of you, but"— she grinned maliciously—"I don't think you have the nerve to strip me right out here on the beach."

"No one around."

She glanced quickly up and down the beach.

"Go ahead and try!"

It would be delightful activity for any number of reasons. I lost my nerve, stepped away, and looked at my model through the viewfinder.

"Not this time."

"Coward," she sniffed.

I began shooting as the morning mists drifted around her. Perfect. Better with the hint of bare breasts than the reality.

I was dazzled by love for her at the moment I shot the best of the pictures.

Since then I've come to understand that photography certainly and perhaps every form of art is sexual activity; the photographer wants to capture the reality whose image has enthralled him and to be captured by it. Moreover, there is no more lovely subject in the world than the human body, especially the body of a woman (even to another woman). Thus, a photo of a woman is necessarily an act of desire and love—a dangerous enterprise often and a delightful enterprise always.

Whether a photograph is obscene or not is the result of the nature of the love that the photographer feels for the model when he snaps the shot. If he is using her, that is obvious in the picture. If he respects and admires her, that is obvious too. The difference between an erotic and an obscene picture, often small and always enormous, is simple to discover and hard to explain, especially to prudes. Like Father Pius.

After a time you stop trying.

(Let me note for the record that when Hugh Hefner, then a fellow Chicagoan, phoned me about working for *Playboy* in 1955, I turned him down flat. I don't find the pictures in that journal particularly immoral, just unreal and dumb.)

"Well"—she shrugged back into her straps—"I think I want a life-size copy to give to the good April for a Christmas present. Foster daughter as temptation. Do you think she'd like it?"

"Yes, she'd like it. No, she wouldn't think it was a temptation. And, yes, she'd want Dad to take a picture like that of her."

"Did he ever paint her in the nude?" She picked up a blue cotton robe from the beach. I helped her on with it, much to her surprise, and adjusted a strap that was not quite in place. My fingers trembled and she drew in her breath. I wanted desperately to kiss her shoulder, but naturally I did not.

It was a shocking question that had never occurred to me before. "I'm sure I don't know," I said huffily.

"I bet he did. I mean, if you're a painter and you have a model like that . . ."

"Did you have a good time last night?"

"Changing the subject, eh? It was all right."

We walked down the beach together in companionable silence.

"You really have changed, Chuck," she said.

"I deny it!"

She ignored me.

"You were always a sweet boy beneath that phony pose of yours. Now you're the sweetest boy I've ever known."

My freckled face was undoubtedly flaming.

"Thank you, Rosemarie," I said awkwardly, striving for a more witty response and unable to find it.

"Your camera was so reverent that for a moment I thought I was beautiful."

"You are beautiful, Rosemarie."

"No I'm not. But your camera, which means you, thinks I am. That's wonderful."

"My camera has excellent taste in women," I said.

I did make a print for my mother and presented it to her, suitably framed, for Christmas.

"Your foster daughter, Aunt April." I handed it to her under the Christmas tree.

She removed the wrapping paper with brisk curiosity. "A photo of Rosie, oh, how exciting."

Rosemarie rolled her eyes at me, saying in effect, you didn't have the nerve, did you really?

Filled with the Christmas spirit I winked at her.

"Chucky, what a darling picture! It's perfect. Rosie, you are *so* beautiful."

"Thank you, Aunt April."

"I told you she wouldn't be shocked."

"Shocked, why should I be shocked, dear? It's not obscene at all . . . look at the way you've caught the drops of water on her, er, breasts . . . it would take a lot more than this to shock me."

The rest of the family crowded around to admire my handiwork.

"You made the frame too?" Jane exclaimed.

"With my own little hands."

"It's the best thing you've ever done, Chuck." My father examined the print with a professional artist's clinical eye. "At least the best thing we've seen yet."

"You could win a prize with it," my mother continued to enthuse. "You should enter it into a contest."

A champagne toast was proposed and drunk to the picture, or as Mom said, "To the picture, the artist, and the model!"

I drank it in Coca-Cola.

"Especially to the model," Peg shouted.

"Especially to the photographer"—Rosemarie smiled at me—"who had the courage to tug the model's swimsuit!"

"To everyone!" the good April announced.

"Rosemarie thinks you probably posed for Dad in the nude when you were younger."

Dad choked on his champagne. The rest of the gang paused in shocked silence.

"Well, dear." The good April was not in the least dismayed. "He would have been a pretty strange sort of painter, wouldn't he, if he didn't want to paint some pictures like that."

"I want to see them!" Peg screamed. "Today."

"Me too." Jane and Rosemarie echoed the shout.

"I'll be damned," I said.

My father was laughing now. "She's delighted, Chuck."

"Well," the good April mused, "I don't know they're all that special. But if you want . . . I'll show them to the girls this afternoon. Chucky, you'll have to wait till you're married."

I really didn't want to look at them at all. Ever.

"I want it understood"—Mom raised a warning finger—"that I did not pose for those paintings, and they are rather good"—she colored—"because of the painter of course, until after we were married."

And then she added a line about which no one dared to ask an explanation. "Well, almost married."

After the private showing that afternoon, Rosemarie slipped up to me. "Don't ask, Chucky Ducky, don't ask."

"I wasn't asking," I said irritably.

"They're wonderful," she said, "simply wonderful."

"I'm glad to hear it."

The healthy attitude of my parents toward the human body, an attitude that had helped produce me, hardly belonged to the same religion as that of Father Pius, my rector in Farley Hall, or of the University of Notre Dame in that era. I never thought my parents' religion would win. But it did. Kind of, anyway.

2

"Hey, kid," Jimmy Rizzo shouted at me, "you want to get into the game?"

I looked around behind me, hoping that there was some other person present who could answer to the name of "Kid." Alas, there was not.

"I don't play softball," I replied with as much dignity as I could.

"Everyone plays softball," Jimmy said with his warm and genial grin. "Take over in right field!"

The St. Ursula team of the Catholic War Veterans was short one man because Tim Boylan was too drunk to walk up to the plate.

"Yes, sir, Captain, sir," I said respectfully.

The vets laughed, Rizzo louder than the rest.

Jimmy Rizzo was pure energy. About my height, maybe an inch taller (which wasn't very tall), with dark skin, curly jet-black hair, a contagious smile that revealed perfect white teeth (of the sort no Irishman could claim), Jimmy was a charmer, a natural leader, an organizer, and a man with, as my father put it, a "great political future ahead of him if he doesn't end up in jail."

The jail possibility arose because the Rizzos were "connected." Though Jimmy's father was a grocer with a small shop on Division Street, his mother's brother Salvatore

"Sal the Pal" Damico was a man of respect, which meant that it was very wise to treat him with respect. Sal the Pal felt that the "Outfit," as we call it in Chicago, needed a new generation of young men who were "serious" and "respectful." "Real war heroes," Sal the Pal had argued in the higher councils of the Outfit, like his nephew Jimmy, should be invited into the organization.

Especially since Jimmy had considerable experience killing people in battles from Guadalcanal to Iwo. Five years older than I was, he had enlisted in the Marines right after Pearl Harbor and won himself the Navy Cross a couple of times. A real war hero, he was. A professional killer for the Outfit? About that there was still some doubt, though the respectable Irish in St. Ursula thought that all Sicilians were criminals. Father John Raven, who always had a multiple agenda, had made Jimmy the organizer and president of the Catholic War Vets in part to keep him away from Sal the Pal and open up to him the possibility of more honorable and honest professions.

Like politics.

Well, moderately more honorable and honest.

Anyway, would I argue with a war hero and a nephew of Sal the Pal? Camera in hand, I trotted out into right field with a fervent prayer that the deity would protect me from pop flies.

I had wandered back to St. Ursula because our new neighborhood one parish west was both too dull and too snobbish for my late-summer loneliness now that I had a job in the city. Naturally, I brought my Leica along to archive Catholic veterans at play. I saw no reason why my temporary duty as a right fielder should inhibit that mission. The Almighty protected me from pop flies that inning, as I recorded Chicago softball in the summer of 1948.

One must note that the only true softball is sixteen-inch, slow-pitching softball like we play it in Chicago—called occasionally in our time "indoor" because it had originated in Knights of Columbus gyms.

In those days before the Windy City League was born, we didn't wear uniforms, just an old assortment of cast-off military fatigues and high school sweatshirts that no longer fit very well, either because our shoulders had become too broad or our bellies too large. I had no trouble wearing my Fenwick sweatshirts. They were still too loose.

"What high school you go to, Red?" Jimmy demanded as he shook hands with me when I came in from right field.

"Captain, sir," I said, "you have just lost one vote when you're up for reelection to be president of this outfit."

"Those fatigues really yours? . . . What's your name?"

"O'Malley, sir, Charles Cronin."

I almost rattled off my serial number. I thought better of it because most of these men were real vets, not phony vets like me.

"Where were you?" he asked as our first batter, encumbered by a large and new beer belly, popped up.

I was too young for someone Jimmy Rizzo's age to know about my exploits at St. Ursula and Fenwick. That was just as well since most of my exploits were pure fiction.

"Germany. Occupation. First Constabulary. State Police, kind of."

"Cushy duty?" he asked without the slightest hint of disrespect.

"Corrupt duty."

"Yeah . . . Anyone ever fire a shot at you in anger— Hey, way to go, Micky!"

Our next batter, a former B-17 tail gunner, had lined a single into left field.

"Once."

"Who?"

"An officer in a black market bunch we'd cornered."

"What did you do?"

He seemed genuinely interested in my story.

"Kept shooting at him," I said, pointing at my camera.

He laughed.

"You'd win a medal for that . . . Then what?"

"A shavetail just out of West Point took the gun away from him. They used my shots as evidence in his trial."

"What did he get?"

I decided that I really liked this Jimmy Rizzo.

"General discharge."

"Figures . . . Hey, you're up!"

Our third batter had dribbled a bounder at the shortstop of the Help of Christians' Vets team. That worthy had heaved the ball into the street. One out, men on second and third and the mighty Casey comes to.

"Hold my weapon till I come back." I gave Jimmy Rizzo my camera. "If I come back."

I had exaggerated when I argued that I did not play softball. In fact, I played it badly, very badly. I understood the game and its strategies—such as they are—but I was innocent of the strength and coordination to apply my theories in practice.

I did know that if I managed to tap a high pitch with my bat, it would fly over the shortstop's head and into left center field. The shortstop would rush for the ball, as would the third baseman, the short center fielder (right shortstop in the real indoor days—if you can imagine a right shortstop), and the left fielder. Given the apparent lack of skill of these paragons and the advanced state of inebriation of some of them, it was not unreasonable to expect that they would mess the play up badly enough for me to struggle down to first base.

The first pitch was high and outside, so I poked at it ineffectually and missed. Deliberately. The pitcher did the obvious. He threw the ball in the same place. I tapped a pathetically weak drive over the shortstop's head as planned and took off at my top speed, which was very slow, for first base. Upon arrival, I heard Jimmy Rizzo

shouting frantically that I should try for second. As I engaged in this folly, I realized that the four fielders who
had converged on the ball were still trying to capture it.
One of them finally picked it up and fired it for home plate
where our second runner might have been tagged out had
not the throw sailed into Massassoit Avenue. I could have
walked to third. So I did. Jimmy had miraculously become
third-base coach. He urged me to hold at third, which I
was only too happy to do.

He thereupon came to bat and hit the ball over the left
fielder's head to drive—if that's the word—me home with
the winning run. Somehow I had not realized it was the
last of the seventh and that we had been down two runs.

Mudville wins tonight.

"Got a couple of good shots of you sliding into third!"
he said, handing me the camera back. "Join me for a beer?"

Naturally I had not slid into third base.

"I don't drink," I replied.

"Bottle of Coke?"

"Only if that pretty little blonde who never takes her
eyes off you joins us."

"You mean Monica Sullivan? . . . You don't miss much,
do you, Charles Cronin O'Malley?"

"We cops don't."

Those were strange times. It was not unusual during the
Depression for unemployed young men with nothing else
to do to hang around street corners, play softball on play-
ground lots and parish yards, and soak up beer like Prohibition was coming back. The difference now was that
most of the young men had fought—or at least served—
in a war. Moreover, the government was paying them to
go to college, something that would never have occurred
to poor kids like Jimmy Rizzo a few years before. The
vets sensed that college would make the difference, that
they could not only catch up with the time they had lost
during the war, but win a share in the prosperity that was
blossoming all around. Their lives now were pregnant with

promise and possibility, with urgency and confidence. They were wild and exuberant young men, not at all like their immediate predecessors, many of them running from memories of horror as much as toward hope for the future. John Raven had organized the Catholic vets in the hope of focusing some of their energy. Naturally, he had turned to Jimmy Rizzo to organize the group.

The goals of those young men were modest: have a little fun, get a degree, buy a home of their own, marry and have kids, live a good and decent life—goals that would have seemed beyond reach in 1939. Most of them were able to achieve all the goals, some spectacularly so.

Some of them had already married, which meant that they had already "settled down"—and put on weight. These were the sober ones at the softball games, some of them with their wives, baby in arms, watching—another innovation in the late nineteen forties.

"Nice hit, Chucky," Father Raven said to me as Jimmy and I walked toward Jimmy's 1937 Chevy. "How's Rosie?"

"Rosie who?" I asked.

The priest just laughed.

Monica Sullivan had kind of materialized next to the Chevy. She handed me a beer bottle, which I passed on to Jimmy.

"He drinks Coke," Jimmy told her.

"Aren't you Jane O'Malley's little brother?" she asked me, never taking her eyes off Jimmy.

"Emphasis on little," I replied.

Monica was a lushly pretty little woman with long blond hair, a sweet smile, and perfect manners.

Not so perfect that she didn't laugh at me. Good. That meant she thought I was cute, though there was no good reason why that should matter.

"Jane is very happy," she said in a matter-of-fact tone from which she never deviated. "Have they set a date for the wedding?"

"Her future father-in-law doesn't think his son should marry until he is able to support a wife and family. That means he must finish med school and internship and residency if he intends to become a specialist. Five, six more years."

"Times have changed," Monica said sadly. "A lot of parents don't seem to realize that."

The rumors I had picked up from Jane reported that Monica was hopelessly in love with Jimmy Rizzo and that her father, Big Tom Sullivan, a pompous and successful banker, had forbidden her to see him. Indeed, Big Tom was supposed to have said that no daughter of his would marry a dirty Sicilian who was so dark that he must have Negro blood in him.

I happened to think that Dr. McCormack was right in principle. I had no intention of marrying till I could support a wife and family. However, the rules did not apply when the bride who had to wait was my sister.

"He's a mean son of a bitch," I said. "He wants to relive his own life in his son. No good parent does that."

Since my beloved Peg was in love with an Italian American boy (though Neopolitan rather than Sicilian), I was instantly on the side of Jimmy and Monica. Besides, I thought that Big Tom was the worst windbag ever to preside over the St. Ursula Holy Name Society.

I had acquired in Germany the bad habit of becoming involved with people who seemed to need help, though there never had been any good reason to think that they needed *my* help. I realized that I was doing the same thing all over again.

But I liked Jimmy Rizzo.

Dusk was settling over the ball field and lights were coming on in the bungalows around the parish grounds, the reassuring routine lights of domestic order and peace. Or so I thought then.

We watched as a couple of guys, between Jimmy and

me in age, helped Timmy Boylan into a Pontiac as old as Jimmy's Chevy.

"What's the matter with Timmy?" I asked.

"ASTP," Monica said dryly. "He's my cousin, you know."

"Yeah," I said.

I really didn't know. I could never figure out the network of relationships in the neighborhood. But I didn't have to, I figured, because the women in my family had all done it for me.

"You remember what the ASTP was?" Jimmy asked, his good humor vanishing.

"Vaguely. Army came around to the high schools when we were sophomores. Really needed bright young men. Give juniors and seniors special training. Get them out of school halfway through the year. Put them in important jobs. Intelligence, that sort of thing."

"By the summer of 1944," Jimmy said grimly, "the Army didn't need bright young men. It needed bodies. So all these kids who thought they were going to be intelligence officers found themselves combat infantry replacements. Cannon fodder."

"After six weeks of basic training," Monica went on, "the Army sent them to replacement centers in France. Poor Timmy was in one of those places for another week. Then they assigned him to the First Infantry Division in the Hurtgen Forest. He wasn't even eighteen years old."

"A replacement," Jimmy continued, "replaces someone, usually a friend of the survivors in the outfit. They hated the replacement because somehow he was responsible for their friend's death so often they did nothing to help him get ready for battle. Tim was in combat for four days before a shell from a German 88 tore him apart."

"Four days to ruin a life," Monica added bitterly. "He was in the hospital for two years. His body is a mass of scars. He's not the same cute, funny boy he was when he graduated from St. Ignatius. He hates everyone and everything."

"I'm not a great fan of the corps," Jim Rizzo said, "but we never did anything like that to people. The kid's life is over. He won't go to school, he won't work. All he wants to do is drink."

My two new friends were more morose than they should have been on our lovely summer evening after a victory over our enemies from the next parish. So I told them about my comic-opera exploits in the First Constabulary. Our encounter with "werewolves" in the Bohemianwald and with Russian smugglers on the road to Leipzig had been ludicrous but not particularly amusing in the actual experience. But in retrospect and with myself cast as a bumbling military cop, they were the material for high comedy. Later in life I would entertain with my stories whenever I had a chance. They never lost anything in the telling.

I left out the more serious events in my hapless military career. They didn't need to know about Brigitta, the faithful woman waiting at the railroad station for her husband who had fought at the battle of Kursk. Nor did I tell them or anyone else about my love affair with Trudi, the sometime member of the Hitler Jugend, or about how we broke the black market ring run by a group of our own officers.

Jimmy and Monica found what I did tell them very funny. The stories grew more comic through the years. On rare occasions I told some people the tragedy as well as the comedy.

John Raven joined us.

"Chuck telling you how he lost the Third World War?" he asked.

"Jane O'Malley says that Chuck earned a Legion of Merit," Monica said solemnly, but then everything she said was solemn.

"Really?" Father Raven was surprised.

I didn't have to tell my confessor everything, did I?

"Pure rumor." I dismissed the story with a wave of my hand.

Jane was not supposed to tell anyone, indeed she wasn't even supposed to know about it.

"They don't give those away for nothing," Jimmy said, a puzzled frown appearing on his handsome face.

"Everything is easy in an army of occupation," I insisted.

"Finally found a pinch hitter who could bring home the bacon, huh, Jimmy?" Father Raven asked.

"One who deliberately fools the pitcher," Monica observed.

She saw too much.

"I won't be back."

"You'd better come back," Jimmy Rizzo warned. "Understand, Corporal?"

"Staff Sergeant, Captain, sir."

"Give you a ride home?"

"No, thanks. Father Raven wants to talk to me."

And I'm not going to intrude on your privacy with the woman you love.

Jimmy helped Monica into the car with attentive reverence. I yearned momentarily for a woman I could treat with similar reverence.

"See you next week, Sergeant Chuck," she said and turned and smiled at me.

My heart turned to butter.

"Yes, ma'am."

As Jimmy's Chevy turned the corner, Father Raven repeated his earlier question. "How's Rosie?"

"Rosemarie is the most beautiful woman I have ever met," I replied. "And doomed!"

"You have a way with words, Chuck."

"You disagree, Father?"

"She has a lot of residual strength and solid instincts, especially in her choice of her foster family."

"We can't stop her from drinking, can we?"

He shrugged his shoulders. "I'm not sure. I hope we can. I hope we can."

Silence for a moment.

"Let's go for a walk," he said, resuming the conversation. "Around the neighborhood."

"Okay."

Darkness had settled in on the neighborhood and with it a sense that peace was slipping down the streets with the steeds of night. A gentle summer breeze stirred the leaves. Eternity and time seemed to have temporarily joined forces to bless our cozy, optimistic little postwar neighborhood.

The optimism was of the sort that makes you cross your fingers, however. The Great Depression was still a vivid memory. A lot of women would pray that night that the Depression would never come back, especially young women like Monica and my sister Jane.

"What did you think of those two?"

"Jimmy and Monica?"

"Yeah."

"So much in love it's painful . . . Beautiful too."

"What chance do you give them?"

"Hey, I'm not even twenty yet."

"That's irrelevant, given your performance in Bamberg."

I was not, as John Raven had often insisted, a born precinct captain. I'd argue that some other time.

"Not all that good. Different backgrounds. Uncle Sal the Pal. Big Tom . . . Even if they get married, they'll have a hard time."

"Love doesn't conquer all?"

"Not a chance. I'm no romantic."

"Most romantic person I know," he said with a snort. "Sometimes, though, love does conquer all."

"Bad bet."

"Maybe . . . The problem isn't Sal the Pal. Jimmy is family. That means you support him. He wants to go a hundred percent legitimate and marry a pretty Irish girl, hey, he's family, know what I mean?"

"Her old man is the problem?"

"He's a pious phony, Chuck, with his manicured fingernails and his wavy white hair and his expensive cologne and his Knight of St. Gregory cape. He's a worse crook than Sal the Pal . . . and more dangerous."

I filed this information away for future use.

"What's he done?"

"Bribery, embezzlement, arson, assault, maybe even murder. Jimmy is on thin ice."

Not if I could help it.

Yeah, I actually thought that on a late August night in 1948. Chucky Ducky the messiah. Bamberg had corrupted me. No, that's not true. I got my poor father out of duty in the jungles of New Guinea when I was still in eighth grade.

"This isn't your world, is it, Chuck—Catholic War Vets?"

"I'm not a war vet."

"Even if you were, this scene is too simple, too optimistic for you."

"I wish it were true, Father. I'll feel terribly sorry for all those good kids when the hard times return."

"Even if you knew the hard times wouldn't return, it still wouldn't be your scene, would it? Always the crazy O'Malley."

"Only sane one."

"These young men and women want love, Chuck. It's a simple enough desire but messy and complicated in practice. They sense that it will be a bit easier because they'll have secure jobs and will be able to afford a decent home, quality education for their kids, a car, and a few conveniences around the house."

"Not all that ambitious."

"No, not at all. It may not make love all that much

easier, but it will change the context of love. This is the turning point for them, Chuck."

"Love is never easy, Father," I said somewhat pompously, "not even for people like the Colonel and the good April Mae."

"Precisely my point."

Uh-huh.

We stopped in front of St. Ursula's rectory.

"But"—Father Raven broke the silence—"God is love."

"So you tell me . . . But not like human love, not erotic or anything like that?"

I was baiting him, because I knew he did mean something like that.

"That bond between Jimmy and Monica that impressed you?"

"Yeah?"

"That's what God is like."

I let that sink in. Not a bad metaphor, come to think of it.

"I do a lot of weddings these days, Chuck. Young people very much in love. Vet weddings, mostly. The link between those two is unique. A sacrament even before they're married."

"If other people don't ruin it for them."

"Yeah."

"Take good care of Rosie," were his last words to me.

"I'll do what I can for Rosemarie," I replied.

He chuckled and walked into the rectory.

Three thoughts struggled for my attention as I trudged back to our home in Oak Park under the warm glow of the moon through the leaf-heavy trees.

I was not and never would be part of the formative experience of men of my generation. I might play softball with them. They might find me amusing. Still, I was an outsider. I didn't know quite why I was an outsider, but I was. Mostly I liked that, but it also made me feel a little sad.

John Raven expected me to save Rosemarie. He loved her too and knew he couldn't save her. Therefore I should . . .

I had made up my mind that I would take charge of the lives of Jimmy Rizzo and Monica Sullivan.

And for good measure I'd try to straighten out Timmy Boylan too.

❧ 3 ❧

The last six weeks of summer I worked as a runner at the Board of Trade. It was a madhouse, a terrifying bazaar in which grown men shouted furiously at one another and gestured savagely over tiny fractions of the dollar as if the barbarians were at the gates and their lives and the bodies of their wives and children were at stake in every deal. As a runner, my job was to pick up slips of paper recording sales from the floor of the pit and see that they were transmitted to the record keepers on the sidelines of the arena.

A runner was in a relatively safe position. It was not his money or his client's money that was at risk. The only danger was that the traders might trample him to death like a child caught in a run of frenzied steers.

Well, no runners were injured in my time there, but there were tales of broken arms and broken legs in the past.

I hated the place with all the power of hatred at my command. It was the disorderly, chaotic life that I detested in its most undiluted form: sweating, violent men risking their fortunes on something only slightly more predictable than the spin of a roulette wheel. I realized from my economics courses that a mature capitalist economy needs commodity markets and that the traders took the risk out of farming for the growers. Fine. But it was still a night-mare world of which I wanted no part.

I was as lonely as I had been in Bamberg. The women in my family were at the lake (where I could easily be if I weren't so stubborn about getting a job), Dad drove up almost every night. I had the big house in Oak Park to myself. So I began to hang out with the Catholic War Veterans, an outsider, listening, watching, noting, some-times photographing. When we didn't play softball, we spent our time at the corner of Corso's drugstore or at Larry Kerrigan's Magic Pub. Larry had turned his hobby of magic into a kind of floor show at the bar that fascinated our crowd, especially the women.

Men in their twenties hanging out on a street corner? It was a long time ago and most of us did not have cars. Women in the bar with us?

Certainly some must find Chuck O'Malley interesting?

Rosemarie and Peg cross-examined me about that sub-ject, with more intensity than I thought was appropriate.

I denied all charges. In truth, however, my comic stories about Bamberg (some of them marginally true) drew an audience of the women that at times was more enthusiastic than Larry's audience. I was definitely cute. Peg and Rose-marie would hear that eventually.

One night, after I had spun my mostly fictional yarns, I found myself sitting next to Tim Boylan, who at that point in the evening was, marvelous to say, still moderately so-ber. In fact, he had survived in right field for all seven innings and hit two homers.

"Was it really like that?" he asked me.

Tim was a tall, handsome black Irishman with thick black hair and eyebrows, dark skin, and a sharply carved face. He looked like he might be a pirate or a boxer or a lawyer on the way to the Federal Bench. The thick twisted scars on his neck and arms and chest underneath his khaki undershirt hinted that he was indeed a pirate.

He had been a great basketball player in his high school

days, good enough to play college ball if his life had been different. Now he was overweight and slow, a shell, no, a ruin of what he had been. Young women avoided him and he avoided them. His deep-set blue eyes were sealed in profound sadness. Yet occasionally they flickered with life and a mischievous smile flitted across his face. It almost made you forget the ugly scar across his forehead.

"High points," I said, "edited for barroom consumption."

A flicker of a smile appeared on his face.

"You're pretty good at the editing. . . . What was it really like?"

"Dull, boring, lonely. Lots of corruption. The people were hungry, sick, beaten. No fun. Not Hurtgen, though."

"I don't know anything about Hurtgen," he said gently. "I don't remember a thing. Just the hospital afterward."

"Oh."

"I was sure I was going to die. I wanted to die. I don't know why. Maybe the pain, though they kept me pretty well doped up. It's a shame I didn't die."

Okay, Chuck O'Malley, what do you say to that?

You say, "I'm sure a lot of people have told you that's not true, so I won't join their ranks."

"Yeah, thanks. . . . Funny thing is that I don't know why I want to die. There's a lot of anger inside me, but I don't know why I'm angry."

"Being torn apart by an 88 shell will do that to you."

"Yeah," he said with a bitter laugh, "I guess it will."

Okay, what do you say now?

Nothing, that's what.

"There's a lot of kids in our family," he continued slowly, sipping cautiously on his beer. "They're going to amount to something. I won't. It's too late for me. I was supposed to be the crown prince. Big lawyer like my dad. Not a chance. Better that they had a son who died a war hero than an emotional cripple who didn't have sense enough to jump into a foxhole."

"How do you know that?"

"The medics told me afterward. Maybe I remember it, I don't know."

He finished his beer glass in a single gulp.

"The war didn't seem to do that to most of these guys." He glanced around the bar. "Some of them were Purple Heart types too."

"Not as bad as you."

"Or spent time in a POW camp in Japan."

"No one in this room."

"Yeah, Chuck, but that's not the point, is it?"

"No, Timmy," I agreed. "It isn't."

I ordered another Coca-Cola.

"What am I sitting here telling you all this stuff for?"

"Because I'm an outsider too."

"You with your camera and I with my ruined body, huh?"

"Maybe, but it isn't really ruined."

"I think it is." He shrugged. "So does everyone else."

I didn't say anything.

It seemed suddenly that everyone in the bar was watching, Monica Sullivan with tears in her eyes. It must have been the first time Timmy had talked seriously to anyone.

"You going to be a professional photographer?"

"No, an accountant," I replied primly. "I'm not a photographer, just a picture-taker."

He threw back his head and laughed.

"So we're both afraid of life, huh?"

"Maybe," I said lamely.

"Tell you what, Chuck O'Malley. When you become a photographer, I'll become a lawyer. Deal?"

"It's not a fair proposal," I said even more lamely.

"Yeah, I suppose not."

His exuberant mood disappeared. He hunched forward grimly and began to demolish another beer. In one long gulp.

"Well, anyway, thanks for listening. See you around."

He stood up and lurched out of the bar into the humid summer night, perhaps our neighborhood's first and only Flying Dutchman.

"You said exactly the right thing," Rosemarie said indignantly as we lolled in the waters of Lake Michigan the following Saturday. "He had no right to propose that deal."

"I know," I said sadly, as I splashed her with water.

She splashed back, naturally.

I had arrived that morning at a tense summer home. A very somber Peg had picked me up at the South Shore Yards to drive me to the beach in our funny-looking new Studebaker about which I said, not unreasonably, that you couldn't tell whether it was coming or going.

"What's wrong?" I demanded.

"Nothing."

"Fight with poor Vince?"

"Certainly not."

Vince was my Neopolitan classmate from St. Ursula and Fenwick who was in love with Peg. He was a football star at Notre Dame and certainly had to be lurking somewhere in the vicinity on a summer weekend. The only trouble with Vince was that for stupid reasons of social class and nationality he felt inferior to the O'Malleys, especially as we became more affluent.

How could anyone feel inferior to the crazy O'Malleys?

"Rosemarie?"

"You're too damn smart for your own good, Chucky Ducky."

"Rosemarie got drunk again last night," I observed, "embarrassed you and Vince, and you and she had a shouting fit?"

"Shut up!"

"Yes, ma'am."

"Fool around with Monica Sullivan's life and Timmy Boylan's. Leave mine alone."

"Yes, ma'am."

I glanced at her. Tears were flowing down her lovely face.

"Sorry, Chuck."

"It's okay, Peg."

"It was really bad. She was terrible. She's very contrite today. I don't know whether that means anything."

"It means she's sorry. . . . It hasn't happened recently, has it?"

"No . . . Almost a year. I thought it was over. . . . That's why I feel so bad this morning."

She pulled the car over to the side of Highway 12 to dab at her eyes.

"I shouldn't take it out on you. And I shouldn't have said that about Monica and Tim either."

"I'm not really fooling around with their lives," I said meekly, though indeed that was exactly what I was doing.

"I know that. I think it's wonderful that you're helping them."

"I'm not helping them!" I said, raising my voice. "I'm just listening to them."

"It's still wonderful," she said as she eased the car back on the road.

"I don't even know why they want to talk to me."

"Don't you *really*, Chuckie?"

Her normal good humor was back in place.

"Nope."

"It's obvious."

"Oh?"

"Because taking care of people is what you do!"

She was wrong, but I saw no reason to argue.

"I need help with a metaphor," I said, changing the subject.

"A metaphor?"

"Right. . . . If you're a cougar slinking through a forest and Rosemarie is a timber wolf charging at prey, what's Monica Sullivan?"

Peg laughed so hard I thought she'd have to stop the car again.

"Chuckie! How wonderful! Am I really a sleek, strong, beautiful cougar—whatever a cougar is?"

"She cougar," I added.

"I completely agree that Rosie is a timber wolf, that's perfect!"

And just when I thought I had begun to understand women!

"Well, let me think about Monica. She's not easy. How about a filly, all prim and proper and dignified and determined to win any race she runs?"

"I'll take that under advisement . . . Now don't go telling Rosemarie that I said she was a timber wolf."

"Why not? They're beautiful creatures."

"And dangerous."

"Only when you threaten them or their cubs . . . Promise me you'll be nice to her today, please?"

"I've been nice to her ever since I came home."

"I know. And you wrote her such nice letters while you were away."

Naturally Peg had read all my letters to Rosemarie. I had taken that for granted.

"Did I?"

"She feels so bad today."

"Embarrassed, worthless?"

"Terrible . . . Promise?"

"Sure."

So I was very nice on the beach and in the water as we bounced up and down on the waves under the hazy sky and a searing sun.

Rosemarie had insisted on anointing me with suntan cream because, as she said, redheads have to take good care of their skin.

I did not resist. How could I? During the process I thought that, if God approved, heaven for me might be Rosemarie's gentle fingers rubbing suntan cream into my body.

I offered to return the favor. She glanced at me skeptically and offered me the bottle.

"Only my back, Charles Cronin O'Malley."

"If you say so."

I then proposed to the Deity that if He didn't mind we could split the time in heaven so that she anointed me for half of eternity and I anointed her for the other half.

"You have very tender hands, Chuck," she said with a sigh. "It's like you're rubbing cream into a baby's skin."

"Anytime."

In the water she had turned to the subject of Monica, Jim, and Timmy. Dazed by her beauty and the intimacy that the heat and the humidity of the day created, I recounted my stories, this time with very little editing.

Then she said that I had done the right thing in rejecting Tim's offer.

"Of course," she said as she struggled to pull me under the water, "you are going to be a photographer. Absolutely. But not to save someone else who won't take care of himself."

I let her pull me under because it seemed a pleasant experience. Then I had to pull her under to even the score.

We are acting like young lovers, I thought. But we're not that. Nor will we ever be.

Still it was fun.

And she was so very, very beautiful.

"Is it true that Mr. Sullivan told Monica she had to move out of the house if she didn't stop seeing Jim Rizzo?"

"Yes," I said, gulping water. "He's given her til Labor Day to make a decision."

"What do you think she'll do?"

She suspended the wrestling because gossip was now more important.

"It will be hard for her. She loves the younger children. Her mother is hysterical. Jim is willing to suspend their, uh, courtship for a while."

"So you think she'll drop him?"

"No, I don't think so."

"Good for her! Those prim little fillies can run pretty fast when they want to, can't they?"

She pulled me under the water again. Naturally, Peg had told her about my metaphors.

"But," I said, struggling to the surface, "it's those timber wolves you gotta watch."

"They're very good to their mates and their children," she gurgled as her head went under.

A point well taken, but how did she find it out so soon?

In those days young women rarely moved out of the family home until they married. It would be a grave scandal in the neighborhood.

"Big Tom is a big jerk," I said, twisting her arm behind her as I prepared to dunk her again, mind you only in reprisal.

"If I can be of any help with them, Chuck," she said as we wrestled, "I'd be glad to do whatever I could."

I almost told her that she was a high school senior who couldn't control her drinking. However, a benign angel talked me out of it.

"That's a good idea, Rosemarie," I said, "an excellent idea. I'll see what happens!"

Her face lit up with joy. So I kissed her and then dunked her. She came up sputtering. I kissed her again and pushed her under.

The kisses were very mild.

"What are you two doing out there?" Peg shouted from the beach.

"I'm trying to drown your obnoxious brother!" Rosemarie shouted happily.

Peg and Vince charged into the water to join us. We frolicked till the sun went down.

As far as I was concerned the day could have gone on forever.

Some of the time, I informed God, we'll want to play in the lake. I assume you have one up in Heaven.

That night the four of us—Vince and Peg, Rosemarie and I—went to a Dan Dailey/Jeanne Crain film about a band leader. Then we went to a soda parlor where I ate three dishes of ice cream. It was, I had to admit, a delightful evening. Rosemarie was on her very best behavior, funny, charming, intelligent. Vince, of whom I hadn't seen much since my return, alternately talked about Notre Dame and gazed adoringly at Peg.

He thought Notre Dame was wonderful, great priests, great guys, great life, great football team, great school. I had my doubts about all of it. Vince did protest too much.

"Who's going to win the election?" Peg demanded, tired of the praise for Notre Dame.

"I think it's time for a change," Vince said. "But I'm a Democrat, so if I were old enough to vote, I'd vote for the haberdasher from Missouri."

"Dewey is a funny little man on a wedding cake," Peg added, quoting our mother's judgment.

"But he's going to win," Rosemarie said. "Everything says that. The stupid Democrats are split four ways."

(Strom Thurmond was running on the Dixiecrat ticket and Henry Wallace on a left-wing Progressive Party ticket.)

"It looks like the race is already over and it's only August," Peg sighed. "I think elections are exciting."

Time for Chucky Ducky to weigh in.

"The race is not over and Dewey won't win," I announced. "Bet on it."

They all insisted that I was wrong, didn't know what I was talking about, didn't read the newspapers, had been away from America too long.

"Three malted milks say I'm right," I insisted.

"You won't pay," Peg sneered. "That's why I never bet with you. You always weasel out."

"I won't this time. . . . Incidentally, ma'am, may I have a chocolate malted milk with double whipped cream and don't forget the butter cookies."

So the bet was made. I won it, naturally. And collected.

Smart political analyst? No, lucky guesser who wanted to make trouble on a pleasant August evening when we were all so very young.

More interested in and better informed about politics, if I may say so, than many subsequent generations of young people.

Peg and Vince went for a long walk on the beach. Rosemarie protected me from the embarrassing necessity of proposing the same thing for us by saying that she was tired and was going right to bed.

Michael was in the other bed in our room when I stumbled in.

"On a date, Chuck?" he said, with a touch of totally unjustified amusement in his voice.

I hadn't known he was coming back from his seminary summer assignment.

"No," I said curtly, "just went to a movie with Peg and Rosemarie and Vince."

"That isn't a date?"

"Certainly not."

"Why not?"

"Because I didn't ask them, they asked me."

"It would only be a date if you invited Rosie?"

"Right," I said, turning off the light and climbing into my bed.

"I'm glad that's cleared up."

The punk was becoming dangerous. I'd have to watch out.

As I struggled to come down off the excitement of the evening, I thought about Vince and Peg. The bond between them was strong, not as tensile tough as that between Monica Sullivan and Jimmy Rizzo, but tough enough. They would marry. Maybe a year after Vince's graduation from Notre Dame. She would have finished her sophomore year in college.

I had mixed feelings about such a marriage. She was

my beloved sister, he my best friend. They were too young to marry. Yet in those days, in the aftermath of the war, men and women married young. Half of Jane's class at Rosary had engagement rings when they were sophomores, almost all of them by the time they were seniors. My children refuse to believe, as a matter of solemn principle, that people married so young when we were growing up. In the years before and the years after our time marriages occurred much later. But our generation was reacting to the Depression and the war and grabbing, almost desperately, at a chance for happiness before the Depression came back or we went to war with the Russians.

Parents reacted differently. The colonel and the good April were delighted at the prospect of Jane's marriage right out of college. They would be equally delighted if Peg married at the end of her sophomore year. She could continue her violin training at the Conservatory even after marriage. They viewed my determination to postpone marriage till I could support a wife and family as distressingly stuffy, even old-fashioned.

Other parents, however, foolishly tried to resist. Big Tom Sullivan objected to Jimmy Rizzo's Sicilian background, Dr. McCormack complained that Ted was not engaged to the daughter of a surgeon like himself. They also used, however, the secondary argument that their child was too young to marry.

I was on their side as far as my own life was concerned, but I realized that I was voting in the minority among my generation. Peg a mother at twenty-one?

I didn't like the picture.

Moreover, I realized as sleep claimed me that if I should abandon my principles, I could have myself a wife in a couple of years.

Rosemarie?

Sleep snuffed that image out. I cannot remember whether it came back in my dreams. Probably it did.

I went back to Oak Park on Sunday night with Dad,

delighted with the respite of the weekend and dreading the grain pit the next morning.

"You're certainly a good influence on Rosie," Dad said to me.

I came close to saying, "And she on me."

Instead I said, "The poor kid has terrible problems."

I felt like someone on a slippery water slide who wanted to get off. *Now.*

Jim Clancy was always in the middle of the grain pit, his vast shirt soaked in sweat, his little face twisted in a diabolical grimace, his tiny paws waving frantically above his mountainous body—a troll come down out of the Black Forest.

Small wonder that poor Rosemarie was a mess.

"You're O'Malley, aren't you?" he demanded one day at the end of a trading session.

"Yes, sir."

"Like it here?"

"It's all right, sir."

"It's a place where they separate the men from the boys," he whined, proud of the originality, as he saw it, of his turn of the phrase.

"Yes, sir."

"My daughter says you're smart, tough. Real man."

"Thank you, sir."

Was that what she thought of me?

"You want a seat here? I'll buy you one."

Not for all the Rosemaries in the world.

"That's very kind, sir, but I'm still in school."

"When you get out, we'll talk about it. Right?"

"Yes, sir."

"You'll like it here. I can see it in your eyes. You're a real fighter."

"Thank you, sir."

A real fighter I was not. Nor could I survive, I told myself, tensions so stormy that many traders had to lose themselves in drink or sex during the long afternoons after the trading sessions ended.

And by none of the standards available to me was James Clancy a man. If to be unlike him was to be a boy, put me on the list.

So I read William Butler Yeats and James Joyce (*Portrait,* which I loved) and books on the business cycle on the El riding back and forth from the exchange and De-Paul.

I read Sigrid Undset (who died that year) and John P. Marquand's *Point of No Return.* I sat alone at the Rockne to watch *All the King's Men* and *The Third Man.*

Was there ever a cinema shot to compare with the face of Orson Welles in the first shot of Harry Lime?

The film has always haunted me. I dig out the videotape every once in a while. The drab despair, the poverty, the hunger, the determination to survive, were like what I had seen in Bamberg. The first time I showed it to my wife, she asked, "How did you stand it, Chuck?"

"I counted the days till I would go home."

There was more to it than that, however.

I hummed the tunes from *South Pacific,* I thought of Rosemarie, no, I fantasized about her every time I sang "Younger Than Springtime." I played softball (poorly), marveled at Larry's tricks at the pub, listened to the problems of my new friends, and tossed restlessly in bed at night as I tried to figure out what life meant.

It was not a bad summer, all things considered. Metaphysics and epistemology were marginally interesting and the homework requirements were negligible. Since DePaul was a Catholic college, ND would have to accept the courses. Or so I told myself.

4

Notre Dame was unimpressed by both me and my credentials.

I had hoped to be admitted as a second-semester sophomore, only a half year behind my high school class. I had taken for granted that the University of Maryland courses I had taken in Bamberg would make me at least a first-semester sophomore. In fact, I was a first-semester freshman.

"You have to take the freshman theology and philosophy courses," the stern-faced, restless Holy Cross priest with heavy aftershave smell who was my "adviser" insisted. "Then the sophomore courses next year. Then we'll see what we can do"—he waved his hand contemptuously at my transcript—"about these other credits."

"But I have four philosophy credits from Bamberg . . ."

"Those courses were not in *Catholic* philosophy. They're worthless."

I was dismayed. With a dismissive wave, the "adviser" had told me that my hard work in Germany had been a waste of time.

"But, Father . . ."

"This is our university and we run it the way we want to run it, young man. If you want credit for these pagan philosophy courses, you can risk your immortal soul at a state university."

"Can I appeal?"

"It won't do you any good. Our philosophy and theology requirements are never waived." He scowled at me in contemptuous disapproval. "The trouble with you postwar veterans is that you were never in any danger. The real veterans did not complain about the way we run our university. Men like you want to take the university away from us."

The basic problem between me and the Golden Dome folk was that I didn't understand a split in my own character. Or perhaps I should say that what seemed to me to be a seamless character appeared in their environment a badly bifurcated personality.

I wanted the orderly life, but I did not want a life of externally imposed order. I would make my own order, there was no need for the outside world to inflict its order on me.

Moreover, I wanted an existence in which I could predict today what I would be doing a year from today with little fear of being in error. That did not mean that I wanted to exclude art and music and literature from my life. I may have deplored the chaos in our family, but I surely did not reject its musical and artistic concerns. I was not, I told some of my Notre Dame friends who admitted they couldn't quite figure me out, an artist but I wanted to be able to enjoy art.

"But what good does it do?" one of them asked, his handsome fair-skinned Irish face wrapped in a puzzled frown. "I mean, how will art help your career?"

That said it all. I had avoided, as best I could, the enticing Rosemarie Clancy because I thought she was crazy and drank too much. At the Golden Dome of the National Championship years I encountered a different kind of madness, one that was not personal, but institutional.

To put it succinctly, it was a madness that believed passionately that education could be accomplished without a need for thought.

Father Pius found me reading *Ulysses*. I would catch up with Rosemarie even if I would not see her.

"That book's on the Index," he wailed. "You can't read it without permission of your confessor."

Father Pius assumed that his role authorized him to enter anyone's room without knocking at any time of the day or night.

"I have his permission," I replied.

That was that, except the rector made one more mark against me in the notebook he kept.

This is the same Charles Cronin O'Malley who was careful not to lie to anyone while he was suckering Special Agent Clarke, the FBI bounty hunter who wanted to turn Trudi and her mother and sister over to Red Army rapists.

"Why did I do that?" I asked myself after he had left my room. I was pretty sure that Joyce had never been condemned by the Vatican. Why did I not look it up and inform the rector he had made a mistake?

I'd get a check against my name anyway and it would be a waste of time.

I even struggled through *Ulysses* a second time and pondered Molly Bloom's outburst at the end. It suggested that sexual pleasure was as important to women as to men. Maybe even more important.

It was a scary idea.

And a glorious one too.

Did women yearn for sex as much as men?

I would learn over the years that the answer is yes and no—yes, they do, but no, not the same way. Even now I'm not sure, from day to day, that in practice I understand what that answer means.

I also felt vaguely that maybe Molly's yes said something religious too.

In that early part of my Notre Dame interlude, I had persuaded myself that I liked the school and was happy in my choice. But my anger was already building up, preparing for an explosion.

The assumptions of the system were simple enough: if you gathered together a group of young men, kept them under strict disciplinary supervision, constrained them to sit through sixteen required philosophy and theology courses, pressured them to receive Communion everyday and go to confession often ("hit the rail," "hit the box"), minimized as best you could their contacts with young women, warned them against the dangers of reading forbidden books, and imposed on them strict habits of study and memorization, then you would produce devout Catholic laymen who would be successful in the world of business and profession.

It seemed to work. The young men complained about the regulations and the boredom of the required courses; engaged in drunken orgies when they were off campus (the high jinks at the Christmas bashes of the Notre Dame Club of Chicago were already legendary in the late nineteen forties); and treated their dates like raffle prizes of whom they were shortly to be deprived.

However, the monastic spirituality and the course requirements did appear to turn out graduates who remained loyal to the church. And they were indeed successful in their chosen careers.

That most never read a book after they graduated, that many teetered on the brink of alcoholism, and that a considerable number were incapable of sustained intimacy with their wives—none of these seemed to cause the Holy Cross priests any second thoughts.

In fact, there was never much doubt about our religious affiliation. We were Catholics, what else could we be? And our success in the postwar boom required only that we stay sober long enough to hold a job. The self-congratulations of the priests who ran the Catholic colleges in those years like they were second-class seminaries were not merited.

Like everyone else in the late forties, they were riding the wave of history and taking credit for it.

These are bitter reactions long after the fact—and I suppose they reveal how deep my anger was. At the time, I was troubled and confused.

And unhappy. At first I was caught up in the excitement of coming home, seeing my family, admiring our new house on Fair Oaks in north Oak Park (technically we lived in St. Agedius but we still went to St. Ursula's because Dad was building the new church), renewing friendships with my classmates—many of whom were ND students— and cheering myself hoarse at the pep rallies and football games. Moreover, I had a sense of moving forward again toward my life, behind schedule perhaps but at least moving. There was now a neat and orderly path mapped out for me. The days of confusion and uncertainty, of folly and comedy, were over.

Within the first couple of months, however, I began to realize that I had been happier in Bamberg. After my basic training I had more freedom in the Army than I did under the Golden Dome.

That time was also the most confusing in my young life. I had virtually given up the camera and the darkroom. My business courses were competent but boring. I hated the dry casuistry of Healy's *Moral Guidance* and the high-flown unintelligibility of Farrell's *Companion to the Summa*—the theology textbooks on which my generation were introduced to the Catholic heritage. In philosophy classes we studied Saint Thomas and his answers to the questions posed centuries later by such enemies as Descartes, Hegel, Kant, and Spinoza—obviously stupid from the explanations we were given of their positions. Marx, Freud, Dewey, William James, all of whom I had read with great curiosity in Germany, were dismissed as so patently wrong and so completely unimportant as not to deserve refutations.

Nor did one dare to ask probing questions in most of

the philosophy and theology classes. Such questions, indeed almost any questions, were a sign that the questioner was losing his faith and deserved both prayer and a failing grade.

Our "Apologetics" course was designed to produce answers to all the questions that "non-Catholics," clever and dishonest objectors, might raise against our "Holy Catholic Faith." By refuting such carping, we proved that our Church was the only true faith and that all other religions were lies, heresies, and infidelities.

Could you be a Protestant and still save your soul?

Yes, if you remained in good faith because of your "invincible ignorance," but, in the words of our Apologetics teacher, "It's hard for me to see how an intelligent and well-educated Protestant can remain in good faith. You've read our answers to them. Would they not convince an intelligent and sincere man that Protestantism is an indefensible heresy?"

Fortunately, no one took these classes very seriously. The young men dreamed of weekends, girls, and beer. Only the few of us who were a little less certain about the goals of our lives might be frustrated by an education half of which consisted in memorization of answers to test questions that passed out of our heads as soon as the tests were returned.

If you didn't drink and didn't have a girl and had no plans to let off steam on weekends, you were a little strange. You might even start to think; that was an inadvisable response to Notre Dame of the nineteen forties.

Notre Dame in the era was a men's locker room with all the noise and the smells and the dirt and the crudities and the foul words about women that one would expect to find in a locker room, a boisterous, raw, rank den of coarse and horny animals.

The noise and the smell especially affronted me, worse even, it seemed to me, than a military barracks.

There is nothing wrong with men's locker rooms (I will

not attempt to comment on what women's locker rooms might be like but rather be content with my male fantasies on the subject) except when one claims that the locker room is in fact a university.

I'm not sure that the all-male Holy Cross Order of priests realized how crude our locker room manners and mores were. Those few men who might have found them offensive probably thought that by hitting the box and hitting the rail often we exorcised our gross behavior as well as our moral guilt.

Their seminary, I reflect now, was probably a men's locker room too.

The Holy Cross sisters administered St. Mary's College across the road and were patronized by the priests and were often the target of mean little jokes about "Sister Mary Holy Water C.S.C." It was assumed that since they were women they were inferior and that their women's college was inferior. Actually, as I would learn later, the young women were better educated than we were.

I rode the South Shore home to Chicago and the Lake Street El to the Ridgeland stop where Peg or Mom would pick me up in one of the several family cars that now seemed to clutter around our big Tudor house—including a now grotesque Cadillac with tail fins.

I would try to find a South Shore train on which there would not be many of my fellow Domers. Bad enough that I had to put up with their inanity all week long without having to listen to them babble about booze and broads on the train. I read a lot of fiction in defiance of the anti-intellectualism of the school. Waugh's *The Loved One*. Greene's *The Heart of the Matter*, Mailer's *The Naked and the Dead*, each one of them a heavy hitter. I also reveled in Christopher Fry's play *The Lady's Not for Burning*. I fell in love with the play's heroine and fantasized about saving her, though the hero beat me to it.

In our new home I had a room and bath of my own for the first time in my life. We would sing (*Finian's Rainbow*,

Kiss Me Kate) and talk and laugh and dream. I would dread the return to Notre Dame, not clear in my own head why.

"Are you happy there, darling?" Mom would ask.

"More or less."

"You look"—Dad would frown over his port—"stifled. Are they getting to you?"

"There are times," I would admit, "when it all seems pretty dull."

"Maybe you just ought to come home and go to the Pier," Jane would say. "They leave your private life alone there."

The University of Illinois's Chicago campus in those days was on Navy Pier.

"What private life?" Peg would laugh.

"You ought to take pictures again," Rosemarie would conclude the litany of advice. "I can't believe you've given up the camera."

Rosemarie?

Sure, she was still part of the family. Her long hair had returned after her brief surrender to Dame Fashion. With the exception of our walk on the beach the day of my photograph of her, I was never alone with her during the first year after I came home from the service. I did not want to be alone with her. She was more lovely, more mysterious, more fragile than ever—sometimes just an adolescent girl and sometimes a dazzlingly beautiful mature woman, so beautiful, so graceful, so seemingly self-possessed that you gasped for breath when she walked into the room. And as doomed as ever, I thought. I firmly resolved that I would have nothing to do with her.

Save her, as John Raven had suggested?

An overpoweringly sweet temptation. She seemed to be in desperate need of a savior.

Not me. I had played that game once.

It was still almost impossible not to drink in her love-

liness. Surely none of my friends at the Dome had a girlfriend like my friend who was a girl.

So we became quiet friends. We exchanged jokes instead of barbs, literary opinions instead of insults.

And Peg, herself now an equally stunning beauty,
beamed happily that her brother and her best friend were
civil to each other and seemed even to enjoy each other's
company.

I learned only from Vince about Rosemarie's escapades
at Trinity—she was suspended twice for drinking exploits
at school dances and would have been expelled if Monsignor Mugsy, at the goading of my parents, had not intervened to earn her "one last chance."

I learned, as I say I don't remember how, that her
mother had died in an accident two years ago: she had
fallen down the basement steps of their house at Menard
and Thomas.

A voice whispered inside my brain, "I bet that bastard
pushed her."

It's a theory I treasured for a long time.

Then Sunday evening would come and my spirits drag-
ging, my heart heavy, I would put on my Ike jacket (worn
even at the coldest times of the year) for the ride on the
El and the dirty orange South Shore back to Notre Dame
to make the eleven-thirty curfew deadline.

I am, as should be evident to the readers of these pages
by now, neither a hero nor a rebel. I have usually been
able to make my peace with whatever system in which I
found myself. I make friends easily with my equals and
win over my superiors. At Notre Dame I found no diffi-
culty in making new friends in my own class and renewing
friendships with old friends.

A tall, blond kid in a football letter jacket stopped
me one day during the first semester. "You're Chuck
O'Malley, aren't you?"

I had a sudden impulse to run, an impulse that was very
hard to resist. Working up the remnants of my courage, I

accepted his outstretched hand. "I deny all knowledge of the subject."

"You look even smaller without a football helmet. I'm Ed Murray."

· I knew *that*. All too well.

"I think I have to find a goal line real quick."

"If you do, remind me to down the kickoff in the end zone."

In our laughter that damp November afternoon a friendship was born that would last a lifetime. My only regret is that he now believes the myth about the game at Hansen Park instead of supporting my version of the story.

So Ed and Vince Antonelli and I became a threesome. Some of the time. I didn't join them on their drinking parties and I didn't date with them.

The Holy Cross priests did not respond to my charms the way Coach Angelo Smith had at Fenwick or General Radford Meade in Bamberg. Somehow, I was written off early as a bad influence.

I think the reason was my refusal to go to mass every morning. A refusal that was both uncharacteristic and ostentatious.

There was no rule requiring daily mass attendance, though there had been one in the past (when the school was almost indistinguishable from a seminary). However, the practice was strongly encouraged. In fact, you were required to get out of bed and sign a register by the chapel door to indicate that you were in the dorm at the beginning of the day. You could then go back to sleep if you wanted to; but, as the hall rector would say, you might as well hit the rail.

It was acceptable for you to receive Communion, available before mass as well as during the service, and then bounce back into bed—a violation, as we would learn in later years, of the symbolism of the Eucharist, but at Notre Dame in 1948 we didn't know from symbolism.

The rector kept a careful record in his notebook of those

who turned their back on Jesus. He must have run out of pages putting checks after my name.

Whence this stubbornness, this refusal to go along, that doomed my efforts to win friends in the Holy Cross community?

I don't know, not even forty years after.

"You are a revolutionary, O'Malley," the rector screeched at me in January of 1949, "a troublemaker."

"No, Father," I said respectfully. "I don't make trouble at all. I don't drink, I don't smoke, I don't date. I keep my part of the room neat. I study hard and get good grades . . ."

"And you swagger back to your bed in the morning as if you are proud to turn your back on Jesus."

"It's not a rule, Father."

"And you encourage others to stay away from morning mass."

"I never say a word about it, Father."

"It's your bad example that does the devil's work."

"I don't think so, Father."

"We're keeping an eye on you."

"Yes, Father."

Even today I have a hard time comprehending why I was so stubborn, especially since I often went to daily mass with Mom at St. Ursula when I was home from school.

Looking back, I'm sure there were many sensitive and progressive Holy Cross priests in those days, intelligent teachers. There were even some literate students. It was partly my fault that I didn't find any of them. Moreover, the school was in a minor crisis, adjusting to the shift in enrollment back to unruly and callow adolescents from the mature and responsible vets, many of whom lived in the Quonset-hut married-student housing. The "vet years" were described as a golden age for many years. Even today there is a memorial plaque on the campus to the "vetville" Quonsets.

If I had brought a wife along with me, I would have lived in one of the Quonsets and could have risen from bed whenever I wished. Somehow a wife dispensed you from the control of the Holy Cross Order.

I suspect that it had something to do with control of one's passions. The married vets had an approved "outlet" for their sexual desires and hence did not need the discipline of campus life. Whereas the unmarried vets needed to receive Communion every morning lest they succumb to temptation.

Was my confusion and dissatisfaction caused by sexual frustration? Would I have been better off if I had a relationship with a girl like Vince had with Peg—affection, including heavy necking and petting, combined with respect and hope for the future?

Sure I would, but I distrusted women, or more precisely I distrusted myself with women. Based on my experiences in Bamberg, I lost self-control almost instantly.

I had never known the carefully contained dance of ordinary dating with its limitations and rituals, the fine drawing of invisible lines that separated foreplay from the main event.

Nor had I known the reassurance that for the time being someone did care about you.

Yes, dating probably would have helped, but my belated crises about the meaning of my life probably would have persisted.

5

Life was not all bad despite my disenchantment with the Golden Dome. I reveled in Truman's election victory, defeating *Time* and *Life* and the little man with the mustache who should have been standing on a wedding cake instead of running for the presidency. I had been predicting this victory since I arrived at the school, much to the annoyance of my Republican hall mates. My prediction was based no more on sound political analysis than when I had made my bet at the soda joint in Michigan City. However, as the campaign wore on, my instincts began to tell me that Thomas E. Dewey was a loser. I rubbed it in on Wednesday morning at Notre Dame, putting my physical well-being at some risk. The local conservatives seemed to think that the Devil had won a victory over God.

That weekend I collected my three malted milks and consumed them at one sitting in Pedersen's Ice Cream Parlor at Chicago and Harlem. "Double whipped cream and don't forget the butter cookies." My friends also gave me a framed copy of the famous headline from the *Tribune*: "Dewey Defeats Truman!"

"You were brilliant, Chucky," my sister informed me.

"Incredible!" Rosemarie agreed, her eyes glowing.

"Lucky," Vince sniffed.

He, as the Irish would say, had the right of it.

That evening I wandered over to the Magic Pub, searching for my softball friends from summertime. I had appeared there a couple of times on earlier weekends, only to find that they all had disappeared into the serious life of the post–Labor Day world. I had heard, however, from John Raven that Monica and Jimmy had broken up—thus for eternal bonds—and Timmy was drunk half the time and had stopped going to his shrink.

When Big Tom had ordered Monica to drop Jimmy or move out of the house, Jimmy, true romantic that he was, suggested some time off so that Monica could think about what she was doing before she moved out. Monica, a realist like most women, wanted no part of it. Take me now or never. Let's give it time. It doesn't need time.

So they parted, temporarily, Jimmy had said. Permanently, Monica had asserted.

"Idiots!" I had exploded to Father Raven. "They didn't ask me!"

That was going a bit too far. Who the hell did I think I was?

"Oddly enough, they didn't ask me either."

The only familiar face in the Magic Pub was Timmy, sitting over in a corner by himself.

"I was wondering where you were, Charles C. I thought you might have become so enamored of the Dome that you spent all your time there."

Enamored, huh? Literate guy, if a drunk. But so, I would learn as my life went on, were a lot of Irish drunks.

"Hardly," I said as I sat next to him.

"Seen through it already, huh?"

"I liked the Army better."

"You were in it at a relatively good time."

"Can I tell you a story about Bamberg?"

"Sure, I got nothing else to do but listen."

"What do you think of this picture?"

He took it in his big hands and pondered it carefully.

"Who's the woman?" he asked slowly.

"The wife of a German Panzer officer who was in the Battle of Krusk. Big tank fight. Missing in action. She's at the railroad station waiting for him."

"Much chance of his coming back?"

He handed the picture back to me with a shudder.

"Hardly any. Good old Uncle Joe killed most of the prisoners off, one way or another."

"Yet she's at the station waiting for him?"

"Everyday."

"What do you call the picture?"

"Fidelity."

He took it from my hands and inspected it again.

"Good title. . . . Well, our deal is off. You're going to be a photographer whether you want to or not."

"That's not the point."

"Yeah, I suppose not. . . . Never came back, did he?"

"He did come back."

"Really? Was she there?"

"Oddly enough, she wasn't. She was working for us by then as a translator. There was an important meeting with this fellow Adenauer who is the new head of the German government. They needed her."

"So who did meet him?"

"She sent me over to cover for her."

Timmy Boylan laughed loudly, the second time he had done that.

"Who else? So you saluted him and called him 'Captain, sir,' and brought him back to your headquarters and a tearful reunion?"

That was too close for comfort.

"Something like that. . . . The point is that he was barely alive after those years in Uncle Joe's prison camp. Still jaunty, but mostly dead. Since she worked for us, he was an American dependent of a sort. So we took him off to our base hospital and fixed him up."

"Lucky guy. . . . I suppose they all lived happily ever after?"

"You know better than that, Timmy."

"Even with a woman like this, he did an imitation of me?"

"Something like that."

"And?"

"And one of our shrinks straightened him out."

"Yeah?"

"Yeah."

"I see what you're getting at. No way. I got rid of my shrink a couple of weeks ago."

"Our guy in Bamberg was a friend of mine. We both did a lot of work in the USO darkroom."

"But you're not a photographer, right?"

"Right. . . . Anyway, he's out of the Army now and has just opened up an office here in Chicago. He was on the phone the other day to make sure I hadn't been arrested for impersonating a veteran."

I gave him Dr. Berman's name, address, and phone number, written neatly, as is everything I write, on a three-by-five card.

Timmy looked at it, cocked his eye at me, and put it in his pocket.

"No promises, Charles C."

"No promises."

As I left the Magic Pub with my fingers crossed, on both hands, Timmy ordered another beer.

Was it not brilliant of me to link up Tim and Dr. Berman?

It was indeed. I'm proud of the idea. I would be even more proud if Rosemarie had not suggested it to me when I told her about Dr. Berman and Kurt.

That Sunday I went to the eleven o'clock mass at St. Ursula's. Our old softball field was now a vast hole in the ground. The work had at last begun on the "new church" that Dad had designed for the parish (for free) back during the Depression. I prayed during mass that it be finished before the Depression returned. John Raven said the mass and preached about commitment and opportunity, though I don't remember the exact words he said. This was standard stuff for John. It usually made a lot of people frown thoughtfully, as though it was something they knew they should hear but really didn't want to hear.

Cynically I suspected that the scene in front of the church after mass rather than the sermons was what drew everyone from fifteen to thirty to church—or in our case to the gym that served as a church till Dad finished his new building. The vestibule, the steps, the sidewalk, even the street, became like the plaza in front of the cathedral in some European countries. It was a place to see and be seen, to find out what was happening, where everyone was going, what the latest gossip was. Adolescent girls huddled together, giggling and pretending not to notice anything or anyone else as they chattered. They did not, however, miss a thing. Their male counterparts stood listlessly as far away as possible exchanging animal noises. The sexes were more likely to mix among my generation than among the vets, especially the unmarried ones. Our local politicians wandered about shaking hands and celebrating Truman's victory. The clergy, especially Msgr. Mugsy Branigan, the pastor, made sure that they said hello to everyone. Monsignor Mugsy celebrated not only Truman's victory but, more important from his viewpoint, the triumph of the Fighting Irish of Notre Dame the day before.

"Your friend Vince is really good, Chuck," he informed me.

"For an Italian," I replied.

"You weren't at the game?"

"I had to come home and settle some family disputes."

The pastor knew me well enough to know that both of my comments were designed to pull his leg. He was a master of the art and had told my father once that I was the only one in the parish who could match him.

"How's Rosie, Chucky?" John Raven asked me.

"She went to the nine o'clock mass with Peg."

"I know that . . ."

He wandered away, as if he were disgusted with me.

"Chuck!"

Ah, someone was glad to see me—Monica Sullivan cautiously navigating the steps in high heels and a New Look coat. The New Look was Christian Dior's return to femininity in the postwar world, rounded shoulders, a tucked-in waist, padded hips, and a long, pleated, flouncy skirt that fell to about ten inches from the floor. It was alleged that it was a revolution against the square, manlike, utilitarian fashions of the Depression and the war. It required many yards of fabric and determined cinching of the waist. The women in my family had signed on to it immediately.

"Thank goodness," Mom said with a happy sigh, "we don't have to pretend not to be women anymore."

"I hadn't noticed that pretense," Dad said.

Then he quickly added, "The women in this family look beautiful no matter what they wear."

"I like them in two-piece swimsuits." I registered my opinion. "Maybe next summer they'll wear those bikini things that the French are doing."

There were loud protests that this would never happen.

"You look gorgeous, Monica," I observed. "The New Look was designed for women like you."

She blushed. "Thank you, Chuck. For a punk you are very thoughtful."

Monica was indeed gorgeous, a well-tailored, nicely rounded little blond doll, fresh out of the pages of *Harper's Bazaar*. It would take considerable effort, my lewd imagination suggested, to remove the various layers of expansive fabric and repressive lingerie, but it would certainly be worth the effort. Jimmy Rizzo was an idiot.

I almost said that.

Instead I said something almost as bad.

"I hear you dumped Captain Rizzo."

"You heard correctly," she said calmly, not fazed by my crude comment. That meant she wanted to talk about it.

Why to me?

Why do women trust me as a confidant?

I never could figure it out, but they do.

"Too bad," I said.

She shrugged. "I was ready to move into an apartment," she said, "to get away from my father. That would have torn our family apart. I wanted to do it because I love Jimmy . . . loved him. He wanted me to hold off for another year so I could be sure. He didn't want me to have any regrets. What kind of a love is it that worries about regrets?"

"Maybe a very sensitive and caring love," I said, having no idea where the words came from.

She paused to reflect on what I had said, as though it were something important.

"Do you really think so?"

"I don't know anything about love, Monica. Except I recognize it when I see it."

She drew a deep breath.

"Would you say that to your little Rosie?"

Unfair! Besides, Rosemarie was a good four inches taller than Monica.

"Rosemarie," I said firmly, "is my foster sister. Moreover, if any man tried to do that with her, his life and health would be in serious peril."

"She is certainly breathtakingly lovely."

"Furious temper."

"Maybe I should have beat up on Jimmy!" she said with a fond smile.

"Right! Slap him! Hit him! Punch him in the stomach! Kick him! Stomp on him! That's the way to deal with your ex-marines!"

"I could never hit him, Chucky," she said sadly. "I love him too much."

"My point."

"Did you know that he could go to law school at Michigan or Princeton? On a scholarship?"

"Jimmy Rizzo an Ivy Leaguer?"

"He looks quite civilized when he dresses up."

"I'll take your word for it."

We both laughed, unindicted coconspirators.

"You think he did the right thing?"

"Certain kinds of Italian American men," I said, making it up as I went along, "see themselves as gallant knight-errants. You happened to find a particularly gallant one. Maybe he knows a little bit more about you than you think he does."

"Maybe," she sighed. "Anyway, Chuck, thanks for listening."

"Anytime."

My next stop was Marco's drugstore corner. The neighborhood was stark and barren under a somber gray sky, a bungalow belt in need of postwar retouching. The leafless trees reached to heaven like souls in purgatory pleading for release this November.

The boundaries of life were still circumscribed by neighborhood boundaries. Where else did you go than to the corner of the neighborhood drugstore?

Why the drugstore?

Who knows?

In fact, the customs were changing as more and more of the vets bought old jalopies like Jimmys' 1937 Chevy. It became possible to have several drugstore corners in neighborhoods surrounding your own. A member of our softball team boasted that he had twelve corners where he could hang out. His bride-to-be made him promise to give them all up. Wives tended not to like street-corner societies.

"Didn't catch you at church this morning, Captain, sir," I began.

"Nine-fifteen in the chapel," he said with his usual genial smile. "Didn't want to bump into certain people."

"If I were a couple of years older, I'd want to bump into her," I said.

He thought that was very funny.

"How the hell is it going at Notre Dame? Still like it?"

"Hate it passionately."

"I figured you would. . . . You don't belong at a place like that."

"Where do I belong?"

He laughed again. "I don't know, Chuck, someplace special where you can appear out of the mists and disturb people's consciences."

"Is that what I do?"

"Yeah, that's what you do. . . . You see, I gotta give Monica time to make sure. It's like investing in a future down at the exchange."

"Risky."

"Too risky the other way, you know?"

"Maybe . . . Don't give her too much time."

"You gonna steal her on me?"

"She's a one-man woman, Jimmy," I said, once more making up the words as I went along. "You're the one man. For Monica it's either you or no one."

"You're kidding?"

"It's obvious."

It was indeed, though I had noticed it only in front of St. Ursula's an hour before.

"Then I don't have to rush."

"You do have to rush. If she gives up on you, she'll give up permanently on men."

"Maybe you're right."

I didn't say what I was thinking—that if I were as much in love with a woman as he was with Monica and she loved me as much as Monica loved him, I would be driven out of my mind until we could take off each other's clothes and jump into bed. Jimmy should ignore Uncle Sal and Big Tom and follow his gallant instincts to carry off the fair maiden.

What right did I have to that opinion? What did I know about love?

Enough, as I had said, to recognize it when I see it.

Jimmy was finishing up college and managing one of Uncle Sal's restaurants.

"I sure wish I'd had a year or two of college before I joined the Marines," he said with a shake of his head. "I never thought I'd be a collegian. Seemed part of another world. Now they want me to go to law school."

"Where?" I said, playing dumb.

"DePaul, Kent, Michigan, even Princeton. Can you imagine me in Princeton?"

"If you comb your hair . . ."

Self-consciously he reached for his thick black hair, which was perfectly combed.

"You bastard," he said with a laugh. "You're a hell of a one to talk."

"It's useful for scrubbing pots and pans. . . . What does your family want you to do?"

"Uncle Sal says when I graduate from college in June I can take over all his restaurants. He insists that they are a hundred percent legit."

"And your parents?"

"Uncle Sal is family. He's been good to us. But they want me to go to law school."

"Is anything the boys run a hundred percent legit?"

"Yeah. Absolutely. But not a hundred percent of the time, you know?"

He raised his hands in the familiar Italian gesture that means, in effect, what more can I say?

"What do you think Monica would say?" he continued anxiously.

"Monica loves you, Captain, sir, as any idiot can tell. Hopelessly. She'll love you no matter what you do. But I think she'd agree with your parents. Moreover, if I dare say so, Captain, sir, she'd fit in just fine at Princeton."

"She'd fit in perfectly," he said proudly, "anywhere."

"At a gathering of the wives of the boys?"

He frowned. "I see what you mean. . . . Hey, I'll drive you home."

"I can walk," I said. "I need the exercise."

Our house seemed empty. But as I prowled around looking for family, I found Rosemarie, curled up on a sofa reading *War and Peace*. She was clad in the young woman's fatigue uniform of the day—full skirt (red plaid), bobby socks, saddle shoes, blouse, and sweater. Her casual loveliness took my breath away.

"Hi, Rosemarie, where's everyone?"

She didn't exactly live with us. However, there was an empty room on our third floor that was dubbed "Rosie's room." She could drift in and out of our house with no questions asked.

"Huh?" She stirred on the couch, distracted by my interruption.

"O'Malley, Charles Cronin, ma'am, serial number—"

"Don't be silly, Chucky."

"I was only wondering where everyone was."

She put her finger in place and sighed, causing her delectable breasts to move up and down beneath her sweater and my heart to skip several beats.

Lusting after her, I warned myself, is almost incestuous.

"Oh . . . Don't you think I'd make a good grand duchess, Chucky?"

"A grand grand duchess," I said, reclining in a chair at a safe distance from her.

She sighed again and sat up on the couch.

"What did you want to know?"

"Whether my parents and my siblings have deserted me forever."

"Oh, *that*! Peg and Jane and the good April are out shopping. Michael is singing at the cathedral. Your dad is meeting with contractors. I'm the chatelaine. Do you know what a chatelaine is, Chucky Ducky?"

"A low-level grand duchess . . . Go back to Tolstoy. Sorry to interrupt you."

"Okay."

She stretched out on the sofa and returned to Moscow in 1812.

"Napoleon," she informed me, "was a jerk."

"A brilliant jerk."

"Hmm . . ."

Silence.

Why did she have to be a drunk!

"Rosemarie," I blurted without thinking about what I was going to say. "Why do women, especially older women, turn me into a confidant?"

She closed Tolstoy again, but did not abandon her position on the sofa.

"That's so obvious, Chucky, that if you don't see it, I can't explain it."

"Try."

She sighed in protest, put a bookmark in *War and Peace,* and rearranged herself on the sofa.

"You're a good listener and you're smart and you're sweet and you care about people and you're cute. Kind of a magic little good-luck charm. Now don't try to tell me that you're none of those things, because you're all of them, even if you are the most stubborn boy I've ever known."

"Oh."

"Who was confiding in you today?"

"Monica."

"Monica Sullivan?"

"Yeah."

"What do you think of her?"

"Diminutive but lush."

She laughed and bells pealed somewhere in the distance.

"Look who's talking diminutive!"

"I'm taller than she is!"

"Not much . . . If she's got any brains she won't let that James Rizzo get away."

"I agree. The problem is him."

"As the good April says, it is always the woman who has to slam the door."

I had never heard her say it, but I had no doubt that she had said it.

" 'Lush' is a good word for Monica," she commented after a moment's judicious reflection.

"I kind of thought so too."

"Am I lush?"

Aha, a challenge!

"Absolutely not!"

"Then what am I?"

As usual the word came without thought.

"What about lithe?"

Another moment of judicious reflection.

"I kind of like that."

"I thought you might."

"Just a minute." She sighed and rose from the sofa.

She returned shortly with a tray that contained four ham and cheese sandwiches on rye and two mugs of hot chocolate.

"You'll get your ice cream when you've eaten your sandwiches."

"Yes, ma'am. Thank you, ma'am. I didn't say I was hungry, ma'am."

"O'Malley, Charles Cronin, Master Sergeant, Army of the United States, you are *always* hungry."

"If I hadn't come up with the word 'lithe,' would you have fed me anyway?"

"I knew you'd come up with something sweet, Chucky Ducky. I just wanted to see what it would be."

"The word," I said, building on my success, "implies that you are not a Juno or a Venus but a Diana."

"Blarney . . . Diana rising from the sea?"

"She doesn't rise from the sea."

"I know but I'd like to. . . . Kind of Diana on the half shell."

Where does a high school senior come up with that kind

of allusion? But then why was a high school senior reading Tolstoy?

"As I remember the painting, she didn't have any clothes. Naked Diana on a half shell?"

"Chucky," she said with a faint blush. "You're impossible. . . . Eat your lunch and then I'll drive you downtown so you can take the South Shore back to that horrible place."

"I can take the El."

"I know you can take the El. But if you want your ice cream, you'll let me drive you downtown, understand?"

"Yes, ma'am."

"I won't try to seduce you, Chucky Ducky, I promise."

"Wow! I was really worried!"

"I hate that place. Every boy down there looks at you like you're a potential slave being paraded naked across a stage."

"Not an inaccurate observation . . . Even Vince?"

"No, Vince is an exception, but he has to be."

"Right."

"That Mount Carmel boy you knocked out at the football game, he's a nice boy too. . . . What's his name?"

"Ed Murray. And I didn't knock him out."

"Yes you did, Chucky Ducky. He knocked you out when you scored the winning touchdown, then you knocked him out on the kickoff."

Instead of trying to argue with this utterly false legend— a bootless task—I tore into the second sandwich.

"Three for you, one for me."

"Fair enough."

I was distracted from my nourishment, but not greatly, by the observation that Rosemarie's eyes were dancing with merriment. She thought I was funny.

"You didn't add 'funny' to your litany of my admirable qualities."

"I didn't want to hurt your feelings."

She donned her silver fox jacket and led me out to her Cadillac.

"You had a car in Germany, didn't you, Chuck?"

"A jeep at first and then my very own Buick."

"You should have one here."

"Can't own one at Notre Dame unless you have a wife."

She merely laughed at that.

On Washington Boulevard as we rode downtown, she asked, "You really hate it down there, don't you, Chuck?"

"I'm not wild about the place."

"You're homesick."

It was a flat statement, not a question.

"Kind of."

"More so than when you were in Bamberg."

"Maybe."

"Your family is only two hours away here."

"Yeah, but the other five days of the week are worse than Bamberg. In Bamberg I was free. Down at the Dome, I'm not free."

"You don't belong there," she insisted as we paused for a stop light at Cicero Avenue.

That was the second time today someone had told me that.

"Where do I belong?"

"I don't know. . . . Someplace where they appreciate you."

"I've planned to go there as long as I can remember. The real Notre Dame is nothing like my dreams."

"I know."

With the light fading on a dismal November Sunday and my hopes fading with them, there's nothing like sympathy from a lovely and sensitive young woman.

Careful, Charles C., you're asking for trouble.

Yeah, but such nice, warm trouble.

"Maybe I'll get used to it."

"You could go to the Pier or DePaul or Loyola and live at home. They leave your private life alone. And you'd be with the family."

That possibility sounded appealing, just at that moment very appealing.

"I have to try it for a year."

"You'll never be happy down at that terrible place."

"Maybe . . . Where are you going to college, Rosemarie? Sorry I never asked."

"The University," she said promptly.

"What university?"

"In this city there is only one university—the University of Chicago!"

"That Communist place!"

"Don't be a naïve bigot, Chucky."

All right, I won't.

"Aren't you afraid you'll lose your faith?"

"If I haven't lost it at Trinity High School, I'll never lose it. . . . Don't worry, Chuck, I'll be an Irish Catholic all my life. I wouldn't know how to be anything else."

That settled that.

"I'll wait and see how I feel at the end of the year. Maybe I'll get some good courses."

"Loyola and DePaul would take all your courses from Bamberg. You'd be a junior like you should be."

That was probably true. And they wouldn't take the crap I was picking up at the Dome. I was wasting my money.

But, no, I wouldn't quit. An O'Malley never quits, Mom always said.

However, she defined "quit" very loosely.

"I guess I have to figure out who I am."

"Like everyone else."

"Like everyone else, Rosemarie."

Silence.

"It's not fair," she exploded passionately.

"I agree. . . . Only what is it that's not fair?"

"You're always helping other people to be happy and you're not happy yourself."

That, I thought, was an exaggerated statement of my virtue.

We turned onto Warren Boulevard, which paralleled Washington Boulevard, probably the only two one-way streets in the city.

"It will work out, Rosemarie," I said finally, breaking an agonized silence. "It will just take time. Maybe I have to adjust to the postwar world."

"Well, there's never going to be another depression. That's what my father says and he knows business, despite everything else."

What was "everything else"?

"Does he?"

"You simply have to realize, Chuck," she exploded again, "that you're special."

I wasn't special. I had a quick smile and a quicker tongue and unlimited nerve and I was considered "cute." So I charmed people at Fenwick and in the Constabulary, but not at the Golden Dome.

"I can't see myself that way, Rosemarie."

I expected her to blow up at me.

Instead she said, "Someday you will."

When we arrived at the South Shore Station on Michigan Avenue at Randolph, I had a headache and felt melancholy. Despite the headache, I wished Rosemarie were driving me all the way to Notre Dame.

She hugged me and kissed my cheek. A sisterly kiss. Too sisterly in fact. I noticed in the dim illumination of the street lights that her face was wet with tears that I did not deserve.

"Thank you for the ride, Rosemarie."

"See you at Thanksgiving, Chuck."

On the interminable train ride, I alternated between elation at Rosemarie's affection and agonized confusion over who I really was.

However, it was November, the purgatory month, wasn't it?

6

There was happy family news at Thanksgiving when Jane and Ted announced that they would be married during Christmas vacation. Ted finally had the nerve to stand up to Doctor, as his father was always called—with a tone of reverence required in one's voice.

"You're inviting Monica Sullivan?" I asked Jane during a moment's respite from our noisy celebration.

"Sure," she said. "We're good friends and we both teach at St. Ursula. Why do you ask?"

"Maybe you should ask my friend James F. Rizzo, late captain of the United States Marines and currently captain of my softball team."

Jane considered me cautiously.

"They've broken up, Chucky."

"I know that."

Jane might be a lightweight as her younger sister often suggested, but when it came to matters of the heart, she was quick.

"That's a very good idea." She nodded and smiled. "An excellent idea . . . You're dangerous, Chucky."

"Who me?"

"Have you heard the latest?" Peg informed me a week later at the final Notre Dame football weekend (this time a contest with the hated Trojans). "Dr. McCormack will double Ted's allowance if he drops psychiatry and goes into a surgical residency. Poor Janey doesn't know what to do."

"Do they need money? Doesn't he have the GI Bill?"

"They don't really need the money, not yet. But Ted is nervous about rebelling against Doctor; more money might be an excuse to drop the fight. Then Doctor and Mrs. Doctor will own Ted and Jane for the rest of their lives."

"Psychiatrist heal thyself."

Ted was a slender young man of medium height (well, he was taller than I was) with a boyish face, sandy hair, and a ready smile. He moved quickly and decisively and exuded the confidence that the Navy looked for in its fighter pilots. When he turned on his charm and his blue eyes sparkled with enthusiasm, I thought he should have run for public office instead of becoming a doctor.

Despite his vigor and assurance, he was no match for his overbearing father.

Peg nodded solemnly. "Jane isn't an alley fighter like me, poor thing."

Dr. McCormack divided the human race into two categories—surgeon and all other. He was convinced that his son would marry down if he wed Jane. In Doctor's world there was little difference between an architect and a bricklayer.

"There's nothing wrong with being a bricklayer, dear!" Mom's normally smooth brow furrowed during one of our conversations on the subject of Doctor. "Your great-grandfather was a bricklayer."

"And Doctor's father was a saloonkeeper," Dad responded. "A fact conveniently forgotten, it seems to me."

Dad was a distinguished architect now and Mom was the daughter of a doctor. But Grandpa Cronin was not a surgeon, you see. Ted was quite capable of flying fifty missions in a F4U Corsair during the war without his father peering over his shoulder, but not capable, in Doctor's estimation, of choosing a wife or a professional specialty.

Ted had revolted on the first point and had started a revolt on the second; but now the apron strings were being tightened. Jane had no idea how to respond to the pressures and could not imagine that she and the psychiatric profession had been lumped together as the Enemy of Doctor's wisdom.

"When he's a successful psychiatrist," the good April announced to us, "his mother and father will simply love Jane."

My father had started to open his mouth and then closed it slowly. His wife's analysis was wrong, but there wasn't much we could do to help Jane. As Peg had said, she was not qualified to be an alley fighter.

Jane was as naïve as Mom and infinitely more innocent. She had charmed her teachers all through school just as I had before I ventured to Notre Dame and took it for granted that older folk would collapse in the face of her laughing effervescence. Now she was often in tears as a result of Doctor's snubs.

"Can we do her alley fighting for her?" I asked Peg.

"Charles the Bold," she laughed. "But, seriously, Chucky, maybe it will come to that. You and me and Rosie."

When I returned for my Christmas parole from Notre Dame, the O'Malley house was in that advanced state of chaos that weddings demand. I wisely kept my mouth shut, though there were scores of hilarious comments I might have made. Alas, they would not have been seen as funny. I withdrew to my room and strove to memorize answers for my philosophy and theology exams in which it would be required that I repeat verbatim sections of the textbooks. Liberal education in a Catholic university in the year of Our Lord nineteen hundred and forty-eight.

I ventured forth into the winter cold a couple of times to visit Marco's corner and the Magic Pub. The corner was deserted the first two times but my friends from the Catholic War Vets filled the pub and greeted me warmly.

Everyone wanted to know how Notre Dame was. I told them that it was too early to tell. However, neither Jimmy Rizzo nor Tim Boylan were there.

I did find Tim on the corner of Menard and Division, however, shivering in the cold.

"No action here tonight, Charles C.," he said. "All sensible people are somewhere that's warm."

"And if they're outside they're not wearing Ike jackets like we are."

"Two misfits, huh, Charles C.?"

"I don't know about you, Timmy, but I feel like a misfit."

"Serves you right for going down to the Golden Dome."

"I guess so."

"Your friend Dr. Berman tell you I was seeing him a couple of times a week?"

"Certainly not. That would be a violation of professional ethics."

"Are you going to ask how it's coming?"

"Not unless you want to tell me."

He laughed.

"Okay, I want to tell you, so ask."

"How's it's coming with Dr. Berman?"

"He's a hell of an interesting little guy. I really like his Jewish style. Best shrink yet."

"So?" I said, imitating the Doctor's style.

"So I'm still a bundle of anger that would be better off dead. But I'm talking to him and feeling . . . well, feeling good about doing it, to tell you the truth."

"I'm glad to hear it."

"Are you going to tell me to stick with it?"

"If you want me to."

"I do."

"Okay, Timmy, stick with it."

"My whole future could depend on him, huh?"

"No, your whole future depends on you."

Silence in the cold darkness.

"I suppose that's right. . . . Well, I'm going somewhere where I can find some liquid warmth."

"Merry Christmas, Tim."

"Yeah," he said with a sneer, "Merry Christmas, Charles C."

As I walked back to Oak Park I wondered where the words I said to Tim came from. Was someone whispering in my ear?

John Raven had told me once that in the confessional or the rectory office words leaped out of his mouth that seemed to come from somewhere else.

"That happens to me all the time," I said.

"I don't doubt it, Chuck."

"So I should be a priest?"

"I do doubt it, but don't take my word for it."

Anyway, I said to whoever was in charge, thanks for the help.

I slipped into the house and quietly climbed to my room. I was caught, however, and informed by Mom that I would have to be fitted for my tux the next morning. Wisely I agreed without comment.

I'm sure the subsequent laughter was aimed at me.

The next night I found Jimmy Rizzo on the same corner.

"Why aren't you at the Magic, Captain, sir?" I demanded.

"Too many people ask me about Monica."

"Good enough reason."

"She won't even talk to me now. I never knew your Irish women could be so stubborn."

"You haven't been very observant."

"I love her more than ever."

It was a pathetic remark to a guy five years younger. So maybe I should be a priest after all. That would solve a lot of problems.

"You're waiting for her to call you and back down."

"Yeah, I guess so."

"Then you don't understand her or really love her."

Silence.

"I'm turning down the law schools."

"Don't."

"Uncle Sal will pay me as much next year as I would earn as a lawyer in ten years."

"You don't know that for sure."

"I don't think I'd make a very good lawyer."

"You'll make a great lawyer. . . . What's your deadline for accepting Princeton?"

"March first."

"Uncle Sal pushing you?"

"Not really."

"Promise me you'll hold off till then."

Maybe, just maybe, we could celebrate a solemn high reconciliation at Oak Park Country Club.

He hesitated.

"Okay. No harm done, I guess."

As I walked home I wondered whether there was a chance in hell that I would ever go to Princeton if I had the chance.

Doctor behaved abominably during the preparations for the wedding. He forbade Mrs. Doctor (as his wife was always called) from attending the tea and the shower for Jane. He threatened that they would not come to the wedding. He ordered Ted's cousin, a former major in the infantry, not to participate, an order that the major ignored.

No one in our family could understand Doctor's behavior. What did he have against us?

I kept my analysis (Doctor loves being mean) to myself since I figured Chucky Ducky's wit and wisdom would not be well received under the circumstances.

Ted finally admitted, his head bowed in shame, that from the moment of her birth the two families had planned that Ted would marry the daughter of a fellow surgeon with whom Doctor had gone to medical school.

"So why didn't you marry her?" I piped up, breaking my vow of silence.

He grinned at me, the F4U pilot once again.

"I can't stand her, Chuck. And she can't stand me. She congratulated me fervently when she heard about Jane."

"Good for her!" I said.

Dummies! If they had left the two young people alone, it might have worked out. Too bad for them. Good for Jane.

Why were parents so stupid?

Would I be stupid as a parent?

I addressed a brief prayer to the Deity that I be a parent like my parents.

"They'll grow to love Jane, I'm sure," my maternal Dr. Panglossa asserted.

Doctor and wife finally relented and promised that they would come to both the wedding and the rehearsal dinner. The latter in 1948 was much less elaborate than such events came to be subsequently. Only the wedding party and the immediate family were invited. Doctor should have scheduled it at Butterfield Country Club, to which he belonged, or at Nielsen's restaurant on North Avenue. However, he was furious because Mom and Dad had decided that the reception after the wedding would be at Oak Park Country Club to which Doctor did not belong.

I don't remember the reason for this decision. Perhaps it was to show the Protestants who still dominated Oak Park that we were as good as they were.

Anyway, Doctor informed us that the rehearsal dinner would be upstairs at Hayes' at North and Harlem (on the Elmwood Park side of the four corners). There was nothing wrong with Hayes'. It was a great place to go after a date for a bite to eat, I was told, since I never really had a date.

"The food is very nice," Mom insisted, "and the upstairs is very quiet."

"A lot cheaper too," I added. "Surgeons have to be careful because they don't make much money."

"That's not very nice, Chuck," Mom warned me.

"Yes, ma'am."

"But it's true," Peg whispered in my ear.

My cougar sibling was convinced that the reception would need some "spontaneous" extra entertainment beyond that provided by the orchestra (big band music, of course). Therefore, she insisted that Rosemarie and I practice our spontaneity, accompanied by her on the violin. She permitted herself a gigue from Niccolò Paganini as a solo.

"Peg," I said when she was finished, "that was sensational!"

"Thanks, Chuck," she said with a pleased smile. "I worked awfully hard on this thing."

"Too good for Doctor," Rosemarie said, now definitely the timber wolf.

We all giggled.

Doctor and Mrs. Doctor were not at the rehearsal. The women in my family were painfully distraught that we might make hideous blunders in the ceremonies that would be a blot on the family tradition. Given a chance, they would have forced us to practice over and over again till midnight.

Fortunately, John Raven turned the rehearsal into comedy. Our clan dissolved into laughter, which was never far away from the crazy O'Malleys, no matter how serious the circumstances.

"Do we really want Chuck in this wedding party?" he asked. "He'll never be able to walk down the aisle at the right speed."

"Great idea!" I agreed.

"But, Father," my foster sister protested, "he looks so funny in a formal suit!"

"A point well taken."

General laughter.

"And we'll make him comb his hair," Peg added.

More laughter.

"I won't invite any of you to my wedding!" I threatened.

Still more laughter.

Everyone but me was worrying about whether Doctor

would show up at Hayes'. I wasn't worrying because I knew he wouldn't.

Sure enough, neither of them came. Mrs. Doctor called the restaurant before we arrived to report that Doctor was "in surgery" with an emergency.

Poor Ted was humiliated.

I whispered to Dad, "Be sure you send him the bill."

Dad, who had kept his fury at Doctor to himself, under the same restraints as I was, whispered back, "I thought of that before you did, Chuck, and I will."

The next morning was one of those bitter cold winter days in Chicago on which the pure blue sky, the clean white snow, and the crystalline air made you forget for a moment the icy bite when you walk out of the door of your house.

The nuptial mass was a huge success, mostly because the women of my family were dazzling. I noticed also how strong and handsome my father was in his formal suit. A tall bald man with a wonderful red beard, he looked dangerous but was as gentle as a mother with a newborn child—until someone pushed him too far.

I worried about him. He had lost weight since our days of poverty because he could devote time to exercise. Yet there was a touch of anxiety in his eyes that I had not noticed when we were poor. The demands of a successful business were taking their toll. I had to do something about that.

A mysterious decision, about which I was not consulted, had decreed that Rosemarie and I were paired.

"You look fabulous, Chuck," she whispered. "Really cute."

"You're so beautiful," I replied, "that I'm speechless."

Which was the honest truth. In her dark green bridesmaid's dress with red trim, quite modest save for a slight hint of décolletage, my foster sister did indeed render me inarticulate, something that doesn't happen very often.

Even today when I take the wedding pictures out of my files, I gasp.

After the bridal procession, Doctor and Mrs. Doctor, two short and overweight people, he egg-bald, bustled down the aisle. I resolved, quite uncharitably, that we would get him good before the day was over.

Monsignor Mugsy presided over the exchange of vows. John Raven said the mass. His sermon was about as candid about sexual love as you could be in those days.

I pondered the possibility that I would be the groom on some such occasion.

No, it could never happen.

My sister, my foster sister, and I, in unspoken agreement, headed right for Doctor after the receiving line finally ended. He had declined to participate in it.

I was an ant who hardly merited notice. But Peg and Rosemarie were so beautiful that he had to acknowledge our presence.

"It must be wonderful to be a doctor," the good Margaret Mary began, her eyes wide with fake admiration.

"Yes, it is," Doctor said, puffing up. "The wonderful aspect of being a physician and surgeon is that you wake up every morning with the knowledge that you're going to do good things for people all day long."

"And get paid well for every good thing you do," Rosemarie, the soul of worshipful innocence, continued.

Doctor simply nodded proudly.

Peg really went too far when she said, "And every penny of that goes into keeping the American economy going despite that man in the White House."

The dummy missed it all. Doubtless he told Mrs. Doctor later that we were three very bright young people.

I figured that the cougar and the timber wolf were waiting for the clown to speak his lines.

"A tremendous achievement for a shopkeeper's son," I said.

Doctor had hesitated at that one and decided it was a compliment.

"I thank God for His blessings every day."

"What did your father sell?" Peg had asked, all wide-eyed innocence.

"Groceries," Doctor had replied shortly.

Rosemarie, drat her, beat me to our punch line.

"That was after Prohibition wasn't it, Doctor? My father said your family owned a very nice saloon before Prohibition."

"There's nothing wrong with owning a saloon, Rosemarie dear," Peggy said in an admonishing tone.

"Some very respectable people own saloons," I chimed in.

At that point the good April bore down upon us and chased us up to the head table for grace.

"I'm so happy that you're being nice to Doctor," she bubbled.

I glanced back at Doctor. He was frowning, as though he were trying to figure out what had happened to him.

"We vindicated our family honor," I said to Rosemarie, as we waited for Monsignor Mugsy to say grace.

"We sure did. . . . But I feel so sorry for poor Ted."

"Don't," I replied. "He gets to sleep with Jane tonight."

She cocked an eye at me. "Take off her clothes and play with her and then sleep with her. I hope he plays with her for a long time!"

"Rosemarie!" I was genuinely shocked.

She laughed recklessly.

Doctor and Mrs. Doctor decamped before the wedding cake was cut.

Then the dancing began. I was forced to dance with all the women in my family, each one of whom complimented me, doubtless a new policy of using the carrot instead of the stick.

"Well," Rosemarie murmured as she held me close. "At least Janey won't have to sleep in a cold bed tonight."

"Rosemarie!"

"Well, that's what a wedding ceremony is about, isn't it, even if we pretend differently."

"I'll be glad when this whole business is over," I said, trying to change the subject.

"Only for a while, Chucky Ducky. Before you know it, Peg and Vince will be walking down the middle aisle. Then, who knows, maybe your foster sister will find a man."

Rosemarie's wedding! How dare she!

"Like this music says, I'll dance at your wedding," I said, realizing that I was caught in a spasm of jealousy.

"You bet your life you will," she said with a giggle.

Had Rosemarie made up her mind that I would be her husband? If she had, would I be able to resist? Would I even want to resist?

Did I want her to marry someone else?

Before I could wrap my mind around that question, the orchestra stopped playing and took its break. Promptly the O'Malley trio began its spontaneous and unrehearsed performance. We sang songs from Sigmund Romberg and Rodgers and Hammerstein. Rosemarie and I did a duet of love songs from *The Desert Song,* which we played for laughs. Then Peg won sustained applause for her interpretation of Paganini. Finally Rosemarie sang a hilarious version of "I'm Gonna Wash That Man Right Outa My Hair," which strongly hinted that I was the man who was going to be washed. I had no choice but to play along as her straight man. Thunderous ovation. Then the orchestra reappeared and she scurried back to the head table to accept kisses from the new Mrs. McCormack and warm handshakes from her husband.

"Not part of the program, was it?" Dad said with a sly grin.

"A lot of things aren't part of the program, Dad," Peg said with a saucy shake of her brown curls.

"So I noticed. I don't want to know what you guys said to Doctor. . . . Not till tomorrow anyway."

Then the day's second major event happened. The orchestra was playing "I'll Dance at Your Wedding." Rosemarie had nudged me with a sharp elbow. Before I could ponder what role I might play at her wedding and whether I would be there at all, Monica Sullivan and James Rizzo, by accident it seemed, encountered one another on the dance floor.

He opened his arms in an invitation. She collapsed into them.

Jane glanced at me and smiled. We'd won.

They stayed together for the next dance.

Then, from somewhere offstage, Big Tom Sullivan appeared, tall, distinguished if a bit fat, silver-haired, his face red in fury. He pulled Jimmy away from his daughter and shoved him. Then he tried to drag Monica back to their table.

As one person, Peg, Rosemarie, and I leaped from our chairs and ran toward the confrontation. Dad, Monsignor Mugsy, and Father Raven were running too.

Jimmy, his face grim, his fists clenched, did nothing. Monica tore herself out of her father's grip. Just then the enforcers arrived. Dad and the monsignor led Big Tom out of the room. It all happened so quickly that most of the guests didn't notice. However, it was the talk of the parish on Sunday.

Father Raven turned and saw the three of us.

"Guess we didn't need the Seventh Cavalry this time, huh?"

"How dare that man try to ruin Janey's wedding!" Peggy said through clenched teeth.

"Well, he didn't. . . . And, by the way, I'd hate to have the three of you avenging angels angry at me!"

All in all, it was a good day. I dealt with Rosemarie's suggestive hints by ignoring them.

❧ 7 ❧

Chicago was locked into snowbanks and deep freeze at the beginning of January. My welcome back to the snow-blanketed Notre Dame campus was appropriate for the season. My roommates had been expelled and I had been put on warning.

"We found beer and whiskey in your room during the vacation," the rector crowed triumphantly. "Whiskey!"

"I don't drink, Father." My stomach turned just as it had at the farmhouse in the Bohemian Alps when we captured the so-called Werewolves and in Trudi's apartment when I found their identity papers. "You know that. Everyone knows that."

"You've been given a second chance." He shook his fist at me. "Against my advice and recommendation. One more offense and you will be summarily expelled."

His lips lingered lovingly on the word "summarily," almost as though it were a woman's breast.

"Fine," I said, pushing by him into my now mostly empty room. "Will I have any roommates this semester?"

"We don't intend to expose anyone to your bad example."

Privacy, peace, and quiet to study and to read. I felt sorry for my buddies, but they were probably better off.

How long, I wondered, would I survive before I did something stupid and got caught?

Doing what?

Something worse than drinking. Maybe caught with a girl in my room.

All I needed to do was to find the girl. And that was a most unlikely occurrence.

That night I dreamed about Trudi, the first dream in a long time.

I survived the next month mostly by reading books on the photographic masters—Steiglitz, Cannon, Adams, Weston—that I had found in the library and by returning to my camera (Leica) to archive the Notre Dame campus at winter. As I look at the shots today I realize with a shock that they are some of the most stark and barren pictures I have ever made. I daresay they revealed the inexplicable emptiness in my soul, a depression that echoed the ultimate barrenness of Notre Dame's locker-room Catholicism.

I look at the pictures and ask myself what that poor, troubled young man needed.

The answer is readily given. He needed love.

Since many of the men in my hall had pictures of their girl (or girls) pinned to their walls or propped up against their desk, I deceived myself into thinking I should have a similar picture too, if only to assert my masculinity in this crude, smelly locker room.

After considering this possibility for a time and wondering where I would find an appropriate picture of a young woman, I had a brilliant idea.

The picture of Rosemarie!

Well, why not? Give them something to talk about!

The print of Rosemarie, five by nine, brightened the room and occasioned a good deal of comment from other young men who drifted into my room, after the news of it got around, explicitly to see the picture.

"Great tits!"

"Breasts."

One or two, more acute than I would have expected, said, "It's not dirty, it's beautiful! It's not a pinup at all."

"It's pinned up. Well, actually tacked up."

"You're really good at picture-taking, O'Malley."

Father Pius did not agree.

After he had lunged out of my room, I picked up the pieces, pondered the wreckage, searched through my negative files, found the right one, and walked over to the photographic lab.

This time I made a sixteen-by-twenty print, bought a frame for it at the bookstore, and placed it prominently on my desk. Father Pius would think twice about smashing a picture frame.

He would not hesitate, however, to smash a life. Or to try to smash it.

The snow continued. The cold persisted. The South Shore became unreliable. I went home only one weekend in that terrible January. I learned that Monica had moved into an apartment on Austin Boulevard with another young teacher from St. Ursula and that her father had hired private detectives to shadow her.

"There's a rumor," Peg reported, "that Jimmy is going to Princeton Law School next year and that Monica will go with him."

"Presumably after a marriage ceremony."

"Of course," my sibling said haughtily.

"Good."

"And they say that Timmy Boylan is much better."

"That's good."

"So what's the next project, Chucky Ducky?"

"Surviving the winter in South Bend."

8

"It is infinitely better, Charles," Christopher Kurtz said, smiling amiably at me over his glass of Coke, "to marry than to burn."

"I don't plan to go to hell." I sipped more of my malt. "Not at the moment at any rate. Could I have another malt, please?"

As the last two total abstainers in the University of Notre Dame (or so it seemed), Christopher and I usually had our serious talks in the Huddle, Notre Dame's soda parlor.

"Chocolate is your substitute for sex." Christopher shook his head in feigned dismay. "It's not fair that you don't put on weight."

"A lot less harmful than sex."

"Not as interesting." He adjusted his conservative brown tie, on which, by some miracle, no drop of Coke ever fell.

"I didn't say that it was."

"You'll never hear it from your religion teacher, Charles, but what Saint Paul meant was not that it was better to marry than to go to hell but that it was better to marry than to burn with passion."

"Who's burning with passion?"

"You are. For Cordelia Lennon. You devour her with your eyes whenever you're with her."

"She's eminently devourable." Suiting my words to action, I set to work on my second malt.

"You don't have to be so obvious about it." He smoothed his long, perfectly groomed auburn hair.

"So obvious that she notices it?" I paused in my assault on my surrogate for sex.

"Of course she notices it, Charles." Christopher pointed a lawyer's accusing finger at me, his gray eyes sparkling with delight. "The young woman is neither blind nor stupid."

"I don't want to embarrass her."

"She's flattered, not embarrassed. My point is that no useful purpose is served for you or for her by silent adoration."

"I don't want to become involved again, unless I'm ready to marry."

Christopher and I had become such close friends that I had told him about Trudi.

"When someone burns as fervently and as obviously as you do, Charles, he is ready to marry."

"I'm not persuaded."

"Men our age marry when they decide it is time to go to bed with the same woman more or less permanently. They usually marry the woman who seems the best choice of those available at the time. It's as simple as that."

"Cordelia?"

"You could do a lot worse."

Indeed I could. I pondered Christopher's wisdom. He was the only man my age, indeed the only man besides my father, from whose wisdom I thought I might learn.

"When I'm in my middle twenties and ready to support a family."

"She won't wait that long. I don't think you can wait that long either."

Cordelia was as stable a young woman as I could imagine, a small, delicate, pretty blonde with a fragile face and an astonishingly voluptuous body. She didn't drink either and might meet us in the Huddle before the afternoon was over.

I had not told Christopher about Rosemarie, although he and everyone else were fascinated by the perhaps naked girl whose picture was prominently displayed on my desk.

Was I aware that it was strange that I had told my first close male friend about my mistress in Germany but not about my foster sister?

You bet.

"I can't see the point in a marriage when you are not ready to support your wife and children."

"What about all the guys at Vetville?" He nodded his head in the direction of the Quonset-hut village where the married students were permitted to continue their family life, despite the fact that they were students at the quasi-seminary that was Notre Dame in March of 1949.

I'm sure the administration hoped that they were not engaging in too much sex with their wives. Or at least not enjoying it too much.

"I don't happen to approve," I said primly.

"The world has changed, Charles." He clasped his hands behind his head and grinned like a young high school teacher with a slow but appealing student. "They have calculated nicely the costs and the payoffs and find the venture into marriage and family while still in school to be profitable. Do they seem unhappy?"

"They are taking terrible risks with the future."

"Don't we all when we breathe?"

Whence came my conviction that marriage was inappropriate until financial responsibilities had been secured? My father had certainly endorsed such a position when we were growing up, but only casually and without overwhelming conviction.

"Love, Chuck, does not conquer all. Write that down in one of your notebooks."

"Does it help?"

"It sure does!" Dad had grinned like a very contented

canary after consuming a delectable cat. "Without it you can't conquer much of anything."

Surely mild advice on which to build a whole life program. My strategy was to minimize the amount of hardship over which love had to triumph. It seemed a not unreasonable approach.

The problem was that hormones don't always agree with head. My deep-brain subbasement devoted to delightfully lascivious images was jammed now with various elaborately detailed effigies of Cordelia Lennon in the advanced stages of both undress and sexual arousal. Such pictures had not crowded out phantasms of Rosemarie, but did compete with them vigorously.

"You're telling me that I should marry Cordelia because she's attractive and available and I want to go to bed with a woman. That does not, Christopher, sound much like love."

"A girl in hand," he said, waving his own hand negligently, "is worth two in the thicket."

It was characteristic of Christopher Killian Kurtz that he would say "thicket" to avoid the possible double entendre of "bush." If ever in my life I met a gentleman, he was the one.

In him I had found the friend that I could cite to Rosemarie as my equivalent to her Peg—if I ever introduced Rosemarie to Christopher, a possibility that didn't seem likely.

Christopher and I were an odd pair. Christopher was a German Republican from the North Side of Chicago, God help us all. The West Side and the South Side Irish might poke fun at one another. They agreed, however, that for all practical purposes there was no North Side. And German Republicans? What are they?

In fact, as Christopher explained to me with twinkling eyes, the Germans were once the largest and most influential nationality group in Chicago ("Because, Charles, we were the best educated and most cultured") and possessed a strong religious tradition of their own ("more intelligent and reasoned than your Irish enthusiasm").

I would later discover that the Chicago Germans, like all American Germans, were subject to suspicion and prejudice during the First World War even though they were as loyal as anyone else. It was a trial from which they never recovered, as a group, their full confidence.

He was serious, intellectual, rational. I pretended to be a comic and a cutup and, while I had read a lot of serious stuff, I didn't wear my intellectual interest on my sleeve as he did. He was always immaculately dressed, either in his Navy ROTC uniform or a suit, vest, tie, and brightly polished shoes. I was a slob, often unshaven, whose shoes were always scuffed and whose ordinary dress was a mixture of military castoffs and Maxwell Street second-hands. I joked with the professors who permitted questions. He worried about serious issues. He had an almost unlimited friendship network and I was something of a loner, save for my occasional companionship with Vince and Ed Murray and their football-team friends.

I met Christopher in a class on Catholic fiction taught by a layman from whom Vince had told me I'd learn more about religion than I would in any of the religion classes. The first book to be studied was a depressing effort called *The Woman Who Was Poor* by a man named Léon Bloy (I pronounced his name Lee-on Blow). It ended with a statement that I was to learn was very popular with a certain kind of intellectual or would-be intellectual Catholic in those days: "There is but one tragedy and that is for us not to be saints."

"What do you think of that, gentlemen?" demanded the teacher. His voice was slurred and I would later discover that he was drunk most of the time, a phenomenon that did not prevent him from being the best teacher I ever encountered.

There was silence in the classroom. Snow was falling

again outside, as it always falls in the South Bend snowbelt during winter.

"How about you, Mr. Redhead? What's your name?"

"O'Malley, sir. Charles C. O'Malley."

"Well, Mr. Charles C. O'Malley, what do you think of the ending of the book? . . . You have read it, haven't you?"

"Terribly depressing book, sir, much more so than *The Heart of the Matter.*"

Was I showing off? Me? Charles C. O'Malley?

"An interesting literary judgment . . . but the last sentence?"

"He's wrong, sir." I slipped into my usual half-fun, full-earnest mode in which I could defend with deadly seriousness a position I had initially espoused as a joke.

"Wrong, Mr. O'Malley?" The teacher arched his eyebrows, delighted that there was at least one character in his class.

"The only tragedy is not to be happy. I believe that God made us to be happy not to be saints."

The auburn-haired young man with the long nose in the brown business suit who was sitting next to me glanced up with a curious eye.

"Are not saints the most happy people in the world?" he asked mildly.

"That's what the sisters told us in grammar school, but the faces on holy cards don't look happy."

There was a titter in the room.

The professor positively beamed. "Anyone want to comment?"

The fop, as I thought of him, next to me said gently, "I'm not sure that we should judge saints by holy cards. If you're really a saint, you must be happy."

It was like throwing a slow curve ball to a home-run hitter.

"Your name is . . . ?"

"Kurtz, Christopher K. Kurtz."

"Ah. Now, Mr. Charles C.—"

"I'm a Democrat."

"Indeed. That is interesting information. Now Mr. Charles C. O'Malley, Democrat from, I presume by your disreputable accent, Chicago, how do you reply to Mr. Christopher K. Kurtz, who I suspect is also from Chicago?"

"With all due respect"—this would be the only fun class in the university, of that I was now sure—"to my distinguished colleague, I think he has it all wrong. You have to be really happy before you become a saint. I mean you work all your life at being as happy as you can and then toward the end, maybe you get to be a little bit of a saint."

That was not bad for the spur of the moment, was it?

I noticed that some of the other guys were writing it down. My distinguished colleague from Chicago stared at me thoughtfully and wrote it down too.

Our teacher was now contemplating me very carefully. "Have you ever seen any serious suffering, Charles C. O'Malley?"

"Yes, sir."

"Could you describe it to us?"

"I was in the Army of Occupation in Germany. Near my office was a railroad station in which the prisoners came home from Russia, the few who did come home. Women would wait for the train every afternoon for their husbands or fathers or sons, their poor faces bruised with loneliness and grief. Occasionally the man they were waiting for would be on the train."

"I see. Were some of them happy, those women who came back day after day?"

I had never thought of the question. But naturally I had an answer. "They would be a lot happier if their man were on the train, sir; but I thought there was ... well, a sort of faith that put purpose in the lives of some of them. And purpose gave them a little more to live for than a lot of other people had. . . . They didn't complain, sir."

The classroom was as silent as the Holy Cross priest's graveyard at midnight. I didn't quite like what had happened. The man had tricked me into thinking and I'd managed to sound more profound than I really was.

Anyway, the discussion floodgates opened. I enjoyed the rest of the class, because it seemed almost like I was teaching it.

"Have a drink with me?" Christopher Kurtz asked when the class adjourned.

"I don't drink."

"Neither do I."

"We must be the only two left in the university. We'd better close ranks."

So I met the best male friend I ever had.

Christopher put on his double-breasted overcoat, white silk scarf, and galoshes (really) and we trudged through the snow toward the Huddle. In an apparent concession to collegiate style, he didn't wear a hat. I was dressed in combat boots and a parka with pockets big enough for my Leica and four or five rolls of film—my usual outer garb from December to the last April thaw. As he talked, he gestured with his hands, a sideways motion cutting through the air like an auto salesman or a precinct captain or a priest.

I remember that he said something about the relationship between happiness and sanctity being the most important religious question in the life of a layman, maybe in the religious life of anyone. I thought to myself that it was strange that two young males, walking across a barren campus as the temperature plummeted toward zero, would discuss sanctity.

"You'd almost think this is a Catholic school, Christopher. We're talking religion after class, and the class wasn't even religion class."

He laughed and turned up his coat collar against the wind. "Someday it will be a Catholic university, Charles. Men like us will make it so."

"Why aren't you studying to be a priest?" I demanded. "Anyone who talks as much as you do about God's love ought to be a priest."

"Why?" He brushed the fallen snow off his thick hair. "Do priests have a monopoly on religion?"

I admitted that they didn't.

He had attended Quigley, the high school seminary, for four years before coming to Notre Dame. He felt that his vocation was to be a layman, representing the Church and Christ in the world of work.

"Only sisters and priests have vocations," I replied promptly. "Like my brother who goes to Quigley now."

"What year?"

"Third."

"Is he a better human being than you are?"

"I'd never admit it."

"Every baptized person has a vocation, you and I as much as your brother or my classmates who will be ordained."

I didn't really believe any of it, but I was fascinated by the naturalness with which this young man discussed God and religion and church. As naturally as we would later discuss girls at the Huddle and back in my room.

That first day of our friendship, in my room, I at my desk, Christopher sitting on my bed, almost without realizing what I was doing, I told him about Trudi.

"You never heard from her again?"

"Not a word."

We were silent for a moment. His eyes flicked as they had done before to the shot of Rosemarie on my desk. "Is that her?"

"No, that's just a friend of my little sister."

"Beautiful woman."

"Pretty girl."

He shrugged his right shoulder, a signal I had already learned that he didn't agree but was stipulating the point so our discussion could continue.

"Why do you think Trudi disappeared?"

"I've asked myself that a thousand times. I don't know. . . . Maybe because she figured that it wouldn't work out if we were married and she came to America. A lot of other German girls her age thought the opposite. . . ."

"Would it have worked out?"

"Maybe, probably not, I don't know."

The Angel of Judgment breaking into the room, Father Pius, my hall rector on another rampage, broke the conversation.

"I've caught you this time, O'Malley. Remember you're on your last chance." He fell to his knees as if he were about to pray and poked his head under the bed oblivious to Christopher's feet.

"Where's the beer, O'Malley? I know it's here." His eyes shone with a holy light, a young monk going to the lions.

"Try my desk, Father."

He rampaged around the room, shoving aside chairs, tossing jackets and sweatshirts on the floor, pulling up bed sheets. "I'll find it, never fear."

He too glanced at the picture of Rosemarie, with disgust and anger. "You're evil, O'Malley. We'll get you yet."

"Good luck."

Unable to find a trace of the forbidden beer, he swept toward the door.

"You forgot to check the girls in the closet, Father Pius."

He knew that there were no girls in the closet and he knew that I knew that he knew. Yet he could not prevent himself from yanking open the closet door and pushing around the mess inside.

"Maybe they're lying on the floor, Father."

He jerked my pile of army fatigues off the floor and threw them back with disgust.

"I guess they must have sneaked out when we weren't looking."

"You'll laugh out of the other side of your mouth when

we finally catch you." He lunged toward the door to the corridor.

"Father Pius." I raised my voice just as he propelled himself through the door.

"Yes?" His face was contorted with rage.

"Knock next time."

He slammed the door so forcefully that the picture of Rosemarie fell off my desk.

"Father Pius, my hall rector," I explained to Christopher.

"So I gathered. He's supposed to be nuts. Be careful of him."

"I don't drink and I don't have any girls in the room, worse luck for me." I resorted Rosemarie to her proper place. "Why should I worry about him?"

His right shoulder went up. "He doesn't seem to like your friend."

"That's his problem."

"Just so long as he doesn't make it your problem. . . . Anyway, Charles, let me ask you a favor."

That was the language of Chicago politics that we both understood.

"Sure."

"Would you write up in a short article the scene in the Bamberg Bahnhof you described in class today?"

"Sure . . . why?"

"We have a little magazine, for students around the country. We're always looking for good stuff."

"You won't use my name?"

"Not if you don't want us to."

"Okay."

He had the delicacy not to ask why I did not want my name used. I could not have answered the question anyway. I suppose the truth was that I did not want publicity, even the most minimal, to interfere with my dreams of private bliss.

Which, when you consider what was to happen to my life during the next four decades, was pretty funny.

I checked out Christopher Kurtz with Vince.

"A really nice guy, Chuck. Everyone likes him. Not the student politician kind either. He's not running for class president. He probably ought to be a priest."

"He has a vocation to be a layman."

"Huh?" Vince rubbed his dark jaw. "What does that mean?"

"I'm not sure. So you think if he wants to be a friend, it's all right?"

"Sure, why not?"

"Don't tell Peg."

"I don't tell Peg everything." He was flustered but happy at the mention of that magic name.

"You'd better or you'll be in real trouble."

So I wrote the article and Christopher and I became close friends. I learned that he was a determined student who worked very hard for his B grades. He planned to be a lawyer and then perhaps a federal judge, "to bring Christian values into that sector of human life."

I got A's without much effort and performed in class with an easy, not to say obnoxious, flare. And I wanted to be an obscure accountant of whose existence everyone else was unaware.

The contrast was not lost on me. So great was my respect and admiration for Christopher that my conscience was a bit troubled, not sufficiently however to inhibit my outrageous performance in the Cath Lit class.

It was mostly French Cath Lit or, as I persisted in calling it, Frog Lit.

It required no great effort to stir up sedition in that class. I was not your typical Chicago Irish anti-intellectual Notre Dame drunk. I had grown up in an atmosphere in which books, art, and music were respected. I had read, had I not, James Joyce because a young woman had written me a letter when I was in Germany in which she said that the last waterfall of "yeses" was powerfully erotic. I was familiar with Greene and Waugh.

But the whole gloomy gus Frog crowd, as I told Christopher, turned me off. Péguy, Claudel, Bernanos, Mauriac, Bloy—the entire creepy bunch were grim, depressing, and a waste of time.

Occasionally, when attacking the Frog "crowd," I remembered the French noncom at the checkpoint outside of Stuttgart and shivered with a memory of the fear of that night.

It was easy for me to adopt the pose of the anti-intellectual and disrupt the class, much to the delight of the professor. He was especially pleased the day I savaged *Diary of a Country Priest* and its ending: "everything is grace."

"That little bitch was grace, sir? Come on, isn't the author unfair to God? She's a devil, not a grace."

The prof beamed appreciatively. "It requires great literary taste, Mr. Charles Cronin O'Malley, to make such a tasteless observation."

Even Christopher laughed at that.

Many years later after I saw Robert Bresson's film adaptation of Bernanos's novel, I reread the book and marveled at my youthful insensitivity. Gloomy it surely was, and also a masterpiece. By then I had learned that grace is indeed everywhere.

I gave Christopher my first and only draft of my article "Faces in the Bahnhof" that day.

He glanced at it quickly. "It's easy to see why you're a photographer, Charles."

"I'm not a photographer, I just take pictures."

The next day he cornered me after my English composition class.

"The editor liked your piece, Charles. Liked it a lot. Could I introduce you?"

"Why not?"

So I moved to the fringes of the *Compact* group.

Headquartered in two windowless rooms in the basement of old Sorin Hall, a building that I argued would forever smell of the unwashed bodies of Holy Cross priests from yesteryear, *Compact* was a joint Notre Dame–St. Mary's venture. Such a phenomenon was rare in those days when the administrations of both schools thought that the existence of the other was a personal affront and that the presence of members of the opposite sex in such proximity was a threat to the eternal salvation of their respective student bodies.

"Cordelia, this is Charles O'Malley." Christopher was smooth at introductions, as at everything else. "Charles, this is Cordelia Lennon, the editor of *Compact*."

"Do sit down, Charles." Her voice was soft and low. "That was a beautiful piece. Were you really in Germany for two years? . . . You look so young."

"I was born at a very early age."

Her laugh, as fastidious and delicate as her voice, was more enthusiastic than my flip response merited. Could it be that I disturbed her as much as she disturbed me?

It was a possibility that merited further exploration.

Cordelia (definitely not Delia—which is what she would have been called in St. Ursula—as I found when my first attempt at the nickname was gently but firmly corrected) did not fit my image of an editor. Rather she looked like a model from the pages of *Vogue*'s special section on freshmen college fashions, a model perhaps for the tan sweater and skirt she wore. She was short, no more than five feet two, doll-like in her seeming fragility, with soft white-blond hair bound tightly in an elegant roll on the back of her head, the lightest of blue eyes, and a body that, especially in a sweater, made it hard for you to keep your eyes above her chin.

She was a graduate of the Convent of the Sacred Heart and "ladylike" in the precisely disciplined fashion that such quasi-novitiates developed in their students. The kind of girl you wanted to take home to mother.

To my mother, whose daughters and foster daughter were too vivacious ever to be inhibited by convent discipline?

Ah, that was the question—which, to admit the truth, I asked myself that very first day.

"Christopher said that I might be able to persuade you to help us with our little magazine?" She fluttered her hand at the confusion in the office. "I don't like to impose, but it is a such an important Catholic apostolate and your article shows such sensitivity and taste."

Me? Sensitivity and taste? I felt ashamed of my smelly sweatshirt.

"You bet."

"That you have taste?" Her eyes twinkled.

"That I'd be delighted to help."

"We'll be very grateful indeed, Charles."

One learned very quickly that despite her china-doll appearance, Cordelia's personality was not fragile. She not only supported *Compact* with her family money, she ran it with a steadfast hand. Indeed, of all the characters who hung round the offices, she and Christopher were the only ones who worked seriously at the job.

Her editorial decisions were delivered in an almost inaudible voice with a tonal question mark at the end, but they were both definitive and final—and as far as I was concerned unfailingly tasteful. You could tell that she had made up her mind when she put on her rimless glasses.

Another shortsighted woman in my life!

When she asked you to do something, it was always in the form of a polite, not to say diffident request. But you did it as if you had been issued a royal command.

Like my mother?

Not really. As appealing as Cordelia was, she did not have the wit and the slightly demented giggle of the good April.

At least not near the surface of her character.

She was a music major at St. Mary's, a diligent student of the piano, firmly convinced of her talent and her promise as a concert pianist, a conviction with which no one disagreed.

I listened to her play a transcription of a Bach prelude for me in a music room in St. Mary's the week we met.

After the first few passages, it was evident that her friends and teachers were not telling her the truth. Cordelia had "taken" music since preschool and was technically perfect. All the notes were in the right place. But her playing was innocent of spirit and energy—wooden, in fact, and dull. Of training, she had a lot; of talent, very little.

The comparison with Peg was inevitable. My sister was, except when in defense of Rosemarie, a mild-mannered, sweet-tempered young woman in whose mouth butter would find it hard to melt. But put the violin bow in her hands and she became a frenzied, almost frightening, dervish. Peg had immediate access to the ice and the fire, the demons and the angels, in her young soul. Despite her technical skill, perhaps even because of it, Cordelia Lennon was innocent of access to her own depths.

Perhaps the convent had imposed a barrier that would never be broken.

How did her piano compare with Rosemarie's voice?

Rosemarie, who was she?

As I listened to Cordelia's passage through Bach, both authoritative and mechanical, I fantasized about the various diverting ways one might strip her, not merely of clothes, but of inhibitions.

For the purpose of improving her skills as a pianist. Obviously.

In bed I would call her "Delia" or even "Deal" and make her like it.

Like I say, I was twenty.

I had determined to take her to bed?

Not at all, but it was a diverting fantasy as I listened to her stolid progression through the Bach themes.

When she was finished with the piece, she rested her fingers on the piano keys, tilted her head, and smiled demurely, awaiting my verdict.

"I don't know much about music, Cordelia." I rose from

the bench on which I had been sitting. "Our family isn't very musical. But it sounded great to me."

Three lies.

But she was beautiful and I was twenty.

Then I kissed both her tiny hands.

Really? Yeah, really.

A flush slowly crept down her cheeks and throat.

"How elegant you are, Charles. Thank you."

Elegant and arguably out of my class.

"Isn't it wrong to lie to her?" I asked Christopher later.

He crossed his hands thoughtfully underneath his chin.

"What do you see her future to be like?" he asked.

"Marry someone, maybe a Notre Dame athlete. Kids, family, home in Kenilworth or Lake Forest."

"Anything wrong with that?"

"I don't suppose so."

"She'll play for parish recitals and maybe the organ in church. She'll direct little musicals and choruses. And she'll always have a nostalgic memory of how she gave up a career in the concert world for family and love. Her regrets will be occasional at most. Why take away her dream?"

Why, indeed.

"She's pretty damned determined."

"We don't lie to her. We tell her she's good and she is, as good as the best teachers and the most industrious practice can make her. There's only a couple of us who know better and we have no obligation to say what we know."

"Would the right kind of man—"

"Unlock her depths?" Christopher sighed. "Marriage doesn't do that very often, Charles. Besides, what if there are no depths there?"

I thought to myself that it might be fun to search for them.

A notion that returned on that raw, windy March day in the Huddle when Christopher suggested that marriage to

Cordelia might be a happy alternative to being consumed with passion.

"You're saying that because Cordelia is available and I'm horny I should marry her. What about love?"

His right shoulder rose a quarter inch. "Would you ever hurt her?"

"Of course not."

"Would you be faithful to her?"

"Sure."

"I think"—he searched carefully for words—"that at our age we don't know what love is. Probably we're not capable of it. If a girl is attractive, if we think we can't live without her in our bed every night, and if we have the right answers to both those questions, then we've gone as far as we can on the road to love."

It was clear-eyed realism on a subject about which we are not programmed to be clear-eyed realists. I was convinced that he'd missed something important. Ought not some weight be given to the fact that I liked and admired Cordelia, indeed was fascinated by her delectable mixture of femininity and toughness?

There was another factor that had escaped Christopher's realism, but it would take me years to comprehend it.

"Why don't you marry her? You obviously like her."

He smiled easily. "Not my type, I guess. She doesn't affect me like she so patently affects you. Incidentally"—he lowered his voice—"the woman herself has just entered these premises."

We met every afternoon at the Huddle, away from the chaos of the *Compact* basement offices, to discuss the magazine in relatively quiet circumstances.

Above the fur-lined collar of her blue coat, her face glowed from the wind. Cordelia was even more radiant than usual. My heartbeat increased noticeably.

Maybe Christopher was right. Why not date her for a while? I gulped. That would mean asking her for a date, a ritual at which I had less practice than sexual intercourse.

"Here're the galley sheets for your article, Christopher."
She removed them from a book she was carrying in gloved
hands and sat between us. "They seem fine, but you still
have time to revise."

As she removed her gloves and the matching scarf that
protected her perfectly groomed hair from the wind, I
moved my Leica from her place on the table and picked
up the book. Maritain's *Art and Scholasticism.*

"I do wish you'd let me see some of your pictures,
Charles." She fluffed her hair deftly.

"Soon. . . . What's this book about?"

"It's very interesting." She folded her hands, a pious
novice. "It's about the relationship between God and art.
When an artist makes something, he's really acting for
God and like God. That's what you do"—she smiled and
actually winked at me, the hussy—"when you make a picture, just as Eric Gill does when he makes a statue."

Eric Gill was an English Catholic artist, greatly admired
by the *Compact* crowd, a convert, as all the English Catholics they admired seemed to be.

"God snaps the shot?"

She nodded briskly. "You and God."

"I never noticed Him peering over my shoulder."

Christopher brought a Coke for her and yet another malt
for me.

"Charles! You know what I mean. . . . Thank you very
much, Christopher."

Later in my life another woman would explain *Art and
Scholasticism* in different terms that made much more
sense. I still found the book itself impenetrable.

Cordelia and I had a minor argument about using my
name with the article. I still declined. I didn't want to be
associated with the *Compact* bunch. I went over to the
basement of Sorin every day because I liked Christopher
and was half in love with Cordelia. I wanted a lot more
time to figure out what I thought about their magazine and
the people who worked on it with them. As I worked on

their addressograph file I played the role of the typical Notre Dame goon, which was not altogether a false part, because I was wary of being identified with the rest of them.

Why? I ask myself almost four decades later.

I page through some of the old issues of the short-lived magazine. From the vast wisdom of hindsight, I can say that the articles and the poetry were fresh and notably less naïve than most college writing I've seen since then. We discussed complicated religious and social issues with enthusiasm and confidence if rarely with mature intelligence. But, dear God, we were not angry or cynical.

I hated the addressograph. I still smell the plates, an outhouse smell I protested to Christopher, who praised my aptitude for striking metaphors. How are you supposed to put in alphabetical order plates on which the type is backward? My passion for neatness and order was profoundly affronted by that diabolical machine and the mess it made.

But that's what Cordelia wanted me to do.

I think of Cordelia's glowing face on that March afternoon and of the delightful twist of her torso as Christopher helped her off with her coat. I close the pages of the magazine and sigh.

They were a mixed bunch, a couple of ex-seminarians like Christopher talking about the lay vocation—which seemed to me then to be a compensation for having left the seminary; some vets in combat boots who claimed to be "Catholic Workers" and "socialists" and treated me with contempt when they found that I was part of the occupation army; a few very intense young women, mostly from art or music or drama at St. Mary's, some of them very angry. A young nun and an elderly priest were the "moderators" though they seemed to take their orders, like everyone else, from Cordelia.

None of the girls were as attractive as she was—the vets drooled over her—but I never bothered to look very closely at them.

They were part of the "joint YCS"—Young Christian Students—of St. Mary's and Notre Dame. They fancied themselves the intellectual and literary elite of the schools, although the rest of the student bodies were unaware of their existence. The group was based on the Young Christian Worker movement, I was told, founded by a Belgian priest named Cardijn before the war. They met every week to discuss the Bible and social problems. They thought of themselves as the link between the Church and the world. They insisted that to "play their role" effectively they must be professionally "excellent"—"really good at what we do," Cordelia would say gently. "Whether it be law or music or philosophy or,"—with a nod at me—"photography."

"Picture-taking."

They'd all laugh. Chucky Ducky the team mascot and envelope addresser.

Compact was the national magazine of the group, mailed to "college chapters all over the country" with stamps purchased by the money of Dennis Lennon, Cordelia's architect father.

"He's a very gifted man," my father said slowly when I asked about him. "He designed some brilliant churches before the war. Inherited money, so he can pick and choose his commissions. I've met him a couple of times and admire his work. I'm not sure he represents any trends for the future though, not that it's necessary to do that. You're dating his daughter?"

He sounded astonished.

"Ogling her."

"Nothing wrong with that."

My father never criticized a rival or a colleague, a rare trait in all professions and especially rare in his. I interpreted his comment to mean that Dennis Lennon was good but stuffy.

I often wondered whether the group would have existed

at all if it had not been for Cordelia's good looks and money.

And willpower.

Why was I skeptical?

I didn't understand the philosophy books they gave me to read—Maritain, Gilson, Simone. I could make neither head nor tail out of Simone Weil, who was their heroine, or Charles Péguy, who was their hero. *Cross Currents,* their favorite magazine, might as well have been written in Russian for all the sense I could make out of it. *Commonweal,* their second favorite magazine, struck me even then as being priggish and dumb. In later years they invariably attacked my own work. I did not (and do not) have a very metaphysical mind, but I knew I was not stupid. In fact, I had better grades than any of them, little Miss Lennon included. So I suspected they didn't understand much more about what they were reading than I did.

I was dubious that there was a Catholic answer for all the questions the world was asking. They saw the world in hues and shapes that did not allow for its complexity.

I was more interested in women than in ideas.

Cordelia especially.

And, finally, I was afraid to be labeled a religious zealot.

"That's all right," Christopher would assure me. "There are many different vocations. Didn't Jesus say that in His father's kingdom there were many houses?"

"Did He?"

"He did."

"Smart man."

Yet they fascinated me. They represented enthusiasm, energy, dedication, and a side of my religion of whose possible existence I had not dreamed. They were not the last of this "new breed" of Catholic I would encounter during my life.

And, I reflect, as I gingerly open a yellowed copy of the journal, they saw what would come with the Second Vatican Council more clearly than most of us, perhaps more clearly than they realized.

In March of 1949, Cordelia—and Christopher—were much more important to me than Jacques Maritain or Charles Péguy.

"Finally"—she adjusted her glasses to examine the last item on her agenda—"it does not seem that there will be many YCS members coming to our convention on Easter Monday. Only a few high school seniors have enrolled and we were counting on them."

A "movement" that was going to change both the Church and the world was forced to rely on high school seniors, brats Peg's age, to fill out their ranks?

And Rosemarie's age?

Rosemarie who?

"I suppose"—she touched her tightly bound hair, a gesture that said she was labeling a phenomenon so that she could understand it—"that their moderators discouraged them."

Cordelia's categories for organizing the world were reasonably broad and moderately flexible, so long as she could express them precisely.

"We want quality not quantity," Christopher said serenely that afternoon in the Huddle.

"And brats that age might be disciplinary problems."

"We'll put you in charge of them, Charles . . ." She smiled lightly. "Anyway, this issue of *Compact* will be ready for the meeting. Maybe"—the same hint of a wink—"we'll have a lot of interest in its one anonymous author."

"Modest."

"Scared," she said, accurately enough.

"Prudent." As always Christopher was the peacemaker.

I saw a notice of a Mozart concert that night on the Huddle's bulletin board next to our table and acted impulsively.

"Are you going to listen to Mozart tonight, Cordelia?"

"I might." She regarded me with a faintly quizzical smile.

"Might you go with me?"

"I might." She reached out and touched my hand.

"Uh, I don't have any tickets."

"There's never a shortage of tickets for serious concerts at Notre Dame, Charles. I have two anyway, so you'll be my guest."

"He accepts," Christopher interjected. "With delight."

My heart beat wildly as I bent my head against the wind and hurried back to my room in search of decent clothes.

I had come to a turning point.

❧ 9 ❧

The small concert hall at St. Mary's was almost empty.

"Are we too early?" I asked the lovely young woman in a dark brown jersey dress who was, on her initiative be it noted, leaning on my arm.

"All concerts here attract the same small group of people, Charles," she whispered. "The same for lectures. That's why the apostolate of YCS is so important. The Church is the mother of all culture and it must no longer abandon its children. Mozart was Catholic."

"And a Mason," I added.

She glanced at me in surprise. Charles the Uncultivated was not supposed to know that.

"You're a very interesting young man."

"That's what my hall rector says."

I had been able to recall enough images of how Dad was attentive to the good April so that I was not a complete dullard on this my first real date. I don't know whether Cordelia expected my minor courtesies, but she always smiled and said "thank you."

Even when I helped her off with her coat and whistled, quite spontaneously, at her dress.

"Few enough dates here," she laughed. "A girl should dress up for one, particularly at a concert."

"I'm not complaining."

When we were seated and she opened the score for the first serenade, I looked around again.

"This isn't fair, Cordelia. Those musicians"—I pointed to the quartet, all young, who were tuning up their instruments—"will have to perform to a nearly empty house."

"If you're a good musician," she said, putting on her glasses and considering the first page of the score, "you perform your best for an audience of one. Besides, to be crassly commercial about it, their pay doesn't depend, thank God, on the size of the audience."

"What's the matter with Catholic schools that they can't do better than this?"

"I bet that they don't do any better at IU or Purdue. Maybe worse at Purdue."

"It's still terrible, like you said . . ."

She closed the score and took off her glasses.

"Charles, did you know about the concert or even the Chamber Music Series until you saw the notice on the bulletin board in the Huddle this afternoon?"

"Caught that, did you?" I said.

"Did you?" She frowned at my evasion.

"No."

"And you're brighter than most of the boys at Notre Dame and you've read more."

"I see your point. A lot of work to do for the YCS?"

"A lifetime, but that's all right; we'll win."

"Well, I'm lucky. I found both the series and a lovely musician to take to it."

"Shush." The violinist had lifted his bow. And then in a whisper, "Thank you."

Cordelia Lennon had been taught all her life that music was work. If you were invited to a chamber music concert, you dug the scores for the program out of your personal collection or you found them in the college library and you settled down to following every note.

Need I say that among the children of April Cronin O'Malley that was an unacceptable response to music?

"Poor dear Mozart wrote the music to be listened to, not studied."

I thought about that line of the good April, hesitated, decided to ignore its implications, and then, despite my decision, I reached over to my date, took the score out of her hands and closed it. Then I took one of her tiny hands firmly in both of mine and moved it in the general direction of the armrest on my seat where I firmly imprisoned it.

She stiffened, looked sharply at me, then smiled happily. I freed one of my hands for a moment, took off her glasses and put them in her purse. Obediently she leaned against my arm.

The poor kid was as frightened about this date as I was. That made me feel even more tender toward her.

The two of us relaxed and reveled in the music.

At the end of the recital, hand in hand, we approached the quartet. "Don't apologize," she whispered. "Just thank them."

"Yes, mother."

She snickered and squeezed my hand.

So we thanked them and asked them where they had studied and where they were going on their tour and wished them luck. The girl who played the viola thanked us in her turn, in a rich New York Jewish accent. "We really appreciate people like you."

"Is it too cold to go for a walk?" I asked my date as we left the hall.

"Certainly not."

It was indeed too cold, but there wasn't any other way to find any privacy in the Notre Dame world of those days. Neither of us was aware of the cold anyway.

On your first date with someone you think you are beginning to love, the gloves that separate your hands hardly exist.

I don't remember what we talked about. Everything and anything, I suppose.

"From the first time I saw you I wanted to take you out."

"And from the first time I saw you I wanted to go out with you."

Perhaps, I thought, this is going a little too fast.

"Time to be walking back. Eleven o'clock curfew tonight."

How dumb can a Catholic school be, even in 1949.

In front of her residence hall, I knew with a certainty that did not admit question that she expected me to kiss her.

The rules in those days said you did not "neck" a girl on her first date.

They also said, however, that the man tried to go as far as he could and the woman tried to draw the line as quickly as she could.

But what if the girl wants to be kissed?

Then, stupid, you kiss her.

How do you kiss her? This was not Rosemarie at Lake Geneva or Trudi in Bamberg. This was a relationship that was altogether different.

Well, I suppose you just kiss her and see how she reacts.

We stopped under a leafless tree, the cold March wind cutting into our faces. I held her hand firmly with one hand and traced the contours of her face with the other. She caught her breath and sagged a little.

I kissed her eyes and the tip of her nose, and her chin, and either cheek, and then, very delicately, her lips. They were soft and waiting for me. She leaned against me.

Then my hormones took over and my delicate kiss became violent. Her response was equally violent. I locked my arms around her and held her as if I would never let her go. She clung to me fiercely.

Still imprisoning her with one arm, I fumbled inside her coat and found a firm mound of breast rising to my hand. There were a lot of layers of protection—dress, slip, heavily armored bra; but there was also warmth and promise.

I gripped the breast firmly and moved it back and forth, oh so carefully. She sighed contentedly and did not attempt to either escape or restrain me. I returned to my assault on her lips, this time with what I thought was devouring fury.

We disengaged by implicit mutual consent.

"Oh, my," she gasped.

"I'm sorry if I hurt you," I said, ashamed of the outbreak of the animal in me.

"You didn't hurt me, Charles. That was very nice . . . very nice indeed."

"To tell the truth, I thought so too."

"You're so sweet."

"And you beat chocolate malts."

We both laughed, relaxing because we had successfully cleared one of the obstacles that we knew we must face.

"You . . . you must have had a lot of experience with women, Charles."

"No, not really."

"Sure?"

"Honest."

"You're not like any boy I've ever known."

"Is that good?"

"Very good indeed. Other boys want to violate me; you want . . ." She searched for the explanatory word to categorize what had happened between us. "You cherish me."

The world melted me.

"No other way to treat you . . ." The words stumbled on my tongue as they rushed out.

"I think I'd better go in now. Thanks for . . . for a memorable evening."

She rushed for the door of the residence hall and then turned and whispered on the wind, "See you tomorrow."

I drifted back down the tree-lined drive toward the highway that separated the two schools in a blissful haze. For the first real date I ever had, I had not done badly at all. I told myself that I might very well love her and that there was a remote possibility that she loved me.

My firm resolutions about waiting till I was twenty-five at least were gone and forgotten.

So serenely satisfied was I with myself and life and the cosmos that I did not see the truck that almost ran me down on the highway.

When I was safe on the other side, I reflected that if the truck had killed me and if I believed the retreat masters at Fenwick and here at Notre Dame, I would have gone straight to hell. I had committed one, maybe many serious mortal sins.

I was not troubled by that thought either. When I had made my peace with God and church in Rome the Christmas before last, I had decided that "necking and petting" were not truly serious sins. They were, I had determined, too natural to the human condition to offend God all that much.

I asked my priest recently if young people confessed "necking and petting" anymore. He rolled his nearsighted blue eyes behind his thick glasses and sighed. "They do not know that such words convey any meaning at all."

Our generation knew them well enough and confessed them often enough, but concluded for the most part that they were no worse than, let us say, a hockey penalty that took you off the ice for a minute or two.

God, we felt instinctively, really did not mind, not as much as did our retreat masters.

"Couldn't one argue," Christopher asked rhetorically, "that such actions are merely part of preparing remotely and then proximately for marital union? Does anyone seriously believe that a couple can jump from a quick peck on the lips to marital surrender overnight?"

"My hall rector does."

"Do you think he ever dated?"

"Impossible."

A lot of other priests and nuns, however, with or without dating experience, continued to warn us that we would go straight to hell.

"How often did Jesus denounce necking and petting?" Christopher continued.

"Not at all, I bet."

"Did you ever wonder how it became one of the most serious of sins?"

To show my hall rector, I went to Communion the next morning and thanked Whoever might be involved for Cordelia.

10

Charles Cronin O'Malley in a white summer dinner jacket? At a rectory in Lake Forest?

Someone surely must be joking.

To make the joke on the future respected accountant even more serious, the dinner jacket fit him perfectly. Yet, his wire-brush hair, barely slicked into place, suggested that he belonged in a bar at Madison and Cicero on the west side and not in the aforementioned rectory in Lake Forest.

It fit perfectly because his parents, convinced imprudently that the Great Depression was over, had insisted on purchasing for him a hastily and specially made white dinner jacket—without any prudent regard for cost.

"We can't have Denny Lennon"—my father was enjoying the purchase of the jacket entirely too much—"saying that an O'Malley looked impoverished."

"Especially since we're not improverished anymore, dear," Mom added.

"I think he looks *so* cute," Rosemarie clucked happily. "Don't you, Peg?"

My favorite sibling eyed me critically: "Unbelievably."

Rosemarie had been thrown out of Trinity the week before graduation because she had piled up her car and several others in the school's parking lot the afternoon of the senior prom. No one in our family wanted to talk about it. Vince, fearful of Peg's wrath, had whispered in my ear, "Drunk out of her mind."

Not only wouldn't the nuns let her collect a diploma, they also had warned Manhattanville about her and her "background," by which they meant Jim Clancy's mob connection. Finally, despite warnings from my father's lawyer, they had refused to forward her grades to other colleges. Somehow, she managed to get into the University of Chicago by passing an entrance exam.

"Moscow Tech," I had sniffed, though I knew full well that the university's reputation as a Communist hotbed among the Chicago Irish was untrue, and indeed the opposite of the truth even in those days.

"If the nuns didn't drive her out of the church," Peg had said bitterly, "the University of Chicago won't either."

I had not said that I thought the problem was her bastard father and not the nuns.

I should like to be able to contend that Charles C. O'Malley felt completely out of place in the Lake Forest environment, Muggins inside the dance instead of standing outside, nose pressed against the windowpane.

That wouldn't be accurate either. I felt perfectly at home as soon as I realized that most of the show was phony; when it came to playing phony games I was as good as the next man and probably better than most.

My love, dressed in modest, long-sleeved black, as Monsignor Redmond insisted in imitation of the requirements for women's dress at papal functions, was playing for us before dinner on a Pleyel piano, bought, as the monsignor assured us, with his own hands in Paris before the war.

(Can't risk the pope getting dirty thoughts from a hint of bosom or elbow, can we?)

The piano was all right, though nothing special. My love, whose admirable breasts could not be totally obscured even by a papal nobility gown, was not only all right but quite special.

Alas, her version of the *Moonlight* sonata (the monsignor's favorite, I was assured) was, God forgive me for it then and now, dreadfully dull. As always, she played with authority and mastery, both utterly innocent of fire.

The poor dear woman (as the good April would have called her in the circumstances) did not lack fire, of that I was now certain. But her demons were not permitted to intervene in her playing and probably never would be, a sad but hardly tragic fact.

However, the monsignor, his pathetic curates, Dennis and Marie Lennon, Alfred Lennon S. J., her brother, and two other Lake Forest couples present for the event not only pretended that they were listening to a womanly Ignaz Jan Paderewski, which would have been acceptable, but the reverential expressions on their faces testified that they actually believed it.

Only the aged English Jesuit, whose first name was Martin and whose last name I learned only much later, and I knew better. He caught my eye once, shrewdly read my face, and then turned away with a ghost of a smile.

You and I, Charles, he was saying, we are the only ones here who are not taken in by it, the only ones with real class.

The old Jesuit was the guest of honor, a thin, haggard man with long, stringy gray hair, bad teeth, and the face of a concentration-camp survivor. He was an Oxford don in a clerical horse collar several sizes too large and a baggy suit that had been neither cleaned nor pressed since the end of the First World War.

He was the close friend and guest of Msgr. David Redmond, the pope of Lake Forest, as Monsignor Branigan had described him with considerable lack of respect. I was told by the Lennons that the visitor was one of the world's great Catholic thinkers, a man of towering intellect and insight, a visitor who shed blinding luster on the United

States and Lake Forest and those lucky enough to dine
with him.

When I finally met the man in the "study"—two stories
high with Gothic arches and stained-glass windows—of
the rectory, I thought he was a caricature, a corpse fresh
from the embalming room, snatched out of his casket, a
bad practical joke played by a cruel humorist.

Then I saw the light in his soft brown eyes and knew
that I was in the presence of genius. I mentally kicked
myself for riding up on the Northwestern without my camera.

It was true, as Monsignor Mugsy had insisted despite
my skepticism, that the Lake Forest pastor did make his
curates wear dinner jackets at his "formal dinners"—two
young South Side Micks fresh out of the seminary looking
as uncomfortable as I was supposed to feel. The monsignor
himself wore the full robes of his office—"papal valet"
Dad had said with a laugh—red cape reaching to the floor,
red cummerbund, red piping in every possible place on his
cassock, red socks under shoes with silver buckles, and
huge red cassock buttons.

"He studied in Rome," Monsignor Mugsy had observed,
sipping a large glass of bourbon with Mom and Dad after
a mid-May golf match, "and thinks he ought to have been
a bishop. A little too ambitious for his own good, I'm
afraid."

The church, I have since learned, honors ambition
mightily, save when it is not denied and becomes too pat-
ent. The presence or absence of talent is immaterial.

As a Jesuit, Alf Lennon was permitted his plain black
cassock. I presumed that the elderly visitor from England
had been granted some kind of special dispensation for his
baggy suit. Or maybe it too was an ornament to Msgr.
David Redmond's elegance.

The pastor's suite—it included the "study," a dining
room, a "master bedroom" (his term), two guest bedrooms,
and a "solarium"—had been put together by a designer

whose instructions must been, "buy the best, the absolute best."

It didn't work. While the size of the study would have been fit for a cardinal (and a rich one at that), the leather-bound books on the shelves that lined the walls were too perfect ever to have been read, the polished oak furniture too bright ever to have been occupied by more than a few people, the thick red carpet too smooth to have been violated by dirty human shoes, the vast desk too neat to have been the site of work.

The Waterford crystal in the adjoining dining room, illuminated already by candlelight, was blinding but excessive by a factor of three or four, and I'm sure that the silver service would have been judged by eyes more practiced than mine to be faintly vulgar.

Dave Redmond, as my father had noted, was "the son of a hod carrier from Bridgeport who didn't have a pot to piss in. You can take the Irishman out of the shanty, but you can't take the shanty out of the Irishman."

For once, the good April, having heard Monsignor's horror stories about Lake Forest, did not protest. Not even at the vulgarity.

Monsignor Redmond had been a seminarian in Rome before the First World War so that made him about sixty. He looked like an overweight and retired British army colonel from India, a balding man who had eaten too much beef, drunk too much port, and played too much polo.

He spoke in the slow, ponderous voice of someone who had seen everything, done everything, and knew everything.

Striving to be both discreet and enthusiastic, we all applauded when Cordelia, flushed and pleased with herself, finished embalming Beethoven.

Would a husband, I wondered, have to tell her that hard work and training were no substitute for talent or for the demons or perhaps the ability to release demons?

Insecure about her lovely body and secure about her dull playing—poor Cordelia.

She was so lovely and so flattered by the congratulations she was receiving that it was hard to feel too sorry for her.

I kissed her hand and she blushed joyfully. "Elegant as always, Charles!"

Alf Lennon cornered the aged Jesuit over champagne (served in Waterford by a manservant who might have been bought with the monsignor's own hands in Paris too) and began a discussion about his own dissertation, on mid-Renaissance English poets, I had been told.

I joined them and tried to look like I understood what they were talking about. In fact there was very little conversation. Alf—"Rev. Mr. Alf" to the host—did most of the talking while his Jesuit confrere appeared to be asleep standing up. I sipped the champagne, which was so tasty as to be more than venially sinful. (I had dispensed myself from my drinking vows for the night.) I resolved that I would have no more than a few sips of all the drinks pressed upon me. I did not want to disgrace either my father or my black-clad love.

"You come from a musical background, young fellow?" the Englishman said during one of the few pauses for breath in Rev. Mr. Alf's lecture.

It required a second or two to realize he was talking to me. No one else had bothered to notice the cute little red-head in the well-cut dinner jacket.

"Fiddlers and horn-blowers, Father. I failed at the flute and try to sing with them sometimes."

He smiled, a generous smile despite his terrible teeth. "I thought so. I noted your rapt expression when you were listening to the young lady playing Beethoven."

"Watching her, Father."

"Quite." He nodded.

Father Alf impatiently resumed his thesis defense.

I decided that the older Jeb was a good guy even if he was an Englishman.

Father Alf, lean, balding, intense, was a bit of a bore. No, that's not fair to the man. He was an enormous bore, but hard to dislike. I felt sure that when he was finished with his work he would know more on the subject than anyone in the world.

It was impossible to dislike any of the Lennons. They were gentle folk who treated me without the slightest hint of the condescension that I had expected, almost hoped for. I also understood—or thought I understood—a lot more about my spring nymph.

Her father must have been almost fifty years older than her, her mother perhaps forty-five years older. Theirs had been a late marriage and Alfred their first and presumably only offspring until the unexpected arrival of Cordelia.

Her parents were tall, distinguished-looking people, with white hair and an atmosphere of gentle abstraction, as though they had been lost in grave and dignified thought for a couple of decades, mystics maybe or great philosophers, profoundly earnest and serious. They loved their bright little daughter with obvious pride—when they noticed her. They were easily gracious to the rather amusing little fellow that she had brought home for the weekend, though I suspect they wondered, if they thought about him at all, whether he might be a leftover from her eleventh birthday party. A year or two ago, wasn't it?

"You're most welcome, Charles. It's so nice to have young people in the house again."

"You must think of it for the duration of your visit as your home as much as our home."

Cordelia could have kept me there all summer and they would not have minded.

Perhaps they would not have noticed.

My Cordelia was not starved for love so much as she was starved for laughter. If she was grimly determined to do great things for God and Church and Art, the reason was that her parents had already done great things—her father as an architect, her mother as a painter—and she wanted to be like them.

Interpreting Dad's evaluation of Dennis Lennon and extending it to Maude Kane Lennon, I suspected that Cordelia might be too much like them already—too much seriousness and not enough flair.

Well, I could make up for the latter without much problem. Right?

At the dinner table, I was seated between Maude Lennon and one of the hapless young priests—"monks" had been brought in to hear confessions, the monsignor explained, so that the curates might attend. The word "monks," spoken in his solemn, sententious baritone, suggested men seized from the basement of a monastery or perhaps from a remote cloister in northern Wisconsin.

Neither of my dinner companions required any small talk from me, though the priest glanced at me curiously now and then as if he wondered what kind of odd fish I was.

Indeed no conversation was required of any of us. Monsignor Redmond presided over the table like an interlocutor over a minstrel show.

Although he had told us beforehand that the secret of his "little dinners" was good conversation, by conversation he meant questions and answers between himself and individual guests. He directed questions seriatim to guests and reflected ponderously on their responses.

I figured that he would not even notice me, much less put me in the witness box.

"Now, Martin [to the English Jesuit], would you agree with what some of my friends in the State Department tell me, that Germany will not be a great power again for this century?"

"We should never underestimate the Hun, David."

Right on, Father.

I tried to read the expression on Cordelia's face. What did she think of this marvelous charade? Probably nothing much. It was simply there. Dinner at the rectory was as neutral and unanalyzed as the giant oak trees in the garden of her house.

"I, for one," the monsignor continued, "can't say I'm sorry. Like you, Martin, I've been through two wars with them and that is enough for a lifetime."

The curate next to me shifted uneasily. Monsignor noted his movement and withered him with a single look. Obviously, you not only listened to and agreed with the pastor, you kept perfectly still when he was talking.

"They are a resilient people."

"Now you, young man." He meant me. "Are we to understand that you are a friend of our gifted young pianist of earlier this evening?"

Damn the priest next to me. His movement had attracted the monsignor's attention to my red hair.

"A colleague, Monsignor. We work on a school magazine together."

Cordelia continued to be unreadable.

He raised a shaggy skeptical eyebrow. "Are we to presume that you are the editor of this worthy publication?"

"No, Monsignor, Miss Lennon is."

"Really? How extraordinary! And what then *is* your role?"

"I'm her slave, Monsignor. She tells me what work she wants done and I do it."

There was a moment of dead silence around the table: I had broken a rule. I had said something that might be funny. Damn it, Cordelia, smile.

"Remarkable, remarkable. And where might you be from?"

"Chicago, Monsignor, it's a city down the Northwestern track from here."

Cordelia wasn't smiling, but the English Jesuit was actually grinning. I dared not glance at the young priest next to me, but his colleague across the table was struggling to contain laughter.

Into the valley of death rode the Light Brigade. Right?

"Yes, indeed. It is safe to presume that you are a practicing Catholic?"

Did I see a quick frown line on my beloved's fair brow?

"Yes, Monsignor."

"You have a parish?"

"St. Ursula, Monsignor."

"Ah, yes, poor Monsignor Meany, God be good to him. I can't for the moment recall who replaced him."

Why was I on the grill? Was the guy jealous of me? Had he been ogling Cordelia during her recital? Why hadn't I kept an eye on him?

"Monsignor Branigan, Monsignor. The school superintendent."

"Yes, indeed, I remember now. Hmm. A man of considerable energy."

And, by implication, not enough seriousness. No friends at the State Department.

I'll get him, Mugsy, I promise I'll get him.

"Your father is a working man, I presume?"

"No, Monsignor."

"No?"

"He doesn't like to work, so he became an architect."

Alf Lennon actually laughed. I now liked him immensely.

My nymph was biting her lip. Angry because I was being disrespectful? Or because I had never told her that our fathers shared the same occupation?

"Imagine that! Are you aware of this young man's father, Dennis?"

"I can't say. . . . What is his first name, uh, Charles?"

"J. E. O'Malley, sir. John the Evangelist O'Malley. Really."

I added the last for Cordelia, across whose beloved brow there were now two frown lines.

"I seem to remember . . . Didn't he win a prize recently? . . . I remember reading about it somewhere."

Cordelia turned to consider her father. Surprised? Or merely loving him.

"The Liturgical Arts award for church design last year, sir. The new St. Ursula Church."

"How extraordinary. . . . Now, Martin, wouldn't you say that the most serious problem the world faces is the persistent power of world Communism, far more serious than Fascism ever was?"

Thus my father and his prize were dismissed, but I had been freed from the gridiron with nothing worse than a draw to my credit.

"Only if the terrible poverty in western Europe cannot be undone, David."

"That is the position of Secretary of State Marshall, whom I am informed, authoritatively, I might add, is viewed with considerable reserve by the State Department professionals. Not a Communist exactly, I hasten to add, but certainly not unsympathetic to their cause."

"The misery in Germany and France and in my own country," his guest replied, "is considerable. Recently some progress has been made, but I fear for our future unless there is more."

"The Labor government in England, of course . . . Well, you're safe, as we know, from external invasion because of the blessed English Channel." He finished his fish course, long since disposed of by the rest of us, and waved away the proferred white wine. "The red wine now, please. . . . But the rest of Europe, would it not be ripe as a plum for the picking should the Red Army elect to move, save for the presence of our brave young fighting men?"

This was getting to be too much. Even for me. Especially for me.

"Quite possibly, quite possibly." The visitor dug into the roast beef, blood rare, as if he were not sure when he would eat his next meal.

"My sources tell me"—the monsignor heaped his plate high with potatoes, one shanty-Irish trait he had not been able to shed—"that our army is in splendid shape, spoiling for a fight, and that if old Uncle Joe, as I believe the late President Roosevelt called him, should be so incautious as to attack, we would promptly drive them all the way back to the Pacific."

"Charles was in the Army in Germany, Monsignor, for two years."

Cordelia.

Traitor.

"Who? Oh yes, the inestimable Mr. O'Malley."

"Charles O'Malley, Monsignor. Charles C. O'Malley."

"Indeed. So you were in the service in Germany, young man?"

"An elite unit, Monsignor." Cordelia, small bite of beef on her fork, was a witch.

"Astonishing. . . . Is this true, young man?"

"I was in the Constabulary, Monsignor." I put my fork down. "A kind of mobile military police unit, responsible for order in the countryside. Perhaps like a mixture of state police and National Guard in this country."

"So you would be familiar with the condition of our troops. They are, I presume, battle ready?"

"No, Monsignor." I picked up my fork and wolfed down a substantial mouthful of potatoes. I never denied that I was shanty Irish. "They're not."

"Truly?" The man seemed genuinely agitated. "I should think they would be prepared to resist an invasion."

"Cordelia was right, Monsignor. I guess my outfit was an elite unit, fancy blue braid and putties and helmets and yellow scarves. And to tell you the truth, we would not have been able to form a skirmish line that would repel an attack by the Little Sisters of the Poor."

The English Jesuit whooped with laughter. Denny Lennon really and truly smiled. Not only did my love's lip corners turn up in approval; her eyes shone. The curate next to me seemed to be choking.

Charles C. O'Malley never had the sense to quit when he was ahead.

"In my squad—I was a sergeant, Mr. Lennon, which will show you in what shape the army is—at least six men didn't know how to remove the safety from their weapons. Nor was I about to teach them because I was afraid that if they did release the safety they might shoot me in the back by accident."

I was even farther ahead now. Time to quit.

So, I didn't quit.

"The only reason to be hopeful is that our intelligence reports indicate that the other side is in even worse shape than we are. As I'm sure your reading of history discloses, Monsignor, armies of occupation have always been demoralized and barely effective at anything besides black market trade."

Now everyone was super solemn. Had I gone too far or had I scared them?

To hell with it.

"Remarkable." The Monsignor considered me gravely. "I shall have to inquire of my friends in government whether the situation may be rather more grim than they are willing to admit. . . . Now, Martin, let us hear about your new work."

The elderly Jesuit's new work, it seemed, was about love. Most of the discussion, like all abstract reflection, was far above me. Cordelia listened with rapt attention.

It seemed that the Jesuit was responding to two men— "Bishop Nygren" and "DeRougemont," both of whom had thus far escaped my attention. The question was whether love could be totally unselfish or whether it always must involve some self-seeking.

Angels on the head of a pin, I thought with some disgust.

One form of love, I could not determine which, was called "agape" the other "eros."

Love, it seemed to me then, was obviously love; debate

about such ethereal questions was ridiculous. If you had ever been in love, you know what love is, right?

Wrong, Chucky Ducky, dead wrong, but you were too young then to be expected to know any better.

Perhaps also too much "in love."

Much later, the table having been cleared, the monsignor sat up straight, glanced around as if taking a roll call. "Well, now, Martin," he said sighing as if he had played a vigorous game of touch football. "What's your solution?"

I glanced around the table. With the exception of my intensely attentive beloved, everyone seemed to be dozing.

"I don't know that I have a solution, old fellow; it may be one of those ultimately insoluble puzzles, a maze from which there is no escape, if you take my meaning. Still, I wonder sometimes whether one might not come moderately close to an answer—know the direction of it, you see—if one says that love, of God or of another human, is not so much the desire to possess the other totally as the desire to be possessed totally by the other . . ."

Bang.

I knew he was right. I would check the notion with Christopher when I was back in the shadow of the Golden Dome, but I was back in the shadow of the Golden Dome, but the strange old Jesuit had put his finger on it. I didn't like his solution, not one bit, but he had said it all.

"Now that is a very striking thought, Martin. If I may, let me see if I can find some reaction among our friends round the table. Let me see . . . Cordelia, my dear, you are young and the young are supposed to be wise in the ways of love. What do you think of Father's definition?"

"Not a definition certainly"—the Englishman, coughed modesty—"just the hint of an explanation, if you take my meaning."

"Well, yes; Cordelia, how would you react to his hint of an explanation: love is the desire to be possessed totally by another?"

"The other," she corrected him, her eyes shining brightly. "I find it an extremely challenging insight, Monsignor."

She didn't look at me, understandably I suppose.

"Very interesting indeed." His eyes swiveled around the table and found me again. "Ah, yes, Charles, our expert on armies of occupation. Have you given any thought to this matter?"

"A little, Monsignor."

"And how are you affected by the description of love as the desire to be totally possessed by another?"

"The other." If he didn't see the difference, he didn't know from nothing.

"Of course." He waved his hand.

"Frankly, Monsignor, I think that Father is absolutely right. That's what love is."

Everyone around the table seemed to have awakened and to be staring fixedly at me.

"And?"

"And, Monsignor, if being possessed totally by the other is what love is, then love scares the hell out of me."

The assembly gasped.

The Jesuit applauded.

Monsignor Redmond suggested that Maude lead the ladies into the study, "all we have for a drawing room, my dear; we'll join you shortly."

When we followed them into the study half an hour later, the Jesuit clapped me on the back. "Jolly good, old fellow, jolly good."

"Keeps David on his toes. Good thing too," Dennis Lennon murmured.

After she had planted a chaste good-night kiss on my lips later in the evening, Cordelia seemed to agree. "I'm so proud of you, Charles. So proud."

So, I hadn't done too badly after all.

I lay in bed in my guest room wide awake for hours. At first, I fantasized about Cordelia, only a few doors away down the corridor. Somehow, it was hard to be too detailed in my images about a young woman who was sleeping in what had been until recently her nursery.

Then I thought about what was really on my mind—love as the desire to be totally possessed.

Did my beautiful sleeping Cordelia want to be totally possessed by me? By anyone indeed, but in the present set of circumstances by me?

She certainly thought she did.

And did I want to be totally possessed by the other—whoever the other might be?

Not on your life.

A couple of nights after my improbable adventures in Lake Forest, I was back where I belonged, in the rough-and-tumble world of the St. Ursula chapter of the Catholic War Veterans. To be precise I was sitting on the running board of Jimmy Rizzo's ancient Chevy, guzzling from a Coke bottle while Monica Sullivan sat next to me, a bottle of beer in her hand.

Somehow, in Monica's pretty little hand, a beer bottle seemed elegant and refined.

"The men in that red Ford," she said, pointing to a car parked at the outer limits of right field, "are the private detectives my father has hired to watch me."

"For what?"

"Some evidence that I've lost my virginity, I suppose."

"That's not exactly against the law."

"I know. But if Jimmy and I should be sleeping together that would somehow prove that he's right."

"I don't understand."

"Neither do I, Chuck. It's an obsession with him. . . . He's forbidden everyone else in our family to speak with me. I'm under interdict."

"Do they obey it?"

"Mom calls me on the phone when he's not around. She begs me to give 'that Dago' up."

"Hardly calculated to be an effective plea."

"No, but she's beside herself with grief. I am very sorry for her. It's terrible for all of us."

I was sitting on the running board with the captain's lady because my talents were not required in right field any longer. Tim Boylan, trim and alert again, was back in left field, and Danny Cummins, our left fielder, had been moved to right. We hadn't lost a game yet and would probably win the Catholic War Veterans city championship. We were dusting off the team from St. Lucy's this evening. With the lure of the championship cup (less than ten dollars on the trophy market!), softball had become a serious business. Charles C. O'Malley was thrown into the breach only when we were so far ahead that he couldn't blow it.

I accepted this rebuff with characteristic fatalism.

This would probably be the last summer for the Catholic War Veterans. The war had been over now for four years. Most of them had college degrees and jobs and many had wives and children. The postwar world would not survive into 1950.

It was a sound prediction. I did not anticipate that in a year there would be another war, one that would quickly be forgotten, but which would cause grave problems for my generation and for my family and friends.

I had come to the reluctant conclusion that the Depression would not return for a long time. That should have made me happy. Our family was unlikely ever to be poor again. But all my plans had assumed that the postwar prosperity could not last. What was left of my plans?

I was working for O'Hanlon and O'Halloran, Certified Public Accounts, during the summer. I earned less than I had the previous summer. The job was exactly the opposite of my stint on the exchange. The work was smooth, orderly, and efficient. It was also boring. My responsibilities demanded nothing more than the accounting skills I had earned in my courses at Bamberg. Indeed the senior partners, reliable, sound, honest men, had learned their accounting at DeLaSalle High School when they were adolescents. The firm had a superb reputation. It would do your work more quickly and less expensively than some of the bigger and more prestigious firms—so long as there was nothing complicated in your operation.

In other words, the firm was steady, moderately prosperous, safe, and dull.

Really dull.

That's what I thought I had wanted when I had planned my life out during the Depression. There was always work, I believed, for accountants.

Dull work.

Once again my plans had somehow not fit reality.

Since I was quick at what I did, I had lots of time to fantasize about life and about what my life would look like in ten years. The fantasies were not all that appealing, save for the images of Cordelia that often inhabited them. Even if my workaday life were dull, Cordelia at home waiting for me would make all the difference in the world.

Wouldn't she?

I realized the irony of my advice to Jimmy Rizzo and Tim Boylan that they should take risks; I was not taking risks myself. I argued that I was not averse to risk taking, but what were the risks I was supposed to take?

Wasn't I taking enough of a risk in courting Cordelia?

"So what happens next?" I asked Monica Sullivan.

"Nothing is definite . . . I mean it is definite that James and I will marry. I have, as your sister Jane says, slammed the door shut on that."

"Ah," I said.

"Next time you see me, I might just have something on this finger."

"High time."

"That's what I say too."

"James will probably go to Princeton Law School in the

fall. After he gets settled down there he will come back and we will be married."

"Good news . . . *Probably* go to Princeton?"

"He has not turned down his uncle's offer of managing a chain of restaurants. He could always get his law degree at night. It takes only another year."

"You get along with his family?"

"Of course. They're sweet, lovely people. Even Uncle Sal seems to like me."

"You both should get out of town, Monica."

"I know that."

"So slam the door on that too."

"Not quite yet."

Before we could continue the discussion, our side had retired the St. Lucy guys, one, two, three. Jimmy and Tim joined us on the running board.

"Flirting with my girl, Sarge?" Jimmy asked.

"She's much too old for me," I said. "Besides, I don't see any ring that proclaims that she's anyone's girl."

The guys laughed, Monica blushed happily.

"I'm his girl all right, but I am much too mature for you, Chucky. Anyway, I wouldn't want to have Rosemarie angry at me."

More laughter. I had given up trying to persuade people that Rosemarie had not staked a claim on me. Or vice versa.

"Keep an eye on that finger for a while," Jimmy said enthusiastically.

"I hope you get it wholesale. I know a good place where you can get it wholesale."

I didn't, but that's what they expected me to say.

"Sorry to edge you out of right field, Charles C.," Tim said with a wicked grin. "It's your fault for sending me to that Jewish friend of yours."

The neighborhood was celebrating the return of the old Tim Boylan. It was even said that he was dating, more or less, a nice young woman from St. Catherine's, a certain Jenny Collins.

"No good deed goes unpunished."

"What about Rosie Clancy?" Tim continued. "Are you dating her or are you not?"

"Rosemarie," I said evenly, "is kind of like a foster sister in our family. It would be incestuous to date her."

"She sure is pretty," Jimmy protested.

"Have you noticed that too?"

"You're up, James," Monica informed him.

"Try to get on base for a change," Tim warned him. "First base will do; I'll drive you in. . . . You've noticed his hitting slump, Charles C.?"

"Slump?" I said in feigned disbelief. "Love should make people hit better, shouldn't it?"

"Brat!" Monica slapped my arm very lightly.

"Who, me?"

"So you're not really dating anyone?" Tim persisted.

"As a matter of fact, I am," I said, knowing full well that the story would be all over the parish the next morning. "A girl from St. Mary's named Cordelia Lennon."

Dead silence.

Jim beat out a ground to get on first base. Tim went to bat.

"Can't we get rid of those spies?" I asked Monica, mostly to deflect conversation about Cordelia. "Call the cops or something?"

"They are cops, Chuck, off-duty cops earning a few extra dollars. I'm very nice to them and that makes them ashamed. I don't mind. . . . And tell me more about this Cordelia."

"Not much to tell. She's blond like you, though pale, almost ice blond. She's a musician and her father is an architect. So we have a lot in common. She's very intelligent and fun to be with."

"What parish?"

"I don't know. They live in Lake Forest."

"Lake Forest? Isn't that pretty rich?"

"I guess so."

"And poor Rosie?"

"We're friends. We've never dated."

"Does she know about Cordelia?"

"Sure, everyone in the family knows."

"How does she react?"

"She doesn't seem to mind."

That was true and not true. Rosemarie did not complain. Indeed, she admired my white dinner jacket and told me she hoped I had a good time. Our timber wolf was polite, correct, restrained. I would have felt better if she had screamed at me.

"Don't you like her, Chuck?"

"Cordelia?"

"No, silly, Rosie."

"She drinks too much, Monica. It scares me."

"People can stop drinking."

"She hasn't."

The guys came back. We were now nine runs ahead of St. Lucy. Before the inning was over we had stretched our lead to thirteen runs. Jimmy and Tim did a little act in which the latter begged him to let me play and the former reluctantly gave in.

I took my Leica out to right field with me.

The seraphs were watching over me again, because no fly ball came anywhere near me.

When the inning was over, I detoured to the red Ford.

"Good evening, gentlemen, would you smile for me, please?"

I leaned through the window of the car and snapped away.

The two off-duty cops no way wanted to smile.

"What the hell are you up to, punk?"

"I'm taking pictures of you for my records."

"You've got a hell of a lot of nerve."

"The commissioner might be interested in these some-day," I said as I strolled away.

Why did I do that?

There's a demon inside me that makes me do such crazy things. I figured it would be a good idea to have a record of the creepy cops who were working for Big Tom Sulli-van.

I didn't expect them to like it.

"What the hell did you do that for?" Jimmy demanded.

"Intelligence work, Captain, sir."

"They'll come after you."

"Not twice."

Whence such bravado?

I would ask Jimmy to drive me home immediately after the game. I would develop the pictures and put them in Dad's safe. The cops could seize the film, but I'd warn them that I had the pictures and would use them if they didn't leave me alone.

The next morning, prints in the safe, film in my pocket, I discovered my rejected Rosemarie in the kitchen drinking a cup of coffee and looking under the weather.

"I didn't know you were in the house," I said.

"Lucky for me, huh?" She grinned wickedly. "I came home from the lake because I have to take some tests out at the University. I worried about it all last night and I didn't sleep so well."

That was her way of telling me that she did not have a hangover. Poor dear woman. She looked so lovely.

"Rosemarie, even after a bad night you look gorgeous in a robe and nightgown."

She beamed.

"You are the sweetest boy in the world, Chuck."

"I know."

My wicked idea suddenly expanded.

I went to the front of the house. Sure enough, the red Ford. I loaded my Kodak, the one Rosemarie had given me when I went to Germany.

I returned to the kitchen. Rosemarie was eating a piece of dry toast. I told her what had happened.

"Chuck," she said admiringly, "you are absolutely crazy."

"You want to help?"

"Sure."

I told her what to do.

"I'll open the safe. Be sure you spin the lock when you close it."

"Absolutely."

She was grinning broadly, loving every minute of our conspiracy.

I thought for a moment. One more precaution. I dialed the Oak Park Police Department.

"I'm Charles C. O'Malley at 1012 Fair Oaks. There is an unmarked Chicago police car parked in front of my house. Illinois license 405–216. I wonder if one of your cars could come over and find out what they want. Thank you."

"I'll run upstairs and get dressed. Then I can drive you to the El after you tell those guys off."

A brilliant idea. Why hadn't I thought of it?

She was back in a couple of minutes, a serious student in a gray summer suit, though a student carrying a foot and a half length of pipe she must have found in the basement.

I gave her the camera.

"Just point and shoot as fast as you can, especially when they're trying to push me around."

"If they hurt you, Chuck, I'll bash their heads."

"Rosemarie Helen Clancy, put that pipe down."

"Okay," she said meekly.

"Unless they get really rough."

"Right."

So I strolled down the stairs and onto our charming oak-lined street.

The two cops were on me at once. I kept my back to

the house so Rosemarie could get pictures of their faces.

The fat one grabbed my arms. The thin one hit me a couple of times.

"We want that film, punk, or we'll beat the shit out of you."

"Sure," I said, keeping my rage under control. "Let me go and I'll give you the film."

Reluctantly the fat one let me go.

I tossed the film on the ground.

"It's all yours, Officers."

"We don't want no more fucking trouble out of you, punk."

"No promises, Officer. My wife has shot a whole roll of film of you assaulting me. Right now she is putting the camera in the safe with the prints I made from that film. Moreover, there's an Oak Park police car on the way. You know what they think of your kind. They've got your license number so they'll make sure you go back to Chicago where you belong. I don't think you should come back. But if you do I'll bring charges against you. Lots of charges."

"You fucking punk," the thin one said furiously.

"You try to break into the house it won't do you any good because you can't get into the safe. Before the day is over all the prints will be in our lawyer's office. You'd better be on your good behavior from now on."

"Let's beat the fuck out of him," the fat one said.

That would bring on Rosemarie with her pipe.

"That would be most unwise."

"Don't be an asshole," the thin one said to his partner. "Let's get the fuck out of here."

"Thank your lucky stars that I'm not bringing charges against you now. Like I say, the Oak Park police don't like your kind messing around."

"Fuck you," the fat one said.

"I think I see an Oak Park police car. . . . And you can tell Big Tom Sullivan that there's a veteran of the First

Constabulary Regiment who is tougher than he is."

They scurried into the car and drove off just as the OPPD turned the corner. I pointed at the red Ford. I'd talk to them later in the day and tell them about these guys, so they would have a record.

Rosemarie, her eyes glowing with excitement, came down the stairs, key to the convertible in her hand.

"Let's get out of here," she said, as if she were a character in a mystery movie. "That sure was fun."

"It's lucky for them they stopped hitting me," I said.

"I was halfway out the door."

"I figured."

"What was the point of it, Chucky?"

The answer that sprung to my lips was that I was bored. It was a dangerous answer so I suppressed it.

"I figured it was a good chance to get a little leverage against Big Tom."

Only then did I start to tremble.

"Charles Cronin O'Malley," she said as we approached the Marrion Street El station. "You're crazy."

"Yeah, I guess I am."

"Stable accountant indeed!"

"Rosemarie," I said fervently as I climbed out of the convertible. "You're a good one to have around in a crisis."

She grinned.

"I always told you that."

❧ 12 ❧

Cordelia dropped me.

I didn't quite understand why then and I still don't.

It was the end of June. I was working at O'Hanlon and O'Halloran Certified Public Accountants and attending night school at DePaul. I ate lunch twice a week with Christopher at Berghoff's (he was working at his father's law office) and played handball with him once a week in the late afternoon—winning occasionally now.

He gently suggested that perhaps Cordelia and I might triple with him and Vince and their two dates. I said I would ask her whether she wanted to.

I never did ask her.

She and I talked on the phone every day and went to Orson Welles's *Macbeth* at the Studio Theater downtown.

It was hard in those days to sustain a romance at opposite ends of the city when neither you nor your beloved drove a car.

I considered asking Peg to teach me how to change a tire and asking Mom if, in exchange for yielding to her by now persistent request to invite Delia for dinner, I might borrow her car on weekends for my pilgrimage to the North Shore.

I knew I was deeply in love with Cordelia and she with me. My triumph at the rectory dinner table, of which I was now inordinately proud, had swept away the last imaginable obstacle.

Our kissing in the Northwestern station the night we watched Orson's magnificently hammy performance was as violent as the public circumstances permitted. I thought that she was even more passionate than I.

Then, in the middle of the next week, when I came home from DePaul to our house in Oak Park—I could not quite come to terms with the fact that we no longer lived in the tiny apartment on Menard Avenue—there was a letter on my desk, pink, scented letter-size stationery, thick vellum paper. The return address in fine Gothic script said "Cordelia Elizabeth Mary Lennon, Lake Forest, Illinois."

No one else was in the house as I opened the envelope with fingers that ought not to have been trembling but were.

The letter is beside my computer now as I write this chapter. The colors have faded from the paper and from the neat, Convent-of-the-Sacred-Heart script.

Dear Charles,

I know you would want me to be direct.

I think that we ought not to see each other during the summer. I suggest this not because I don't love you. I do love you, very much, perhaps too much for my age and my plans.

I do not say that we should break up. The words are too harsh and besides it is inaccurate. I want us to be friends and perhaps even lovers again. When we're both back at Notre Dame in the autumn, I would very much like that we sit down and with clearer heads talk about the future, about *our* future.

This decision of mine—it's really a request because it would be unjust for me to make the decision alone—is not the result of your visit to our home before the end of school. You were wonderful then. My parents and brother adore you. Alf says I'm lucky to have found someone like you at Notre Dame of all places!

(Notre Dame isn't Jesuit, you see!)

Nor have I stopped loving you. Please believe that I love you as much as ever. You revealed my womanliness to me for the first time. I will always remember with a thrill of excitement the touch of your lips, tender yet insistent, on my flesh. You are the most important person in my life. With God's help, I hope you always will be.

But—there always seems to be a "but," doesn't there, my darling?—I am only nineteen and in the summer between my sophomore and junior years I have to finish college, do my graduate work, at Juilliard if they'll have me, and begin my concert career before I think about marriage and family. I know you too have long-range plans.

Neither of us is ready for marriage yet, Charles. I know we have not discussed it, but our passion for each other will certainly lead to marriage sooner rather than later. We both know that, even if neither of us has so far had the courage to say it. I do not want to ruin your dreams and I know you don't want to ruin my dreams. That's why, for the summer, just for the summer, I think we should pause, relax, and examine ourselves and our futures with a little better perspective than we have now.

I said to you once that the woman who shared your marriage bed with you would be fortunate indeed. I still believe that, with even more conviction now than on that memorable day in the basement of Sorin. I don't want to hurt you. If you disagree with this request of mine, please, please, let's talk about it now.

Remember that no matter what happens, I'll always love you.

Cordelia

Among the many emotions that churned through my head when I put the letter down and sat on the edge of my bed was relief. I resolved that I would examine that later.

The next day in the crowded, noisy Berghoff's, with its tart smell of sauerkraut, I read parts of the letter to Christopher.

"What do you think?"

"The question, Charles, is what do *you* think?"

"Yeah." I put the letter aside and dug into my potato pancake. "I guess that is the question. I don't know what I think. I love her of course . . ."

"Enough to dismiss that letter as nonsense and continue relentless pursuit of the fair lady?"

"What will happen if I do that?"

"I think it is a fair bet that she'll stop running. Even now she's not running very hard."

"A little more pursuit is all that is needed?"

"I should think so."

He held a glass of root beer in his right hand and watched me carefully. Damn him, he saw too much.

"Funny thing . . . I felt relief when I read this." I pointed my fork, on which was impaled a large hunk of potato pancake, at her letter. "I'm not heartbroken like I ought to be."

"Not yet totally possessed by the other?"

"No, Christopher. Decidedly not. What if she's right?"

His face was impassive. "Yes, what if she is?"

"You think I'm a fool?"

"I think you're on the spot. She's yours if you want her. She's also absolutely correct: you're headed for the altar, not right away, maybe. A year or two, no more. Do you want that?"

"I don't think . . . I'm not sure."

"This is an honorable way out"—he tilted his glass toward the pink vellum—"and an easy one at that."

"We could always get back together later on."

"Some enchanted evening?"

"Why not?"

"It's not impossible. Not likely either. If you want her, now is the time, not later."

That night I drafted a careful response and then copied it for my file of saved paper. The copy, in a fifteen-cent spiral notebook with a lot of other observations from those days, is on my desk now, under the pink vellum letter.

Dear Cordelia,

. A number of possible replies to your letter ran through my head:

a) You bitch.

b) I didn't know we were dating seriously. Maybe it's some other guy.

c) It's up to you, kid. See you around.

d) If you think it's that easy to get away from me, you've got another thought coming.

I rejected all of them, the last most reluctantly. The first does not reflect the love I feel, the second would be a lie, the third is silly.

So I decided to write the truth, which is as follows:

You might be right. We're both young and we both have plans and dreams. A summer off won't hurt in the long run. Let's try it anyway. You can count on me showing up in the office of *Compact* the first day of school in September, with all kinds of passionate longings in my head.

Until then I love you and propose to continue to do so.

Charles

I read it to Christopher on the phone.

"Faint heart never won fair lady," he said.

"It's fainthearted?"

"Ingeniously so."

"That's how I feel, I think."

"If that's how you feel"—his voice was impassive—"then send it."

I did.

Rereading the letter now, I think it is a very clever exercise in cowardice.

What would have happened if I had taken the Northwestern up to Lake Forest, enveloped her in my arms, and claimed her as my own forever? What would have happened if I said we'd work out the dreams together?

Would we have been happy together? Would we have worked out our dreams so that the compromises would have been happy ones, better than the separate dreams because they were joint plans and commitments?

Would our passion have withered and died?

Was she just a delightful spring fling?

Or a lost opportunity?

I don't know. I'll never know.

In my most responsible moments, I conclude that it was an enchanting interlude in both our lives that ought to have ended and would have ended eventually anyway.

Maybe that mature reflection is correct.

Maybe not.

At any rate I mailed the letter and settled down for a long summer of loneliness.

13

The red Ford was not in evidence at our next softball game—this time against St. Agedius, near the O'Malleys' Fair Oaks Avenue home. Agedius was Ursula's most hated rival. Spoiled rich kids, we had insisted in grammar school. As evidence of the charge, we compared their grass softball field to our gravel field.

If one acquired a knee burn on the St. Ursula field, one picked at ugly scabs for a couple of months.

However, and despite the lovely homes around their field, the Agedius vets were pretty much like us, though their cars were newer.

"No red Ford," I said to Monica as I sat next to her on the running board of Jimmy Rizzo's Chevy.

"Whatever did you do to them, Chuck?" she asked in awe.

"Scared the living daylights out of them."

"How?"

I considered the pros and cons of telling her some of the details and decided it might help her to know that there were two crazy people on her side.

I exaggerated a little, as I often do. In my narrative, Rosemarie actually came down the steps with the iron pipe. It was not exactly a lie. If the thin cop had hit me once more, she would have been all over him.

"Chuck," she said in horror, "you didn't really do those things, did you?"

"I'm afraid we did."

"Why?"

"Get rid of the red Ford. Show certain people that you have allies."

"Poor Daddy would never understand something like that."

"He'll think twice about sending cops after you and everyone else."

"Daddy used to be such a nice man," she said sadly. "Then he made all that money during the war and it seemed to change him. Isn't that sad?"

"Very sad."

So she still loved her father. That must be kept in mind.

Tim Boylan introduced me to his new date, a certain Jenny Collins, a lovely lass with long black hair and a great smile. She treated Staff Sergeant O'Malley, Charles Cronin, with elaborate respect.

"You won't believe what Chucky just told me, James."

"I think I'd believe anything."

"He and Rosie got rid of the cops."

Captain, my captain frowned. "How did they do that?"

Monica recited her version of my story, a version that emphasized our quick wits.

"That the sort of thing you did in the Constabulary?"

"Sometimes."

"No wonder they gave you the Legion of Merit."

"Great hit!" Jenny cried, interrupting our conversation.

Tim Boylan had smashed another home run, increasing our lead to ten runs.

Fascinating events were happening all around us. In Germany, a country I had finally begun to like despite my prejudices, the American airlift to Berlin had worked and the Russians abandoned their blockade. My old friend the Herr Oberbürgermeister of Cologne was the first chancellor of the new Federal Republic of Germany. The Communists were sweeping through China and, as if in reply, the Vatican had announced that it might have found some of the bones of Saint Peter. The British were testing the first jet transport, which they called the Comet. I had never been in an airplane—the Army had put me on troop transports both ways and I almost died from seasickness or at least so I claimed. However, I never wanted to fly in a plane, much less a jet. I vowed solemnly that I never would set foot in one. The Buick Roadmaster appeared, the first car with three or four holes on either side of the chassis.

Naturally, the O'Malleys bought one of them for the good April, so that Peg could inherit Mom's Olds convertible to match Rosemarie's Study. The family thus owned four cars. I resolutely refused one, though I can't quite recall the reason for my high principles.

"What are the holes for?" I had demanded of Dad. "What do they *do*?

"They don't do anything, dear," Mom had replied. "They're just cute."

"Form follows function," I said, quoting Louis Sullivan, one of the most famous of the Chicago School of architects.

"Have you seen the decorations on the Carson's building?" Dad had replied, referring to one of Sullivan's most famous works.

Touché.

"They still look funny."

Dad, I thought, looked more frazzled than ever. Someone had to do something about straightening out the mess in his office.

"They're supposed to look funny, aren't they, Peggy dear?"

"Not as funny as Chuck in his business suit when he goes to work."

And so it went.

At the St. Agedius ball field, Jenny Collins kissed Tim lightly on the cheek as he finished his dash around the bases. He hugged her briefly and over her head winked at me.

"Are you and Rosie together again?" Monica asked me.

Women assume they have the right to take responsibility for everyone's love relationships. There's no point in arguing, I had long since learned, in trying to resist that assumption.

"We were never together in the first place," I said firmly. "She's my foster sister. She is also a very clever, uh, colleague."

Monica smiled, gently, as though she could see my little subterfuge.

"Your heart still belongs to the girl up in Lake Forest . . . what's her name?"

"Cordelia Lennon."

"She's still your summer date?"

No good would come of trying to lie.

"We decided to cool it for the summer."

"*She* decided?"

St. Ursula's heroes finally permitted themselves a third out. The team rushed back to the field.

"Mutual agreement."

"Why?"

I was squirming mentally.

"She wants to be a concert pianist."

"Is she more beautiful than Rosie?"

"No one is more beautiful than Rosemarie, Monica, except maybe you."

She laughed and ended her cross-examination, satisfied apparently that she had figured everything out.

"Thank you," she said, "for getting rid of the spies."

"Anytime."

We won the game of course and then all adjourned to the Magic Pub. Tim Boylan, his arm confidently around Jenny's shoulders, lifted a bottle of Coke to me in a laughing toast.

As the crowd sang "Younger than Springtime," I told

myself that, although my romantic life, never much to begin with, was in limbo, I had accomplished something that
summer. I had helped Tim Boylan and James (as Monica
now called him) Rizzo. As it would later turn out, that was
presumptuous self-congratulation.

The images of the softball games come flooding back
into my memory—the smells of male sweat, beer, the
grease in Jimmy's car, and Monica's perfume. The noise
of our cheering supporters, the hollers of triumph as we
swarmed off the field, Jimmy's crisp commands as he
barked instructions, Monica's gentle tones, the shots in the
pub after our victories, the cries of horror as I dropped fly
balls in right field, the noises in Kerrigan's after the game,
the songs from *South Pacific* that rocked the walls of the
pub. Especially "Younger than Springtime." The glow in
Jenny Collins's green eyes as Tim pounded around the
bases, the sun sinking behind the rising walls of our new
church, the eager young faces of the vets who had escaped
death and were now escaping the Depression, Father
Raven's approving smile.

The images fade. We were all so young and so hopeful.
Admittedly, I never quite fit. I was not a real vet, I was a
rotten athlete, my language, son of the good April that I
was, was much milder than that of the other vets. They all
liked me—who wouldn't like poor little Chucky?—but I
was odd, unusual, different, headed down a different path.

Do I learn anything from recalling those images? I don't
know. Maybe like that French novelist I am recalling those
memories and writing about them so I can capture them
in the net of eternity.

Still, that's what it was like when I was twenty.

❧ 14 ❧

"Do you know this boy Christopher that's a friend of Vince's?"

Rosemarie in swimsuit and robe had come from the beach. Peg had, as usual, picked me up at the train on Saturday morning. I was sitting on the porch staring balefully at the pretty blue lake—sometimes Lake Michigan elects to be pretty.

"Sure," I said.

"What's he like?"

She sat down across from me, her head cocked to one side, a usual pose for Rosemarie when she wanted to learn something that you know.

"He's my closest friend down there, a thoroughly admirable young man."

"Oh," she said, as if she were disappointed.

"Why do you ask?"

If I were not an idiot, I would not have had to ask.

"Well . . . Vince wants me to triple with him and your old friend Ed Murray and some girl from the South Side."

The last clause hinted at a generalized suspicion toward anyone from the South Side, a required attitude among us more civilized West Siders.

"You'll have a good time," I said as casually as I could.

"He's a German and a Republican and pretty serious but he can be fun too."

I was naturally furious. What was Christopher doing? How dare he date Rosemarie?

Hold on, Chucky Ducky. He doesn't know about Rosemarie and he certainly doesn't know the name of the girl in the photo. Peg doesn't know about him either. Moreover, she and Rosemarie think I'm still in love with Cordelia. I had kept my relationships neatly compartmentalized.

"You don't mind if I go out with him?"

Yes, I mind. I'm in a rage.

"Not at all," I said benignly. "I think you'll like him and I know he'll like you."

"I probably won't have much fun," she said, rising from the chaise.

You'll have too damn much fun.

"I bet you do."

Isn't our hero mature and generous?

When I saw Christopher at our next weekly lunch, he seemed embarrassed.

"I almost died when I saw she was the girl in the picture."

"You didn't say anything about it?"

"Charles, I'm not a complete idiot. You never told me the name of the girl in the picture."

"What did you think of her?"

He ignored the question and went on with his explanation.

"Vince and Ed said they wanted me to triple with them and a girl who was a friend of your sister, whom by the way I have never met before."

Peg had undoubtedly put them up to it. Since I was involved with Cordelia, Rosemarie must look elsewhere for a summer romance. Peg had never heard of Christopher from me. Vince and Ed were too dumb to catch the nuances. It was enough for them to be told that I had a date of my own.

"So what did you think of both of them?"

"You really grow up with those two?"

"Yeah."

"Absolutely dazzling. I could hardly believe my eyes."

"So you had a good time."

"I certainly did. Your Rosemarie is a beautiful, brilliant, exciting young woman."

Yeah.

"I'm glad you did."

"You don't mind? I'm not trespassing on your territory?"

"She's a foster sister, Christopher, that's all."

He frowned.

"I would have thought from the picture that there was more to the relationship than that."

"Not at all."

"You sure?"

"Yep."

"Neither of them mentioned you."

"Why should they?"

"Ed and Vince must have told them that we are friends."

My sister and my foster sister were playing their cards very carefully.

"That wouldn't have made any difference."

"You're sure?"

"For the final time, yes, I'm sure."

I had no right to complain, absolutely no right to complain. But I was furious. However, I kept my mouth shut.

The next weekend Peg asked the inevitable question when she picked me up at the Yards.

"How are you and Cordelia doing?"

"Who?"

"The girl up in Lake Forest our parents got the summer formal jacket for."

That was one way of putting it.

"She dumped me."

"*What?*"

"She just washed me right out of her hair." I did an imitation of Mary Martin and Rosemarie singing that song.

"Why?"

A highly personal question but I was now under obligation to respond to the catechism.

"She thought we were getting too serious."

"Usual baloney . . . Were you getting too serious?"

"She thought so."

Very gently, "Do you love her, Chuck?"

"I thought I did. Not enough to disagree with her judgment, I guess."

She nodded sympathetically.

"Did she love you?"

"I think so."

"A lot?"

"Hard to tell. Maybe."

"Once you've found him, never let him go."

"I'm sure the good April would agree with that sentiment."

"What was her reason?"

"She wants to be a concert pianist. Marriage and motherhood, she said, would interfere."

"Is she good enough?"

"Let me explain. She has had a first-rate education and has sound technical skills. But she is different from your fiddle playing in one important respect."

"Violin playing . . . And what's that?"

"When you do Paganini a very considerable fire in your soul explodes. You and the fiddle come alive with passion and power. The wild woman inside of you, the cougar, comes alive in the music. Poor Cordelia can't do that."

"Why?"

"Dull parents, I think. Not like ours."

"Did you tell her that?"

"Come on, Peg."

"All right, all right. Did she break it up or just postpone it?"

"A bit of both. We'll reexamine the relationship in September."

"What will happen then?"

I sighed.

"Unless I'm prepared to insist, it's finished."

"And if you do insist?"

"Then she'll cave in."

Peg's turn to sigh.

"Chucky, what an awful situation."

We turned into the gate at Grand Beach.

"Maybe I fell in love too quickly. I don't know."

"Would I like her?"

"Probably."

Silence.

Peg drew a deep breath.

"Will you insist?"

"I don't think so. Too noble maybe. Or perhaps too proud."

"More likely too wise."

We got out of the car.

"Maybe."

"She has to find out herself that her dream can't come true."

"That's what I think too."

Inside the house, I warned her that this information should not interfere with Rosemarie dating Christopher. I did not doubt for a moment that Peg was debating that subject in her agile mind.

"We wouldn't have started that if we had known."

"I have no claim on Christopher and no claim on Rosemarie. Let it play itself out."

She inclined her head in a quick nod.

"I guess that's the only fair thing to do."

"Right."

I went out on the porch to glare at the lake, feeling very

sorry for myself. Would a friendship between Christopher and my foster sister grow and flourish? I didn't think so. She was a little too wild for him and he a little too staid for her. Maybe, however, it was a match made in heaven. If it wasn't, I shouldn't be the one to tell either of them.

In later years such serious thoughts about a woman going into her first year of college would have seemed absurd. But it was the late nineteen forties, the postwar world. Young men and young women seized almost brutally the first chance for happiness that came along.

On the porch I opened my textbook on the business cycle, a course I was taking at DePaul. Why go to night school for a course that Notre Dame would never accept—DePaul was viewed at the Golden Dome as little better than a high school? Because I liked school when I was able to pick my own courses and because I was curious. About everything. Perhaps I would always be taking night-school classes.

The book explained why the Depression had not returned. Demand for goods and services had been pent up during the Depression and the war—fifteen long years. At the end of the war, Americans had a lot of money available because of wartime full employment. They wanted cars, homes, radios, fridges, washing machines. They married quickly and immediately began to have children. The result was a strong surge of prosperity. The author of the book refused to predict an end to the postwar expansion.

So I had been wrong, dead wrong. America would need architects for a long time. I felt good about that. I was glad I had been wrong.

But what did that mean for me?

I was still baffled by the contrast between my boring job, which I had come to hate, and my propensity to reckless adventure. The incident with the cops who had been haunting Monica Sullivan proved that my behavior in the First Constab was not the result of the long distance from home. I was a little crazy after all, worse even than the rest of the crazy O'Malleys. Not quite as bad as my foster sister.

Something would have to change soon.

At supper Mom, all innocence, asked, "Have you seen that little girl from Lake Forest lately, Chuck?"

Aha, the monstrous regiment of women was conspiring again.

"Not for a while. I'll look her up when we get back to Notre Dame."

"Would I like her?"

"Sure. She's the kind people bring home to mother."

In fact, the good April, come to think of it, would insist that Cordelia was "lovely" but "maybe a little too serious."

"Doesn't it depend a lot on who mother is?" Dad asked with equal innocence.

So! Peg had told them that Cordelia and I were no longer an item, but had not revealed the details. It was just as well that my failure in love was out in the open.

"Maybe," I replied.

I did not want to dim the family joy over the news that Jane was pregnant, so I elected to play down the whole matter. Chucky Ducky with a broken heart? Don't be ridiculous.

"I've never told you about supper at the rectory in Lake Forest, have I? You won't believe it!"

So I recounted my adventures with David Redmond and the Lennons in rich and perhaps somewhat exaggerated detail. My audience laughed and laughed and laughed.

"Chucky, you never said that!" the good April protested several times.

"I did too."

I left out the dialogue about love.

"She does seem kind of sweet," Rosemarie said gently. "I imagine her heart is broken."

"Sweet she is. Whose heart isn't broken when a romance comes to an end? But her heart would be more broken if she gave up a chance at a concert career."

"Once you've found him, never let him go," Peg insisted.

"You're certain the young woman has no great musical talent?" Dad asked cautiously.

"My idea of young talent is my obnoxious little sister on the fiddle. Poor Cordelia, for all her training and dedication, is not in the same league."

"Violin," Peg corrected me.

"She has to find that out for herself, doesn't she, dear?"

"Exactly, Mom," I replied.

"She does sound sweet, but maybe a little too serious," Mom said, bringing that episode in my life to a close.

I had not admitted, had I, that I too had suffered a bit of a broken heart? Chucky Ducky conceding the pangs of unrequited love?

Nonsense.

But then why did I feel so sorry for myself?

✌ 15 ↩

My second year at Notre Dame, such as it was, changed my life.

I sought out Christopher the first day of class and demanded that he teach me to play tennis the way he had taught me to play handball. "I break even with you now in the pits, so the challenge has gone out of it."

"You don't break even the way I count," he grumbled.

"You count wrong."

So, the first set I lost 6–love. In the second I worked myself up to 6–2.

"Closing in on you," I insisted, as I sunk into the grass outside the court, wondering if I was really too young to have a heart attack.

"You're becoming a regular jock, Charles," he laughed.

"You forget I was a quarterback on the city champs. Just wait, I'll be good enough soon to beat you and my sister."

"Five years if ever to beat me. Never to beat Peg."

That's right, he knew Peg now.

"How are you and Rosemarie coming along these days?"

"Rosemarie? We haven't dated for the last month. Don't they tell you anything around your house?"

"Not a thing."

He could wait till Judgment Day for me to ask why he and Rosemarie had broken up.

"She's a wonderful girl"—he broke the silence—"absolutely spectacular—beautiful, bright, funny, everything a man could want with one exception."

"And that is?"

"She wasn't ready to fall in love with me."

"A shame."

"Or anyone else."

"Oh?"

"There is only one man in her life, I'm afraid."

All right, I rose to the bait.

"Who?"

"Who?" He feigned great surprise. "Why, darling Chucky, who else? I entertained her for a time this summer because we could talk about him. . . . Chucky said this, Chucky did that, Chucky said the funniest thing, isn't Chucky amazing . . . et cetera, et cetera, et cetera."

"Damn her! She has no right—"

"Ah, but Charles, my boy, she does, you see. That's the wonderful irony of it all. You have the right to ignore her adoration, but you have no right to demand that she stop it."

"Shit."

He raised his right shoulder, a little higher than usual. "Mind you, I have no objection to hearing your praises sung. After all, I have been known to engage in such melodies myself on occasion. I won't argue that the young woman is in error, even if her portrait is essentially one-sided. Still—"

"Shut up, damn it. I don't want to hear about the little bitch."

He laughed genially. "I fear that you will hear about her, one way or another, for a long time to come."

The last time I had seen Rosemarie was the Thursday before the Labor Day weekend. Mom was not ready to trust her daughter and her favorite foster daughter to my care at the wheel of a car. Despite my adventures on the autobahn, I was, by my own admission, something less than the world's greatest driver.

About my adventures on the autobahn—carrying Trudi and her family to Stuttgart, breaking up the black market ring, needless to say, I had told no one, except John Raven and Christopher.

So, we drove together from Oak Park to Lake Geneva to collect Rosemarie and Peg from the former's house, the scene of my prom triumph. Rosemarie, whose car was being repaired for reasons that were not explained to me, had spent a few days with her father, "poor dear man."

I tried to argue that they were both adults, were they not, going to college, and could ride the Northwestern and the South Shore. In those days before the expressways it was a day-long venture to Lake Geneva and then all the way down to the Dunes.

"They're only children, dear."

"Rosemarie is enough of an adult to rent an apartment in Hyde Park and attend an immoral, pagan, Communist university, isn't she?"

"That's next month, dear."

I should have known better than to argue.

It was late morning when we arrived at the Clancy house at Lake Geneva. It had been repainted since I was there last. The landscaping had changed too. Even the pier that had been the scene of my heroics had been extended.

The girls, in slacks and blouses, were waiting for us, both quiet and withdrawn. Jim Clancy, in yachting jacket and white flannels and a captain's cap, seemed less evil this time and more pathetic—a lonely man desperately seeking love.

"Didn't see you in the pits this summer, Chuck." He rubbed his little hands together disconsolately, as if he missed me.

"I work at O'Hanlon and O'Halloran this summer."

"First-rate firm, you won't go wrong if you stay with them."

"Yes, sir."

"What do you think about the Cubs this summer?"

"I don't think they'll ever win the pennant again."

"As bad as your White Sox, huh?"

"Maybe worse."

"Bad times for Chicago teams, eh?" He sounded like the deterioration of Chicago sports was breaking his heart.

"The Big Red will be back," I insisted, still believing that the Chicago Cardinals' triumph a few years back had not been a fluke.

"I sure hope so. Any winner would be fine now."

Dear God, his eyes were sad.

"Business good, April?" he asked as I piled the six suitcases necessary for three days at Lake Geneva into the trunk of the Buick.

"Too busy, Jim, but Vangie loves it. And the house at Grand Beach is just wonderful. You must come and see it sometime soon."

Over my dead body.

"That'll be nice, like the old days"—he grinned despondently—"when the four of us were together, huh?"

"Thank you, Daddy." Rosemarie pecked his cheek. "We had a lovely time."

"Thank you, Mr. Clancy," Peg echoed her, with what seemed to be notable lack of conviction. "It was very nice."

"Sure you can't stay for lunch?" Jim Clancy's eyes brightened as though the idea had just occurred to him. "I have some wonderful steaks. I could throw them on the grill." He glanced nervously at his watch. "Have you on the road inside the hour."

"How wonderful, Jim dear," Mom said. "It would be so nice, but I do have to keep our schedule. You know what the Labor Day traffic is like."

"Sure, sure." His face fell. "I understand. Maybe next time. . . . Have a great Labor Day, kids!"

I felt sorry for him, a wretched, lonely little man. But I didn't want my sister staying at his house. Somehow, he was even more sinister when he was sad.

Peg took over at the wheel. Rosie slipped in quietly next to me.

"Did Chucky flunk your driving test, Mom?" Peg asked as she steered the Buick out of the Clancy grounds.

"He's doing very well, dear. He needs a little more practice, that's all. Maybe we'll let him drive a little on the way to the Dunes."

"I'll walk."

"I had a Buick of my very own in Bamberg," I said, my masculine ego offended by the suggestion that I was not a competent driver. "I drove it all over the autobahns, day and night, and never had a single accident. Except when I banged up my knee by bumping into it in the dark."

Peg and Rosemarie laughed, feebly, I thought.

"If you want, dear, we'll buy you your own little Buick."

"Only if it has four holes."

"There's the pier, Chucky," Peg tried again. "Remember?"

"What pier?"

The one I vomited on.

"Did you have a nice time, darlings?" Mom interjected. "The weather was so nice for a change."

"Good tennis," Rosemarie murmured.

"Neat boys in Geneva town?" I asked.

"Creeps," they replied together.

"Drips," Peg added for emphasis.

We were on the outskirts of Gary, shrouded in steel-mill smoke, before their spirits returned.

Yeah, they had a hell of a good time at Jim Clancy's.

On the side of the tennis courts at Notre Dame, Christopher interrupted my reverie.

"Are you sure you don't love her, Charles? I know she's kind of strange at times . . ."

"Absolutely certain."

Christopher was too much of a gentleman to challenge my savage reply.

"How about Cordelia?"

"I guess I don't miss her as much as I thought I would." I pondered this truth, acknowledged for the first time. "Out of sight, out of mind. I guess I wasn't that much in love after all."

"It comes and goes at our age, doesn't it?"

"Sure does."

"Are you going to look her up?"

"I suppose I should."

"Soon?"

"Right."

"Today?"

"All right, Mom!"

So I showered and hiked over to Sorin Hall. Nothing had changed in the offices of *Compact*. It was still a scene of disorder and confusion presided over by the strong-willed little editor, who today was wearing a light gray skirt and blouse, very professional.

"Charles!" She jumped from her swivel chair and extended her hand.

I took the hand and kissed her lips, briefly, very briefly.

She was flustered and not displeased.

"Sit down, sit down," she urged me. "Tell me about your summer."

I made it as funny as I could, which, considering the summer, was not all that funny.

Her parents were at Harbor Springs still. Alf was back at West Baden, the Jesuit seminary. She had performed successfully at a junior contest at Ravinia Park. Her mother thought that she ought to go to Florence next year to study there. She did want to graduate first, however.

She was pretty enough and pleasant enough. Yet I could

hardly believe that we had embraced so passionately in the same room a few months before.

She didn't ask me to work on the magazine and I didn't volunteer. We promised to stay in touch.

The fires were banked, the embers were cold, the flames were out. That was that.

Yet, her lips had told the truth when I touched them with my own. If I wanted, I could pour a little gasoline on the coals and we would have a conflagration again.

Why bother?

No good reason occurred to me.

Why did the mating drive have to be so powerful? Why could not man and woman do nicely without one another? It would be a much more sedate world.

I had not given up on Cordelia. Now wasn't the time. Moreover, let her make the first move.

Ah, Chucky, weren't you the clever lover?

I was still living in Farley Hall, still under the ministrations of the manic Father Pius, still in a room by myself. The reason given—which I did not question—was that my status was still unclear.

Later I suspected that Father Pius was setting me up.

My new adviser told me that I had been reclassified as a "provisional junior" and that my DePaul and Maryland philosophy courses had been accepted. If I took two extra philosophy or theology courses, I would be reclassified yet again as a second-semester junior in the spring semester. I would be only a year behind Ed and Vince. With summer school, I might even be able to graduate a year from January.

I was delighted. My advanced economics courses were more interesting than anything I had taken the year before. I intended to concentrate on business-cycle theory. Much later I would read an article by Norman Rider about the Depression that sustained my thesis in a way about which I had not thought. His data showed that one quarter of the women who had reached puberty during the worst year of the Depression were infertile, so great had been the impact of poor nutrition on their reproductive systems.

Bodies were affected by economic disasters in ways we didn't imagine then. Souls too, mine included.

Christopher and I also signed up for another fiction course (American Fiction) with the prof we had the year before. Astonishingly he did not remember either of us.

It looked like an exciting year.

Vince was waiting for me in my room when I returned from my brief encounter with Cordelia.

"How you doing, guy? Are we gonna win this year?"

"I guess," he sighed. "Practice sure does wear you out. How you doing?"

We had drifted apart in the year I had been at Notre Dame. No, it would be more accurate to say that we had been separated when I went to the service and had never renewed our friendship. I hung around sometimes with him and Ed Murray, relatively sober and relatively intelligent members of the football subculture. But my interests and their interests were not the same anymore. Christopher who could get along with anyone had actually become a closer friend to Vince than I was.

I kind of assumed that he and Peg would marry eventually and that we'd be brothers-in-law for the rest of our lives, so I didn't worry about the hiatus in our friendship.

"I'm good," I replied to his question. "Liking it here more this year than last."

"You washed up with that gorgeous little blonde?"

So, she is gorgeous after all? Vince would know.

"Let's say the romance is suspended for the moment. Neither of us ready yet, you know the line. What about you and . . . what's that girl's name again?"

"Peg." He grinned. "You so and so!"

"Yes, I do see her occasionally. On the tennis courts mostly."

"Where she beats you?"

"Calumny."

"It's, uh, kind of, well, I uh . . . want to talk about Peg."

A warning siren went off in my head. I'd better be a little more serious than usual.

"Talk."

"Well, I think I love her."

"*Think!* Vincent, don't think about it long. As a man of the world in these matters, let me assure you that you do love her and that you thereby demonstrate very good taste."

He slumped down on the edge of my bed, his head sunk in his hands, not the posture of someone in love.

"I think I want to marry her."

"I should hope so. That's what people do when they're in love. When?"

"Like maybe a year after I graduate." He shook his head sadly. "Or two years. I don't know."

"Two or three years from now. Why not next year?"

"She's too young."

"She's as old as the proverbial hills."

I sat back on the chair behind my desk, feeling I was almost that old.

"I don't know whether she wants to marry me."

"She doesn't speak of it and if she did, I'd probably not quote her. But, take my word for it, she does."

"I don't have any money."

"You'll get it."

"Yeah, but a man should be ready to support a family when he marries, you know?"

"Nonsense, my dear Vincent,"—I waved an airy hand— "absolute nonsense. Look around this university. The rules have changed."

I was well aware that I was giving advice that I had refused to follow myself.

So what? I was telling a friend what he wanted to hear and what he should hear. Do as I say, not as I do.

"Yeah . . . but . . ."

"Have you talked to the ineffable Margaret Mary about these questions?"

"Gosh, no." His eyes widened. "I'd be afraid to."

"Talk to her. Why do you have to do it all by yourself?"

"We've never discussed marriage, Chuck, I mean I'd have a hell of a lot of nerve if I brought it up."

"Then, my good man, get yourself a hell of a lot of nerve. How long have you been dating? Three years now? Four years this prom season. Isn't it time to let the poor girl know that your intentions are honorable?"

"She knows they're honorable." He blushed.

I couldn't imagine either of these innocents in a scene like mine with Cordelia. Not yet anyway.

"I didn't mean that, dope. I meant it is time to hint broadly that you want to be a permanent part of her life."

"Yeah?" He lifted his head out of his hands. "But what if she doesn't want me?"

"Does she give any signs of that?"

"Well . . . no, but—"

"But, what?"

"But . . . I'm an Italian, my father's a tailor, we still don't have much money. Your family is wealthy and Irish and I'm not sure that . . ."

Dear God, the poor goof.

I stood up, walked over to the disconsolate halfback, and bent down to his ear. "I have something to say to you, Vincent. I will whisper it, but don't you forget it. Bullshit," I whispered softly. "Again I say to you *bullshit!*"

"Yeah?" He brightened considerably.

"Yeah. I have with my own ears heard the woman of the house, the good April, refer to you as 'poor Vincent.' Better even than the Good Housekeeping Seal of Approval."

"Yeah?"

"Do you think you would be let into the house if she didn't approve?"

"Well . . ."

"Having committed the ultimate miscegenation of marrying a West Side Irishman, how could she draw the line at an Italian?"

I almost said that we were not rich, but from Vince's point of view we were.

He left my room happy. Peg owed me one.

I felt enormously satisfied with myself. June wedding in 1951. Peg would be young, only a junior in college, and a lot of violin work ahead of her. But she'd stick at it and they'd be happy.

The scenario would write itself very differently in the next twelve months.

But that autumn of 1949 few of us had even heard of Korea.

On a sunny Indian summer Thursday morning in the first week of October, I was reading Sherwood Anderson's *Winesburg, Ohio* in front of my blown-up photo of Rosemarie and looking forward to the celebration of my twenty-first birthday that night in Oak Park. I'd catch the South Shore after my last morning class, cut the silly religion class that was my only Friday obligation (Christopher would respond to my name at the roll call), and spend the weekend with the family—thus avoiding the insanity of the Michigan game the coming weekend.

I was happy when the team won and even listened to the games on the radio, but I couldn't take the pep rallies and the cheering sections and especially the drunken alumni in the stands.

The gloom of Winesburg was interrupted by the rector and Father Clarke and Father Tierny, the prefect of discipline (dean of students to you moderns).

They burst into my room without knocking or warning.

"We've caught you at last, O'Malley," the rector chortled. "And you're on warning."

They rushed to my bed and pulled a dozen bottles of beer from under it.

"You will be on the three o'clock train," the prefect of

discipline announced happily. "Good riddance to you."

"This will make a man out of you," said Father Clarke.

"The university will be free from your evil soul!" Father Pius exulted.

Rosemarie's picture would no longer desecrate his hall. They turned around and marched out.

That was that. Caught, tried, judged, and executed within thirty seconds.

Could I appeal? Sure. Would my appeal be granted? Not a chance. Maybe, if I were contrite enough, they might take me back next year. I was in no mood for contrition.

Need I say that it was not my beer? Nor that of anyone in the hall as my neighbors assured me when they came back from class to find me packing. Someone had planted the beer and tipped off the rector.

Who? Did I have any enemies that hated me that much? I doubted it then and I still doubt it now.

The rector who wanted to get rid of me and was driven to it by the naked shoulders of Rosemarie?

Almost certainly.

Close to tears, Christopher helped me pack, promised to send on my books and laundry, and rode with me in the taxi to the South Shore station.

"I'll ask my father if we can file suit—"

"Don't bother. I don't belong here, Christopher. Father Pius did me a favor."

"It's so goddamn unfair."

"Not your language."

"Appropriate language."

We shook hands at the station and promised we would not let Father Pius interfere with our friendship.

I thought, as the train pulled away, that maybe he ought to go back to the seminary. But if anyone could make something of this lay-vocation stuff, it was Christopher.

We stayed in touch, talking on the phone once a week, eating lunch and playing handball or tennis during the summer till he graduated in the spring of 1950. Since he was NROTC he owed the Navy a few years. He asked for a commission in the Marines, against all my advice.

"Family tradition, Charles. My father fought at Belleau Wood; anyway, I get seasick. It'll only be three years."

He was a lieutenant in the Marine division that landed at Inchon a few months later, the last real victory the American military has managed to win. Shortly after he went ashore with X Corps at Wonson on the other side of Korea. Somehow he had already become a captain.

I prayed for him every night, without much confidence that my prayers made any difference.

❧ 16 ❧

During the melancholy ride to Chicago on the South Shore for my twenty-first birthday party, while an autumn rainstorm obscured Gary and East Chicago and Whiting and Hegwisch, I tried to sort out my life.

I was shattered, ashamed, guilty. I had done nothing wrong, I had been framed, yet still I felt guilty.

How can you be ashamed when you're innocent?

Authority, I would later learn, has the power to make you ashamed when it decides, however unjustly, that you are guilty.

If enough people tell you that you are a criminal, then you begin to think and act like a criminal.

I knew in my head that I was right when I told Christopher that I didn't belong there. But Notre Dame had been part of my program since I saw *Knute Rockne All American* during my grammar school days. I had served in the Army for two years to make Notre Dame possible. Now it had been snatched away from me by a madman.

What was left of my grand design? How would I put the pieces back together?

I had failed my parents; they would be ashamed of me; how could I face them at the birthday party tonight; how could I tell them that I had let them down?

Ridiculous self-pity, you say? Sure was. The O'Malleys

were nothing if not loyal to one another. Mom and Dad had never been convinced that I belonged at Notre Dame. There were lots of other colleges that would be delighted to take my government money. What difference did one lost semester make?

My carefully arranged plans had been disturbed. I was losing time. My frantic (now I'd say compulsive) effort to make up for the years wasted in the service had been ruined.

Then I realized that my parents would be hurt because I was hurt.

That infuriated me even more. The worst pain of all was knowing that my pain, impossible to hide even if I tried—and I told myself I would try—would hurt them more than anything else.

Okay, Charles C. O'Malley is an adult. He will take this like an adult. He will laugh it off to protect his parents and his brother and sisters.

No, he doesn't want a final meal. No, he won't require a blindfold.

Many young men were expelled from Notre Dame in those days (and for years after) on similar charges, most of them willing to admit their guilt, some arguing still that they were covering for friends. They all agreed one way or another with the comment of the third priest. It had helped them to mature, to grow up, and to become a man.

It didn't do that to me at all. Rather, it made a fervent anticlerical out of me.

Many years later, at a professional convention, I asked a young Holy Cross priest, wearing a brown suit and a plaid tie as had become the fashion in that era, what had ever happened to Father Pius.

"Oh, he's doing parish work out in the Pacific Northwest. He had a nervous breakdown, let me see, about 1955."

"How did they notice the difference?"

The young priest eyed me thoughtfully. "Crazy all

along, eh? I wouldn't be surprised. I've only met him a couple of times but the legend is kind of weird."

"Ah."

"Well," the priest continued, "it seems he was caught one day by a group of students planting a couple of six-packs under someone's bed. Turned out that he'd been doing it for years and no one in the community became suspicious. There were so many expulsions at Notre Dame for drinking back then that the superiors didn't notice how high his rate was."

"Any reason for this unrecognized zeal?"

"This particular kid kept a picture of his girlfriend on his desk. In a scanty swimsuit, as I remember the legend."

"And the others who had been expelled?"

"Were you one of them?"

"Funny you should ask."

"There was no way of knowing after the fact . . ." His voice trailed off.

"I had a picture of a woman with bare shoulders on my desk, Father."

"My God!"

"That's what I said too."

Notre Dame was not the only Catholic institution that entrusted the supervision of the lives of young lay men and women to deeply troubled religious in those days—and much later. It was probably not the worst offender either. Religious orders ought not to permit themselves to be suckered into the position where they are trying to regulate the lives of laity the way they regulate the lives of their own members. They can't do it effectively. Moreover, they turn people away from the church when they try.

Many, many years later, Father Hesburgh called to offer me an honorary doctorate. "Chuck, we'd like you to give the commencement address this spring. And flatter us by accepting an honorary doctorate."

"I have a long history with Notre Dame, Father."

"Well, we can let bygones be bygones, can't we, Chuck?"

"No," I said.

"I had hoped you might welcome a reconciliation after all these years. Forgive and forget, you know what I mean?" ·

"Forgive and forget, Father?" I thundered. "I was innocent. I did not drink then. Everyone knew that. I was expelled unjustly. If the university is willing to publicly apologize and change my record then I'll think about your degree."

"Well"—he tried to placate me—"we'll certainly change the record to read that you withdrew instead of being expelled. But that was so long ago—"

"It was only yesterday, Father," I shouted. "I want an apology."

"Well, I don't see how—"

"Then stuff your honorary degree you know where."

I was still shaking with rage when I hung up the phone.

When I told my priest the story, the good Father Blackie clapped his little hands with leprechaunish glee. "Good enough for him, says I," he exclaimed. "I wonder how many of their generous contributors are men they threw out long ago."

"Men who now say that the experience made a man out of them," I continued, still angry.

"We churchmen, particularly if we are in religious orders, are like the Bourbons. We never learn and we never forget. We expect the laity, of course, to do both. As you must do now by calling poor Father Ted and apologizing to him."

"No!"

"Yes."

So I called him back, apologized, and accepted his offer of an honorary degree.

"It is a kind of an apology, Chuck, isn't it?"

"I'm sure it is."

"And the senior class wants you to give the commencement address."

I laughed and said I would. Later I was told that it was the funniest graduation address in the history of the Golden Dome. Chucky Ducky forgives and forgets? Well, more or less.

My outburst shows how great was the pain as I rode home on the South Shore that lovely Thursday evening. And how long the hurt from such pain can endure.

I dreaded the front doorbell. I'd have to tell them that I was thrown out, probably because of the photo of Rosemarie.

Mike threw open the door and rushed back to his viola.

The family chorale struck up "See the conquering hero comes!" from Handel's *Judas Maccabeus*.

Sad sack that I was, I couldn't help but grin.

"I am not the frigging Duke of Buckingham!"

"Chucky!"

The walls were hung with banners: "Chucky the Prize-winner!"

"Chucky Wins!"

"Twenty-one and Winning!"

"A Voting Citizen and a Winner!"

"All the Way with Chucky!"

What the hell!

I was embraced by everyone. Mom, a happily pregnant Jane, Peg, Dad, Mike, Ted, wished me a happy birthday and congratulated me on my victory.

No Rosemarie?

I looked around. Indeed, no Rosemarie.

Except an enormous, much-larger-than-life blowup of my shot of her, hanging on the parlor wall with a vast gold and blue ribbon on it.

"What have I won?" I asked. Did they consider my expulsion from Notre Dame a victory? No, they didn't know about it. Unless Vince had phoned Peg and I had sent word through Christopher that he was not to spoil the party.

"First prize!" Peg hugged me and shouted gleefully. "First prize and a *thousand* dollars!"

"What?"

My father endeavored to restore some order. "The two she-imps submitted your picture of Rosie to *Life*'s college photographer contest. You won, going away if you ask me; you get a thousand dollars and a full-page picture credit in *Life,* which is not a bad achievement for someone not quite twenty-one."

"Huh?"

"We did it! We did it!" Peg exulted. "We won Chucky his first first prize!"

"You brats!" I protested, as happy as they were.

My head was whirling. How much could you crowd into one day? Expelled, celebrated, rewarded. Someone please turn off the merry-go-round.

I danced with the three women and sang, hollowly, the Notre Dame "Victory March" with them.

The prize and the expulsion were for the same reason. Someone had a sense of humor.

"Why did you bring your two duffel bags home?" Mike pointed at my khaki luggage. "And all your clothes?"

I didn't want to tell them.

Suddenly it was as quiet as a wake.

"Have you finally left that terrible place, dear?" Mom asked softly.

"Well . . . yes."

"Hooray," Jane shouted uncertainly.

"Why?" Peg demanded.

What do you do now? Ruin the party? No.

"I just don't belong there."

"They threw you out," Peg insisted, her eyes blazing. "The dirty bastards."

"Right on both counts."

"But, dear, why?" Mom was badly shaken for the first time in all my life.

"For drinking."

"But you don't drink!"

"Ironic, isn't it?"

"What happened?" Dad was grim-faced, angry.

"A priest, my hall rector, never did like me. I think he framed me. They all came in and found beer bottles under my bed. I was on probation because they had thrown out my roommates last year for the same offense."

"That's crazy, son."

"Bastards!" Peg screamed, beautiful in her rage. Lucky Vincent.

"I know it's crazy."

"Why didn't he like you?" Mike frowned, still too innocent in the ways of the church he hoped to serve.

I thought of the picture. Because of Rosemarie.

That was an irony I would keep to myself.

"Didn't like my red hair, I guess."

My family was as supportive as I knew it would be.

Dad: We should sue.

Michael: Rotten Christians. Disgrace to the priesthood.

Mom: You were never happy there, dear.

Jane: It's their loss. Someday they'll know that.

Peg: (Words of consolation muffled in a sobbing embrace.)

Mom: Well, I'm glad that's over with. It just wasn't the place for you. Now you're free from them.

My family had converted Notre Dame's expulsion into an honorable discharge. From what?

They also gave me a prize and a thousand dollars and a picture in *Life*.

I was not a photographer, only a picture-taker. Okay. You're still in *Life*.

I did feel free, honorably discharged. Free to ride on the mad merry-go-round. Back in Riverview again.

Dad: Where will you go to school now?

Me: Wait till the next semester and enroll in DePaul, I suppose. All the colleges are too far into the first semester now.

Peg: (suddenly intelligible) No! The University of Chicago! Oh, Chucky. (Another hug.) It starts tomorrow!

Dad: You could try it, son. Nothing lost if you don't like it.

Peg: (brightening dramatically) And you can take care of Rosemarie!

Mom: (faint reproving tone) Perhaps Rosemarie could take care of Chucky too.

Just then, giddy and light-headed, battered by surprises and still on my personal Flying Turns, I wanted someone to take care of me.

I took a very deep breath.

"Don't tell her until I'm sure they'll accept me."

17

The next day I walked in the cold rain from the Sixty-third Street El Station to the Classics building to take my "aptitude examination." I was a late applicant and would take it by myself in a tiny, grimy classroom presided over by a single bright-eyed young "proctor." He gave me the huge stack of paper and informed me that I would have six hours, which included my time out for lunch, if I felt eating was more important than gaining admission to the university.

"I've been in the military," I replied as I took off my rain-soaked Ike jacket. "I can endure privations."

"Good for you," he said sarcastically. "I'll see you here at four o'clock. I must continue to work on my dissertation."

"Aren't you afraid I'll cheat?"

"I'd like to see you cheat on that examination!" he said with a sneer. "Our tests are cheatproof. . . . Incidentally, almost none of the late applicants attain adequate grades in this examination."

"I will," I assured the closing door as I sat down to begin my work.

The test was long indeed but easy. My various educational background—Fenwick, the University of Maryland, Notre Dame—had prepared me well. I finished it a half hour ahead of time, removed three Hershey bars from my Ike jacket and munched on them contentedly. They'd have to take me in—if I wanted in.

As I ate I glanced over some of my essays. Ah, the Irish gift of glibness, what a blessing! If the rest of the University would be this easy, I'd have no problem here.

"Breeze," I said to the proctor, when he returned as I finished off my last bite of candy. "Finished two hours ago, but didn't want to walk out on you. I think I'll like it around here. A lot easier than Notre Dame."

I took my leave whistling "Younger Than Springtime."

The rain had ended and the sun had returned. I turned to "The Last Rose of Summer" as I walked over to the El.

That night, my father came to my room. I was lying on my bed, deeply morose again. What a terrible mess I had made of the first twenty-one years of my life. Already I hated the University of Chicago, but it was my last chance.

He sat down on the chair next to the bed. He was holding a stack of typescript.

"I have something here," he said uncomfortably, "that your mother thinks you should read."

"The good April's wish is my command," I said, trying to sound happy.

"It's something I wrote while you were away," he said, frowning nervously and rubbing his forehead. "A kind of a memoir. For our children and grandchildren. We were going to kind of leave it for them after . . . well, when we're not here anymore."

"That sounds like fun." I sat up and reached for the manuscript.

"But we think you ought to read it now." He pulled the pages back, not quite ready to give them up. "In your, ah, special situation . . . We'd just as soon you didn't mention it to the others."

"Cross my heart and hope to die!"

He laughed uneasily.

"There's some material in here about our courtship . . ."

"Great." I continued to reach for the pages.

"I think I look pretty dumb . . ."

"The good April disagrees, I bet."

He blushed and relinquished the text to me.

"Naturally . . . I was not all that clever a suitor."

"You won the girl, isn't that what counts?"

"Come to think of it, I guess I did. . . . You'll probably think us dreadfully old-fashioned."

"Not as old-fashioned as I am."

He smiled, pleasant memories of the pursuit of April Mae Cronin doubtless flitting across his imagination.

"You'll have to judge for yourself. . . . Your mother wants you to read it—and I agree with her. . . ."

"Of course."

"Naturally." He grinned as would an unindicted coconspirator. "We both feel that you will understand a good deal more about Rosie if you realize what her parents were like when they were your age . . . or maybe a little older."

"I'm interested in my parents, not her parents."

"We think you should know more about them."

"Fair enough."

"Two other matters, Chuck." He paused with his hand on the doorknob. "A man should always assume that his wife's pleasure is more important than his own."

I nodded. I already knew this from my sorry affair with Trudi. Yet, it was useful to hear it again.

"And I know why I wasn't sent to New Guinea."

"Who told you?" I demanded hotly. "Rosemarie? She was the only one who knew and she was guessing!"

My father grinned; he had caught his contentious son in a mistake.

"The congressman you talked to," he said. "I'm sure I'd be dead if you hadn't. Thank you for giving me another chance."

He closed the door softly.

I pounded the bed in frustration. Couldn't you keep anything secret?

I was, needless to say, greatly pleased that he had found out about my Sunday-morning visit the month after Pearl Harbor.

I picked up the manuscript.

I assumed then that this was one more part of their on-going campaign to persuade me to "take care" of Rose-marie. Only much later would I realize that it was more of a warning about what I might encounter if I did fall in love with her.

John's Love Story

❧ 18 ❧

1918

I died the first time on the parade ground of Camp Leavenworth on November 11, 1918. The armistice ending the Great War (later called World War I) had already gone into effect. But I didn't know that because I died before they announced it at morning assembly.

It was my own fault I died that day. I should have been nowhere near Camp Leavenworth.

I had graduated a year early from St. Ignatius College, lied about my age in my rush to don the uniform and fight the Hun, and at the age of seventeen years and nine months was inducted at Fort Sheridan and shipped off to Kansas. I was three days past my eighteenth birthday that morning I slipped noiselessly to the parade ground. If I had not been in such a rush to defeat the Kaiser and waited till my eighteenth birthday, I would not have volunteered—all chance of glory was lost—and would not have been stricken by the Spanish influenza two hours after the war was over.

I knew I was dying from the flu when I dropped my rifle and sagged toward the ground. I had seen other men, their faces black, collapse during assemblies the past week, many of them dead before they hit the ground.

My only thoughts, as I was overcome by sudden exhaustion and—I can think of no other word—peacefulness, were that I would not mind dying if I had just one chance to paint a portrait of a woman I loved.

Which shows what a romantic I was in those days.

Dumb eighteen-year-old kid, I was sure it would not happen to me. But I was still scared, we all were. The flu was sweeping the country. It was, we were told, the Black Death all over again. Almost everyone in the world might die.

I figured I would miss the others.

Even when two of the men in my wooden Spanish-American War barracks had succumbed, I was sure I was immune. In the letter I had written to my mother the night before I assured her that there was nothing to worry about, the flu was abating, the war would be over soon, and I would come home.

Hence, I was surprised when I suddenly felt very tired as our lines formed up that morning. I had learned to sleep on the thinly covered wooden bunks and had bounced out of bed at reveille wide awake and eager for the day. I was no lover of the military life, despite my father's record in the Spanish-American War and my grandfather's in the Civil War. A couple of months of training had disillusioned me. In the next war, I told myself, neither I nor my children would be taken in by the craziness that drove men to enlist.

Which shows how wrong you can be.

I was happy and eager that crisp morning as the sun came up in a clear sky over the plains of Kansas. I knew I'd be getting out of the army soon and could go home again—not exactly covered with honor perhaps but at least possessing an offer of a commission.

The Spanish flu hit you almost instantly. One moment you were feeling fine, the next moment there was a sudden weariness, and the moment after that you collapsed—quite possibly dead.

Twenty million people died in the pandemic, not counting the victims in India after the plague had stopped everywhere else (as abruptly as it had started the previous summer), in the rest of the world, one percent of the human race, far more than had died in the war. In the United States half a million died, about one half of one percent of the population. The virus hit the United States in late August in Boston, leaped across the country in October, and then disappeared in late February. A hundred thousand died every month. My mother told of counting the crepes on the doors as she rode home from the Loop on the Washington Boulevard bus—sometimes three and four in a single block.

The country panicked, as might well be imagined. Schools were closed, meetings canceled, plants shut down. There was a terrible shortage of coffins. What might it have been like if there were television or even radio in those days?

Don't expect to find much in the history books about the Spanish influenza. It was a far worse disaster for America than the war, but no one wanted to remember it when it was over. Or to think about the possibility that it might come back again.

A lot of people, they said later, died of pneumonia that was caused by complications from the flu itself. Sulfa and penicillin would have saved many of those lives as they did the lives of men and women infected by later and milder varieties of the flu.

But no wonder drug could possibly have saved those who died almost instantly.

As I did.

I do not even think I felt the ground as I hit it. Terrible weariness invaded my body, the rifle slipped out of my hands, I thought about painting a woman I loved, even saw her face momentarily, and then slipped toward the dust from which I had been told the previous Ash Wednesday I had been made.

Then nothing, not even blackness.

Nothing at all.

Then from a very great distance a pounding. And soft voices. Southern voices. Damn, why couldn't they talk good, Chicago English like we civilized people did?

I was angry that they were disturbing my nap. I tried to shut out the sounds of their voices and the raucous pounding of hammer on wood.

What the hell were they making at this hour of the night?

"Thirty more today," one of them said. "Shit, we're going to run out of ground to bury them in."

"And wood to make these coffins."

"Did you ever think someone might be making a coffin for you tomorrow?"

"Just my luck, I'll get it my last hour on this duty."

"We won't catch it as long as we wear these masks, that's true, isn't it?"

"Do you believe that shit?"

They both laughed uneasily.

Bad duty. Making caskets for flu victims. But that was no excuse for the noise. Why wouldn't they go away and let me sleep?

"This redhead kid is the youngest I've seen yet. Can't be more than sixteen."

Bastards. I was eighteen. And three days.

I thought of waking up and telling them. I decided against it. Ignorant rednecks.

"Doesn't matter how old you are. He's as dead as the rest of them. Come on, let's toss him on the box and load him on the truck."

I was aware that I was lying on a flat surface, flat and hard and that I was terribly cold. Too hard and too cold to be my bunk in the barracks.

What did they mean, dead?

I wasn't dead. Just taking a nice nap, that's all.

Then I felt myself being lifted up, like a sack of turnips. No, not turnips. Potatoes. That's the right word, a sack of potatoes.

I was dumped unceremoniously into a box of some sort.

"Big kid—don't hardly fit."

"I reckon he don't mind much. Give me a hand with the top."

What the hell was going on? Were they putting me in a coffin?

I'd better wake up and stop them.

I tried to sit up. My body wouldn't respond. I tried to open my eyes. They wouldn't move. I tried to talk. My lips were frozen together.

Then I heard nails being pounded above my head. A lid being attached.

Why fight it? It was only a nightmare. Go back to sleep. Forget the whole thing.

"Get Joe Pete and Jimmy Jack to help."

"Hey, you guys, this is a heavy one. Give us a hand and we can get the hell out of here."

Ridiculous mistake. But it didn't make any difference. I'd nap for a few more minutes and then Mom would wake me up and I'd rush for the bus down to St. Ignatius.

The box was lifted up and carried some distance, jostling me uncomfortably. Then it was dropped abruptly on another platform. Like the slow train to Wisconsin.

What a joke! They thought I was dead.

Well, a little bit more sleep and it would all go away like the foolish dream that it was.

Then I saw the woman's face again, not pretty exactly, not in the ordinary sense of that word. No, her face was etched in vitality and character, a special kind of beauty all her own. A lovely elegant body to go with the face. I would paint that too . . .

Not if I let them bury me alive.

I still thought it was a dream. No one was really trying

to bury me alive. But even in a dream you fight them when they want to bury you alive.

I tried to pound on the top of my coffin.

At first my fists wouldn't move. I tried banging my head against the sides. It moved slowly back and forth, just barely hitting the wood.

I smelled the wood for the first time. Like sawdust in a meat market.

"Y'all hear anything?"

One of the hillbillies.

"You're crazy, Jim Bob, they're all stiffs."

"I don't know. I thought I heard something."

"Naw! I don't hear nothing."

"Come on." A third voice. "Start the fucking truck. Let's get these stiffs over to the graveyard."

I pulled my fists out of the bonds in which they seemed to be trapped. Almost without instructions from me, they began to pound the top of the coffin.

"Lordamercy!"

"One of them's trying to come back from the dead."

"Fuck the colonel! Let's get the shit out of this place!"

I heard them starting to run. That's fine, hillbillies. Run away and leave me in this thing.

I threw myself against the side of the coffin. It seemed to tilt. They had not piled it on the truck too securely. I heaved again and the casket sailed through space and crashed to the ground.

The lid flew off. I sat up and yelled, "Come back, you damn fools!"

They kept on running.

I felt very tired again and considered lying down again, just for a few more minutes.

But the sun was sinking and I was cold. I'd take the nap back in my bed.

So I lurched out of the casket and looked around. I was in front of the icehouse—so that's why I was so cold.

No shroud? The rumor was right: They'd run out of them!

I trudged back to my barracks. No one was around. In the mess hall for supper.

I fell into my bunk and back to sleep.

Later that night I was carried by stretcher to the base hospital, which looked like a brick Gothic castle, where I was an object of curiosity for an hour or two—someone returned from the dead.

Then the horror of the sick and the dying all around distracted the doctors and nurses from me. I was deposited in a cot in a corridor with a high ceiling. Later that night, in the dim light of a kerosene lantern, a doctor leaned over me. "You're lucky, son. You've no right to be alive. It's all gravy for you from now on."

Since then I've often wondered how many other cases there might have been where the haste and fear that followed the Plague of the Spanish Lady caused unconscious men to be diagnosed as dead, perhaps even to be buried alive.

I stayed in the National Guard for more than two decades, but never did work up the nerve to ask a doctor whether there were any records of similar cases. I guess I didn't want to know.

Is my recollection of waking up in the icehouse the product of a fevered mind? Maybe I was in the hospital all the time. The next morning when I woke, weak and still sick, but over the worst of the flu, I wondered that myself. Maybe it was all part of the same nightmare.

I didn't ask the hospital staff. They were too busy with men who were sicker than I was.

But in the disorderly stack of papers in front of me as I write this little memoir, there is the yellowed telegram my parents received from the War Department informing them of my death on November 11, 1918.

Underneath it is the telegram two days later telling them that I was still alive.

Giving up on the uncertain long-distance phone network, they boarded the Santa Fe and rode down to the base. I had no idea till I met them in the corridor of the hospital that they had been told I was dead.

"This should have an important effect on the rest of your life, John." My mother was always one for deriving morals from events. "You'll understand how important it is to be in the state of grace."

"Yes, Mom," I said dutifully.

"We would have missed you." There were tears in my father's eyes.

"I would have missed you too."

"The Blessed in heaven do not miss anyone," Mom said piously.

I was too weak to argue.

After they returned to Chicago, I tried to sketch the face of the woman who had kept me alive, as I already was thinking of her. It was surprisingly easy to capture her face. Later, back home, I filled in the colors.

"That's a very pretty girl, John." My father rarely paid any attention to my paintings. "She looks like someone I know, but I can't quite place her face. South Side, maybe?"

"I don't know any girls from the South Side."

"Someone you met in the service?"

"I wasn't in the service long enough to meet any girls . . . she's just someone I imagined."

He warned me about the dangers of the temptation of Pygmalion and then, unnecessarily, given the classical education I had received at St. Ignatius, told me the Pygmalion story.

"I don't really think she's so pretty, Dad." I considered the young woman with brown eyes. "Interesting maybe. A bit of an imp. Lots of fun."

"Don't let your mother see her."

"I won't."

We laughed together, sharing the secret that no girl would ever, in my mother's eyes, be good enough for me.

I did not tell my father that there was strength and character in those brown eyes as well as merriment. She would not let me die.

But she was not real and her face, I assumed, was one that I would never encounter in real life.

Nonetheless, I fantasized about the body, a willing body, I told myself, that went with that face. However, I never did try to add the body to my painting. Or even to sketch it.

Well, maybe a few lines on a sheet of paper during the duller classes at Armour Tech.

Lovely, lovely lines.

Did the experience of waking up in my own coffin during the flu epidemic really affect my life as the Army doctor and my parents suggested that it might?

I had none of the medical ill effects of the infection that plagued so many people—cardiac problems and Bright's disease and TB. Emotional effects?

Once you've been practically dead, do you live a little more frantically because you are aware of your own mortality? Or do you approach life with a much more relaxed attitude?

I'm not sure what my pattern is. I know that I've never been as ambitious as my parents or my kids. If I departed from Camp Leavenworth with any change in personality or character, it was with the conviction that life was meant to be enjoyed—a notion that made me pretty different from most of the Chicago Irish of my generation.

Maybe it was the beginning of an outlook that would later win my family and me the name "crazy O'Malleys"—a name that was richly deserved and, despite my wife's feeble protests, deeply enjoyed.

I did *not,* however, learn to stay away from places I ought not to be in. Hence, I would die twice more. Once in Jim Clancy's Duesenberg AA2 on a back road in Wisconsin during the summer of 1925. And later in the Black Horse Troop in December 1941.

So, I died twice more.

This memoir is about how I came back to life after the Duesy cracked up. I learned only many years later how I survived after Pearl Harbor and I still can't quite believe it.

But this story is, as I say, about the Duesy. And the girl with the brown eyes who brought me back to life.

19

1925

I was listening to a jazz trio playing "Black Bottom Stomp" in a speakeasy at Twenty-sixth and Oakley when Jim Clancy came charging in, bright-eyed, charming, enthusiastic, and almost three quarters of a foot shorter than my six feet one.

"You gotta see my new car," he shouted, waving the keys at me. "A Duesy!"

He was still my "Jim-in-the-box," as I described him to my mother after my first day in first grade, a comic face, with a hint of sadness in it, that kept popping up, looking eagerly for attention and laughter, my closest friend, my boon companion, my jester and my master of the revels.

I held up my hand, motioning for silence. I wanted to see the new car as much as anyone wanted to see a new car in those days, I more than others because it would be a frequent means of transportation for me. Jim would gladly loan it to me for a date—if I ever had a date. But the jazz group—horn, trombone, clarinet—was too good to interrupt.

The Blue Note had opened in Chicago a few years before. New Orleans musicians had migrated to Chicago in big numbers so that Chicago had become the second jazz capital of the nation. Louis Armstrong, then in his middle twenties, had come to the Lincoln Garden's Cafe over on

East Thirty-first Street with the King Oliver Band and the "Dippermouth Blues." Now, in 1925, even the neighborhood speaks were likely to feature a trio of competent Negro musicians—who would never have been admitted as patrons. The group who played at Twenty-sixth and Oakley, in the heart of Heart of Chicago (as that neighborhood, south of Pilsen and west of Bridgeport, was called), was better than just competent.

Jim sat on the edge of the chair, impatiently jingling his keys, an overactive elf, while I signaled for a beer for him.

He downed it in a single gulp. Then the power of the rhythms seemed to take possession of him. He put the beer mug on the ancient table in front of him and slipped into what seemed like a trance. The engine racing inside of him turned itself off and he became a little boy enchanted by something wonderful.

If only, I thought, that enchanted little boy could escape more often.

The speak was in a corner building on the first floor. The windows along the Twenty-sixth Street side were boarded up. In the front you entered a perfectly respectable little candy store. Behind the store, you walked into a narrow passage with a locked door on either end through which you were buzzed. Then you came into a large, dimly lit room that had once been quarters for the family of the storeowner.

The speak was permeated by the faint smell not unlike that one could encounter in a rarely cleaned men's washroom—possibly because the air had not been circulated since the passing of the Volstead Act.

Everyone in the city knew it was a speak, including all the cops in the district. But the owners paid their "tax" to the local police and their cut to the Capone mob, which provided the booze. The narrow passage was mostly for atmosphere.

As was the dark room, the rickety old tables and chairs, and the jazz group. Maybe even the smell.

Jazz was an important part of my life, almost as important as painting—and far more important than architecture and engineering, which was how I earned my living. My musical tastes were catholic—I would spend a night a week during the season listening to the fading Chicago Opera Company at the Auditorium and another night at Orchestra Hall to listen to Theodore Thomas and the Chicago Symphony.

My parents, tolerant of anything their only child did, were baffled by my interest in art and music.

"There's nothing like that in either of our families," my mother would say, as if she were talking about a hereditary disease.

"That's all right, mother," Dad would say reassuringly. "The boy is a very successful engineer."

Actually, I thought of myself as an architect. That word, however, my parents could not bring themselves to say. Architects were Protestants who lived on the North Shore. The firm for which I worked, Hurley and Considine, called itself an "engineering company," even if its offices were in the Rookery, the first Chicago skyscraper (designed by Burnham and Root in 1886 and remodeled by Frank Lloyd Wright in 1905). They had hired me, however, because they wanted, first of all, someone to draw pictures of their projects and secondly someone to actually design them.

So at twenty-five, the year of the big eclipse and the Scopes Trial, I had worked on both the new double-level Wacker Drive and the new Soldier Field—a fact about which my children are openly skeptical since they are convinced that both structures existed from the creation of the world.

"I'm practically engaged," Jimmy said in a stage whisper that was louder than the clarinet. The three other patrons of the speak turned and frowned at him.

It was not the first time that Jim, a classmate at St. Catherine's grammar school and St. Ignatius College (actually a six-year high school that later split into St. Ignatius High and Loyola University), was "practically engaged." I sighed to myself. If my mother should hear about this relationship she would be even more concerned about my becoming "another stodgy old Irish bachelor." Until the previous year, no girl was good enough for me, and Jim Clancy was a suspect companion because he "ran around with fast women." Now I was being pushed to find myself a bride and to "meet some nice girls like the ones Jim Clancy knows."

Mom's fears were not unjustified. My existence was comfortable enough. I had started to put on weight and, alas, to lose some of my red hair. But the weight was controlled by swimming a couple of days a week at the Illinois Athletic Club (whose star swimmer, a kid named Johnny Weissmuller, was setting world records) and the baldness, should it get worse as it probably would, by wearing caps (which along with plus four knickers were in style for men in those days). Women were interesting of course and I planned to marry one eventually and to raise some children.

But I was in no hurry.

And I was still looking for the brown-eyed girl who had called me back from the grave.

I had painted her face many times, usually destroying the canvas afterward. I'd even experimented with sketches of her slender, graceful body—with marvelous long legs— but gave that project up as too dangerous.

Did fantasies about my brown girl, as I called her although sometimes I painted her in blue clothes, impede my search for a bride?

I suppose they did. I told myself often enough that it was impossible for a flesh-and-blood woman to compete with a fantasy.

But I would still glance out of the El windows in the morning on the way to work, hoping that she might be standing on the platform.

"You gotta meet her." Jim leaned toward me, smelling of the beer he had consumed. "She's tremendous. You'll love her. Great musician. *And* she has a gorgeous friend."

I ordered him another beer with a wave of my hand and waited for the trio to wrap up its cadenza. They were, as I have said, only a little better than run-of-the-mill. But I've never heard records that were as good.

When Mom would talk about "stodgy Irish bachelors," Dad would chuckle because he had been a stodgy bachelor until he met her in St. Catherine's rectory.

After the famine the Irish turned to late marriages, a complete change from the very early marriages of the first half of the nineteenth century (I'm not much on history, but my older son is. So when I talk about history I'm quoting him. And God help me if the quotes aren't accurate!). They brought the custom with them to this country. My father was forty-five when he married my mother, who herself was thirty-eight. "We just barely had time to produce you," he would laugh.

"Charles!" Mom would reprove him for his allusion to the facts of reproduction—which were always ignored in our family.

His father, my grandfather, had been a famine immigrant who served in the Civil War and worked on the Northwestern railroad. Most of his family had been wiped out in the cholera epidemic of the eighteen eighties. Dad had gone to work at fifteen for the city, the protégé of a Republican alderman (Chicago had some of those in the old days) and fought his way up to the job of a commissioner on the Cook County Board. Only when he had reached that level of security did he begin to search for a wife. Mom's family came after the Civil War, one at a time, each child of the eleven working to pay the passage of the next. Like so many women of her generation, Mom worked as domestic help for a wealthy family in South Oak Park, an occupation about which she never spoke. Then she became a housekeeper at St. Catherine's rectory, a dignified and honorable, if perhaps not so well-paying, position.

I suppose that she viewed it as a permanent job. Her younger sisters had already married and moved to Boston. She was probably resigned to lifelong spinsterhood. Then my father, the nephew of the pastor of St. Catherine's, decided that it was at last time to marry, having barely survived the climb up San Juan Hill in the Spanish-American War, and she caught his eye.

Now, years after their deaths, I wonder about that courtship, its hesitations and fears, its awkwardness and its sudden burst of passion that brought them to the altar—my mother, as I would later determine from the parish records, already two months pregnant.

Well, maybe I was premature, but I kind of doubt it. They celebrated their wedding anniversary not on the date it is recorded in the parish books but four months earlier.

I must say I was delighted with the discovery. John E. O'Malley, a love child.

Each generation thinks it has discovered sex for the first time in history and that it was produced not by sexual love but by spontaneous combustion.

Dear God, how strong the passion must have been between my parents to have overcome their fears and inhibitions so that they produced me.

I have often wondered whether I was conceived in the old rectory at St. Catherine's.

I sure hope so.

After their deaths I stood in the tiny room in the rectory in which she lived the summer she conceived me—a cubbyhole in the third-floor attic with a small window next to a great oak tree and the rose window of the church. On humid days before air-conditioning it must have been a steamy oven.

All the better to stoke the fires of human passion.

Without which I would not have come to be.

In their wedding picture, they are a striking couple, my father tall and solid, my mother almost as tall and full-figured. They must have quite overwhelmed each other.

Ignorance, inexperience, fear, guilt—all must have melted like candle wax.

And right next to the church too.

I suppose his uncle, the pastor, figured things out later when I arrived. I wonder if he ever admitted the rectory love affair to himself. What did he think, for example, when he poured the waters of baptism on me, not only a child conceived out of wedlock, but conceived in his rectory!

It will be said that only a wild romantic would ponder such possibilities.

A wild and crazy romantic.

Later my own family would earn the name "the crazy O'Malleys," a label in which we all exult, save for my would-be accountant older son who always aspired to be the white sheep of our clan.

My parents were still a striking couple in 1925, both erect and vigorous with snowy white hair.

Hints of their past would occasionally appear. When Mom would worry that I was a "stodgy Irish bachelor" in the making, Dad would chuckle, "Just like the man you married."

"You were never stodgy," she'd fire back at him. Then coloring a little, she would add, "And you're not stodgy now either."

And they both would chuckle.

I was too young then to understand.

That they loved one another, after their own fashion and with their own rhetoric, there was never any doubt. They were companions and friends, sharing the same prejudices and joys. They didn't like "foreigners" or Democrats or "flappers" or "vulgar South Side Irish."

They did like the Catholic church, Republicans, and "respectable" people.

As a Republican Dad thought Calvin Coolidge was one of the greatest leaders in all history, a truly honest president and a decent man (the highest compliment of all). He did not say that Coolidge was a welcome relief to Republicans after the corruption of the Harding years. Nor did he comment on the Republican party's commitment to Prohibition, a subject that was not discussed in our house. Ever.

Like every other good Irish Catholic family we ignored the Noble Experiment.

I resisted the temptation to observe that the Experiment was bringing wealth to many good Italian Republicans like Al Capone.

Dad's job brought them enough income so that they did not have to worry about money. Much of that income would be considered illegal today, but the rules were different in those days. Dad considered himself an "honest politician," a rarity among Republicans and, according to him, an impossibility among Democrats.

Like almost everyone with a few dollars in 1925, he invested in the stock market, though cautiously and conservatively.

"There's always our Union Carbide stock to fall back on," he would say when Mom worried about the unpredictability of the market. "That's our nest egg. If Union Carbide fails, the whole country will fail."

Which it did.

Technically, I was a Republican too. But in the secret of the ballot box, I had already become a Democrat and for reasons of profound political conviction: I objected to Prohibition. It was, I told my father, an attempt by Protestants to deprive the Catholics of their inalienable right to consume the creature. They intended to force us to be virtuous for our own good. Dad would mumble but not disagree. Later when most Catholics ended up as Democrats, the reasons given were the appeal of FDR and the Great Depression. But those were after-the-fact excuses. Prohibition is what made Democrats out of us.

Anyway, Dad earned a decent living as a Republican. We lived in a big old Victorian house on West End Avenue with a live-in (Negro) butler and maid. There was enough money to pay for my tuition at Armour and my trips to Europe each summer to paint, enough even to buy a car. However, we did not buy a car because Dad saw "no point in it." He was correct, I suppose. The Washington bus (double-decker, open in the summer) was one block south of us and the Lake Street El two blocks north. We could take the Northwestern to Twin Lakes for summer vacation, the Aurora and Elgin to golf courses in the western suburbs, and the El to Wrigley Field to watch such stalwarts as Rogers Hornsby and Hack Wilson.

Dad was very careful with a buck, just like my older son. I never did acquire that virtue. The reason I didn't buy a car was that I didn't want to offend Dad, who would have taken it as a judgment on his own wisdom. I bought a LaSalle when I married. Then, six or seven years later, when the LaSalle collapsed, I couldn't afford a new car.

My kids can believe that I didn't own another car till I was over forty because they were around then. My grandchildren either don't believe it or figure that was about the time autos were invented.

So when I needed a car I could always call Jim Clancy.

The trio finished their composition and I applauded. Jim joined in as he always joined in when I did something.

I gave the trombonist five bucks and whistled the opening theme from *Rhapsody in Blue,* which was played for the first time that year and was, I felt even then, a masterpiece. He responded on his instrument.

"That Mr. Gershwin writes like he was a Negro man," the trombonist laughed.

"He must have listened to a lot of you for many years."

"Sure sounds that way."

Jim grinned at the black man, his contagious winning grin that made everyone want to laugh, and slipped a bill into his hand, a twenty at least.

"Did you give that trombonist five bucks?" Jim asked incredulously as we walked through the candy store. "No wonder you never have any money. You should have let me take care of it."

"Five bucks wouldn't be much toward a down payment on a Duesy," I responded. "Or even a Ford."

"That's different." He frowned at me. "The Duesy is an investment."

I was fond of Jim, but I had no illusions that he was sensitive to irony, a fact that did not prevent me from often inflicting my irony on him.

He was short, only about five eight, and handsome, curly black hair, with a lock hanging over his forehead, bright blue eyes, pale skin, a dimple in his chin, and a quick winning smile—a cute little boy with, alas, a hairline receding much more rapidly than mine.

He worked at the Board of Trade, in a seat that his mother, a widow with lots of money and delusions of social prestige, had purchased for him. He was at that time reasonably successful at riding the waves of the exchange but not nearly as successful as he would later be. Even with his mother's ample funds and his own profits and the sale of his Stutz, he ought not to be able to afford a Duesy.

I'm sure he had found a deal. Jim always found deals.

My eyes winced in the bright spring sunlight and winced again at the sleek silver car with enormous whitewall tires (the spare tucked in next to the engine), thickly spoked wheels, and bright red hubcaps. Sports cars haven't changed all that much in their shape since 1925. Later they would add superchargers to the Duesys that would let you drive them at 150 miles an hour. In 1925, Jim couldn't get his much over eighty.

"Like it?" he asked.

Jim was an enthusiast about everything, a young man

of boundless energy and vitality, a jack-in-the-box always ready to pop open and laugh at you. I liked him partly because I realized that his enthusiasms were a balance to my more languid approach to life and, partly because I admired his verve and drive. He was fun to watch in action.

Maybe I patronized him a little too, but I was young and didn't realize that you didn't act that way with your friends.

"You bet I do. . . . Does the new girl come with the car?"

"She doesn't even know about the car." Holding his boater straw (not strictly appropriate because Memorial Day was a week away), he climbed into the front seat. "Hey, that Boston Store box has your name on it."

I knew before I opened it that it would be a boater straw hat of the most current fashion.

"Thanks, Jim," I said simply, having learned long ago to graciously accept his generosity.

Not only was Jim astonishingly generous; he also knew how to lavish gifts in such a way that it seemed as if you were doing him a favor by accepting his gift.

"Can't have you wandering around Italy looking like a hillbilly. . . . Put it on, I think it's the right size."

It fit perfectly, well, as perfectly as a boater ever fit anyone.

"All the girls in Rome will chase me when they see it."

"Hey, you really like it?"

"Perfect."

"April will love it on you, Johnny."

"April?"

"My fiancée. Almost. She plays the harp. Come on, let's go. Better put the boater back in its box. Two harps."

"At the same time?"

He turned on the engine and honked impatiently at a horse-driven garbage wagon that had pulled out of the alley in front of us. In the mid-twenties many wagons were still drawn by horses—produce, milk, ice, garbage.

"One's an Irish harp. That's smaller. She even sings in Irish."

He spun the car around the corner and roared down Twenty-sixth Street toward Western Avenue.

"Is she from Ireland?"

"No, from St. Gabriel's."

"Back of the Yards?" I asked in mock horror.

A date from West Africa would offend my mother only slightly more than one from Canaryville.

"You'll like her. She's great. So's her friend. They're going to be up at Barry for the Memorial Day weekend. You will come, won't you?"

We wheeled down Western, racing north at forty-five miles an hour.

In those days, you might pass a couple of cars every block. The only obstacles to high speeds were the doggedly moving streetcars. The police were no problem at all, not if you had a few bucks to pay them off.

"Barry is a dull place."

Barry Country Club was a summer resort run by my father's Knights of Columbus Council. It was a great assembly place for the West Side Irish, and a useful marriage market. The golf course was adequate, but the rest of the place was a summer camp at the most, not a country club.

"After Europe I suppose it's not much," he admitted.

Jim's enthusiasms were vigorous, but transient. He was never unenthusiastic, but the objects of his energy changed rapidly. Sometimes I would not see him for weeks, and then he would pop up and bounce across my path with a new project about which he was deeply excited, whether it be west suburban property or a handball match.

I invited him to come to Europe with me every time I booked a ticket on the *Lusitania*. His mother would not permit him to go because she was afraid that shipboard life would have a harmful effect on "little Jimmy's delicate health." As far as I could see, the delicacy existed in her mind only.

"I suppose I could stand it for a weekend," I said. To tell the truth I felt sorry for him.

"Great." He ran a yellow light and careened around a green milk wagon, scaring the poor horse that was pulling it half to death. "You'll really like her friend too. I'll pick you up at your office after work on Friday?"

The Board of Trade closed down at one-thirty. So that afternoon Jimmy was legitimately free to drive his new silver car. We worked till five-thirty. But no one cared when I came or went so long as my drawings were done on time. Normally I finished my work before lunch and did my own sketches in the early afternoon.

"At home after supper," I said as we leaped around the corner of Jackson Boulevard and roared west at fifty miles an hour. I held on to my corduroy cap. "I should eat with the folks."

They would be so delighted that I was going up to Barry that they would not have minded my missing the evening meal. But I figured that it would be one less dull evening if we arrived late.

I knew from experience to be skeptical about my friend's "swell" girls.

"Great!" he hollered above the noise of the Duesy's 4250 RPM. "We'll have a swell weekend!"

We made the trip from Western to Austin Boulevard—four and a half miles with maybe a dozen stoplights—in six minutes. We didn't stop for any of the red lights.

Jim dropped me off in front of our house on West End and then roared back to Austin Boulevard. He and his mother lived at that time in a suite in the Chateau Hotel at Lake and Austin, across the street from the El Station (his cars were parked in a garage around the corner on Mason and Lake). In those days, a suite in an elegant apartment hotel was considered a fashionable way to live.

"Does Jim have another new car?" Mom demanded. "It makes a terrible noise. Is it a Ford?"

Mom thought all cars were either Fords or Packards.

"No, it's a Duesenberg."

"Is that an expensive car?"

"Probably worth ten thousand brand-new."

In the mid-nineteen twenties a new Ford cost between two hundred and fifty and three hundred dollars.

"Where did he get that kind of money?"

"He didn't get it, Mom. He bought the car from the estate of a bootlegger who offended Al Capone."

"No!"

"Well, something like that."

My parents were so happy that I was "finally" going to spend a weekend at Barry that they soon forgot about Jim's "bootlegger" car.

They also admired my new boater.

"He is the sweetest boy," Mom admitted, "when he wants to be. He doesn't have to do things like that."

"He genuinely likes giving things to people." I tilted the hat at a rakish angle and wondered what "April" would be like. "No strings attached."

"There are always strings attached to gifts." My father glanced up from his evening paper. "That's not always bad."

I settled down on the porch with my sketchpad and began yet another drawing of the girl with the brown eyes. One part of my soul was convinced that she was real and that somehow, someday, I would meet her.

I finished the sketch long before dark. We were on daylight saving time by then, the fourth or fifth year of that experiment of which my father disapproved because it was contrary to nature.

The trip to Twin Lakes, on which they were setting so much store, almost never occurred. Friday at noon Jim called my office (we had one phone, in the outer office) to say that a business matter had come up and that he couldn't make it till late Saturday night.

"I'm really sorry," he said, his voice racing at top speed, "but it's a very important matter."

"Well, maybe when I get home from Italy—the end of August."

"But the girls have already gone up. They'll be terribly disappointed. Couldn't you ride up on the train tomorrow morning? They'll meet you in the hack at Genoa City."

The original station wagons were called depot hacks.

"I don't think that would be a good idea."

I had no desire to entertain two of Jimmy's "swell girls" for most of the day. And, judging from past experiences with Jimmy's "business opportunities," possibly the whole weekend too.

I was most particularly not interested in a girl from Canaryville who played not one but two harps.

And probably never heard of Jelly Roll Morton's "Red Hot Peppers."

"Please, Johnny," he begged, the sound of tears—authentic but not to be taken too seriously—in his voice. "Just this once. As a personal favor. I'll owe you one."

It was an old argument, one he had often used on me and always with the same effect. There was enough Irish politics in my bloodstream that I could not resist an appeal for a personal favor.

"All right," I said, "for the last time."

And I thereby changed my life.

20

"What does the *e* stand for?" the rhapsody in blue demanded.

She had leaned against the hood of the depot hack, folded her arms, tilted her head, and cocked an eyebrow at me.

"The *e*?" I stumbled as my face grew warm.

"John E. O'Malley. Jimmy wouldn't tell us what the *e* stands for."

I hesitated. "Edward."

"If you don't tell the truth once," she smiled, half fun and full earnest, "how can someone believe you ever again?"

"Evangelist," I gulped. "As in John the Baptist. You know John the Evangelist and John the Baptist."

"How cute!" She clapped her hands. "Vangie for short."

I would have jumped back on the train and returned instantly to Chicago except for one reason.

The young woman in the blue summer flapper dress and the helmetlike blue hat (and blue gloves) was the girl with the brown eyes from my dream.

"And what is your middle name, Miss Powers?" I tried to regain my balance. Admittedly, there was a glint in the dream girl's eyes but she wasn't supposed to be a hoyden.

"I'm *not* Miss Powers." She waved her hand at the gorgeous willowy blonde standing in the background. "She is Miss Powers. I'm Miss Cronin. You can probably call me April."

"April what?"

I was taken aback for the second time. I had assumed that the quiet blonde was Jim's girl. How could it be that he was practically engaged to the young woman who had pulled me back from the grave?

"April M. Cronin." She lifted my duffel bag and tossed it, effortlessly I noted, into the backseat of the hack.

"Mary?"

"Close . . . get in, you don't plan to stand out in the heat all day, do you?"

I was suddenly wounded by sexual desire, demanding, powerful, pervasive. My eyes, working on their own initiative, stripped away her clothes.

She sensed my searching evaluation and turned away, flustered but not displeased.

"Where's the driver?"

My unruly imagination would not put her clothes back on all weekend.

"I'm the driver, am I not, Clarice?"

"You certainly are," the sleepy blonde agreed.

"Do you want to drive, Mr. O'Malley?" She held out the keys, which I would have accepted from her at peril to my right arm. "Don't you trust a woman at the wheel of an auto?"

"I'd trust her more than I'd trust myself."

"He's not so bad, is he, Clarice?"

"We'll have to wait and see."

Clarice seemed to have stepped out of the pages of a fashion magazine; her white dress, hat, and gloves might have graced a mannequin in Marshall Field's windows. Her face and figure were perfectly shaped, a model or a movie actress, perhaps, a fantasy woman, cool, reserved, aloof, unattainable.

The kind of woman Jim could be expected to pursue.

Instead of my brown-eyed, vivacious tomboy.

My imagination ruled out of order any consideration of an unclad Clarice. It was too fascinated by April M. Cronin.

"Well," that latter worthy demanded, "are you going to ride with us or are you planning to walk to Twin Lakes?"

She and Clarice were already in the front seat of the Chevy. Gingerly I got in behind them.

"I'll ride with you, of course. And count myself lucky to be borne to Twin Lakes by such fair damsels."

She turned around to consider me, an examination almost as obvious as mine of her.

"I suppose, April M. Cronin, that if you are driving this station hack, you are not only a competent driver but an excellent driver. And does the *m* stand for Mae with an *e*?"

"Hmpf," she snorted, turning back and starting the ignition. "You're a good guesser. And my confirmation name is June. Also with an *e*. April Mae June Cronin, the whole of spring."

Clarice giggled.

I later learned that her confirmation name was in fact Anne with an *e*, an inevitable name for an Irish woman who has already honored the Blessed Virgin with a previous name. The claim to the third month of spring had been made up out of whole cloth. I charged her with the very falsehood that she had denounced in me.

"But that's different," she said calmly. "You knew I was making it up."

That was that.

One of her traits, I was to learn over that Memorial Day weekend, was that she combined a stern code of moral principles, sterner even than my mother's, with great flexibility of application. In a lesser person than April Cronin such a combination might have been called hypocrisy. In her case, however, the blend seemed to fit neatly into her character and personality.

I received a hint of another trait as we bounced over the gravel road from Genoa City to Twin Lakes.

"You've known Jimmy a long time, haven't you?" she asked as she guided the station hack with competence matched only by her confidence.

"Almost all my life. We went through St. Catherine's and St. Ignatius together."

"Isn't he the sweetest boy?" she demanded enthusiastically. "So kind and so generous and so much fun?"

"He certainly is," I said, determined to match her enthusiasm and still baffled by the harsh fact that my best friend was in love with this astonishing creature.

She then spent at least five minutes praising Jim, periodically interrupting her litany with demands for agreement from Clarice, "isn't that true, Clarice?"

Clarice always agreed.

And I mumbled my hypocritical assent to the praise.

That night at the dance hall down the lake from Barry (about which more later) she flipped the coin over. "Poor dear Jimmy, he's so sweet and so much fun. I'm sure he'll grow up soon."

Innocence and shrewdness, naïveté and cunning, were mixed in her seamlessly, although you had to listen closely to catch the shrewdness and the cunning.

That hot spring morning I wondered how "almost engaged" she was and how I could possibly survive in life without her.

"You play two harps, Miss April Mae June Cronin?"

"Only one at a time."

"Will we be fortunate enough to hear you play one of them this weekend?"

"After I dragged the Irish harp up on the train—that's the small one—"

"I know what a Celtic harp is."

She ignored the interruption. "—I'd play it at the drop of your funny hat. In fact, I'll play it even if you don't drop your hat and even if no one comes to hear me play it. Isn't that true, Clarice?"

"You never need much persuasion." Clarice spoke her longest sentence.

"See, Vangie?"

"No one calls me that."

"Someone does now."

I didn't like the nickname but I liked the tone in her voice when she said it. It somehow hinted at an invitation, the exact content of which was yet unspecified.

She couldn't, I told myself, be all that much engaged.

Still, Jim was my friend. I had no right to poach on his territory. He had been generous to me all my life. Now it was my turn to be generous in return.

Except boater hats and rhapsodies in blue are not quite comparable.

I could, however, legitimately hope that his enthusiasm would wane, as it almost always did, couldn't I?

And in the meantime, I could at least keep my oar in the water, couldn't I?

Would it not be practically immoral to take my oar out of the water?

She and Clarice—she was careful to do a joint autobiography—were both from St. Gabriel's. Their fathers were doctors on the staff of Mercy Hospital. She was the youngest of five daughters, all married except herself. Clarice was an only child, just like me (she apparently had been fully informed on my background). They both had attended St. Xavier's Academy. Clarice had spent some time in a finishing school in Switzerland ("as if you needed to be finished, Clarice, when you're already perfectly beautiful," praise without a touch of envy) while she had, at her father's insistence, gone to Normal over on Sixty-seventh Street. ("Daddy thinks I should be able to teach music because he doesn't think anyone can earn a living playing the harp.")

She'd been in Ireland last summer, learning about the

Irish harp and enough of the language to sing some songs in Irish.

"Gaelic?" I asked.

"Irish," she responded, ending that part of the discussion.

She had finished at Normal only last week and would begin teaching at the academy (St. Xavier's, was there any other?) in the fall.

She would be twenty-one in August and had been warned by her mother and father to avoid West Side Irish men at all costs.

"Poor dears, they're so dull."

"Your parents or West Side men?"

"My parents are *not* dull."

"Am I dull?"

"I haven't made up my mind yet. . . . You paint, don't you, Vangie?"

"Nothing so romantic, April Mae June Cronin; I'm an engineer, maybe you could even say an architect, though my parents think that is almost as bad as being an artist. I mess around with oils and watercolors in my spare time as a hobby."

"If I let you listen to my music, you have to let me see your paintings."

"That sounds like an ultimatum."

"It is," she said firmly. "What do you paint?"

"Landscapes, homes, women."

"With their clothes off?"

"April!" Clarice protested piously.

"The landscapes?"

"Certainly not."

"Oh, you mean the women? Not usually."

"But sometimes?"

"Well, I had a course at the Art Institute . . ."

"I've often wondered how an artist could concentrate on his work. Or if they do concentrate."

"Don't you concentrate on your music when you're singing a love song?"

"I don't sing to naked lovers."

"April!"

"It's a perfectly legitimate question."

April Cronin was a flapper, almost by definition. She wore a flapper dress (flapper clothes, according to a newsreel I had seen, weighed no more in aggregate than twenty-four ounces) and drove a car and probably smoked (as it turned out she didn't and the suggestion that she might infuriated her). She was by the standards of 1925 a thoroughly modern young woman. But she was also an Irish Catholic flapper from Canaryville who had attended the academy and would soon teach there.

The woman in my imagination on November 11, 1918, was mysterious, but she hadn't given me any advance warning of the directions of her mystery.

"I suppose it depends on who the model is. In the classroom, it's titillating and awkward for about thirty seconds, then it's just another assignment. If the model were a woman the artist loved and they were alone in his studio, it might be another matter."

"You've never done that?" she persisted, as she turned the car down the road at the outskirts of Twin Lakes.

"Not yet. I'll admit it's an interesting possibility."

It was on the tip of my irresponsible tongue to ask her if she would like me to paint her. I'm still not sure that I could not have gotten away with it that morning.

"Well, at least you're honest about it."

"God made women's bodies very beautiful."

"You've noticed?"

We all laughed.

It was a very hot morning for late May, but not yet hot enough to explain why my shirt was drenched with perspiration. April Mae June Cronin was a disconcerting young woman.

She parked in the lot behind the Barry dining hall.

"Are you tired from rising early and coming up on the train?" she demanded as she opened the door for me—very much the official driver.

"I wouldn't mind a little nap."

"Ten minutes." She glanced at her watch. "Then we play tennis. The golf course is already too crowded and we want to spend the afternoon at the lake, don't we?"

"Yes, ma'am. . . . Ten minutes?"

She grinned affectionately. "Fifteen, but don't be late. We'll meet you at the tennis court."

I lugged my bag up to my second-floor room in the Blackstone, as one of the wooden buildings with screened-in porches was wistfully called. It was nothing more than a resort cabin, painted white with green trim, that had been divided by clapboard partitions into small, Spartan rooms that smelled always of disinfectant.

I was distracted in my unpacking by an image of a painting of a naked, no, a half-naked harpist—concealed and revealed behind the strings of her harp.

I sternly reminded myself that Jim considered himself "practically engaged" to April Mae Cronin.

❧ 21 ❧

Fortunately for me there is no snapshot of us before or after the tennis match.

In white blouse and long tennis skirt, April Cronin was a terror on the clay. She played to win, and win she did, but with disconcerting fairness and courtesy. Her calls were always in my favor and her praise for my successful volleys fulsome. I'm going to beat you, she was saying in effect, but I'm going to be sweet and gentle and ladylike in the process.

Only don't get in my way when I rush the net.

Clarice watched from a bench. Was she bored or was she merely quiet?

I debated that question through the whole Memorial Day weekend and finally concluded that she was simply a very quiet girl. If I had met her without her ebullient companion I might have been stunned by her beauty. But in the presence of the energetic April, one hardly had time to notice any other woman, no matter how attractive.

I do have a snapshot, taken the next day, perhaps after mass, of the four of us. Two snapshots. Like my firstborn son, I am a paper saver. Unlike him I do not have my past neatly organized and catalogued. He helped me to organize my records for this exercise in trying to remember times past. On the back of the second picture, he has penciled in with his maddeningly neat block printing the accusing word "duplicate."

Clarice and April are both wearing flapper hats and dresses, short skirted, free flowing, and designed to pretend that woman did not have breasts. Jim and I are wearing boater hats, double-breasted dark coats, and wide white trousers, the kind that, for reasons that now escape me, were offensive to conservatives in 1925. My children laugh at the picture.

Jim and I are rather stiff and formal. Clarice seems cool and at ease with the camera. April is grinning happily.

I wince when I look at her. She is surely pretty, perhaps beautiful, and very much alive. I remember the desire I felt for her that day and my guilt over my betrayal of Jimmy.

I'm sure my mind was churning that morning. Had our embrace the night before been a violation of our friendship?

Had it been sinful, a question about which I normally did not worry when I kissed women.

But there had never been a kiss like that.

I didn't know what April thought. However, she had tripped up to Communion at the foot of the "pergola" on which mass was said on Sunday mornings.

She picked her way through the crowd of people with the same balance and grace with which she drove me off the tennis court the day before. On the court her backhand was fair, but her forehand was murderous.

"If you practiced," she said after winning the second set 6–2, "you'd be a very good player."

"Good enough to beat you?" I slumped into the bench next to the silent Clarice.

"I didn't say that." She wiped the sweat off her face with a towel. "I'll go get us something to drink."

There weren't handy Coke machines everywhere in 1925. April pulled three tin cups out of her tennis bag and sauntered off to the well behind the caretaker's house.

"She's a remarkable girl, isn't she?" In the absence of her friend, Clarice suddenly became articulate.

"Breathtaking." I continued to gasp for breath.

"She is very talented and yet is a swell person."

"And delights in beating men on the tennis courts."

"Naturally."

I pondered Clarice's languid form. She was interesting, no doubt about that, but definitely not the young woman who had haunted me back to life in the morgue at Camp Leavenworth.

"How close is she to engagement?"

"Engagement?" Clarice curled her lips. "To whom?"

"Well, Jim, I suppose."

"Really!" She frowned. "I can't imagine what would make you think that."

"She's not contemplating marriage with Jim?"

"Contemplating?" She shook her head in dismay at my ignorance. "Even if she wanted to marry Jim—and I'm quite sure she does not—he would never marry her. She scares him."

"I think she would scare most men." I tried not to sound relieved.

"She doesn't scare you, however."

It was a statement of conviction, not a question.

"Oh?" I confess I was uneasy.

"You rather enjoy her."

Clarice was not only articulate, she was perceptive. And I was a little frightened. I didn't want to be captured, not that easily.

"Can't someone be frightened and amused at the same time?"

Clarice merely laughed. It was a nice, warm laugh that melted her icy beauty and made her human and appealing.

I felt a trap closing in on me.

"You made Clarice laugh." April bounced up, her three tin cups in delicate balance. "You really *are* a charmer.

Here, don't spill it. I'm exhausted from pushing on the pump."

We sat side by side, with me in the middle, and silently sipped on the cool, tart well water.

April could not long remain silent. She turned toward me and examined my face closely.

"Have we met before, John the Evangelist O'Malley?"

"I don't think so." I decided not to stare back into her astute brown eyes.

"I guess not." She relaxed against the bench once more. "But somehow you look familiar."

"Maybe you met me in a dream."

"I don't dream about men . . ."

The three of us laughed.

"And you always tell the truth."

"You knew that wasn't quite true. . . . Still, maybe you are someone I dreamed about. . . . How could I dream about someone I don't know?"

"Maybe this is a dream and you'll wake up again."

"Indian philosophy," she snapped impatiently.

Impressing me again.

She then decreed that, unless we wanted to eat lunch in the dining hall, it was now time to enjoy the beach.

I dutifully agreed.

Commodore Barry Country Club was named, like the Knights of Columbus Council that established it, after Commodore John Barry (1745–1803), the "founder of the American Navy." His ship *Lexington* defeated the English ship *Edward* in the first sea battle of the War of Independence. Irish-born John Barry was thought to prove to those who doubted it that Catholics were as good Americans as anyone else—a fact widely questioned in those days.

Barry, as the place was always called, was a country club only in name. The KC Council had purchased the summer estate of a Milwaukee beer baron and a nearby golf course. The baron's home became the clubhouse and his servants quarters' the Drake. Two other wooden "cabins" were crowded around the grounds—the Commodore and the Blackstone—and a guest house at the far end of the estate became a separate dwelling for priests, of whom there were always more than enough in the course of the season.

The "beach" was an artificial spit of sand at the edge of a small lake that straddled the Illinois–Wisconsin border. Most sunbathing was done on a wooden pier that extended precariously into the lake at the foot of the "pergola," a concrete platform with a stone roof over the boathouse. It was also the site for Saturday night romancing and Sunday morning mass.

Across the road was a subdivision of small summer homes owned by members of the KC Council.

It seems astonishing today that we could accept and take for granted summer living conditions that now would be intolerable.

The clubhouse and the Drake were equipped with running water and an occasional tub and toilet bowl. The other buildings offered only nonpotable water in washbasins. Drinking water came from the outdoor pumps. One "bathed" in the shower house, appropriately divided by a thick wall into "gentlemen" and "ladies" sections, both of which were crowded all day in high summer.

We made do with privies scattered conveniently around the grounds, "outhouses" in the term of the day. And we took them for granted. Some of the older people, my parents' generation but not so fortunate, had known such sanitation mechanisms when they were growing up in Chicago. The memory of the outdoor toilet was sufficiently alive that one adjusted to its reality with little effort.

The next generation, raised with inside plumbing, would not tolerate such arrangements even in the summer.

It takes only a generation to undo all previous human history, at least when sanitation is the issue.

After a weekend at Barry I would amuse myself at the drawing table on Monday mornings by designing vast and elaborate bathroom facilities for the resorts of the future. In retrospect, it seems that, if anything, my imagination was too restrained.

Men were obliged to wear ties in the dining room, no matter how hot it was. Some of them even wore ties on the golf course and tennis court.

Officially there was nothing to drink on the grounds. The Volstead Act was still in force. What Herbert Hoover would call a few years later the "noble" experiment continued, its only effect the enrichment of bootleggers.

Moreover, the police in southern Wisconsin were less tolerant of speaks than the Chicago cops—although there was a roadhouse off on a side road from the highway to Kenosha, an establishment filled with young people from Barry on Saturday nights.

Since Barry was Catholic, there was always enough forbidden booze within its boundaries on a summer weekend to supply a speakeasy for a month. It was simply taken for granted that you would bring your own drinks up on the train or in your car.

If the truth be told, I had arrived at Genoa City with two bottles of single-malt scotch, which, I was willing to wager, would be the best booze available to anyone at Barry all weekend.

I wondered if April Mae June Cronin drank. I assumed that she did not.

I was wrong again.

She and Clarice arrived at the pier in huge floppy hats and "beach pajamas," a fashion innovation of the year. While heaven knows these garments were opaque enough, their loose fit and alluringly colored fabrics did convey a hint of the boudoir.

The older generation contended, with some validity, that they were merely an excuse for flappers to wear trousers.

Clarice carried two copies of *Reader's Digest*. April was reading *The Great Gatsby*.

They arranged themselves and their paraphernalia on

two deck chairs near the pier and settled down to their reading.

I strolled over.

"Good book?" I asked.

She glanced up. Her eyes narrowed as she inspected me. I was wearing swim trunks instead of the one-piece body suit that was still expected from male swimmers if they did not want to cause unfavorable comment from their elders.

"Poor dear man." She tapped the book, apparently deciding that my chest and shoulders were acceptable.

"Me?"

"No, Mr. Gatsby. And I suppose Mr. Fitzgerald too . . . have you read it?"

"Yes."

"Do you like it?"

"He's a fine writer and I think what he's writing about really exists. Even in Chicago."

"Are you like him?"

"Fitzgerald or Gatsby? No, I don't think so. I like to drink, but I don't get drunk."

"Which reminds me, you did bring something to drink, didn't you? Otherwise we will have to wait till poor Jimmy comes."

Another illusion down the drain.

"Single malt."

"Yummy."

A towel draped over my shoulders, I sat on the grass next to her and opened my copy of *Arrowsmith,* I must confess that I didn't pay too much attention to Sinclair Lewis. My mind was completely occupied by April Mae Cronin.

It was distracted by fantasies about how she would look in the swimsuit beneath the beach pajamas, but not so distracted that I did not worry about Jim.

I had Clarice's testimony, undoubtedly accurate, that Jim's suggestion that they were "practically engaged" was an overstatement. Moreover, I agreed that a woman like April would scare Jim half to death. Very likely she was a passing enthusiasm.

Still, Jim needed a good woman, I told myself, to bring some stability and happiness into his erratic life. We had been close friends since first grade. It would be immoral . . . well, at least wrong . . . for me to court April until he made up his mind that he wasn't interested.

She would keep, wouldn't she?

And I was leaving for Rome in ten days. When I came back, the romance between Jim and her would be long over. Then, if I still wanted to, I could begin my pursuit.

Would I still want to? Did I want to even now?

The answer was a clear yes. April was a woman to spend your life with.

I stirred uneasily, the stodgy Irish bachelor in me protesting against such a hasty decision.

Well, I replied to him. There's no rush. I *am* going to Rome in ten days. When I return, we'll see.

The only trouble with that strategy was that April might find someone else while I was away.

I was furiously jealous.

She wouldn't dare.

I sighed. It was all too complicated.

"Something wrong, Vangie?"

"Hot, that's all," I replied.

I sure was.

As one grows older, I have noted, there is a tendency to think it was hotter in summers when you were growing up than it is in the present, a judgment for which the weather records provide no substantiation.

So, I checked with the Weather Bureau. Memorial Day 1925 was the hottest in history—a high of 93.

In southern Wisconsin, it might have been a degree or two cooler.

So my sense of being on fire was not all internal.

"I think it's time for a swim. Clarice?"

"Fine."

The two of them trundled off to the "ladies" beneath the pergola. You did not remove your beach pajamas in public, even if you were wearing a swimsuit. Worse luck for my racing imagination.

I awaited their return with, as the reader might imagine, considerable interest.

In the space of a half decade, enormous progress had been made in women's swimwear—revolutionary progress, compared to which the recent appearance of the bikini is only a small adaptation.

Even during the war years, the presumption among those who designed such garb was that one was simply not supposed to see women's flesh on the beaches. The swimming "costume" was just that—a dress with a skirt that reached below the knees and stockings that protected everything below that. You could sit on the beach in such garb and stand in the water, but you certainly could not swim in it.

By 1925, however, young women like my two charges were wearing one-piece jersey suits that reached only to mid-thigh, exposed a considerable amount of back and neck, and clung to the parts of the body that their flapper dresses denied.

Scandalous, delightfully so.

When Clarice and April emerged from the pergola, every eye on the pier and the beach turned toward them, a fact of which I'm sure April was very well aware. Her suit was light gray, Clarice's light blue, both with broad white belts. They walked toward me with confident indifference, as though they appeared on the street every day in such dress. In fact, it was surely the first time that they had worn the suits and they were very anxious about public reaction.

"They might as well be stark naked," an elderly woman whispered behind me.

She exaggerated, but in terms of recent fashions her point was well taken.

Clarice was surely the more beautiful, a trim, flawlessly curved body, an ideal of youthful beauty for any era. April was taller and more slender. But her legs were splendid and her breasts, now clearly outlined by the swimsuit, were full and firm, as I had hoped they would be.

"You both look lovely." I rose to greet them and tried to smile approvingly.

"Thank you," they said together, blushing at my compliment.

"It's the first time we wore these"—April was a bit flustered—"and they're, well, kind of embarrassing, aren't they, Clarice?"

"Yes, they are."

"You feel like you almost don't have anything on, and you know that a lot of older women are watching you and don't approve and—"

"There's one thing you have to say about such swimsuits."

"What's that, Vangie?" She cocked a suspicious eye, expecting that I would say something to which she would have to object.

"You can swim in them."

"Right." She grabbed my hand. "So let's swim!"

I was unceremoniously yanked into the lake. The muscles in her bare arms and legs, I observed as I plunged into the lake, were solid and strong.

Twin Lakes is little more than a glacial mud puddle. It requires only a week or two of warm weather to heat it up for swimming. But that Memorial Day weekend it was still at least twenty-five degrees cooler than the air.

I screamed in vain protest and tried to pull away from her.

"Coward," she shouted and abandoned me.

Swim she did, with a sure, even stroke, out into the lake twenty or thirty yards. I followed.

"Don't you wish that every day was the first day of summer?" she said when I caught up with her.

"If it were the day I first met you, it would be wonderful indeed."

"Blarney." She swam back toward shore.

I followed her in. She and Clarice appropriated a place for themselves on the pier, tucked towels around themselves, and settled back to luxuriate in the warmth of the sun. I stretched out on the pier and indulged in my ability to nap whenever and wherever I wanted.

April Cronin had exhausted me, I told myself as I drifted into a world where there were no moral choices necessary between friendship and love.

I was awakened from dreams, I fear about firm young breasts, by a shattering blast of cold. Water was rushing up my nostrils and into my throat. I was drowning in the Arctic Ocean.

I sputtered and wheezed and somehow managed to come up for air.

April Cronin was guffawing at me. "Time to get up, sleepyhead."

"You pushed me off the pier," I said, furious at her.

"You looked so funny when you hit the water." She backed away from the dangerous light in my eyes.

I grabbed her and shoved her under. She broke free and surfaced, bubbling and laughing.

"Beast!" she shouted, dove under the water, and tackled me.

It was a glorious wrestling match. I was stronger than she, but she was a sturdy young woman, quick and determined, and not in the least afraid of me.

So, I suppose, have young people begun their summer romances since the species began.

Then our play turned serious and demanding, fun transformed into sexual invitation and response.

We stopped abruptly. I felt foolish and ashamed.

"I'm sorry," I muttered. "My fault."

"I started it," she said sheepishly, her face averted. "I guess the water isn't cold enough."

"Not nearly cold enough."

The two of us stood there, water up to our chests, afraid to look at each other, afraid to speak, caught in a mix of pleasure, guilt, and possibility. Time seemed to stop. There was only April Cronin and John O'Malley and an encompassing lake. All the possibilities of the moment and of a lifetime rushed through our imaginations. A playful relationship had suddenly become somber. It would be playful again perhaps, but never quite as innocent.

We had ventured to the far side of innocence in a single day, indeed in a few hours.

We might not speak of the violent emotions that had captured us during our play, but we both knew about them and we knew that, whatever else happened between us for the rest of the day and beyond, those emotions would be the context of our future.

It was terrifying and wonderful.

"I think it's colder farther out," she said. "I'll swim this way." She gestured to her left. "You swim that way."

"Yes, ma'am."

The water was not cold enough to make any difference.

Nor was my repeated mental resolution to sail for Rome the second week in June.

22

After supper, as the sun went down, April played her Irish harp and sang on the terrace in front of the clubhouse.

Almost everyone was there. No movie theater, no TV (though a transatlantic television broadcast had taken place that year), no taverns, no transportation for many of the guests: April was the only show in town.

She wore a plain white blouse and skirt and looked like an angel come down from the empyrean.

I fell completely in love with her while she played and sang. Her voice was sweet, clear, and pretty—not quite good enough for a concert stage, but wondrous in the fading twilight of a Wisconsin Memorial Day. She was a wonderful actress, putting herself into the various roles her show demanded.

And she was marvelous with the Irish harp.

All right, she didn't have to know about Jelly Roll Morton or ever hear of the "Dead Man Blues."

I sat on a stone bench near her and fantasized about a painting of a bare-breasted harpist, now bathed in the colors of twilight.

Her program was ingenious. She began with a medley from *RoseMarie*, then did "One Alone" from *The Desert Song*. Then she sang the Irish American songs that everyone expected—"Irish Eyes Are Smiling," "My Wild Irish

Rose," "Mother Macree," and (not strictly Irish American) "Danny Boy." Then she did a lovely ballad in Irish that made you want to cry, as do most Irish-language songs, regardless of their content. Then she turned to an aria from the final act of *Figaro,* and finally, just to prove she could sing anything, she offered a Gershwin medley, ending with a raucous, honky-tonk, speakeasy rendition of "Lady Be Good."

I told myself that she sang that just for me.

Afterward I carried her harp back to the Drake for her.

"You're a swell singer," I told her.

"Good enough for parish musicals and family concerts," she said firmly. "Not much more."

I considered denying that statement and decided that with April Cronin denial of the truth would not work.

"You could be a concert harpist."

"In an orchestra, maybe. But Dr. Thomas already has more harpists than he needs. It's all right, Vangie, I don't mind. You do what you can do and enjoy it, instead of feeling sorry for what you can't do."

"You sound like a wise old woman."

"Do I?" I saw her white face glance toward me in the dark. "By the way, you shouldn't look at me that way when I'm playing the harp. . . . Well, it's all right to *look* at me that way. But it shouldn't be so obvious."

"I'm sorry."

"Don't be. I was flattered. But it's hard to sing and play when you're wondering if everyone else knows what's going on in a man's mind."

"Oh. I was only thinking of a painting."

"An *immoral* painting." She had made her point and was now teasing me.

"Not necessarily."

"Yes it was."

We had arrived in front of the Drake and were facing each other in the glow of the single pale streetlight.

"I don't know whether I should ask about the painting," she said.

"It would be a portrait of a lovely young woman playing a harp in front of a stone house on a hot summer night with the colors of twilight all around her."

"With her clothes on?"

"Some of them."

There was a pause.

"No," she said finally.

"I wasn't proposing such a painting . . . and even if I were, it wouldn't be dirty."

"I know that." She took the harp from my hands. "But the answer is still no."

"Forever?"

She walked up the steps to the porch. "I didn't say that either. . . . I'll wake up Clarice and we'll meet you down by the pier. I'm terribly thirsty."

"I understand. Bring your tin cups."

She chuckled and disappeared in the darkness.

For the rest of the night I forgot about Jim.

The three of us sat at the end of the pier and demolished one of my bottles of single malt.

April Cronin drank like I did, slowly and carefully savoring the taste of each delicate sip.

"Nothing like Celtic whiskey," I said, "after Celtic music."

"Scotch whiskey after Irish music." She jabbed at my ribs. "Bring Irish the next time you come up here."

"When are you returning?" I asked politely.

"Weekend after next." She added a touch to her tin cup. "You too?"

"I'm sailing for Rome in ten days."

"Oh."

"I want to paint Roman churches and ruins. With those two terrible new buildings on Michigan Avenue we're entering an era, I fear, of silly decorations. Maybe I'll learn in Rome how to do decoration that has taste."

"Like poor Mr. Sullivan did at Carson's?"

"Yes."

So, she knew about architecture too. Was there anything that this astonishing girl did not know?

"You mean Tribune Tower and the Wrigley Building?"

"Wedding cake and in the city that produced Burnham and Sullivan."

"And Mr. Wright."

"Yes and Mr. Wright too."

"And John the Evangelist O'Malley?"

"Not the same class, I'm afraid."

"But good enough?"

"Yes, I suppose so."

I risked a question about jazz.

"*Well,* I don't happen to think that the Red Onion Jazz babies are better than the Red Hot Peppers."

"You've heard both bands?" I asked incredulously. "I bet neither of them play at White City."

"I don't go just to places like White City. Why, I even heard Bessie Smith sing 'St. Louis Blues' at the Arcadia."

Which was more than I had done.

"So you like jazz?"

"I find it very interesting. . . . I bet you'll tell me. Other boys won't. What does the word mean?"

I refilled Clarice's empty tin cup.

"Most Negro people will tell you"—I tried not to stumble over the words—"that it is a slang word for 'lovemaking.' "

"How interesting!" April gulped and sipped at her drink.

"How terrible!" Clarice murmured, swaying slightly as she drew the tin cup to her lips.

"The music," I went on lamely, "works only when the musicians are in close harmony with one another, almost like lovers when they are, er, making love."

"I see." April sounded dubious. "Well"—she took a deep breath—"my mother says there's nothing wrong with lovemaking when you love someone."

"April!" Clarice's voice was slurred. "Nice girls don't talk about such things."

"My mother also says that love without lovemaking is almost as bad as lovemaking without love."

"April!"

April's mother was frequently quoted on matters of controversy. I had begun to suspect that on some occasions the quotes were made up to fit April's own opinions.

"I'm sure she's right," I said agreeably.

"I hope lovemaking isn't as difficult as 'King Porter Stomp.' "

"It is reputed to be even more fun."

We both laughed nervously.

"Well, thank you for explaining what the word means."

"I hope it doesn't turn every jazz piece into a temptation."

She paused to consider that observation.

"No more than they already are."

It was my turn to gulp.

While we were exploring my place in the history of Chicago architecture and the meaning of jazz, Clarice was guzzling my single malt like it was water. Once when she reached for the bottle, April gently stopped her arm.

Obediently Clarice stopped drinking. She was pretty drunk by then, however.

"I'm sure you'll enjoy your trip in Rome," April said piously. "Maybe you can have an audience with Pope Pius."

"He'll be up at Castelgandolfo where they go in the summer. Anyway, why should he want to see an engineer from Chicago?"

"Who designs buildings and paints pictures."

"Which are not immoral."

"Only suggestive," she laughed. "Pour me a little drop more."

"A little more than that," I said, filling her cup halfway.

We sat on the pergola and watched the stars at peace

with each other and the world. In the distance on the other side of the lake, a jazz band was playing in the local dance hall, not very good jazz by Chicago standards.

I wished that the night would last forever.

Why the hell should I go to Rome?

"What time is it, Vangie?"

I pulled my watch out of my watch pocket and peered at it in the darkness. "As best I can make out it's eleven-thirty."

"Good. We mustn't drink after midnight if we want to receive Our Lord in Holy Communion tomorrow."

"You receive every Sunday?"

My parents were of a generation that made its Easter Duty with fear and trembling. I wasn't quite so frightened of Holy Communion—or perhaps not so convinced of my own unworthiness.

"Every day. Naturally."

A daily communicant who would not exclude the possibility of modeling for a "suggestive" painting. More and more interesting, this April Cronin.

"You think you're worthy to do that?"

"Certainly not," she said promptly. "No one is worthy to receive Our Lord. Ever. But Communion is food for our soul, so we should take it every day, just like we take food for our body. It makes us less unworthy, doesn't it, Clarice?"

Clarice was sleeping.

"Oh, dear. I'm afraid we've kept poor Clarice awake by our chattering. I think we'd better walk back to the Drake."

We had to guide "poor Clarice" back to their cabin.

"Wait here," April whispered to me. "I'll put her to bed and come back."

"Wonderful."

She returned in about ten minutes. I was so preoccupied by my fantasies that I did not hear her until she was next to me.

"Tired?"

I jumped. "Certainly not."

"Scare you in the dark? Are you afraid of the dark, Vangie?"

"No, I am not. . . ." Then I remembered the rules. You tell the truth to April Cronin. "Well, maybe a little. You surprised me. I was thinking."

"I won't ask about what. Do you want to walk over to the dance hall?"

"Sure."

"We won't be able to drink anything, not even water, if we want to receive Communion tomorrow."

"All right . . . Is Clarice asleep?"

She linked her arm with mine; we followed the dimly lighted path toward the even darker highway.

"The poor dear. She's really very, very intelligent. But her father is such a terrible man. He still spanks her and won't let her do anything or be anything. It's really quite terrible."

"Beats her?"

"And fights all the time with her mother, who stands up for Clarice some of the time. I don't know what's going to happen to the poor dear."

"Her father let her come up here for the weekend?"

"He's away in California. He spends a lot of time out there. If he knew she spent a weekend away from home without a chaperone, he'd be furious."

"You seem to be a fine chaperone."

"Would you trust me," she giggled, "to protect your daughter?"

"Absolutely."

"You would *not,* not if you were real old."

I thought about it. "I still think I'd trust you."

We paused on the highway, gravel of course, to let our eyes adjust to the darkness. Only two cars passed us during the twenty-minute walk to the dance hall.

They were playing the Charleston as we walked up to it.

"Oh, good! I just love the Charleston, don't you?"

"I've never danced it. It looks kind of wild."

"Don't be a stodgy old bachelor." She patted my arm.

"That's what my mother says."

"She sounds like a very wise woman."

"This place smells like the stockyards."

"Careful, sir"—she grinned at me—"you're talking about my neighborhood. Besides the smell—"

"I know . . . it's what puts the color in your skin."

We chuckled together and plunged into the maelstrom.

The Twin Lakes dance hall was a rickety old building that had been built in the eighteen eighties and was probably run-down the day the construction was finished. It was as hot as a furnace room at the South Works and filled with gyrating, undulating, sweat-smelling young bodies.

We had hardly pushed our way inside when my companion, who smelled quite sweet I had noted on our walk through the hot night, began to gyrate and undulate with the best of them.

Her legs were quite breathtaking when disclosed, almost up to her hips, by her bouncing skirt and slip. Such revelations hindered my efforts to learn the dance.

Nonetheless I finally did the Charleston right—because April Mae June (as I still thought) Cronin was determined that I would learn to do it right.

"You stare at my legs," she said when we had settled into a more relaxed fox-trot number, "like you've never seen a woman's legs before."

"Never more spectacular legs, that's certain. But it's the astonishing woman who walks on them that fascinates me."

I gripped her hand a little more firmly as I said that.

"That's very sweet . . . still, no man has ever looked at me before quite the way you do."

"I'm sorry—"

"Don't be. I'm not angry, just a little unnerved."

"Me too."

"What would the painting be like?" she asked.

"Which painting?"

"Of the nude harpist, silly."

"Oh, her!"

"Yes, her!"

"Well, she'd be well protected by the harp, of course. But the viewer would be able to see that she had firm and full and very lovely breasts."

After I had spoken, I realized that I had drank far too much single malt.

"Well, *that* certainly wouldn't be immoral, not very immoral anyway."

We huddled a little more closely.

"I suppose you stare at me because you're an artist and examine shapes and forms closely."

"That's part of it, I'm sure. But your shapes and forms are special."

"Silly." She pushed me away a little and then nestled in more closely. "I hope they do the Charleston one more time. I want to make sure you have learned how to do it right."

They did play it once more and I did do it, if not exactly right and not intolerably wrong.

Then they played the Black Bottom, which my mother had said no self-respecting girl would dance.

Nonetheless, April danced it and made me dance it too.

Then, astonishingly, there was a waltz.

"My kind of stodgy old bachelor music."

"You're none of those things." She snuggled into my arms. "Are you thirsty? I'm terribly thirsty."

"I have another bottle of single malt back in my room."

"I meant thirsty for water." She frowned disapprovingly. "But we're going to Communion tomorrow, aren't we?"

"I guess."

There was no reason why I wouldn't go except I didn't want to seem too pious.

"A little thirst isn't much compared to the terrible thirst

Jesus suffered on the cross for our sins, is it?"

I murmured my agreement.

The words were nunish piety, but they were nonetheless authentic on the lips of April Cronin. There was no contradiction in her soul between such notions and the Charleston and discussing the breasts of a half-naked harpist. My son the seminarian (my younger son) tells me that it is the Catholic genius to be able to say "both . . . and." Heaven knows April Cronin was in that respect as in many others the most Catholic person I ever met.

Finally the band played "Show Me the Way to Go Home"—the hit song of the year and now the sign that the party was over. April, who had kind of taken over the dance floor, led all of us in singing the song. It sounded like we were all so drunk that we could hardly walk. In fact, although bottles were passed constantly around the dance floor, no one was very drunk.

I had sweated off my part of the single malt by the end of the first Charleston.

April decreed that it was necessary to remove our shoes and socks (she performed the latter operation after my head was chastely turned away) and wade along the lakeshore under the stars. I rolled up my trousers and tagged along after her.

That was when I said it was a shame Jim was not with us to enjoy the fun and she said that someday he might grow up.

I continued to slosh through the water, not certain how to reply or whether to reply. I remembered again that she was Jim's girl, at least to the extent that if it hadn't been for him I would not know her.

Looking back on it, I realized she was telling me in her sweet fashion that there were no claims staked on her yet. Perhaps she was even hinting that all was fair in love and war.

I was innocent of how the love game was played, mostly because I hadn't played it much. So I didn't hear what she was telling me—the same message I had heard earlier from Clarice. Or maybe I did hear it and could not bring myself to betray Jim.

We were friends. He knew her before I did. And he needed to find a sensible, stable wife more desperately than I did.

So I thought.

Or so I told myself I thought.

We put on our shoes when we arrived back at the pergola.

The Barry grounds were as silent as a cemetery. Everyone else was in bed. From a far distance I heard a baby, disturbed in the middle of the night, protest with a routine wail.

"Wasn't that fun?" she demanded with enthusiasm appropriate for the beginning and not the end of the evening. "What shall we do next?"

"April Mae Cronin," I said, taking her collarbones in my hands, "you are one of the most remarkable women I have ever met. I've known you for sixteen hours and already it seems like sixteen wonderful years. Nonetheless and with all due respect for your beauty, talent, and vitality, I don't give a—"

"Careful!"

"I was about to say I don't give a hoot what you do. I'm going to walk you back to the Drake. Then I'm going to the Blackstone and sleep till I wake up even if it's the day of the Last Judgment."

"Maybe you are a stodgy old bachelor," she said giggling.

I set her on the darkened path to the Drake and gave her a shove. "Walk, woman, and walk quickly."

"Yes, sir." She giggled again, so tired herself that she was close to mild hysteria.

We giggled together as we struggled up the hill to her cabin.

"You're silly," she said with mock seriousness. "I'm

going to tell old Mr. Hurley that his prize artist is silly."

"He knows it already . . . now, good night, young woman, and don't wake me till just before mass."

"You can wake yourself." She giggled again.

If there was anyone listening they would have been convinced we were both drunk.

Perhaps we were, but not with alcohol.

At the bottom of the steps up to the screened-in porch, hardly realizing what I was doing, I bent over to kiss her. Somehow her face was turned up waiting for the kiss.

I intended only a mild touch of lips. After all, I hardly knew her.

Her response indicated that she intended no more.

But energies more powerful than our intentions were working under the hot, starry skies. In the time it takes an eyelid to flick we were in each other's arms, our bodies pressed against one another in a desperate lunge toward unity. Our lips seemed frozen together as though they were sealed in a permanent bond. Despite her smell of human sweat and the distant taste of whisky on her lips, she was unbearably sweet to my mouth. Her body fit against mine as though we had been designed to embrace one another.

Her allotted twenty-four ounces of women's garb was soaked with sweat and hence hardly any barrier to the feel of her pliant woman's body, solid and soft in just the appropriate places.

We clung together for what seemed an eternity, neither one of us wishing to end the ecstasy.

Which we felt, naturally, was unique to us and experienced by no other couple in human history.

"Oh my," she whispered when finally, somehow, we parted. "I've never been kissed that way before."

"Me neither."

She was shivering.

"You're a swell kisser. A lalapazoo." She rested her head against my chest. "And if you dare say you're sorry, I'll hit you."

"I didn't mean—"

"No apologies." Her fingers against my lips silenced my regrets. "It was wonderful. Scary, but wonderful."

"I agree," I mumbled, feeling clumsy and awkward.

"One more, very gentle kiss"—she touched my lips with hers and then quickly backed away—"and I'm going to my room and dream the rest of the night away."

"Pleasant dreams, April Mae June Cronin."

"My confirmation name is really Anne. With an *e*. I'm sure the dreams will be pleasant."

She ran up the stairs and through the screen door into the darkened porch without ever looking back.

I walked back to my cabin and into the damp cubbyhole that was my room on the third floor—with the only window opening not on the outside but on the porch, humming "Sweet Georgia Brown" exultantly to myself.

I had never before so completely overwhelmed a woman.

And never had I felt myself so completely a man.

I pulled off my clothes in the darkness, and lay on top of the soggy sheet, hands behind my head.

The woman was mine. It might take time and there would be obstacles. But she was mine.

I thought I would be too excited to sleep, but I was wrong. In a few moments, I was in a pleasant dream world filled with compliant women. Guilt lingered on the fringes of this paradise, but made no difference at all.

Then the fire alarms went off and I knew that Jim had arrived and that my exultation of a few hours before was finished.

23

"Did you see the look on their faces when they came tumbling out of the Drake?" Jim was ecstatic. "The old women especially. They thought the world was coming to an end."

We were milling around on the lawn between the pergola and the statue of Commodore Barry.

"And the young ones, hey, don't they look great in nightgowns?"

"No one looks great when they've just gotten out of bed."

In fact, I hadn't seen anyone. As soon as I had heard the alarms, I knew it was another one of Jim's practical jokes. I rolled over on my bed and cursed Jim, the Kenosha Fire Department, and the rising sun that had poked its way into my room and seemed determined not to leave.

I had begun to worry about Jim's jokes. When we were younger they seemed to be part of the same innocent fun as his generous giving of gifts—jack-in-the-box high spirits. In his mind gifts and jokes were different sides of the same coin: Peter Pan playing Tinkerbell. But as we grew older the jokes, innocently intended perhaps, became somewhat less innocent in their effects.

I wanted my Peter Pan to grow up, but not to lose his flair for frolic and surprise.

I listened to the rush of people fleeing my building and

imagined the same sounds all over the grounds.

Then, knowing I would not go back to sleep, I struggled out of my bed, shaved as best I could, put on my seer-sucker blue suit, blue tie, and boater hat, and ventured out as though I were prepared for mass.

Looking back on it, I suppose I was foolish. A suspicious person would have wondered how I knew it was a false alarm.

"You shouldn't do things like that," I said to Jim when he rushed up to me, brimming over with excitement at his coup. "What if one of the firemen was hurt or what if an elderly person had a heart attack?"

His face fell, as I knew it would. When I didn't rejoice with him over one of his successful practical jokes, Jim was heartbroken.

"But no one was hurt and no one had a heart attack. You sound like my mother."

I sounded like my own mother too.

"That's not the point," I said wearily. "Turning in a false alarm is against the law. What if there's a real fire emergency here next week and the clubhouse phones Kenosha for help and they won't come?"

"Ah, heck, Johnny, that won't happen." He shoved his hands into his jacket pockets and hung his head, as he usually did when I reprimanded him. "No one was hurt. And it will give them something to talk about all day. You know how dull it is up here. And the firemen will moan about it all during their picnic this afternoon. I'll send them an anonymous contribution. Everything is all right."

"All right, but promise me that you won't do it again?"

"Sure, Johnny, sure. Anything you want. I didn't mean any harm."

In fact, he didn't mean any harm. He turned to practical jokes only when he was discouraged about something or unhappy, usually unhappy with himself.

"He does silly things," my mother had often said, "just to get attention."

"Seems to me that he gets more than enough attention from that doting mother of his," Dad would respond.

"I mean real attention." Mom would end the discussion. She meant, I think, attention that didn't involve domination and control, but she didn't have the vocabulary to express her astute insight.

At St. Ignatius I would defend poor Jim against those who did not like his practical jokes.

"He's a mean boy, Jack," one of the young Jesuit Scholastics said with a harsh frown. "His jokes aren't funny. They're cruel."

"It's not cruel to paint a mustache on a statue of Saint Aloysius Gonzaga," I argued.

"You think it's funny?"

"No, I don't; but I think it's harmless."

When I went off to the Army and he took the seat his mother had bought for him on the Board of Trade, he seemed to quiet down. The excitement of the grain pits apparently replaced the fun of sending hearses to people's homes, pulling fire alarm boxes, or phoning emergency calls to police stations.

While I was in Armour, there were rumors in the neighborhood that he had tipped off federal agents about speakeasies and then complained to their superiors when no raids occurred.

I didn't want to believe that he'd take such foolish chances. The bootleggers did not like interference in their business.

I didn't ask him about it, however.

"I know you don't mean to hurt anyone, Jim"—I repeated my warning that morning at Twin Lakes—"but promise me you won't do anything like that again."

"All right," he sighed. "I promise. . . . Hey, what do you think of my girl? Isn't she a swell kiddo? Do you like her?"

"She's very impressive, Jim, very impressive."

"Do you think I ought to marry her?" He tugged on my

coat. "I haven't introduced her to Momma yet, but she'll like her, won't she?"

His momma would hate any girl who seemed likely to marry him.

"You have to make up your own mind about choosing a wife, Jim," I said piously.

"Isn't Clarice swell?" He continued to tug on my coat. "She's quiet but she's real smart."

"She certainly is."

"We can have lots of fun this summer, can't we? You with Clarice and me with April. They're swell girls, aren't they?"

"You forget I'm sailing to Italy next week."

"Aw, heck," he whined, "can't you change your plans? I'm going to need help to ask her to marry me."

"I can't, Jim, I just can't. You have to do that yourself."

"If I ask for advice," he begged, grabbing my coat again, "will you give it to me?"

"Sure, for whatever it's worth. Now why don't you duck into our room and shave and get dressed for mass."

"Yeah, sure. I can't let April see me looking like a pig. She sure is swell, isn't she?"

"How did the business go?"

He shrugged. "Pretty good, I'll make some money, but it's not as important as having friends like you and April."

Then why weren't you here all day yesterday to keep me from falling in love with your girl?

He hurried off to the Blackstone to dress for mass— coat, tie, and hat in hand, unless you wanted to be stared at, no matter how hot it was.

I never asked what his mysterious business trips were about. I was afraid that he might tell me that he was financing bootleggers, probably independents since the professionals didn't need financial backing anymore.

Somehow, we missed the girls before mass. By the time I spotted them in the crowd the priest had already begun.

I saw the solemn and devout look on April's face and yanked Jim back.

"Wait till after mass," I whispered. "She won't like to be distracted while she's praying."

"Why?" His small boy's disappointment was almost a whine.

"You said you wanted my help, didn't you?"

"Okay," he grumbled, "if you say so."

The atmosphere at those outdoor masses was not especially reverent. The priest and the makeshift altar on the pergola seemed too far away to be sacred. Since there was no public address system, you couldn't hear the prayers, not that it made any difference because they were in Latin. The crowd was restless and uneasy, eager to be done with the ritual so that the day's amusements could begin.

The humidity was thicker and more oppressive, hinting perhaps at a thunderstorm before the day was over. Since Memorial Day was Saturday, it was not a three-day weekend. The last train for Chicago left Genoa City at six o'clock. After mass and breakfast there wouldn't be much time for golf or swimming or tennis.

There was no sermon, which was a blessing, but there was a collection. Naturally, it was a Catholic church, wasn't it?

Jim put a twenty-dollar bill in the basket.

I tried to sort out my thoughts.

Jim didn't stand a chance with April Cronin. She would be nice to him because she was nice to everyone. He confused her courtesy with love. The most she could ever feel for him was amused affection.

Still, I had to permit him to pursue his courtship. If perhaps she did come to love him, she might save him from his own mistakes.

It did not occur to me to worry about her. She seemed quite capable of taking care of herself. Perhaps I gave her too much credit. Despite her poise and self-sufficiency, she was only a twenty-year-old kid.

A bell tinkled from the altar. The crowd, in unison, pounded its chest, quite unaware, I was sure, what the gesture meant. It was nonetheless a link with the mysteries up at the altar.

The sensible thing for me to do was to sail off on the *Rex* next week and let Jim pursue his courtship of April Cronin. That's what would have happened if I had not permitted him to talk me into coming to Barry for the weekend.

If he was successful, fine. April might bring him some peace and happiness. If he was unsuccessful, I might get in touch with her sometime in late summer or better early autumn. Either way, what would be, would be.

What was wrong with that strategy?

What was wrong with it was that I wanted the woman.

I noticed that she was striding up as vigorously as her ridiculous high heels permitted to receive Communion. I followed her, telling God that if He was upset, it was a problem He would have to discuss with her.

You'll have a hard time winning an argument with that one, I informed the Divine Omniscience, which doubtless already knew that.

I couldn't tell whether she saw me or not when she passed me coming back down the pergola steps. Her eyes were devoutly downcast, but I thought that April Cronin's eyes, even devoutly downcast, would not miss much.

They had no trouble finding us after mass. Both the young women were wearing light pastel dresses with very short skirts and matching hats, pure flapper.

I wanted to take her in my arms and kiss her all day long.

"You look tired, Jim," April began after she had led us to a bench near the lake. "I bet you drove all night. You shouldn't take chances like that. Maybe you should have a nap. Doesn't he look tired, Clarice?"

Clarice nodded serenely.

"I'm fine." Jim beamed at her concern. "Let's have fun."

He opened up the black bag he'd been carrying. "Who needs breakfast. I brought everyone a two-pound box of Fanny Mae's. Bought them at the store at 111 North Lasalle. Aren't they swell?"

"Fanny Mae's!" April grabbed her white satin box like she was an Armenian refugee being offered a loaf of bread after a month's starvation. "I just *love* them!"

She pulled off the top with total lack of womanly delicacy and began wolfing them down.

"I knew you liked them." Jim beamed happily.

"You'll ruin your stomach eating candy that way on Sunday morning." I sounded exactly like my mother.

"Or get fat." Clarice turned up her nose at her friend's gluttony.

"My mother says"—April licked chocolate off her fingertips—"that we come from a long line of skinny women with cast-iron stomachs. . . . Do you think I'm a glutton, Vangie?"

She cared what I thought, but I was pretty sure that if I said that yes she was making a pig out of herself, she would be sorry but would keep right on gobbling down the candy.

"I think chocolate is less harmful than scotch."

We all laughed. April went right on demolishing the two pounds of candy. Clarice and I were content with one or two nibbles. Jim Clancy didn't eat any. The candy was a gift for others, not something he particularly liked for himself.

How could someone be so observant in certain matters and so thick-skulled and thick-skinned in other matters?

"Hey!" He erupted with a new enthusiasm. "You want to play tennis? Doubles? Johnny is real good."

"I beat him yesterday. Why don't you and I play him and Clarice. It should be a swell match."

"Great! Great! Let's get our tennis clothes on. Who needs breakfast."

"I need a cup of coffee," I murmured.

"I'll bring a thermos to the tennis courts," she said. "Come on, let's hurry up before it rains. Jim is entitled to a little fun."

I quickly revised my analysis. She did like him, in a maternal, protective way. A girl with a warm heart could stumble into marriage with those emotions.

Then the bell in front of the dining hall on the other side of the hill began to toll. I glanced at my watch. Official breakfast was already over, though coffee and rolls waited for those who had received Communion at mass. It was still three hours to lunch.

"What's happening?" Clarice looked around nervously.

"It's scary," April agreed. "Like a funeral."

Jim's eyes were sparkling.

Dear God in heaven, he was up to his old tricks again. There was always a second swipe to his elaborate practical jokes. Just when you thought it was over, there'd be one final comic twist—Saint Robert Bellarmine standing up in the crib in the chapel at St. Ignatius College on Christmas Eve, two weeks after the last mustache had been painted on a Jesuit saint.

And now a mustache on the Blessed Virgin.

Prove that Jim had done it? Impossible.

"I smell something"—Clarice grabbed April's arm—"something's on fire!"

"Probably just grease burning in the kitchen," I said, knowing full well that it was a stink bomb or two made from rolls of Kodak film and planted with a slow fuse, most likely in a trash can, before mass.

Jimmy, Jimmy, why do you do things like this to yourself?

I was assailed by a terrible temptation to tell April that it was Jim's idea of a joke. It would destroy his chances with her.

I didn't spill the beans and not because I was feeling all that loyal. If I told her about his jokes, such a disclosure might also destroy my chances with her.

"If it's just grease, why are they ringing the damn bell!"
Poor Clarice was almost hysterical.

Very gently, like a mother reassuring a frightened child,
April extended her arm around her friend's shoulder. "It's
all right, Clarice. Don't be afraid. We'll take care of you.
It's just a little smoke."

"Let's go see." Jim was bursting with excitement. "It's
probably nothing serious."

The aftermass crowd, not yet dispersed back to their
cabins, was already streaming up the hill toward the Drake
and the dining hall, nervous, worried, a little frightened.

As they were supposed to, they were worried whether
the Kenosha Fire Department would race the twenty miles
to Twin Lakes for a second alarm.

Clever, Jimmy, really clever.

"What a terrible smell!" Clarice cried.

"Like the stockyards on the South Side."

"Beast, monster, savage." April jabbed at my ribs. She
smiled while she poked, fiercely enough, a soft, affectionate smile that enveloped me and assured me for the first
time that she loved me as much as I loved her.

Let the whole world burn down.

The bell stopped ringing before we reached it. The
crowd was already breaking up.

"False alarm," someone said. "Second time."

"Just a couple of stink bombs in the garbage."

"They ought to put the one who did it in jail."

"Stick him in a room with his own stink bombs."

Jim's face was purple with suppressed glee.

"See, there was nothing to worry about, dear," April
purred at Clarice. "Just some poor person who has to do
mean things. We should feel sorry for him and say a prayer
for him. Maybe even light a vigil light tomorrow at mass."

Jimmy turned pale, as if he had been stricken with a
stomach infection. "Maybe we should thank the person,"
he burst out. "He's kept the day from being dull."

"He's just a poor sick man, Jim dear. We don't need help to enjoy ourselves."

"May I bring sweet rolls to the tennis courts, please, Miss April, ma'am?"

She smiled at me again, the Lady of the Manor amused by a clever little servant boy. "Bring one for each of us, John the Evangelist. And hurry! We don't want someone to beat us."

"May I eat an extra one on the way, Miss April?"

"Only one." She jabbed at me again, but the poke was light enough to be a caress.

I thought about poking back.

The tennis match was not the runaway I had expected. Clarice was a more competent player than I had anticipated. And Jimmy, who when he was serious could give me a run for my money, acted the clown, showing off for April. Moreover, April, who had routed me with gentle intensity, played the clown back.

I was annoyed with both of them. The more fatuous was their play, the more deadly serious I became. When we were up 5–3, April turned serious enough to win four straight games, one of them with four serves.

"I knew we'd win!" Jim exulted. "Rematch! Rematch!"

"I think we'd better swim while we can." April examined the sky. "It's going to rain."

We gathered our bags and our thermoses.

"Would you carry these back to the kitchen, John?" she asked me.

"Sure."

"I'll help." Jim reached for the coffee jug.

"I thought you might get us a fresh batch of towels, James."

"Right! Right!" He bounded away enthusiastically.

"I'll be right up, Clarice," she said when we reached their cabin.

April waited till her friend had entered the screened-in porch.

"I want to apologize, Vangie," she said solemnly.

"No apologies," I said. "I thought we made that rule last night."

She blushed deeply. "This is different. I'm sorry I ruined the tennis match. I hope you'll forgive me. But poor dear Jim is so tense after his ride up here that I thought we really ought to let him blow off steam. Did you notice how that fire in the garbage upset him?"

There were a lot of things I could have said. What I did say was, "You're very generous and thoughtful, April Mae Anne Cronin."

"I could tell you were upset."

I touched her waist with my hand. "You're wonderful. Now go put on that splendid swimsuit, so I can admire you till the rains come."

"Discreetly admire me."

"I won't drool."

"Beast." Her hand rested on my waist. We stood there for a moment, enjoying each other. I went back to our cabin to dress for the lake, more than ever confident that she would be mine eventually. And then forever.

Like all the confidences of those falling in love, that one lasted for perhaps ten minutes.

If anything she looked more lovely that day than she had the day before.

It was Jim's turn to wrestle and dunk and be dunked. I noted, with considerable satisfaction, that it was a much less ardent struggle than my contest with April.

She feels sorry for him, I told myself with more conviction than I felt, but she loves me. Well, she's beginning to love me.

Then the storm came. Jagged bolts of lightning cut across the black sky. Thunder roared all around us. The rain beat down in torrents. In the city, it would have been one more storm. Somehow in the country it was more threatening and dangerous.

We were driven back to our cabins to escape the rain. The day was pretty much ruined.

"Isn't she wonderful?" Jimmy demanded again as we struggled into dry clothes in our cramped room. "A great beauty, huh?"

"Clarice is more beautiful," I said primly.

"Sure, but no personality. April has great legs and tits and she's lots of fun."

"If you love her, Jim"—I pulled on my socks—"you shouldn't talk about her like that."

"Why not?" He paused, one arm in his shirt. "It's true, isn't it? Really great tits. I mean, I wouldn't say it to her, but can you imagine playing all day with them? Boy, would that be swell!"

How could I explain that it was all right, even normal, to think that way, but that you really didn't talk about women in those terms?

I gave it up.

A kid knocked on our door.

"Miss Cronin says she's going to sing again and that you don't have to come to listen to her but she'll never speak to you again if you don't."

April entertained for another two hours inside the clubhouse, leading us in group song. I stared at her in mute adoration, causing an embarrassed blush now and again. Jim bounced around nervously, moving back and forth from the concert room to the slot machines. He won two jackpots and crowed that he had made all the expenses of his trip.

Finally, at my orders, he slowed down long enough to listen to April's songs. The same look of quiet rapture that I had seen in the speakeasy appeared on his childlike face, peace, joy, and understanding. Why couldn't Jim be that way more often?

Clarice watched the three of us placidly. Dear God, I prayed, find that poor kid a good man.

Then the storm ended. The temperature had fallen

twenty-five degrees and it was time to go home. Jim announced that he could fit the two girls in the Duesy and the harp in the rumble seat. Did I mind taking the six o'clock from Genoa City?

Reveling in my self-pity, I said no, that would be fine.

He would drive me to the train station.

Nonsense. I could ride the hack or the truck. He and the girls should enjoy as much of Sunday as possible.

I was, he told me, really a swell guy. He presented me with a bottle of single malt that somehow had appeared from nowhere.

April walked with me from the clubhouse back to the Blackstone. Neither of us spoke, there was nothing much to say.

She walked up the steps with me and into the screened porch on the first floor, a braver move than I would have attempted over at her cabin.

"You stared at me all afternoon," she said. "I was embarrassed."

"But not displeased."

"I should have been." She looked away from me, embarrassed again.

I turned her face back toward me. "Better get used to it."

She removed my hand from her chin and held it lightly in her own. Our eyes locked.

"It's been a wonderful weekend, John," she said shyly. "It will take me a long time to figure it out."

I embraced her with one arm and drew her to my side. "I don't think either of us will ever figure it out, April."

"I hardly know you"—she leaned against my arm—"yet I feel that I've always known you."

"Your dreams," I said lightly.

"I don't mean it that way. I mean I know you better after thirty-six hours than people I've known for years."

"Do you like what you've discovered?"

"Yes. Very much."

I tightened my grip on her.

"Me too."

We said nothing for a moment, enjoying the peace of our tentative pledges.

"I'll see you in two weeks?" She looked up at me.

"I'll be in Italy by then, or on the boat to Italy."

"I'd forgotten," she sighed. "Or maybe I hoped you'd changed your mind."

There it was. A perfect opportunity.

"I'm afraid it's too late."

"I understand."

"I'll be back in early August."

"And I'll see you then?" She brightened.

Two months seemed like eternity, but not a long eternity.

"You certainly will. And I'll think of you every day that I'm in Rome."

"A couple of days a week will do."

"Nope, every day." I kissed her, gently and tenderly. Now was no time for a repetition of last night's passion.

"Will you write?"

"I sure will."

"Let me know your address."

"As soon as I get to Rome."

I knew the address already, but I wanted to think about whether I should tell it to her.

She kissed me and ran out the door and down the steps.

It was cold on the train riding back to Chicago. I thought that the young women in their light clothes would freeze in Jim's Duesenberg. I worried about an accident.

By the time the taxi dropped me off at our house on West End, I was thoroughly despondent.

My parents were sitting in the parlor, reading the Sunday papers, an obligation as strict as the eleven o'clock mass at St. Catherine's.

"Turned cold," Dad murmured.

"Yep."

"Did Jim Clancy finally arrive?" Mom asked, not all that interested in the answer.

"Yep."

"Did you meet any nice girls?" Mom again.

"Yep."

They both put down their papers, comic sections as I remember.

"Who?" they asked together.

"Her name's April Cronin." I slumped into an over-stuffed easy chair. "She's a Democrat and she's from St. Gabriel's and her cheeks are red from the smell of the stockyards. She's twenty, twenty-one in August, has a certificate in music from Normal, plays the harp and sings, and she'll teach at St. Xavier's Academy in the fall. She has brown hair and brown eyes and is kind of tall and dresses like a flapper. In fact, she is a flapper."

I awaited their protests and warnings.

"Dr. Cronin's daughter?" Dad asked cautiously.

"Yep. His youngest."

"He's quite a remarkable man. Decent fellow."

"Decent" was my father's highest praise.

"They have a lot of money," Mom observed. "Does she seem spoiled?"

"Nope. Not at all."

They didn't even know April Cronin and already, despite her obvious disadvantages of geography and politics, they liked her.

"So?" Dad folded his paper and tilted his head to consider me carefully.

"So I'm still sailing for Italy a week from Wednesday."

"Could I ask why?"

Looking back on that conversation, I realize that something in my voice or my manner must have given away how I felt. Dad had never asked me a question like that before.

"Jim knew her first. He wants to marry her. I'll have to wait and see."

"Is that altogether wise?"

"I don't know."

"Maybe".—Mom always searched for a compromise solution, in that respect much like April—"you should postpone Italy for a few weeks."

"I can't explain why," I sighed. "But my instincts are that I should go away now."

Neither of them replied. But I knew they were thinking what I was thinking.

What if my instincts were wrong?

❧ 24 ❧

With loving concentration on each line, I had drawn a sketch of April on the El train.

The handsome Italian American grandmother sitting next to me watched with obvious approval.

"Pretty girl," she said.

"For Irish."

"You must have some Tuscan blood in you."

"The first bishop of Firenze was Irish."

That ended the conversation.

After I had left my parents and went to my room on Sunday night, I had begun the sketch, working from memory because I was too bemused during the weekend to put a single line on paper.

In my office in the Rookery that Monday morning, I studied the result of my El work. No doubt about it, she was the brown-eyed girl who had summoned me back from the dead at Camp Leavenworth.

But that was impossible. April Cronin had been fourteen years old then, a skinny kid, no doubt. How could she have intervened in my dreams as a young woman of twenty?

I threw my drawing pencil aside. How could she have appeared in my dreams—if it was a dream—at any age?

And she thought she had met me before too.

I picked up the morning *Tribune*. Pete dePaolo had won

the Indy five hundred with the average speed of 101 miles an hour, in a Duesenberg Speedster. Jim, who was obsessed with sports, had probably read the papers and was now determined to push his car up to the same speed. Babe Ruth was back in form after his injury at the end of the last season. Red Grange was expected to break more records at Illinois this coming autumn.

Marshal Paul von Hindenburg was the new president of Germany, the first democratically elected leader of the country. Typically, he was a monarchist. Eight years later he would appoint the absurd little man with the funny mustache as chancellor. Governor Al Smith had signed a law permitting 2.75 beer in New York, Chinese nationalists were rioting in the foreign Concession in Shanghai. The United States was back on the gold standard. The *Ile de France* had been launched and would provide luxury accommodations for a few of the half million Americans who would travel to Europe this summer.

I didn't want to be one of that half million.

I threw the paper back on my desk and thought about the telephone in the outer office. A simple call to the office of the Italian-American line would cancel my reservation on the new *Rex*. I could walk over to their office at noontime and collect a refund on my advance payment.

Instead I heaved myself to my feet, took off my jacket and hung it up, and walked over to the window. Dearborn Street was crowded with delivery trucks, most of them horse drawn.

I pushed open the window and breathed deeply the spring air. The clang of streetcar bells—urging the horse-drawn wagons out of their way—drifted up on the warm spring air.

Despite the faint smell of horse manure, it was a nearly perfect spring day, as soothing and tasty as a glass of the most expensive cognac—clear blue sky, light breeze off the lake, temperature in the high seventies. I planned to finish my work for the day by noon and spend the afternoon strolling along the lakefront from Grant Park up to Lincoln Park.

I'd dream of the wonderful buildings I would design someday for the lakeshore. And dream of showing the plans and then the buildings themselves to an admiring April Cronin.

The Rookery was so named because the building that had been on the site before it was constructed—a temporary city hall after the Chicago Fire—had become the headquarters for most of the pigeons in Chicago. The pigeons decamped from the area when the new building was finished, scared by it like a lot of the citizens of Chicago.

Thirty years later in 1925, Mike Hurley, our senior partner, argued, "I don't care whether it's historic, I still like it."

Hurley was no admirer of Frank Lloyd Wright, who had redesigned the lobby so that it looked like a fairyland of wrought iron. But he grudgingly admitted that maybe we could learn from "that son of a bitch." He had signed me on, he insisted, because "you do his kind of design but with common sense"—from Mike the highest of compliments.

He was an infinitely flexible boss. "I don't care whether you ever show up here in this damn masonry mausoleum, so long as you finish your work on time."

Could I wander off to Italy for seven weeks? No reason why not, so long as the design for the Unitarian church in Evanston on which I was working was finished by August 1.

"Finish it in Rome, or, for all I care, Timbuktu."

"What if I finish it before I leave?"

His wise old eyes examined me. "Don't want to see it. The other partners won't like it if you make the job look too easy. Finish the damn thing if you want, only don't show it to me."

I didn't want the church hanging over my head while I was in Rome, so I had just about wrapped it up. I didn't dare tell my parents that I was working on a Protestant, much less a Unitarian church. They would have been convinced that it was a mortal sin.

It would require another week's work to finish the plans for the Evanston church. But now I didn't feel like bending over the drafting board.

There was no denying it: I was in love.

I sighed and picked up my drafting pencil. I tried to concentrate on the spare, low lines of the church whose minister had told me "half fun and full earnest" (as Mom would say) that Unitarianism believed in "one God at the most." I thought that my first drawing, intended as a joke, looked like a miniature Zeppelin hangar. The minister and his committee loved it.

So, I was stuck with a church that even the great Frank Wright would have thought extreme.

Years later the church won me a national prize, a few dollars that at that time looked like a fortune. Even today the pictures of the All Souls Church show up in books about the history of the Third Chicago School. Seems that I anticipated it by a couple of decades.

As a joke.

In those days I thought of myself as a painter by vocation, an architect only to earn a living. Ironically, my paintings never won much notice (mostly because they didn't deserve much notice) and I've achieved a little bit of recognition for my buildings, particularly for my churches.

Whenever I see a picture of All Souls I remember how lovesick I was in the late spring of 1925—completely captivated by April Cronin in a day and a half.

Instead of the balcony for the All Souls choir loft—two slender steel beams as my joke continued—I drew an imaginary body for the face I had already constructed, imaginary in the sense that it was purely speculative.

No one in his right mind, I told myself as I admired the

curves I had created, would decide to marry a woman he had known for only thirty-six hours.

All right, I'd get to know her better. Postpone the nuptials a long time into the future, till, let us say, Christmas.

There could be no doubt, however, that the more I knew April Mae Cronin, the more I would fall under her spell.

She seemed to like me too, a thought that caused me to drop my pencil and stare out the single narrow window, with what I'm sure was a daffy smile on my face.

A classic case of spring fever, a malady to which I've always been prone.

There remained the problem of Jim.

So, I couldn't phone the Italian-American lines, could I?

What was the "decent" thing to do?

It was the word that represented the gentlemanly ideal for my father, an ideal that I respected. I could not escape the conviction that a "decent" man would give Jim the first chance.

But she was the woman in the icehouse at Leavenworth, was she not?

Yet Jim's future depended on his finding the right wife, soon. Jim would finally get himself into some trouble from which his mother's money could not extract him. "He's too cute by half," my mother would say, accurately I was sure.

There were a few rumors in the neighborhood of brushes with the law.

The most serious of which was a shoot-out in a Negro speak at Madison and Halsted. It was serious not because the police would have been upset over disorderly conduct in the Negro neighborhoods, but because the speak was owned by Bugs Moran, a character not likely to take kindly to someone damaging his property.

The bullets in Jim's big lugar were blanks, and I'm told he turned crimson and burbled with delight when the patrons of the speak—Negro and white—dove under the tables.

No one else was amused. Jim was lucky to escape with his life when the manager of the speak, a gentleman who had spent several years in the Joliet prison on a murder charge, found out that his ammunition was phony.

Typically, Jim could not understand why anyone was upset. A few tables and chairs had been damaged, some hooch had been spilled, nothing more. Jim promptly paid for the damages and left a handsome gift to the manager, who warned him that Mr. Moran would appreciate it if he didn't come back.

Jim often insisted that he didn't like colored people. I think he disliked them because somehow they frightened him. However, he had learned to keep his dislike to himself when he was around me.

On the other hand, he was normally charming with Negroes; he laughed and joked and talked their way without patronizing them.

"They're a hell of a lot of fun," he would say. "Really know how to enjoy life."

The individual Negroes of whom he would say something like that were apparently not the same people as those who scared him.

"And their women." He'd shake his head in admiration. "They really know how to be women! Boy, if they were white, I'd marry one."

I thought that wisecracking with Negro women went too far, but they seemed to find him cute and amusing.

As did white women.

He was a strange blend of acute sensitivity and blind insensitivity. I would try to point out his inconsistency but he could never comprehend my arguments.

My father insisted that "the colored" were every bit as "decent" as white people and that there would be no trouble between the races if each "stayed in its own place."

When I was young, that seemed an eminently reasonable

position—separate but equal in words I had not then heard. But as I grew older, I couldn't understand why if they were equal they had to be separate.

I was afraid that Jim would either end up in jail or have his throat cut by some colored person who didn't find his humor amusing.

I realized even that summer that Jim was at some kind of turning point in his life—maybe because he was losing his hair. His jack-in-the-box mask no longer worked quite the way it used to. It seemed frayed around the edges. His gifts were as charming as ever, but his jokes were becoming more dangerous. He was struggling to grow up but he didn't quite know how to do it and receiving little help from his mother for whom he was always her "adorable little boy."

April's prediction that someday he would grow up was accurate enough as a diagnosis, but problematic as a prognosis.

His only hope, I told myself, was marriage to a woman who would straighten him out, the accepted wisdom about wild young men in those days. He needed someone like April, I thought. I wanted her but I didn't need her the same way. The only decent thing to do was to give him first chance.

I am not given to either idealism or self-analysis. I'm a romantic. I've always insisted that my "decent" response to the problem of Jim and April was romantic and not idealist.

Similarly, in 1942 when I was prepared to go off to New Guinea with the Illinois National Guard in the name of decency, the reasons were less ethical ideals, but romantic dreams.

I was saved from those dreams only because someone was more romantic even that I am and ruthlessly so.

But in 1925, my desire for April, also profoundly romantic, challenged my sense of "decency." I would compromise—cancel the trip to Rome but postpone my pursuit of April Mae until Jim had his chance.

Brilliant solution, I told myself, a credit to a politician's son.

Mike Hurley caught me mooning over the drawing board.

"What the hell's the matter with you?" he barked. "I knocked on the door . . . Hey, am I paying you to design churches or nude women?"

Mike's bark was loud, but his bite was nonexistent.

"Sorry," I sighed.

"Is she real?" He adjusted his half glasses to examine the drawing more carefully.

"Yep." I sighed again. "Met her at Twin Lakes on Saturday."

"She pose for you?"

"Nope. But didn't say she wouldn't. Plays the harp," I added fatuously.

"Don't tell me the Irish bachelor is falling in love."

"It could happen."

"Might be a good thing for you." He smiled his vast, kindly smile and leaned his huge bulk against the door-frame. "Are you still going to Rome next week?"

"Sure, why not?"

"I won't argue," he laughed genially, "but only because I've learned that I never get anywhere when I argue with you."

After he left my office, I worried a little more and then went into the outer office and phoned the Italian-American Line and canceled my reservation on the *Rex*.

I returned to my own tiny cubiculum and put the drawing of April in my jacket pocket, with the same reverence a priest would put the ciborium back into the tabernacle.

I concentrated as best I could, with my heart beating rapidly, on All Souls Unitarian Church of Evanston.

A couple of hours later Jim bounded into my office, as usual without knocking.

"Johnny, I've got wonderful news!"

My startled hand jumped an inch, defacing the decoration I was designing for the center of the choir loft rail.

"Knock, damn it!"

"I'm sorry"—his apology was perfunctory—"I'm so excited that I—"

"Did the Board close down early?" I demanded irritably, as I tried to erase the line I had extended. Then I decided it was an interesting addition and left it there.

"It's two o'clock!" He pulled out his big Bulova watch on a gold chain and examined it. "I've been off work for a half hour . . . and you'd never guess what I just bought!"

He danced around the room like half of a vaudeville song-and-dance team.

"What did you just buy?" I asked, as always never able to remain impatient at his enthusiastic innocence.

He reached in the pocket of his white vest, pulled out a small square box, and flipped open the lid.

"See? Isn't it swell? Awful expensive but, of course, I got a deal! Isn't it really swell?"

"It" was an engagement ring, two carats at least. Churlishly I wondered if he had bought it from a fence.

"For April?" I gasped.

"Sure, who else? Won't she love it?" He clasped the box to his chest. "Johnny, tell me she'll love it."

"I'm sure she'll be impressed."

"And you know, Johnny." He continued to prance around my office like a kid in the lion house at the Lincoln Park Zoo. "You know, you were right yesterday about the way I described her. Those are not nice words to use about a woman you're going to marry. A man should have only pure thoughts about such a woman, especially when she is as pure as April is."

I wasn't so sure that a man could possibly have "pure" thoughts about a woman he proposed to take to his bed. Or that April was all that "pure."

"Women are meant to be desired," I said piously, "but respected too."

How respectful was the drawing tucked away in the darkness of my jacket pocket?

Well, a little respectful.

"You're right, Johnny, you're always right. Tell me that she'll say yes."

A puppy dog begging his master for a bone.

"I don't know her well enough to be able to predict," I temporized. "She certainly seems fond of you."

"You know how important this is to me, Johnny." He sat on the windowsill, precariously poised over Dearborn Street. "Gosh, Johnny, I've done some pretty wild things. Sometimes Mom drives me almost crazy. But if April will marry me, I'll settle down and be as normal and sane as you are. I know that. I can't wait to have a home and a family of my own. And it will be perfect, because Momma will simply love April, won't she?"

"Your mother wants the best for you, I'm sure, Jim."

"See! I knew you'd agree. . . . Do you think we could have a double wedding, maybe after Christmas?"

"A double wedding?"

"I mean—" he popped off the window ledge and bounced around my office again—"you and Clarice. I know you think she's a swell kid."

"I'm not sure she's my type, Jim. Don't count on a double wedding."

"I know you like her a lot," he crowed. "It takes a lot of courage to buy a ring and offer it to a girl. You'll see. You'll be in love yourself soon . . . Hey, you want to come have a drink with me and celebrate?"

"I've got some work I have to finish up." I gestured at the plans for All Souls.

"I know a swell speak on South State Street," he grabbed my arm. "It's hard to get in, but some friends of mine told them that I was all right. They have some really swell strippers."

"Sounds like fun, but not this afternoon, I'm afraid."

"I think I'll head over there anyway." He bounced toward the door. "I've got a lot to celebrate. My life is going to change completely."

He bounced out of my office. I sat back in my chair, troubled and dejected.

During my long walk from Grant Park to Fullerton and then over to the El for the ride back downtown I worried only about Jim and myself. Had I found the girl of my dreams only to lose her to a friend?

I was confident that I could beat Jim out if I tried, maybe looking back on my spring romanticism in 1925 altogether too confident.

But ought I to try? My romantic notions of "decency" (or "honor" if you will) said I ought not.

I rode back down to the Loop, walked over to the Italian-American offices on Michigan Avenue and reinstated my reservation for a second-class berth on the *Rex*. The young woman behind the counter looked at me like I was crazy.

Maybe she was right.

25

I saw April next on a black horse in a parade.

I was on the black horse and she was watching the parade surrounded by a crowd of kids.

"Hi, Vangie!" they shouted.

The kids looked like her. Nieces and nephews.

I did not respond or even smile. I resolutely pretended that I did not see or hear them.

That was like pouring gasoline on the fire.

"Vangie," they shouted again. "Wave back!"

The Black Horse Troop was a rigidly disciplined elite group. Its members did not smile, or wave back, or talk to people on the parade route.

Especially kids. The troop's principal purpose (unacknowledged but obvious) was to awe kids, even twenty-year-old kids (especially twenty-year-old-girl kids), scare the hell out of them in fact, but delightfully. Kids would dream about us the night of a parade—a solemn, portentous cavalry troop in black uniforms with silver breastplates, red plumes, carrying big lances and riding jet black horses.

We were the stuff out of which dreams are supposed to be made.

"He smiled," April shouted as we left her little band behind. "He smiled a little, didn't he, kids?"

"Yes, Aunt April," they responded in obedient chorus as my mount and I sauntered out of hearing.

I thought my heart would burst with love for her.

She knew about the parade and about the Black Horse Troop. She was good with kids. She loved parades. She was a grown-up kid herself.

Then I felt sad for her, a little girl only a few years away from her dolls, she was trying to hold on to the joys of childhood and yet fulfill the responsibilities of an adult woman—an impossible task.

Poor kid. But I would love her all my life. And make her happier than she could believe possible.

When I came back from Rome.

She did love parades! I knew she would. One more love we have in common.

I had been a parade freak as long as I could remember. I think I inherited this obsession from my mother. Though she was the least romantic of women, she took me to every parade in Chicago when I was a toddler.

"Look, Jackie," she'd whisper in mock fright, "here comes the Black Horse Troop! Aren't they wonderful fierce now? Sure, you wouldn't want them to be on the other side in a war, would you now?"

Bug-eyed, I agreed that I wanted them on my side.

The troop rarely led the parades. When the city was honoring a visiting dignitary, they rode in front of his carriage, or later his car. On holiday parades, they came toward the end, both to keep little kids anxious as to whether they'd ever come and because the contrast between the scores of bands, noisy and often ragged, and the solemn troop was awesome.

That's what we were designed to be—awesome. At least to kids.

As a bug-eyed kid, I had worshiped these giant men on their horses—which just maybe came straight from hell. As an adult—or maybe, like my love of 1925, a grown-up kid—I reveled in the worship of bug-eyed kids.

Headquarters Troop, 106th Cavalry (Illinois), we were, truth to tell, not much good at anything except parades. We were allegedly an "elite" unit. What else would you be if you wore silver armor and carried massive lances and rode big jet-black horses? Heavy cavalry, right?

Except the machine gun had made cavalry, heavy or light, obsolete in the first months of 1914. Neither the Uhlans nor the Bengal Lancers nor the Zouaves were of much use in trench war against barbed wire and machine gun emplacements. (In 1939, Polish lancers did charge German tanks, proving their courage if not their prudence.)

In 1940 the Black Horse Troop was told that it was now an armored reconnaissance unit, assigned to exploring the terrain ahead of the advancing 33rd Division (Illinois) in Jeeps and light tanks.

Naturally, we didn't have any Jeeps or light tanks, not that they would have done us much good in New Guinea anyway.

So Headquarters Troop (there were no other troops) was fairy-story cavalry, the only kind of soldier that I ever wanted to be after I was discharged from Camp Leavenworth.

Socialite cavalry veterans had organized the unit after the Civil War, veterans whom I suspect never charged a Confederate earthwork. It enabled them to maintain military titles (most of the troop were officers, I was a first lieutenant in 1925), ride horses in parades, stage a formal ball every year, and field a polo team.

I loved horses as much as I loved parades. Dad kept a horse behind our house on West End until 1920. When I was a little boy, he used to take me riding with him. I learned to ride a horse of my own when I was nine. I tried to enlist in a cavalry unit in 1918, but there were no openings and such was my patriotic zeal that I wanted to be a soldier fighting the Hun even if it meant joining the infantry.

So, when I graduated from Armour I asked Dad to pull

a few strings and get me a commission in the National
Guard and as assignment to the Black Horse Troop.

"All right," Dad grunted, "but I won't pay your hospital
bills if you're a big enough damn fool to play polo."

"I'm not that big a fool," I reassured him. "You can get
hurt with those polo mallets."

My responsibilities required that I spend one Saturday
afternoon a month with the horses, who were quartered
then in the armory in Towertown near the Water Tower,
and participate in one of every three parades. There were
more troopers than there were horses so we took turns
riding in parades, a column of forty-eight two-abreast
troopers, solemn and implacable behind an officer dressed
so splendidly that you would think he was at least a field
marshal.

"Gilbert and Sullivan soldiers," April told me at supper
the next night. Then, noting the hurt expression on my
face, she quickly added, "I love Gilbert and Sullivan."

"Our only role"—I tried to sound self-deprecating—"is
to cause delighted shivers in little kids."

"*Well,* I certainly shivered when I saw those grim men
on their big black horses, riding down the street as if they
had conquered the whole city and everyone in it."

"Sometimes we may even conquer a few hearts among
the maidens of the city."

"Not if you don't ever smile. You're so grim I think
you'd scare most maidens away."

"Not the brave ones."

Jim broke into our banter, anxiously directing the conversation back to himself and a prank he had pulled on
some stuffy traders at the Board.

He wasn't aware of the sexual undercurrent in our conversation. He merely wanted to keep himself the center of
the party.

Clarice knew what was happening, however. She smiled
faintly at our exchange and at Jim's intervention. There
was no ill will in her smile. Rather she seemed content

that her friend was as interested in me as I in her.

Poor Clarice. Was she a doomed soul even then? Perhaps. I was so worried about Jim and so frustrated by the conflict within me between desire and "decency" that I paid no attention to Clarice.

If someone had asked about her then, I would have said that a woman so beautiful could not help but have a happy life.

I felt a little ill at ease in my first month in the troop. The North Shore aristocrats (Protestant) who were the bulk of its members were not my kind of people. They were mildly displeased with me when I pleaded that my professional responsibilities made it impossible for me to try out for the polo team (an untruth of which April Cronin would have thoroughly disapproved). But the son of a politician can get along anywhere and with anyone.

The annual formal ball after Labor Day was, I've always thought, the most elaborate and colorful military ball in human history—even if we were useless militarily. As we rode back up Michigan Avenue after the parade that spring of 1925, I proudly pictured the attention April would attract at the ball at the end of the summer; the vapid North Shore young women would be no match for her South Side Irish vitality.

The Michigan Avenue Bridge had been opened only five years before and Pine Street above the bridge had only then become North Michigan. The Drake Hotel, at Oak Street, new at that time, gave a hint of the splendor the avenue would eventually attain. In 1925, Tribune Tower and the Wrigley Building stood as Art Deco sentinels at the opposite end. The rest of the neighborhood was a backwater between the Loop and the Gold Coast, deteriorating two and three flats, small factories, and two breweries.

I didn't pay much attention to the physical environment, however, as we cantered back to the armory. I worried about April. Or rather, I worried about her and me. She was not pretending not to like me. In fact, she seemed unafraid of violating the strictest of the canons of modesty to make her feelings clear.

She must know I felt the same way. The flames of desire were patently dancing back and forth between us. Moreover, we liked one another. Was this not how young people were supposed to feel when they were about to fix on a choice for a permanent partner?

Yet what would she make of my departing, almost as soon as I had met her, for Rome? Would she think I was seeking only a transient flirtation?

How would I explain to her later—if I were given an opportunity to explain or if there was any point in an explanation?

I was at least sensitive enough to know a woman would not like to be told that I was giving my best friend the first chance at her.

How could I explain my trip at the farewell supper that Jim had set up for the next (Sunday) night?

Jim had arranged for the reservations at the College Inn and then at the Lincoln Garden's Cafe. I was not a fan of farewell parties. They brought out the morose side of my personality, a side I did not like. But April wanted a party, she had insisted the night the four of us went to the movies at the Oriental Theater. That meant there would be a farewell party.

The film we had seen was *Tumbleweed* with William S. Hart and Barbara Bedford—tickets bought beforehand by Jim, naturally.

Each of the four of us had a different style of watching the film—Clarice in dead silence; Jim with guffaws at the broad comedy (Hart throwing the villain into a horse trough); I with cynical comments (noting that Hart seemed more heavily corseted than Barbara Bedford); and April with total abandon to the story (when she was not shushing with some asperity my cynicism).

She cried at the lovely old couple, stamped her feet at the villain's cruelty, muttered angrily when Hart and Miss

Beford permitted their romance to go astray, clutched my hand as Hart galloped through the opening rush into the Cherokee Strip, screamed in horror when it seemed that Hart would be killed, cheered wildly when he finally disarmed the bad guys, and wept yet again when he proposed to Miss Bedford.

In the process, she disposed of all of her two pounds of Fanny Mae's and most of mine.

"I loved it," she cooed happily as we walked out of the Oriental.

"You ate the candy," I said, "the way the man in the newsreel eats everything."

One of the segments had been about a certain Nick Tartaglione, allegedly the world's champion eater.

"You only noticed the bathing-beauty contest," she sniffed.

"None of them were as pretty as you and Clarice."

"You'll forget us after five minutes on that mean old boat. That reminds me . . . Jimmy, don't you think we ought to have a farewell party for Vangie?"

"Great idea!" Jim clapped his hands. "We'll go hear his friend Louis Armstrong play!"

So it was settled. Jim and April both loved parties.

I did too, but . . .

As we rode into the armory, I perceived that the dilemma was insoluble. I would have to run the risk of losing April if Jim was to be given a fair opportunity to win her.

Maybe I'd be able to explain somehow when I returned from Rome. But April did not seem to be the kind of young woman who would take kindly to any excuse for my having spurned her, however temporarily.

I rode home on the open upper deck of a Washington Boulevard bus, depressed and moody. I had backed myself into a corner in which love and honor ("decency," as I called the latter) were in immutable conflict.

A romantic trap, fashioned for himself by an incorrigible romantic—one on a big (and very gentle) black horse.

I would never get credit for my sacrifice, I told myself morosely. If Jim married April, he would not realize that I had made it possible for him to pursue and win her. If I married her after she had turned Jim down, he would never forgive me. More mature men than Jim maintained a life-long grudge against successful rivals.

"Don't expect to receive credit for doing the decent thing," Dad had often said. "Not in this world anyway."

I did expect credit, but I didn't think it very likely that I would get any.

"Another rhapsody in blue," I said to her when Jim and I joined her and Clarice at the College Inn for the farewell party.

(Isham Jones and his band were a fixture at the College Inn in those days and his hit song that year was "I'll See You in My Dreams," appropriate sentiments for the party.)

"A response to a concerto in silver and black." She shook my hand firmly. "Hey, doesn't that sound like a wonderful title? 'Concerto in silver and black'? If I had any talent at composition, I might even write it."

"I'm sure you do have the talent."

"Not what my composition teacher said . . . My nieces and nephews were terribly impressed. They said they'd sleep more peacefully at night with you in the Army. No danger of Amd el Krim and his desert warriors taking over Chicago."

April and Clarice and I began to hum "One Alone" from *The Desert Song*.

"Hey, you guys," Jim protested. "Don't embarrass me. Everyone is looking at us."

We stopped singing.

"I have collected affidavits from my nieces and nephews," my love continued, "that you most certainly did smile at us, only a little smile, but a smile just the same . . ."

"Everyone smiles at clowns," I responded. "Especially silly clowns with very funny South Side faces."

"Will you have to face the firing squad for breaking the rules?"

"You or me. I think it had better be you."

Jim interrupted by producing an enormous flask from his coat pocket and pouring us all a drink.

It was first-rate gin.

Perhaps I should explain to those who don't remember Prohibition that almost no one in Chicago took the Volstead Act seriously—even though the headquarters of the Women's Christian Temperance Union, the power behind the act, was in nearby Evanston. There was not a good restaurant in the city that objected to patrons bringing their own hooch to dinner. Routinely, restaurant managers arranged for empty glasses on every table. If the patrons did not fill them at the beginning of dinner, waiters silently removed them.

The evening was fraught with cross-purposes. Jim was trying to impress the young women with his "contacts" at the College Inn and the Lincoln Garden's Cafe. April and I were trying to arrange an agenda for a summer in which I would be absent. Clarice watched in silent amusement.

Jim had provided corsages and more candy for the girls, buttonhole carnations for himself and me, and the best seats in the house. He was beside himself with happiness at the elegance of the party and as determined that we should enjoy ourselves as a kid who is sharing a new toy with his closest playmates.

"Sometimes," I said to her, "we bring the captured maidens and matrons to a military ball at the Drake in early September. It's a very fancy night."

"Do you wear silver armor?"

"It's hard to dance in silver armor, but we do look splendid in black and gold."

"Elite maidens and matrons." She turned up her nose in disdain. "No South Side Irish with apple color in their cheeks need apply."

"There's always a first time."

Jim cut in with a complaint to the waiter.

"Jimmy." April's tone suggested a kindergarten teacher reproving a mischievous child. "The poor dear man is doing his best. You shouldn't embarrass him."

"I'm sorry. I didn't mean to embarrass him. I'll leave him a big tip." Jim's eyes widened in surprise. How could anyone misunderstand his fun? "Honestly I will."

"Money doesn't erase humiliation."

"Why not? If I had his job, it sure would."

At the Lincoln Garden's Cafe, Louis Armstrong himself came over to meet my party. I introduced him to April and Clarice. Jim, he already knew.

"Miss Cronin is a musician too, Louis," I said (I never could call him "Satchmo"). "She plays the harp, two of them actually."

"Hey." He bowed over her hand. "Maybe the Hot Five should add a harpist."

April was so awed by the presence of fame that she had no riposte other than, "I hope you'll play 'Big Butter and Egg Man from the West.'"

"For you, Miss Cronin"—he bowed again and smiled—"we'll play it the long way."

Louis was twenty-four that summer, as marvelously handsome as he was incredibly gifted. Married to Lillian then and happy in the marriage, he was at the prime of the first phase of his career though even greater achievements were yet to come. Still, his trumpet solo in "Butter and Egg" (the title means small-time big spender) was hailed even then as worthy of Mozart or Schubert.

"You take care of yourself on your trip, Mr. John, you hear?"

"I'll be here the first week I'm back."

"Give this to the band for us." Jim slipped an envelope into Louis's pocket.

"I sure will." He rolled his eyes. "You are one nice man, Mr. Jim."

Jim glowed with pride.

It was at least a five-hundred-dollar tip. Jim did not understand anything about jazz, so he didn't comprehend how great Louis was. But he knew that the Hot Five were class, so he treated accordingly.

Louis winked at me as he walked back to the band, just to make sure that I knew it wasn't the envelope that had brought him over to our table. I winked back.

"Isn't he a gorgeous man," April sighed, "just the most gorgeous man you've ever seen?"

"April!" Clarice protested, almost automatically. "He's colored!"

"I don't care." April lifted her drink. "There's nothing wrong with being colored. Those poor people are every bit as good as we are, maybe better. It's a shame they're not Irish like we are but, as my mother says, not everyone can be Irish and it might be a dull world if they were."

I almost laughed. Then I realized from the serious cast to her brown eyes that she meant every word of it: God had somehow erred in not creating the world entirely Irish, but given that mistake the other people were every bit as good as the Irish, and maybe a little better.

It's one approach to tolerance and equality.

"South Side Irish," I murmured.

"Of course." She smiled benignly at me.

"Isn't he swell!" Jim pointed at Louis who was just swinging into "Butter and Egg." "Isn't he wonderful!"

To my astonishment, Jim left us early at the Lincoln Garden's Cafe. "Momma expects me home for the end of a party she's giving for her friends. You know what Momma is like."

"That's no way to court a girl," I told him as I walked him to the door.

"You know Momma," he repeated. "Hey"—he grabbed my hand and pumped it up and down—"have a swell time in Rome. Meet a lot of swell girls."

"I'll try to enjoy myself."

"Say a prayer for me next weekend, will you please?

I'm going to give her the ring up at Twin Lakes."

"I hope everything works out."

"We'll be married right after Christmas. Momma will like her, I just know she will. Won't she, Johnny?"

"How can anyone not like her?"

"Right. She's such a swell girl. Momma has to like her."

As I walked back to my two dates, I thought that there was absolutely no chance that Mrs. Clancy would like April. On the contrary, she would hate her. And there was not much more chance that April would accept his ring.

Still, women were unpredictable. Who could tell what April might do?

I danced with both of them before I brought them back to Canaryville.

"April doesn't understand why you're going off to Europe," Clarice informed me bluntly while we danced.

She was surely a beauty, light and sweet in my arms. If it were not for April, I might fall for her after all. Romantic that I was, I felt sure I could protect her from her vicious father.

"It's part of my professional training," I lied. "I really must take advantage of the opportunity."

"She'll miss you."

"It's only a few weeks."

"She'll be unhappy all summer."

"I'll write," I lied again.

The next dance was a Charleston.

"I don't do that dance," Clarice insisted.

"I do!" April jumped and dragged me back toward the dance floor. "Now remember, Vangie, up on your heels, down on your toes. Say it after me!"

Dutifully I echoed her. "Up on your heels down on your toes."

After the dance, she observed that I showed some signs of improvement.

"And you don't stare at my legs anymore."

"Yes I do. I've learned to be more discreet."

"Fresh." She dragged me back to the table. "Your turn, Clarice. He really is quite hopeless."

"You don't miss Jim at all, do you?"

"You're entirely too perceptive, Clarice Powers."

Do I have to say that the taxi stopped first at Clarice's house?

I paid off the taxi driver in front of April's house on Emerald.

"Planning on staying in the neighborhood overnight?" she asked.

"On the South Side? My life would be in danger. I'll take the streetcar home—Halsted to Madison."

The homes on her block, the famous and fashionable 4200 block on Emerald, were big and elegant, hiding behind vast trees and faintly illumined by gaslights. The important people who lived on Emerald preferred gaslight to electricity and were affluent enough to have their way. We walked slowly down the street, in no hurry to say good-bye.

Somehow, our hands were linked.

"Were you ever very sick?" she asked. "I keep thinking that somehow I saw you when you were sick, so sick that your face was blue. I know it's silly but I keep seeing that picture."

I squeezed her hand. "I've never been sick in my life, knock on wood. Except, when I was in the Army, I had the Spanish flu. Collapsed on the parade ground. At first they thought I was dead."

"My aunt and uncle died from it," she said softly. "So did lots of people. You're lucky to be alive."

"I know."

We had reached the corner. Silently we turned back toward her house.

"Did it have an effect on your life?"

"Some, maybe. I guess I'm not as ambitious as I might have been. I don't want to be the richest architect in the world."

"Daddy says you're a very good architect, maybe the best at your age in the city."

"How does Daddy know?"

"He asked people, silly!"

Her father was checking up on me? I was both offended and delighted.

"Why?"

"I guess because his daughter came home from Twin Lakes and told him about this funny boy who stared at her all weekend long."

"Lasciviously?"

"What does that mean?"

I felt my face flame. "Lustfully."

"I didn't tell Daddy that."

"Is he mad at you for meeting a boy from the West Side?"

"He says your father is an honest politician, of which there are not many in the Republicans. . . . Are you really a *Republican*?"

"I'm a secret Democrat, but I haven't told my father."

"*Well*, I'm glad of that."

We walked up the stairs to the front porch of the Cronin home, a broad shelf that extended around three sides of the vast house. A big oak tree obscured the pale streetlight. We were alone in almost total darkness.

There was no one else in the whole world. It was a warm, soft night in spring, with the scent of roses in the air. And a delicious woman suddenly in my arms.

If this were not love, then love did not exist.

Our lips met and fused. Our bodies merged, struggling to occupy the same space. Then there was no longer any time. Or any space. The two of us were on a distant star, united in body and soul forever.

My fingers explored her body, delicate throat, firm breasts, solid hips, harsh stays in her corset (yes, even flappers wore them). She moaned softly as I probed but did not try to pull away from me. On the contrary, she clung even more desperately to my waist.

I almost told her I loved her.

Then, in unspoken agreement, we parted.

"My," she sighed. "You bring out the harlot in me."

Not a word that a convent girl should use.

"You're not a harlot," I said, trying to recapture my breath.

"I suppose not. Poor things probably don't enjoy it. I guess I do. I think we'd better say good night now."

"Good night, April Mae Cronin."

"Good night, John Evangelist O'Malley."

Our lips touched again, quickly, carefully.

"Promise me you'll write often."

"Every day," I lied.

It was a long ride home on the streetcar.

26

April is not mentioned once in the diary I kept of my journey to Rome.

I'd like to think the tic-tac-toe doodles (the craze started that summer) in my notebook represented periods when I mooned over her.

In fact, they are doubtless attempts to figure out you could always win the game.

Stuffed in the back pages of the notebook, however, are the love letters I wrote to her from Rome.

The diary rests on the desk in front of me now. My son has pasted a label on it that informs the world in his bold, blunt printing, "Rome Diary, Personal and Confidential. Not to be opened without written permission of author."

The diary can be trusted, I think, in what it says. But its pretense that there was no such person as April Mae Anne (with an *e*) Cronin is dishonest. My resolution to give Jim Clancy a fair chance was honored even in my diary, which no one but me would ever read.

I did not brood about April during my voyage and my stay in Rome. Yet, she was always on my mind, lingering at the edge of my consciousness, like an image for a portrait that I would paint someday.

I didn't mail the love letters, written when my love affair, if that's what it was, with Siobahn was tormenting me. To mail them would have compromised the integrity of my noble decision, as it seemed, to give Jim Clancy his chance.

I won't quote the letters. They are even more embarrassing than my diary. The boy who wrote them, however, was very much in love, more than he realized.

In a way, I suppose you could say that April lurked even in the pages of the diary, her pert nose upturned in dismay at the foolish late adolescent whose heart she had captured.

Consider this excerpt written the third day at sea on the *Rex*:

Until this summer I thought there was no hurry about marriage. Did not my father survive as a bachelor till his middle forties? Now I can hardly wait till I have a wife. I must be candid about this change: It is mostly a biological need that either I did not recognize before—which given the force of the need seems unlikely—or that has suddenly exploded in me. On ship to Cherbourg last summer, I hardly noticed women. This summer I find myself noticing women of whatever age from schoolgirls to matrons in their forties.

Not to put too fine an edge on my desires I want to take to bed almost any presentable woman I encounter, regardless of her state in life. Mind you, I have no wish to force or to hurt such a woman. On the contrary, I yearn to overwhelm her with tenderness and affection.

Can it be that attraction to one woman excites attraction to all women?

This biological need is not unpleasant. I am more alert, more interested in the world, more careful to record my emotions in this diary, and my images in a sketchbook, more friendly, even charming, with my fellow passengers. The quiet recluse on the *Norman-*

die has become a delightfully witty young man on the
Rex.

A young man, I hasten to add in the name of honesty, whose reaction to the bodies of women is that
of a fifteen-year-old.

All true enough, if self-conscious and precious. But not
a word about the woman who had stirred up all this hunger.

There are many pages about Laura, the Bryn Mawr student who was my shipboard romance. I will not quote
them because now they seem embarrassingly infantile. My
sketches of her seem to have been lost long ago. Since I
rarely throw out sketches by accident or mistake, I must
have deliberately disposed of them.

The shipboard romance is a pleasant institution that I
presume arose sometime in the early part of the last century when Atlantic passenger crossings ceased to be a life-
risking adventure. Since there is not much to do on a
crossing and since the odds are against meeting a fellow
passenger ever again, the temptation to fight boredom with
romance is almost irresistible, at least among those trav-
eling in first and second class. Unattached men and women
(and many that were attached) paired off, sometimes with
ruthless efficiency, on the first day and settled down with
one another for the rest of the trip.

Since the voyage is likely to occupy a week at the most,
seduction must proceed quickly if precious time is not to
be wasted. The degree of potential involvement must also
be specified, however implicitly, so that the two partners
need not consume their limited energies in clarifying that
which they are willing to give to one another.

How many such liaisons became liaisons? How much
hasty coupling took place in cramped bunks and dark cabins?

My guess was and is that most such romances were
consummated at least once or twice. Was not that the point

of it all? Did not the whole ritual aim at brief release of tension and satisfaction of curiosity—as well as sweet memories to be recalled in subsequent nostalgia, sweeter usually in recollection than the events had been in reality?

I chose a pretty, fragile girl, prone to motion sickness, homesick because of her first separation from her family, one whom only the cruelest exploiter would proposition. The reason must have been that, however frantic my biological desires, all I wanted was companionship—and perhaps someone to nurture and protect.

Poor Laura. I wonder what ever happened to her. She is probably an affluent and contented grandmother somewhere along the Philadelphia Main Line, with only the most vague memories of her crossing on the *Rex* in the late spring of 1925.

Could I have dragged her into bed with me? It would have been the easiest thing in the world. In her vast gray eyes there was total surrender the first time I took her into my arms. She was a victim looking for a predator, not exactly wanting to be taken, it seemed to me, but helpless to prevent it.

Even without my Headquarters Troop silver armor I was the good knight protecting a fair damsel. Laura and I huddled in each other's arms, kissing and caressing with gentle affection, while we shared our deepest secrets.

Not so deep, however, that I told her about April.

She was to spend the summer in Florence. The last time I saw her was in the old *stazzione* in Rome. We had come up from Naples, alone together in a compartment on the *Settebello*. We had clung desperately to one another on the trip, although not so desperately that Laura had not slept part of the way. We exchanged Italian addresses, promised that we would see each other during the summer, swore eternal loyalty, and kissed passionately before I scrambled off the train.

I'm sure we both meant every word of our vows at the moment we spoke them.

But by the time I had unpacked (matched luggage that had been a going-away present from Jim) and was settled that afternoon in my *pensione* and she caught her first sight of the Arno, those vows were already being transformed into nostalgic memory.

As proof, I cite the embarrassing entry in my diary:

Although I will never see her again, I know that I will never forget Laura and the brief love we shared this glorious spring.

The truth is that, until I opened my diary to use it as a resource for this memoir, I had forgotten her completely.

As more people, especially young people, cross the Atlantic in airplanes, the shipboard romance will disappear. It will be a mixed blessing. The memories that will be lost are sweeter than the actuality. But after a certain age in life, you want to preserve as many memories as you can, especially if you are an incorrigible romantic.

There were two other young women that summer, Siobahn, an Irish girl staying at the same pensione, and Paola, young assistant bursar on the *Rex* whom I encountered on the return trip.

I was cultivating frustration that summer, exulting in my sacrifices in the name of my lost April.

My diary is much more useful in recalling Rome:

There are at least four different Romes. The first is pagan Rome, the ruins of the empire, the Forum, and the other monuments, like Hadrian's Tomb. Although I came here to study the architecture of that world, I confess I find pagan Rome dull. I've never been one to enjoy staring at the monuments of the past all that much. I'll do my sketches and study the decoration, but only because that's the excuse I gave Mike Hurley for the trip.

Then there is ecclesiastical Rome. While it is unthinkable to me that I'll ever be anything but a Catholic, it is the Irish American (West Side Chicago) variety to which I'm committed and not the empty churches, scruffy clergy, and pompous pageantry of Rome's version of Roman Catholicism. I attended a papal audience before His Holiness went up to the hills for the summer. I was utterly unimpressed. What good is all the display when the people of the city never go to church and hate their clergy?

I love modern Rome, the vibrant people, the noise, the smell, the rush of bicycles, carriages, and an occasional auto, the Piazza Farnese, Santa Maria in Trastevere, the train rides down to the beaches at Ostia, the open-air cafes. My sketchbook is always open when I walk through the city. It's probably blasphemous to say so, but I like modern Rome because it reminds me so much of Chicago.

As for Fascist Rome, the Rome of the crowds shouting "Duce! Duce!" in the Piazza Venezia, Siobahn says it perfectly, "frigging musical comedy."

Maybe Mussolini has made the trains run on time, but I can't imagine anything more alien to this city than the Fascist pretense at order and discipline. The Romans love a show and Il Duce provides a show. Otherwise, the city goes on its own languid, corrupt, charming way. The popes were unable to change it. Surely a second-rate journalist won't be able to change it.

Not all Americans here agree.

Siobahn was the girl from Dublin, as brilliant a woman as I've ever known, intelligent, funny, outrageous. She was the daughter of a "barrister," which is what they call a lawyer (imitating the English, I used to tell her), and had inherited from her father a contentious legal mind and, by her own admission, a skill at obscene, profane, and scatological language of which most men would be justly proud.

I find that the only time I quoted such language in my diary was in her comment about the Fascists—and even there I cleaned it up, although she did say "frigging" occasionally when she wanted to tease me.

The first day at the pensione Siobahn discovered I was shocked by her vocabulary. So, naturally, she did all she could for the rest of my time in Rome to shock me even more.

I did not say so in my diary, but, vocabulary aside, she might well have been a product of Canaryville, April Cronin with a brogue.

She was supposed to be studying music in Rome, piano with a "wee gombeen man over in Trastevere who can't keep his filthy hands off my pure Catholic body."

"I sympathize with his temptation."

"Go long with you, you may be a Yank, but you're still an Irish Catholic when it comes to women."

There were a number of participles and adjectives that I have omitted from that quote.

To show her I was not, I swept her into my arms, kissed her solidly, and caressed her forcefully. Which was exactly what she wanted.

"You're a great terrible rapist," she protested insincerely. Again I censor her exact words.

Music was not her main interest in Rome, however. In fact, she was relatively indifferent to it. "My father is after getting me out of Dublin because he thinks I'm a hellion and it's safer to have a hellion daughter in Rome than in Dublin."

That was perhaps not altogether true either. Siobahn was given to raising hell all right—wading in Roman fountains long before Fellini thought of it, drinking wine all afternoon, flirting with every male she encountered at the English Tea Shop at the foot of the Spanish Steps (quoting Keats as she did so)—but, with one exception, chances of getting her into bed were minimal to nonexistent.

"I'm a great frigging Irish prude," she would announce, "terrified of sex and men and the whole frigging reproductive process."

She was a wondrous Irish beauty, a figure from a Pre-Raphaelite painting: pale cream skin, long, shiny black hair, a lithesome figure that hinted at both delicacy and strength, rich blue eyes. More ethereal perhaps than April Cronin, whose exact appearance I could not always recall as the summer wore on (I had virtuously left my sketches of her at home).

"You will make some Irishman a fine, lustful wife," I would respond.

"I might and then again I might not." She would tilt her chin up defiantly and pour us some more wine, a small draft for me and a very large one for her.

"Ah, sure," I'd imitate her brogue, "you'd at least keep the bed warm on a damp Dublin evening."

"If I were after letting him sleep in my bed."

"If you were my woman, Siobahn, you'd have no choice in the matter."

"We'd have to see about that, wouldn't we now? ... And would you ever stop drawing those frigging pictures of me? It interferes with enjoying this wonderful Frascati."

She filled up both our glasses; I closed my notebook and put it on the empty chair between us.

"You're the boss, ma'am."

"Sure, I'm not worth drawing."

"You must know better than that, Siobahn." I toasted her gravely.

"I don't at all, at all," she insisted. "I'm just a fat Irish cow."

I think she half believed that nonsense.

I didn't save any of my sketches of her either, a fact I now profoundly regret.

She was too much for me altogether—too smart, too quick, too unpredictable. And, looking back on it, she was too confused about who she was and what she wanted out of life. She was fun and she was a torment.

"You'd be after having a Yank girlfriend," she insisted that afternoon as we strolled down the Via Veneto, not quite the smart street it would later become or the tourist trap it would still later turn into. "Some immoral Protestant girl with a big body, no doubt."

(I continue to edit her expressions.)

"Woman, I do not."

Well, April wasn't Protestant.

"You're just using me for your own pleasure while you're away from home."

"If it is pleasure I'm after I'd be using you a lot more . . . and aren't you having a fella drinking his heart away in a Dublin pub waiting for you to come back?"

"I do not," she insisted rather too quickly.

It was a hot, languid day. When we arrived back at our pensione behind the Street of the Covered Shops, everyone was at their siesta, the only sensible way to pass the Roman afternoon.

"Like I said, woman"—I imprisoned her in my arms—"if you were mine, you'd sleep in my bed and not just at night."

"Great frigging Yank rapist," she sighed.

Our embrace was more passionate than usual.

"I'm not so sure you could keep me in your bed," she said with a gasp when we were finished. "But it would be interesting to find out, wouldn't it now?"

"It would."

"But it would have to be a damp day in Dublin for a valid experiment, if you take my meaning."

She turned and ran down the corridor to her room.

I wondered what would happened if I followed her. I guess I was afraid to find out.

I went back to my room and, instead of taking a sensible nap, wrote another letter to April. I think I tore it up, but since I don't remember the date of our conversation about a damp day in Dublin, I can't be sure.

It was in the middle of the Roaring Twenties, though we didn't know they were roaring yet. Given the way I came into the world, I can hardly claim that there was a sexual revolution in that decade. It's been my observation that each older generation thinks that something has happened that has corrupted its young—a war, the automobile, jazz, prohibition—and each younger generation thinks that it has invented sex. Both conceits are at best exaggerations. The power of the reproductive urges and the agony of human loneliness being what they are, the young will experiment as much as they can. Free them from supervision and control, even for a few weeks, and their play will become passionate.

Still, there were changes in the Roaring Twenties. Women had the vote now and with it, through some chemistry I didn't quite understand, the right to drink and smoke in public. The flapper was more sexually available and more explicit about her availability than her mother would have been. April Cronin, heaven knows, was more explicitly willing than either my mother or her mother would have been.

· Yet, it was only a matter of degree and sometimes not much of a degree. I'm sure my mother seduced my father with the stained-glass window of St. Catherine's Church lurking outside her window behind the oak tree (for which I am necessarily grateful to her), probably without any overt sexual conversation at all. And as for April Mae, a flapper she doubtless was, but an Irish Catholic (South Side) flapper, which made a big difference.

(I think I have been unfair earlier in this memoir to my father's uncle, who was only a few years older than Dad. I suggested that he would have been shocked and dismayed at my "premature" arrival as a healthy six-pound boy. Now I think he probably smiled ruefully and wondered, perhaps with a laugh over the strange ways of God, whether I had been conceived in his rectory. He may even have shared my delight at the likelihood that I was indeed conceived there.)

That which existed between Siobahn and me in Rome those weeks was probably not untypical of any two young people free from family and community at any time in human history—save perhaps for my romantic restraint, of which to tell the truth I am not completely ashamed even now.

My chivalry (silver armor, black horse, red plume) was put to the ultimate test on an afternoon in late July, perhaps a week before I was to leave Rome. It was unbearably hot, the air still as though all the breezes were taking a siesta too. I awoke from a nap, drenched in sweat and sexually hungry. I wanted her and I wanted her now.

I pulled on shirt and trousers and tiptoed down to Siobahn's room.

I hesitated at the door. I was about to do something that was wrong. Even sinful. Perhaps I ought to bravely resist the temptation.

It was not very sinful, however. And, besides, it was mostly a dream. Maybe completely a dream.

I wish I could say that I thought of my love for April and that caused me to hesitate. Alas for my purity, I had forgotten completely about her.

I knocked lightly on the door.

"Yes?"

"John."

I heard the sound of the key being turned. The door opened. Siobahn, clad in a thin slip and looking tousled from her nap, peered out.

"What do you want?" she demanded.

"You." I shoved the door open.

She stepped back, uncertain but not resistant.

I entered the room, closed the door and locked it, and captured her in a furious embrace.

Her heart was pounding beneath my hands, she was

shivering with fright, but again she did not resist me.

I shoved the slip off her shoulders and continued my assault.

"Please," she begged meekly. "Please, John, don't."

She sounded like she meant it.

She would not, perhaps could not, fight me off. But she still would rather not.

"I love you," I said, at the moment believing it.

"I love you too," she moaned, "but please, not now."

"You mean that?"

"God help me, I do."

There was, I knew, indeed a boy waiting in Dublin, someone she loved as much as I loved April. Lucky boy.

I drew the slip back over her breasts and restored its straps to her shoulders.

"I'm sorry," I said, leading her to the single chair in the narrow room.

"I'm the one who should be saying that," she said miserably.

I kissed her forehead. "I'll never forget you," I said, this time meaning it. "Or this moment."

She shook her head. "You think me a terrible, terrible tease."

"Woman, I do not. And the boy in Dublin is a lucky man."

"Ah, sure"—her crooked grin returned—"so is that frigging lass in Chicago."

When we said good-bye in the Stazzione Termini we exchanged home addresses and promised to stay in touch.

"I'm sorry, Johnnio," she sighed.

"For what?"

"I'm not sure. But what's the point in being Irish unless you can feel guilty at a leave-taking."

"I have no complaints against you, Siobahn."

"Nor I against you, God knows." She kissed me lightly. "Does that lass who's dying to see you back in Chicago play the piano now?"

. "She's not the kind who would die to see anyone. The harp, as a matter of fact. Two harps, one that she insists on calling Irish, thought I tell her it's Gaelic."

"Glory be to God!"

"And that Mick who's pining away in the Dublin pub, does he have red hair?"

"He does, the bastard. And he's in no pub, let me tell you. He's probably chasing some West of Ireland slut out in Salt Hill."

We both laughed, sad at our parting, but not broken-hearted. At all, at all, as she would have said.

We exchanged marriage announcements and still exchange Christmas cards. My wife and I visited her and her family in Dublin when we made our first trip there after the war. She had not changed much, not even her vocabulary, and was obviously happily married. The electricity between us had not changed either.

I was still proud of my restraint. And regretful too.

I was miserable, lonely, frustrated on the ride back to Naples.

But life was quickly renewed when Paola checked me on board the *Rex* and showed me to a cabin with three bunks, though she assured me with a twitch of her eyebrow that I would be the only one in the cabin for the trip.

Diminutive Paola, with dark flashing eyes and an exquisite little body, a bright, budding flower, was not only willing to be seduced; she did everything she could to seduce me on the week-long trip from Naples back to New York. I enjoyed her assaults, truth to tell, and enjoyed my own tactics to keep her at bay. Alas for her, I felt no longing for that sumptuous form, even when it was naked in my cabin, posing at her insistence for my art, with her Carmelite scapular lying contentedly between her large breasts.

My son, whose obsession with such art exceeds mine, has catalogued those operas, in his insolent, insensitive script, as "Nude with Scapular, Watercolor," "Nude with

Scapular, Sketch #1," and so on up to Sketch #5. They are as close to pornographic as any of my paintings have ever come. They are not saved by the scapular, incidentally; it only makes the drawings more lecherous. They are salvaged rather by the innocence in her dark eyes, an innocence that I think was really there and not a phenomenon I saw because I wanted to see it.

Why did I keep those drawings, which might well be thought to be incriminating, and destroyed portraits of Laura and Siobahn that would have seemed, I'm sure, totally innocent?

Probably because the two latter young women had been a threat to my virtue, such as it was, and Paola was an innocent amusement.

Infinitely adaptable survivor that she was, she adjusted to the role, demanding only that I paint a watercolor for her.

I would have had no guilty feelings at all, if she had not wept when I gave her the finished painting.

At twenty-five, I thought I was a mature man of the world, perhaps (in my despondent moments) too old for my fresh young April flower.

Now I realize I was a callow, blundering youth.

Yet there was some slight hint of maturity in my behavior that glorious summer—a summer in which, as I'm sure is obvious, I was gloriously happy despite (and maybe because of) my romantic problems and uncertainties.

As evidence that I was not completely juvenile, I cite this passage in my diary, written on my penultimate day on the *Rex*.

I'm thinking now about New York and then Chicago. Who will I want to call when I disembark? My parents, to assure them that I'm home safe and sound (and with some guilt for having deprived them of my presence in lives which will certainly not last too much longer).

Friends? Jim Clancy, naturally, to see if he has managed to keep himself out of trouble while I've been away.

Who else?

Do I have no friends?

That can't be true. At work, in the neighborhood, in the troop, there are many men who would claim that I was their friend. But I have not missed them, and I suspect that they have hardly noticed my absence. I'm a pleasant enough fellow, but I have no deep friendships. The only friend I worry about is one who is utterly dependent on me.

I suppose the situation is the result of being the only son of loving parents. I never really have needed anyone else.

Perhaps I should marry soon, lest I turn into an utterly secure bachelor who needs and wants no intimacy in his life.

That would be almost as bad as hell.

Maybe that's what hell is.

I phoned Jim from my room in the Taft, immediately after my call to my parents.

"Hey, Johnny, swell to have you back. You meet any great girls on your trip?"

He sounded more agitated than ever before, almost frenzied. Had something gone wrong?

"A few. What's been happening in your life?"

"Banged up the Duesy. Momma was furious. Threatened to take it away from me, but she calmed down."

"That all?"

"Well, there's a great new strip joint on State Street, really swell stuff. I know you don't like that kind of thing, but it's sensational."

"Oh?"

"And a nigger cathouse on Thirty-fifth street. You really

ought to let me take you there. Niggers enjoy it, they don't have moral hang-ups like white women."

"I don't think so . . . what about April?"

"April? Oh, she wouldn't dream of sleeping with me. If she would, I'd stay away from the nigger hookers. Well, maybe I would. Men have their needs, you know."

"Did she take your ring?"

My heart did indeed seem to be in my throat.

"The ring? Oh, no. She didn't take it but she didn't say she wouldn't. So, I keep trying. I think she'll take it by Labor Day. She sure is a swell girl. Maybe when you get back, you can put in a good word for me. She really likes you. Keeps asking if I hear from you. I tell her you don't write much."

She hadn't said either yes or no.

I sat there on the edge of my bed, staring at the phone. Nothing had been solved at all.

~ 27 ~

"She turned him down as gently as she could." Clarice Powers was dancing more closely to me than she had before I left for Europe. I drew her even closer to me, pressing her breasts against my chest. She did not resist.

"So she's not thinking of marrying him," I said, trying to hide my relief.

We were at the Twin Lakes dance hall on the Friday of the third weekend in August, expecting April and Jim the next morning.

"I didn't say that," she murmured into my chest. "She turned him down but left the door open. I don't think she'll marry him, but she feels sorry for him and wants to help him. Besides, no one else has asked her to marry."

I had continued to worry about my phone conversation with Jim. Had he really sounded more frantic than ever before? Or had he been deteriorating before I left for Europe, but so gradually I had not noticed?

My first two weeks back in the States had been frustrating. Mike Hurley wanted me to design another church, immediately. I was obliged to spend a weekend at the armory with the horses. Jim was elusive, in and out of town on mysterious business and too busy with his Board of Trade obligations to spend any time with me.

I didn't feel that it would be right to call April on the phone.

I had hardly been back in Chicago for twenty-four hours when my mother asked me, "what ever happened to that nice young girl from St. Gabriel's you met up at Twin Lakes?"

"Which nice young girl?"

"The little Cronin girl?"

"She's not very little, Mom."

"Have you talked to her since you came home?"

"Not yet."

"Did she write you?"

"I don't think she knew my address."

"You didn't give it to her?"

"She didn't ask for it."

Mom threw up her hands and walked out of the parlor.

As my second weekend back home drew near, no one seemed inclined to invite me to go up to Barry for the weekend. I resolved that I would stay home in Chicago unless someone wanted me at the lake.

Had no one besides my parents missed me?

Jim called my office on Thursday afternoon. Mike Hurley summoned me away from my drafting table. "Your crazy friend Clancy on the phone, Jack. He sounds even crazier than usual, by the way. . . . How did he survive all summer when you weren't around to take care of him?"

"His momma kept him out of trouble."

"You have a nasty wit when you want to," Mike chuckled. "I don't know why you waste time with him."

"I'm an idealist." I picked up the phone. "O'Malley speaking."

"Who else would it be?" Jim sounded genuinely puzzled. "I asked for you."

"I'm terribly busy, Jim."

"Do you have to work on Saturday?" he whined, as he always did when he wanted something from me.

"Probably."

"I thought you were planning on Twin Lakes."

"No."

"I thought you would help me persuade April to marry me."

"No one can do that for you, Jim."

"But you're my best friend!"

"I'm not a marriage broker."

"Oh." He sounded hurt. And manic. Almost desperate. "Well, would you come up anyway? April wants to hear about your trip to Europe."

"Does she?" My heart skipped several beats.

"She thought we'd see you last week."

"I spent all day Saturday at the armory."

"Well, she'd really like to see you this weekend."

Did she or was it Jim's imagination? Was he counting on me to plead his case once he had lured me onto the Barry grounds?

"I don't know that I can make it," I lied.

"Well, we're driving up on Friday night. There's no room for you in the car, so maybe you can take the Saturday train."

"God forbid that Dr. Cronin's daughter would have to ride on the Northwestern."

"What do you mean?" He was puzzled again, irony always puzzled him.

"Look, Jim, I'll see what I can do, but don't count on me, all right?"

"Gee, it sure would be swell if you could join us. Just like old times."

I hung up, impatient with him and impatient with myself. Jim was a nuisance. Why did I put up with him? And if I was going to put up with him, why was I not more tolerant of his peculiarities?

Still, I worried about him. Was he about to have a nervous breakdown? Or, as my father said about a political colleague who had suffered a breakdown, how could anyone tell the difference?

I was also tired of hearing him sing April Cronin's praises. She was, I told myself riding home on the Lake Street El that night, a decidedly overrated young woman.

Why couldn't she make up her mind about Jim and end his anxieties, one way or another?

Even if she did decide that she didn't want his (probably stolen) diamond, I probably wasn't interested in her anymore.

Sweet little Cronin girl, indeed.

"Mom," I said impatiently the second time the subject came up. "She is not little. She's at least five feet seven, maybe five feet eight. And she's not really sweet either. She's a flapper." And then with sudden inspiration, "She dances the Charleston."

"Did she teach you how to do it?"

"She tried."

"I think that was very nice. You weren't a wallflower on the boat."

"I don't do it very well."

Friday morning I packed my duffel bag for the weekend. At breakfast I told Mom that I might just catch the late afternoon train to Twin Lakes.

"That's nice."

"You didn't ask whether the little Cronin girl is going to be there."

"She's not little, is she?"

We both laughed and I hugged Mom as I left for the El. She and April would get along all too well if they ever met one another.

The whole world was conspiring to find me a wife.

I met Clarice Powers on the train with a group of young women from the South Side.

"Welcome home," she said simply, shaking hands with me. "I've persuaded my friends that Wisconsin is more fun than Grand Beach. Easier to get booze."

"In Europe we didn't have to worry about Prohibition."

I would not ask her about April.

"April is driving up tomorrow with Jim."

"Tomorrow?"

"Something came up tonight. You know how Jim is about his mysterious business." Then she added, "Her father doesn't exactly like Jim, but he's not mean like my father."

"He didn't stop you this weekend, did he?"

"Only because he's in California again." Her lips curled into a sneer. "With his California women."

I had no response for that.

When I checked in at the Drake, I asked for the room with Mr. Clancy at the Blackstone.

"Mr. Clancy"—Mrs. Kennelly, the elderly woman clerk (a friend of Mom's from the West Side), did not look up from her register—"has reserved a single room here at the Drake."

In the same cabin with April? I felt my fist clench.

"I see."

The woman looked up at me with kind gray eyes. So she was one of the sources of Mom's intelligence about the "sweet little Cronin girl."

"It's going to be a crowded weekend. We do have a small room at the back of the priests' house."

"I'm not a priest, Mrs. Kennelly."

"You're an unmarried young man."

"The worst kind." I grinned and she grinned back.

"Your mother would be happy, I'm sure, if you became a priest." She turned the register in my direction.

I signed in. "Nowadays she'd be satisfied if I were a married man."

"Happily married." She gave me the key.

"Naturally."

"By the way, John," she called after me, "there are some Gypsies in the area. Fortune-tellers. They seem harmless, but don't leave anything valuable lying around."

"I don't own anything valuable, but thanks for the warning."

My room at the priests' house had probably been a large closet. It was so small that there was hardly room in it for me and the bed. Not a place suited for fornication.

I laughed to myself at the thought. I didn't think it possible that fornication could occur within the precincts of Barry. I wasn't even sure that married love was permitted in its thinly partitioned rooms.

I wandered back to the Drake and, in the fading light, found Clarice—dressed in sports clothes appropriate for a golf course—sitting on a bench by herself.

"Golf anyone?"

"This dress is only for sitting and looking."

"And being looked at?"

She blushed. "Not much to look at, I'm afraid."

"You know better than that. May I look?"

"I can't stop you." She turned her back toward me.

But she didn't seem to object to my suggestion that we walk over to the dance hall.

"All right," she said flatly. "I'll go change my dress. April taught me the Charleston."

Clarice did the wild dance with marvelous grace, kicking her skirt at least as high in the air as had April. Her legs, I noted, as if seeing them for the first time, were incredibly elegant.

"As good as April?" she demanded when we were finished with the Charleston.

"I'm not going to answer that question, Clarice."

She smiled faintly. "I shouldn't have asked it."

Then I asked her about the romance between Jim and April.

As we danced and chatted I considered for the first time the possibility that Clarice Powers might be a young woman worth pursuing in her own right and not merely the beautiful but silent partner of April Cronin.

Her torpid presence in my arms hinted at sultry beaches and luxurious pleasures. Perhaps she merited more careful consideration.

"I'm surprised that no one has tried to give you an engagement ring yet, Clarice."

"Oh, they have." She dismissed the offers with an airy wave of her hand. "I decided more quickly than April. I'm never going to marry."

"Why not? Don't tell me you're planning on becoming a nun?"

"Certainly not," she said, her lips thin with contempt for the good sisters. "I'm not going to give a man control of my life. I don't like men. A woman can't trust men."

"That's not fair."

"I wouldn't make the novena with April last month," she said stubbornly.

"Novena?"

"To Saint Anne."

"As in 'Oh, good Saint Anne, get me a man'?"

"Don't make fun of it."

"I'm not . . . April made the novena? She's only twenty."

"Twenty-one now. You forgot her birthday, didn't you?"

"Guilty."

Saint Anne, the grandmother of Jesus, according to legend, had somehow become the patroness of women seeking husbands, hence the novena before her feast in mid-July (during which, if my calculations are correct, I was conceived).

"She said that she's not taking any chances. And I said that I was afraid that if I went to church with her those nine nights, I might find a husband and I don't want that."

"You certainly dance like a woman who doesn't object to men. And you're a very beautiful young woman."

"That's not worth anything. Most of the time I wish I were ugly."

Spontaneously I put my hand over her mouth. "Don't say that, Clarice."

"Afraid of bad luck?" she said, with a sneer.

"Beauty is a gift that should be treasured."

"You sound just like April. . . . Were you faithful to her in Europe?"

I was stunned. "What kind of a question is that?"

"See!" She smiled knowingly. "Men are never faithful!"

I almost said, "I'm not like your father."

Instead I tightened my grip on her. "Look, Clarice Powers, you're a fine dancer and an attractive and intelligent young woman. I don't intend to permit you to be a bitch. Now to answer your question, which you have no right to ask: first of all, there is no agreement, explicit or implicit, between April and me—"

"You know that she loves you." Her body had become as stiff as the lions in front of the Art Institute.

"I don't know that and damn it, woman, relax."

"Yes, Captain."

"Lieutenant . . . If you mean, did I have minor romances with girls when I was in Europe, the answer is yes. If you mean, did I screw any of them—excuse my language, but I'm being blunt—the answer is no. Was April the reason for my abstinence? I think she was. Does that satisfy your morbid curiosity?"

"I don't believe you."

I stopped dancing and released her. "I won't dance with a woman who calls me a liar."

She stared at me stone-faced. Then her eyes misted, her lip quivered, her marvelous breasts moved up and down quickly. She leaned against me, contrite, beaten.

"Forgive me," she whispered.

"Gladly." I resumed our dance. She was supple and compliant again. "Among your many attractions, Clarice, is that you apologize with grace."

"I don't do it very often," she sighed, still close to tears, "I'm a real bitch."

"No you're not. Understand?"

"Yes, Lieutenant." We chuckled together and the dance ended.

"Sit this one out?"

She nodded. "I'm exhausted. Emotionally."

I led her back to the table and poured her a small drink from my flask.

"More, please."

"No."

She glared at me, then laughed happily. "You're worse even than April."

I raised my glass in a toast.

She responded with a silent toast of her own. And a radiant smile that dimmed all the lights in the stuffy dance hall.

I thought that I could indeed keep this beautiful young woman happy. I could be a stronger influence than her father. I could save her from him and from herself.

I paid no attention to the distant voice of my mother.

"Never marry to save someone. You'll only lose yourself."

"I thought you married Dad to save him," I would respond with a mischievous smile.

"Himself? Ah, sure"—she'd nod her head decisively toward Dad—"he was beyond saving altogether. I married him because I couldn't live without him, which is the only reason for marrying anyone."

The first time I heard it from her, I was astonished. It was a rare expression of passion. Rare and unmistakable.

"The woman was implacable when she made up her mind." Dad would become pleasantly flustered.

Then they would both laugh and our parlor would fill with loving warmth.

I remembered the conversation after I had kissed Clarice good night. She offered me her cheek in front of the Drake. I turned her chin and kissed her solidly on the lips.

"I don't want you to kiss me that way."

"Oh? Then I'll do it again."

Her lips faltered this time.

"Thank you." She turned from me. "April is a fortunate woman."

"Nothing is settled between April and me—as you well know."

She didn't turn back. "I'm sorry I was unpleasant."

"I'll repeat what I said too: you apologize charmingly."

"Thank you."

I watched her walk up the stairs, my young male imagination delighting in her splendidly curvaceous rear end.

I desired her a lot at that moment, and, I think, loved her more than a little.

As I walked over to the celibate stronghold where priests stayed, presumably secure from the charms of women's bottoms, I reflected on my mother's advice. Was it not possible to save someone if you found you could not live without her?

I could hardly argue because of a one-night flirtation that I was unable to live without her. But the woman had great possibilities. Who needed April Mae Cronin?

I did, as it turned out.

The next morning Clarice and I both waited for her in the parking lot, next to the dining hall, leaning, like models in *Vogue,* against the station hack.

The flirtation of the previous night had made us, not lovers, but friends.

"You really love her, don't you?"

"April?"

"No, the Princess of Wales."

"There isn't a Princess of Wales, not yet anyway . . . and I'm not sure I love her. I hardly know her."

"You'd be a perfect match."

"Saint Anne's answer to her prayer?"

"Silly." She poked me just like April would.

"If I love her, Clarice—and I just don't know for sure yet—it doesn't follow that I don't like you."

"I know that." She rested her right hand on my arm. "After last night. I'm flattered. And astonished. But you shouldn't even think of marrying me. Neither of us would be happy. You and April would be real happy, a swell match."

I didn't have a chance to answer because Jim's silver Duesy roared into the gravel parking lot and skidded to a stop next to us with a mighty squeal of protest.

April, clad in outrageous Chinese red and gold beach pajamas, was standing up behind the windshield waving like an empress to her subjects.

She vaulted out of the car, embraced Clarice like a long-lost friend, and then threw her arms around me. "Vangie! Welcome home! You didn't get that suntan in museums! I want to hear all about the trip!"

Her hug was as brief as it was enthusiastic.

"There's not much to tell."

"I want to hear about it all down at the beach. I can hardly wait to dive into the water."

"Did you wear your swimsuit all the way up here?" Clarice frowned in disbelief.

"It made me feel wonderfully wicked!" April laughed enthusiastically. "My mother said that it was all right, so long as I didn't take off the top of my pajamas . . . Do you like them, Vangie? Did they wear anything like this on the beaches of Ostia?"

There was not the slightest doubt: I was hopelessly in love with her.

"We had a swell ride up, Johnny." Jim interjected himself, striving as always to be the center of attention. "I pushed her up to ninety-five. It was lots of fun."

I ignored him. "As to the first question, Miss April Mae Cronin"—I found myself grinning like a silly fool—"I think you in red and gold would stop traffic. And to the second, there was no one like you at any of the Italian beaches."

Except Siobahn, and she doesn't count.

"That's nice, but I don't think I believe you."

"You want to come for a ride later, Johnny?" Jim was

tugging at my shirtsleeve. "Maybe I can get her up to ninety again."

"I don't think so." I shook him off.

April scowled at me. Oh, oh, I had to be nice to Jim or I would be in trouble.

"Come on," Jim persisted. "Maybe before supper?"

"If it doesn't rain, sure."

April's scowl disappeared. "Let's get rid of our bags and run down to the beach." She pulled her bag and her harp case out of the rumble seat of the Duesy. "I can feel the water already. Was it this hot in Italy, John E. O'Malley?"

"It was even hotter." I took the bag from one hand and the harp case from the other, knowing that Jim would never think of carrying someone else's luggage. "Hey, you planning to stay for a week?"

He'd bring candy and buy flowers before the day was over, but somehow no one had told him about luggage.

"Only a big weekend. Just drop that at the door of the Drake, would you, Vangie? I'll meet you at the beach."

"I'm staying at the Drake too!" Jim bristled with pride. "Private room. They're really swell!"

"Oh?" A brown eyebrow lifted in surprise. "Where did they put you, Vangie?"

"In a cabinet at the back of the priests' house. Mrs. Kennelly thought I might make a good priest."

Her eyes moved back and forth between me and Jim, probing us as a precinct captain might when sizing up two voters. "I'm sure you would," she said, responding seriously to my jest. "Maybe if there's no priest here this weekend, they might let you say mass."

"April!" Clarice protested.

"I really don't mean it." April looked guilty. "I'm sure God isn't mad at me."

"Not for long anyway," I reassured her. "It's probably the heat."

"Probably . . . anyway, see you all at the beach!" She

danced ahead of us, her bright good humor recaptured. Almost.

It would be a difficult weekend.

"Isn't she a swell girl, Johnny?" Jim beamed proudly as he watched her disappear beyond the dining hall. "You will help me this weekend?"

Clarice listened intently.

"As much as I can," I said briskly. "See you both at the beach."

I dropped April's bag and harp case with Mrs. Kennelly and rushed back to the priests' house to change to my swim trunks. I wanted a few moments alone with April Cronin before I had to share her with Jim and Clarice.

She was waiting alone on the pier, her feet dangling in the water. Her red swimsuit with a broad gold belt matched her discarded beach pajamas. The girl had expensive taste in clothes.

That was all right, we'd never lack for money. My savings, like those of my father, were in Union Carbide.

"You're dazzling," I said as I sat next to her.

"Thank you, kind sir." She blushed with pleasure. The flush spread from her face to her throat and chest. I wanted desperately to take her in my arms and kiss her. "Why are you and Jim in separate rooms?"

Down to serious business right away.

"I didn't think I could get away this weekend. I'm designing another church—"

"Besides All Souls?"

I didn't recall that I had told her the name of my Unitarian church in Evanston.

"Right. Mike Hurley, my boss, is in a rush for the preliminary drawings. I managed to finish up enough of them to be able to catch the late afternoon train. The only room they had left was in the priests' house. I kind of suspect that Mrs. Kennelly was saving it for me."

That seemed to satisfy her. "Is the room nice?"

"Kind of small. Hardly space to breathe. My virtue is safe there this weekend."

I wondered if she'd be offended by my slightly risqué comment.

She wasn't. After all, she was a flapper.

"I think virtue is safe everywhere in Barry." She nudged me, very lightly, with her elbow. "That's why Mommy and Daddy let me come up here."

"When I was unpacking I thought that it would be difficult even for married people on weekends up here. Pretty thin walls."

"If I ever marry," she said firmly, "and I'm up here with my husband, I won't let thin walls stop me."

"I'm sure it won't stop him either. . . . And what do you mean 'if'? No faith in Saint Anne?"

She nudged me again. "You're terrible."

I captured her hand and raised it to my lips. She gave it to me timidly. "Down payment," I said, kissing each finger respectfully. "More when it's dark. Much more."

"You really are terrible." She glanced around to make sure that our exchange of affection was not stirring too much attention among the older folks on the beach chairs. "Remind me to avoid you in the dark."

But she didn't pull her hand away.

"I'm glad I'm not in too much trouble for not sending you my address."

"Oh,"—she withdrew her fingers from my lips but continued to hold my hand—"I know the address of the Pensione Elizabetta, number 24 Via Nuova, right off the Piazza Venezia where that terrible man shows off to the crowds and behind the Via Bottega Oscura."

"How did you know that?" I tried to pull my hand away from her.

She held on firmly. "I won't tell! I won't tell! But it wasn't your mother. And it wasn't Jim either."

"He probably didn't remember."

"Now," she reproved me gently, "be nice to poor Jim."

"Yes, ma'am . . . I'm glad you're not angry at me."

"*Well*. . . ." She considered. "I was at first. Because I did want to write you. Then I was worried about you. And I prayed for you every night when I said my night prayers—"

"On your knees?"

"Where else? And don't interrupt. Then I did become very angry and—"

"What did you pray for?"

"That no harm would befall you and that you would come safe and healthy . . . and I *said* don't interrupt."

She finally pried her hand loose, but only to slap me lightly on the thigh, an action that sent a manic current of electricity through my body.

"Yes, ma'am."

"Then I said to myself, well, if John the Evangelist isn't writing, he must have a good reason for not writing and I shouldn't be angry. People should trust their friends. And, anyway, his guardian angel will take care of him." Her hand rested now on my thigh, as bold and as brazen an action as one might have imagined in those days.

"So you stopped praying for me?"

" 'Course not."

"Clarice asked me last night if I met any girls while I was away."

It was a sanitized version of Clarice's question, but it would do as a pretext for telling my side of the story first.

"Typical Clarice, always direct. *Well* . . ." Her hand slipped away, fortunately for the remnants of my sanity. "*Naturally* you met girls. You weren't living in a monastery, were you? Or even"—giggle—"a priests' house. If I were in Europe this summer I certainly hope I would have met boys."

She was being tolerant, more tolerant than she probably felt.

"They were all beautiful—"

"Naturally."

"And intelligent—"

"What else?"

"Now who's interrupting?" I slapped her thigh very gently.

She jumped in surprise, but did not protest, not even when my hand somehow found its way to the same part of her body and rested there.

"And charming and sweet and wonderful," she continued unsteadily.

"And I didn't lose my heart to any of them." I removed my hand, with a final little pat.

She laughed. "You get absolution at the priests' house, not here."

"Someday maybe I'll tell you why I didn't write. It wasn't because I didn't want to."

"I wrote you."

"I didn't receive any letters."

"I was afraid to send them."

"As I was to send the ones I wrote to you."

"You wrote me?" Her face became crafty. "I'll show you my letters if you show me yours."

"Someday."

"Why not now?"

"They're love letters, April," I whispered.

"What else would they be?"

Then Clarice and Jim appeared coming down the hill.

"I think I'd better swim." She stood up quickly and plunged into the water with a skillful shallow dive.

Her rear end, I reflected, was not as shapely as Clarice's but it would do.

Oh yes, it would do nicely.

❧ 28 ❧

Jim was cheating.

"How many strokes?" I asked wearily, scorecard in hand.

"Five," he chortled. "One over par, not bad, huh?"

"Are you sure?" I took a deep breath for patience.

"Pretty sure." He smiled innocently. "Let me see." He counted strokes on his fingers. "One from the tee, one on the fairway, a chip shot, and you saw the two puts. Five, right?"

"If you say so."

I had counted three fairway shots and two chips. He should have an eight.

Jim always cheated at sports. It was, I had previously thought, a harmless eccentricity, made all the more innocent because he seemed to believe sincerely in his own version of what had happened.

Now, after a long and trying day in which he had embarrassed both the two young women and me, his systematic dishonesty was preying on my nerves.

He had indeed changed for the worse while I was away. The timing of his jack-in-the-box movements, once flawless, had been disrupted. The joy had gone out of his gift giving (beach towels for all of us in addition to the usual Fanny Mae's). During the summer of 1925, Jim Clancy had somehow become a haunted man; and his haunts had turned him from a happy clown to a tormented pest.

The rest of us had not wanted to play golf. The day was too hot, the water too inviting, the golf course too far away, especially for the complicated logistics of two trips in the Duesy and renting four sets of golf clubs.

But Jim had bragged about his golf accomplishments to compensate for his inability to swim. I knew that Jim was a terrible golfer under the best of circumstances; desperately anxious to prove himself to April and Clarice, he would be even more manic on the course. I tried to veto the expedition but April insisted that if Jim wanted to play golf, then why certainly we should play with him.

Jim had often seemed in the past to experience periods of need to be the center of any activity where there were more than two people—a result of the times when his mother had brought her clever little boy into the parlor to entertain her friends.

There had been no malice in his intermittent need to attract attention. But, while I had been in Rome, the need changed from occasional to permanent. It was still not malicious, I told myself, but it was painful and embarrassing.

I tried to persuade myself that there was not any sexual rivalry in his attempts to divert attention from me when Clarice and April were present. He would have behaved the same way if two men were with us at Twin Lakes.

When he and Clarice joined us at the pier earlier in the day, I was challenged by the girls to render an account of my romantic conquests during my trip to Europe.

I decided to tell the truth, not all the truth of course, but more than they expected me to tell. I gave a comic version of my relationships with Laura, Siobahn, and Paola. It wasn't hard to make the stories sound funny, because they were pretty comic in reality.

After each laugh, Jim, wearing an outlandish and ill-fitting one-piece swimsuit, blue on top and white trunks would interrupt to tell a story about himself, usually abou conversations with Negro women. He didn't say they were disorderly house conversations, but the implication was pretty clear.

Clarice and April listened in silent mortification and then turned back to me for the next chapter in my story.

My comic theme was that I was the clown, not without some basis in fact. Jim's theme was how he had made a fool out of some poor, stupid Negro woman.

It was a strange conversation, three adults being periodically interrupted by an unruly child, patiently listening to the child, and then returning to their own conversation.

Well, the two women tolerated him patiently. I kept my ire under control because I did not want to make matters worse by losing my temper. If April could be patient with him, I told myself, so could I. Even more patient.

"So I said to the nigger, 'Girl, you lose the bet because five nickels make a quarter and four quarters make a dollar.' And she says, 'Mr. Clancy, you sure are one smart white man.'"

Jim guffawed at the end of the story, though it made no sense to the rest of us. Clarice stared at him blankly. April smiled faintly.

"Maybe we have heard enough stories about the Negro woman, Jim." I spoke the words very slowly.

"Yeah, well, as you know, Johnny, I could go on all day with stories about how dumb they are. Poor people, I feel sorry for them. I give them lots of money, don't I, Johnny? Well, anyway, let's go play some golf! It's a swell game."

So we played golf.

None of us were very good. I played in the nineties, very high, without any practice, and with a whole lot of practice maybe on one or two occasions I would lower my score to the high eighties, again very high. Clarice rarely hit the ball off the ground. April had a lovely, graceful swing that suggested that she could be as successful on the links as on the tennis courts if she wanted to. But her sense of the absurd forced her to laugh at herself—and at the rest of us.

"Vangie, you turn so red on your backswing. You'll get high blood pressure if you play this game too often."

"Thank you," I said grimly.

"It was a wonderful drive, so high, so far . . ."

"And?"

"And with curves like your friend Paola."

"All right, let's see what you can do."

She drove into the same area of rough into which I had sliced. Only her drive wasn't a slice. She had deliberately aimed for the place I was, so we could talk in some kind of privacy while we went through the motions of searching for our golf balls.

"See you guys on the green." Jim, now wearing white plus fours, a white vest, and a white cap, waved cheerfully.

When we were alone, however, trudging toward the rough, we were embarrassed and awkward, neither one of us willing to talk about Jim's outrageous behavior.

He was my friend, I told myself, and his performance was innocent. He was deeply troubled about something. And his problem was his mother's fault anyway.

"Are you sure I can't carry your clubs?"

"I'm not an invalid," she laughed. "Besides, if you carried mine, you'd have to carry Clarice's too."

Later, when the weekend ended in disaster, I regretted that I hadn't risen to the bait in that comment.

"What are your parents like?" I asked her. "They seem to trust you completely."

"They're such dear sweet people, Vangie. I'm their youngest, I was born when Mama was forty-four—they're older than your parents—and they've spoiled me rotten. I'm a pampered, self-indulgent youngest child who has never been denied anything all her life. . . . There's your golf ball."

Her self-accusation had been delivered in a calm,

matter-of-fact tone. It doubtless represented exactly how she saw herself.

"You have been well loved, April." I removed my five iron from the golf bag. "None of the rest of what you say is true."

She was silent while I used the iron to blast, not impressively, out of the rough.

"Oh, there's my ball. I drove farther than you did, Vangie dear."

It was the first time she had called me "dear."

"I said that you were not spoiled."

"I heard you." She studied her clubs and selected a six iron.

Her shot was much better than mine. Her ball lay at least fifty yards farther down the fairway, but on a direct line, so that we could walk together.

"You really don't think I'm a spoiled brat? The sisters at school said—"

"They were wrong."

She nodded. "Sometimes I think so too. But, oh, Vangie, I love Mama and Daddy so much. And I know I won't have them with me much longer. You understand what it's like to feel that way, don't you? I pray every night that the Blessed Mother protect them and give them long life. And that I don't do anything to make their last years sad or painful."

I took her arm firmly in my right hand. She turned to face me, brown eyes troubled and uncertain.

"How long anyone lives is up to God, April Cronin. But you'll never make anyone who loves you sad."

Tears formed in her eyes, but she grinned at me.

"Mama warned me that you West Side Irish have clever tongues."

Jim won the golf match with eighty-eight, eleven strokes ahead of me and fifteen ahead of April. Clarice pleaded that I not add up her score.

"I won! I won!" he crowed. "Did I tell you I was a great golfer?"

I'm sure he believed that he was.

"You did very well, James dear," April said in her judicious, King Solomon tone. "But Vangie did well too for someone who hasn't played all summer."

She called him "dear" too.

Traitor.

"But I would win even if he had practiced," Jim insisted, hurt at the hint that he might not be permanently the better.

"Jim always beats me," I said casually.

April frowned, not liking my hint that Jim always cheated.

We deposited the rented clubs in the red-painted barn that served as a clubhouse, drank a quick Coke, and then went out to the Duesy.

Two women were waiting by the car, Gypsies. The older one was slender and handsome, the younger a budding girl, perhaps no more than thirteen or fourteen. Mother and daughter? Older and younger sister?

"Hey, you trash," Jim bellowed, "get away from my car! What have you stolen? I'll have the police after you! Give me back what you've taken! You shouldn't be around decent people."

It was an outbrust like I had never heard from him before. He had always despised Gypsies, but he had always been courteous to them, as he was with Negroes.

"We took nothing, sir." The older woman extended her arms in supplication. "We are not thieves. We only tell fortunes."

The younger woman huddled close to her.

"Give me back what you took"—Jim was livid with rage—"or I'll call the sheriff and have him strip off your clothes and search you."

"Jim," April said mildly, a mother reassuring a frightened little boy, "we left nothing in the car, remember? Mrs. Kennelly warned us about Gypsies."

"Lay off, Jim," I said firmly. "We have no grounds for suspecting them."

My mother had told me when I was a little boy that Gypsies, "like the Irish tinkers," were "poor dear people," who if they stole occasionally did so only because they were so badly treated that they had no choice. She may not have understood the Romany culture, but I agreed with her instinct that they were "poor dear people."

"Grounds?" Jim exploded. "They're Gypsies, aren't they?"

"We tell the ladies' fortune?" The older woman glanced shrewdly at me. "For free? You lady?" She motioned toward April.

"I don't know . . ." April hung back, frightened by the strangeness of the two women.

"Tell mine." I held out my hand.

The woman took my hand and peered into my palm. She was dirty and she smelled of many dank aromas. Yet there was a certain dignity about her. She might be a fake and a thief, but she still had her pride.

"Ah, sir," she murmured. "You are an artist, no? I see difficult times for you, much hard work, but great happiness and then wonderful success."

"Read my palm, please, ma'am?" April extended her hand.

The woman smiled. "Gladly, kind lady."

"They're trash!" Jim was pacing back and forth furiously. "They should be run out of the county."

No one paid any attention to him, which made him all the more angry.

"You are a musician, kind lady," the Gypsy purred, "a good one. You will marry soon and will have many fine children who will love you very much. And a good husband too."

"And me?" Clarice was next in line.

"Hookers," Jim whined. "Frauds and hookers."

The woman examined Clarice's palm closely and

frowned. "You will have a very beautiful child, lady, a daughter, I think. She will do many wonderful things that will make you proud of her."

"Really?"

"Oh yes."

"Thank you very much." I gave the woman a five-dollar bill. "You're very perceptive."

She bowed her thanks, like a slave to a master. Then she smiled, a knowing smile that said, "We understand each other, don't we? You know I'm in the entertainment business."

"Wasn't that astonishing?" Clarice spoke with awe. "How does she know those things?"

"Was it a sin, Vangie?" April was anxious. "The priests say it's a sin to have your fortune told."

"Tar and feather them!" Jim jumped into his car. "If the sheriff doesn't get rid of them, decent people should run them out of the county."

We continued to ignore him.

But I worried nonetheless. Had the nervous breakdown really happened?

"Come on." I tried not to sound too superior. "There's drafting ink on my hands. April's fingers are callused from plucking harp strings; how could you not have a beautiful child, Clarice? And naturally April will be loved by her husband and children."

"Lucky guesses?" Clarice was puzzled.

"Shrewd reading of people." I smiled.

"How did she know I would be married soon?" April was not yet satisfied.

"You're at an age when young women marry"—I gestured easily—"and you're very attractive. She has every reason to think her guess would be pretty accurate."

"And all your sisters were married before they were twenty-two," Clarice chimed in. "You know how much you're afraid that you'll be an old maid if you put off marriage."

"Clarice!" April's face turned as red as the barn behind her.

"Well, let's go eat supper." Jim banged on the horn to get our attention. "I've got some great hooch stored away for after supper. Top quality."

"If April is an old maid"—I opened the car door for her—"the male half of the human race will have gone out of business.

"Vangie!" She continued to blush.

Clarice and I laughed at her, both enjoying April's rare loss of poise.

"Move over." Clarice climbed into the car after her. "I want to take a bath before supper."

"I'll be back in a jiffy, Johnny," Jim promised. "I'll really open her up."

He blasted the horn and roared away.

I watched the Duesy's dust with a vague feeling of unease, like a toothache that one doesn't have yet, but might have in a day or two.

Jim was getting worse. Even if I allowed for his infatuation with April—which somehow seemed to be without passion—and for his frustrations at not being the center of attention for much of the day, he was still becoming stranger.

What would happen to him?

What could I do to help him?

As I waited for him to return, I figured that the answer to the first question was that he would destroy himself and that the answer to the second was that there was nothing much I could do to prevent such a fate.

Despite the heat, I shivered.

How, I wondered, could someone be fated so young in life?

As my son-in-law the psychiatrist with whom I consulted as I was writing this memoir puts it, some sort of semipsychotic interlude probably did occur that summer. The first of many. Even now I wonder whether if I had stayed in Chicago that summer I might have been able to protect him.

I suppose I worried about the same thing as I trudged down the gravel road that summer of 1925.

You see, he didn't come back for me.

I waited a half hour, then forty-five minutes. Finally I realized that he'd forgotten about me—not maliciously of course; something else had claimed his attention. He responded to the new interest, perhaps the hooch he had secreted for after supper. I had simply ceased to exist.

I began to walk back to the "country club."

But April and Clarice should have reminded him.

It was a half-hour walk, under a hot sun and through thick curtains of humidity. My feet hurt from shoes that were not meant for walking on a golf course, much less down a gravel road. With each step, I became more angry at the three of them.

I strode into the ovenlike dining room, and over to the table that they shared with several other young people.

"Where you been, Johnny?" Jim glanced up at me, a big scoop of mashed potatoes on his fork. "Come on, sit down and have some roast beef before it's gone. It really tastes swell."

"What took you so long?" April asked in all innocence.

"I walked."

"What?"

"Jim said that Mr. Evans would pick you up." April's brown eyes were troubled.

"Yeah." Jim gobbled his mashed potatoes. "I met him in the parking lot after I dropped off the girls. He said he was driving over to the links and he'd bring you back."

The conversation almost certainly never happened. But now Jim was convinced that it had.

"Sit down and eat"—April smiled sweetly—"you look starved."

"I'm *not* hungry," I shouted and strode out of the dining

room, conscious that every eye in the room was watching me.

Unfortunately for me, I was hungry. I paused in the clubhouse on my furious march back to the priests' house, and purchased three Hershey milk chocolate bars—five cents each.

The roast beef had indeed smelled tasty.

While I was nursing my anger, determined to keep it alive, and soaking my feet in hot water, Jim burst into my room.

He was wearing a gray double-breasted summer suit, white vest, white straw hat with a gray band, and gray and white saddle shoes.

Despite the obvious quality of his clothes, Jim did not wear them well any longer. His gray tie was improperly tied and the buttons on his jacket were in the wrong buttonholes. Perspiration had already disfigured the jacket.

"You just have to help me, Johnny. What are friends for if they don't help when someone needs it?"

"Friends don't strand you without a ride." My temper was still smoldering.

He didn't hear me, and he certainly didn't remember my walk back from the golf course.

"She has to marry me." Jim sank onto the edge of my cot. "She'll save my life. She really will. She'll take care of me just like Momma does."

"Jim—"

"You'll do it, then?" He leaned forward eagerly. "You'll ask her if she'll marry me?"

"I can't do that, Jim."

"Why not?" He was baffled. "You're my friend, aren't you? And I love her."

"It's not done, Jim. Girls don't like it. It would be counterproductive."

"I don't see why." He lowered his head and began to sulk.

"I can't play John Alden to your Miles Standish."

"Huh?"

Mistakenly I tried to tell him the story that every school-child had heard. Jim quickly lost interest in it. Instead of listening to my explanation of the story, he devoted his attention to biting his fingernails.

"You have to help me," he whined. "You're my friend."

"Let me explain something about women, Jim. You have to adjust your tactics to their tastes. Like this afternoon, you embarrassed them on the golf course when you fibbed a little about your score. And when they wanted to have their fortunes told, you ignored what they wanted and embarrassed them again—"

"I didn't fib, honest, I didn't. I beat you because I'm a better golfer. Gee, I hope you're not mad at me for that. If you'll ask April to marry me, I'll lose tomorrow."

I tried once more. "And when women are enjoying a conversation, you shouldn't break in with your own stories—"

"What does that have to do with April marrying me? Momma will be so pleased with me when I introduce April to her—"

"And you should always offer to carry a woman's luggage and open the door for her before you rush through it."

"I keep forgetting . . ." He waved his hand as if gallantry were an unimportant detail. "Will you ask her tonight?"

I gave up.

"We'll see, Jim."

"That's what Momma says when she means no." He brightened as another thought rushed into his head. "Say, I forgot, we're going to drink my booze back of the hill when it gets dark. They're watching young people at night around here. Meet us there, will you, John. Above the parking lot. It's swell booze."

He bounded out of my room, now totally dedicated to our drinking adventure behind the hill that overlooked the

Barry grounds—and from which you could smell all the outhouses.

If you asked me now what happened to Jim that summer, I'd say that the strain of losing his hair and frustration in his love for April pushed him around the bend—and set a pattern for the rest of his life. He really did love her, in his own Peter Pan fashion. But he had no idea how to manifest that love after he had showered her with presents.

Even my promise of kisses for April would not have persuaded me to join in that adventure—if I were not worried that he might blunder into trouble and lead April and Clarice after him.

He was wrong about the hooch. It was terrible.

I found them in the underbrush above the parking lot, sitting on a Barry blanket. From the murmurs and the soft laughter around us we were not the only ones engaged in violations of the Volstead Act.

A haze, permeated with the fragrance of the privies, had settled on the hill, thick, sticky, irritating. The candle that the girls had lighted cast dim shadows. The ground underneath the blanket was rocky and uneven.

"Have some." Jim's voice was already slurred as he poked the bottle in my direction. "It's swell stuff, the best."

Silently April handed me a tin cup.

With some effort, I didn't spit it out.

"Kind of strong," I said as the roof of my mouth caught fire.

"The best," Jim said again, "my friends give me only the best. I didn't even have to pay for this, would you believe that, Johnny, it was absolutely free."

"A real bargain."

Out of the corner of my eye, I saw April empty her cup into the underbrush. I waited for an opportunity to do the same.

"May I have some more?" Clarice spoke with tipsy courtesy. "It's simply marvelous."

"I told you it was swell booze," Jim proclaimed triumphantly.

He and Clarice finished the bottle within a quarter hour. April and I listened silently to their babble.

"We'd better help them back to the Drake," she said when our two friends had dozed off. "Do you think they'll be sick?"

"After drinking such high-quality gin?"

"Vangie, you're being nasty," she laughed as she struggled to help Clarice to her feet.

"Just ironic."

"Are they sick, do you think, poor dears?"

"They'll be all right when they sleep it off." I pulled Jim off the ground. "Come on, Jimmy boy, time for beddy-bye."

April chortled. "I bet you sound just like his mother."

"God forbid."

At the entrance of the Drake, exhausted from our efforts, we paused for breath.

"What do you want to do after we put them to bed?" April asked.

I realized that I would have her to myself for the rest of the evening.

"Dance hall?"

"I hate to spoil the night for you, Vangie, but I'm not quite up to the Charleston. The pergola? You can tell me more about your trip."

"I think I made some promises on the pier this morning, didn't I?"

"I don't recall."

"Yes you do."

She laughed softly.

✠ 29 ✠

"John?"

"April?

"Are you alone?"

"Completely."

"Good," she sighed.

She emerged from the haze, a white blur in the dark, a sweet-smelling white blur.

"Did you have any trouble putting poor Jim to bed?" she sighed again as she sat next to me on the damp stone bench of the pergola.

"Just dumped him on top of the sheet and left him."

"Poor Clarice," she sighed for a third time, sounding not unlike Siobahn.

Of whom I ought not to have been thinking.

"I don't know what will happen to her," April continued. "Daddy says you do your best for your friends and then it's up to them and to God. Do you agree, Vangie?"

"And their parents."

She shuddered. "Her father is an awful man."

"So is his mother."

"Lets not talk about our friends anymore." She rested against my shoulder. "I've had enough of them for one day."

"Me too."

I drew her close, her back against my chest, my arms around her waist, hands against her belly. She nestled against me easily and gratefully.

She had changed to a simple blouse and skirt—no corset this time, thank goodness.

"I love you, John E. O'Malley. I've never said that to a man before. But I say it now and I mean it."

"I was about to say the same thing to you, April Mae Anne (with an *e*) Cronin." I kissed her forehead. "I love you too."

"I beat you to it," she giggled. "Daddy says that when I make up my mind, I move fast."

"I think my mother would say the exact opposite of me."

"I wanted to say I loved you all day. I was afraid as I walked over here. I prayed to the Blessed Mother to give me courage."

"And she did?"

"Certainly." She nuzzled closer to me. "I would never have had the courage without someone's help."

Our affection that night was quiet and gentle, we were too hot and too tired to be passionate. Brief kisses and soft caresses suited both our moods.

Nonetheless, I did unbutton her blouse, ease the camisole from her shoulders, and kiss her breasts in the dark.

She moaned contentedly as my lips touched her flesh.

We huddled together for what seemed only a few moments and at the same time all of eternity.

Then, knowing that it was time, we stopped.

"I can walk back to the Drake by myself."

"In the dark at this time of night? Don't be silly."

"I can take care of myself," she protested as we walked down the steps of the pergola.

"I'm sure you can, but I'm still walking back to the Drake with you. To the door of the Drake," I hastily added.

We laughed together, knowing that we could trust one another. More or less.

At mass the next morning I noticed that April received

Holy Communion. She noticed that I did not.

"Do you think it's all right to receive Communion after what we did last night?" I asked her bluntly.

"*Well*, I thought about it. Mama says that men and women were made by God to love one another and that everything else depends on the time and the place and the person." She was counting off points on her slender, elegant fingers. "*So*, it seemed that you were the right person and this was the right place and last night was the right time. Mama also says that sometimes it would be wrong not to do things that the priests disapprove. *So . . .*"

"The priests make mistakes?"

"Poor dears, sometimes they just don't understand. *Anyway*, I said a prayer to God before mass. I told Him I loved Him and I loved you and I didn't think it was wrong to love each other the way we did last night, but if it was I was sorry and He should blame me instead of you."

"April!"

"Well, it's true. Mama says the woman sets the tone of what happens between a man and a woman. And I didn't want God blaming you—"

"Do you think God's like that?"

"Of course not, the poor dear. But I think that like other fathers, sometimes He enjoys laughing at us when we say silly things. . . . Now let's change clothes and play golf before it rains or we'll break poor dear Jim's heart."

Priests, God, Jim—they all had been described as "poor" and "dear," with minutely different nuances of voice. I would have to attune myself to those nuances.

It seemed a delightful prospect.

My future looked incredibly bright that morning after mass.

A few hours later it would turn dark.

This time Jim did remember to come back to pick me up after he had dropped the girls at the golf course.

"I want to show you something," he said as the Duesy

rushed by the red barn. "Those damn Gypsies are still around. Look at that!"

An old covered wagon, gaily painted green and yellow but battered and shabby, was parked at one side of the gravel road, in a stand of trees that probably belonged to the farmer whose two-story Gothic house was a quarter mile or so down the road. Two horses, tethered to a nearby oak tree, were grazing on the brown grass. Neither of the two women were visible.

A mother and daughter, or perhaps two sisters, by themselves. Not, from what I had read about Romany, unknown, but still rare.

"Doesn't that infuriate you?" Jim's lips were tight with rage. "Am I glad I hid April's diamond. Wouldn't they like to get their hands on that rock. Well, they won't—that's certain."

"Not all of them steal," I said. "Maybe they're really only fortune-tellers. I don't think the farmer would let them stay on his land if he thought they were thieves, not one of these hard-working Wisconsin German farmers. Come on, let's get back to the golf course. The girls will wonder what happened to us."

"There ought to be a law against Gypsies," Jim muttered to himself as he started the car. "They're trash."

The golf game was a catastrophe; it was almost entirely my fault. I lost my temper on the first hole when Jim reported four strokes and I had counted eight.

"Four," he said cheerfully, after he claimed a four-foot putt as a "concession."

"Eight." I scribbled the number furiously on the scorecard.

"I counted four." He was surprised by my anger. "Well, maybe five."

"I counted eight. April?"

She was taken aback by my curt tone. "My score? Five. Or did you count more, Vangie?"

"I'm not counting your strokes," I fired back, "only his."

I don't have much of a temper. On the rare occasions I do blow up, I calm down almost at once. I don't know what happened to me that day. I was in love with a woman who loved me. I should have been ecstatic. Maybe it was the heat, maybe it was the darkening sky, maybe I had finally reached my limit with Jim, or maybe it was my sore feet.

Most likely, it was the sore feet.

I counted his strokes on each hole. He seemed immune to my watchfulness. Each time he reported three or four strokes less than the actual number and then waited with a look of injured innocence for my reaction.

On the sixth hole I tore up the scorecard. "This is a ridiculous farce, Jim." I threw the scraps of the card on the green. "There's no point in keeping score or pretending that we're playing an honest golf match when you lie about your score on every hole."

"I'm not lying!" he groaned. "Honest, I'm not."

"You don't know what honesty is!"

"John O'Malley," April raged at me. "What difference does it make? It's only a game. Why don't you leave poor Jim alone? You're ruining the day for all of us."

"I'm ruining the day?" Last night she loved me, now she betrays me for an incorrigible liar. "What about him?"

"If you think winning is so important"—she stood tall and determined, an implacable judge—"maybe you should play by yourself and let us enjoy our game."

I was astonished, thunderstruck. Winning wasn't important. Honesty was.

Wasn't it?

"Well, then." I bowed with ceremony appropriate for a member of Headquarters Troop, 106th Illinois. "I hope you enjoy your afternoon."

More angry than I had ever been in my life, I marched back to the red barn, checked in my rented clubs, and on desperately sore feet strode back toward the Barry grounds. I'd catch the noon train to Chicago.

The rain caught up with me in twenty minutes, shrinking my shoes and making my feet hurt even more.

The Duesy pulled up beside me, its cover on for the first time.

"Hi, Johnny." Jim grinned nonchalantly. "Want a ride?"

"There's room here with Clarice and me." April was soaking wet and very sad.

Her compunction infuriated me.

"I'll walk," I snarled at them.

When the station hack pulled out of the parking lot I heard, in the distance, the strings of a harp and a woman's voice singing the "Indian Love Call" from *Rosemarie*.

As Siobahn would have said, the frigging "Indian Love Call."

30

The last week in August 1925 was the most unhappy week of my life.

I was furious at myself, furious at April Cronin, and furious at Jim.

I swore that I would never return to Barry when he was there.

I might court April sometime in the future, but only when she said she was sorry and promised that I would not have to put up with Jim during our courtship.

In my lovesick brain, Jim was her responsibility, not mine.

I stalked out of the living room in our house when dance music was played on our big new Philco. I was especially affronted when they dared to play "Show Me the Way to Go Home."

I glanced at the papers each morning. Nothing much new: forty thousand members of the Klan had marched in Washington. The Navy dirigible *Shenandoah* had exploded in a storm. Bill Tilden had led the United States to another Davis Cup victory. There was a terrible drought in the West and the South. Josephine Baker's "The Negro Review" had opened in Paris, to the delight of Parisians and the shock of proper Americans.

So, what did any of it mean?

I bent over my drawing board and worked.

Summer leaves our part of the Middle West in an embarrassed rush, like a maiden aunt who fears she has overstayed her welcome. One night, as early even as mid-August, there is an especially fierce thunderstorm. Then you wake up, not to the expected return of humidity but to a morning breeze so chill that you reach for your blankets. You look out the window and, although you try not to notice, leaves have already fallen off the trees.

Summer returns and lingers, hearing our pleas that she is never unwelcome. Sometimes she outdoes herself in early October. But after that first August storm, you know that somewhere in the world, winter is gathering its forces and preparing for a return.

It's morose knowledge. The happy suppress it. I was not happy, so I reveled in the end of summer.

My parents were surprised by my now hair-trigger temper and left me alone.

I pictured Mom whispering to Dad, "He's had a fight with that nice little Cronin girl. You know what young lovers are like."

I worked on the Saturday of the Labor Day weekend, not only catching up with Mike Hurley's demands but anticipating them by a week or two. I enjoyed feeling sorry for myself.

I also enjoyed the rain that spoiled the Saturday of the weekend. It served the people at Twin Lakes right.

For all I knew, April and Jim were not there.

I slept late on Sunday morning, went to the twelve o'clock mass at St. Catherine's, and read the papers leisurely on the front porch swing. It was a crisp cool day, suggesting the coming of autumn.

Good. It had been a bad summer for me.

I took a long walk out to the Thatcher Woods Forest Preserve. But there were too many people for me to enjoy a quiet walk in the trees.

Disconsolately I returned home.

"That little Cronin girl phoned while you were out," Mom informed me—with a hint of triumph in her eyes.

"Oh?"

"She's such a sweet thing. She apologized so politely for disturbing our weekend."

"And you told her it was no bother at all to speak to such a nice young woman."

Mom frowned. "Now how did you know that?"

"Did she leave a message?"

"She was calling from the clubhouse at Twin Lakes, the line wasn't too good. You know what long distance calls are like. She said she'd try later."

"Fine." I settled on the front porch to finish *Porgy* by DuBose Hayward. I wouldn't wait by the phone. But I wouldn't take any long walks either.

Dusk and cool night air drove me back into the house with only a few pages left to read.

I was convinced that she wouldn't call.

What had I seen in her anyway?

The phone rang. I let it ring. Mom finally answered it.

"It's Miss Cronin, dear."

"All right."

"John O'Malley," I said formally.

"I need help, Vangie." The connection was poor. She sounded a long way off.

"What can I do?" I donned my silver armor and whistled for my great black horse.

"Come up here."

"Of course." Where was my helmet with the red plume?

"It's too late for the last train. Maybe you can catch the six o'clock in the morning."

The milk train?

For the damsel in distress, why not?

"I'll be on it."

"I think I can borrow the hack. No one will be using it at that hour."

"Fine. I'll be there. What's wrong?"

"You know those poor dear Gypsies?"

"Sure."

"Well, the police put them in jail in Kenosha. They found some stolen property in their wagon. I think Jim put it there. I have the fifty dollars to bail them out, but the deputies won't take money from a woman even though I am of age."

"Dummies."

"Vangie, I'm afraid of what they'll do to those poor women unless we get them out of jail."

"Don't worry, April, we'll take care of them."

After I hung up, I consulted with my parents.

"Impressive young woman." My father smiled tolerantly.

"I never said she wasn't."

"It sounds like the sort of thing your friend Clancy would do."

"It sure does. He's changed a lot this summer. He still doesn't mean any harm—"

"I'm sure not." My father raised his hand. "It does not follow that harm will not be done."

"No, sir."

He resisted the impulse to lecture me about Jim.

"I'll phone our sheriff's office"—he pulled out his watch—"someone is there even at this time on the Labor Day weekend. They'll call Kenosha. They'll tell the deputies up there that Cook County is interested in those women being released on bail tomorrow morning unharmed. That should guarantee there will be no rape tonight."

"You think they're in danger?"

"Certainly they are." He put aside the financial section of the *Herald-Examiner*—reading the Sunday papers was an all-day task for Dad—and stood up. "Excuse me while I see that they are removed from danger."

He returned a few minutes later, glowing with satisfaction. "Well, that's that. Gypsies or not, those women should not be molested."

"Such poor dear people," Mom sighed.

"Be that as it may"—Dad sat down, a man who had worked hard—"I don't think we'd want them wandering about our neighborhood, but they still have the right to be treated like human beings. It's the only decent thing to do."

"Did they reject poor little April's money because they wanted to harm the women?"

"Oh, I'm sure of it." My father waved his hand. "You said they were attractive, didn't you, son? For Gypsies?"

"For anyone." I stirred uneasily. "Was April in danger?"

"I should think so." Dad nodded solemnly. "But I would gather she's a fairly fierce young woman?"

"Would you now?" I smiled happily.

Everyone chuckled.

"*Well,*" Mom sniffed, "I'm certainly looking forward to meeting this young miss."

"We may be able to arrange that."

"Let me see." Dad pulled out his enormous billfold and peered over his glasses. "I have three hundred dollars here. You'd better take two hundred and fifty, just should you need it. I'll write out the phone number of our office, in case you should want any Chicago clout."

I didn't sleep much that night. And when I finally did drift off into fitful slumber, the alarm seemed to ring almost immediately. To catch the milk train on the North Side meant leaving my house by taxi at five A.M.

The pleasant Sunday weather, according to an early edition of the *Tribune* I purchased at the station, would be replaced by another hot day and then an afternoon thunderstorm.

Still I had packed a bag in case there was some reason, or some pretext, to stay overnight.

I realized at the station, as the train slowly chugged in, that I could have just as well taken the North Shore to Kenosha and met April there.

I was too busy being the Black Horse trooper on the phone to think straight.

I sighed and pulled a sketchbook out of my bag. I tried to recall the two Gypsy women and get their faces down on paper.

April was waiting for me at the small, deserted station in Genoa City. Again she was a rhapsody in blue, in skirt and blouse this time and without the hat.

We shook hands formally.

"Thank you for coming."

"Clarice?"

"Her father is home from California. He and her mother had a big fight about Clarice. He wouldn't let her come. I wouldn't stay married to a man like that."

"Neither would I."

"Is that all you brought? I have the hack, but we'll have to hurry. They want it back by ten."

"I'm sorry I didn't think to take the North Shore and meet you in Kenosha."

"Do you want to drive?" She offered me the car keys.

"I don't know how. I ride horses, big black ones."

"And wear silver armor." She smiled tentatively.

"With a red plume, which I seem to have forgotten."

The ice had been broken, thank God. Now to continue with the repair work—while not, mind you, giving up my knight role. I put my bag on the backseat, but kept the sketchbook on my lap.

"There are two Hershey bars on the backseat," she informed me. "In case you need breakfast."

"You're entitled to one of them."

"I already ate three." She closed the door and glanced at my open sketchbook. "The Gypsy women?" She started the car. "It looks just like them."

"Romany women is what they would call themselves," I said pompously. "Maybe I'll do a painting and call it that."

"I'm sure it will be beautiful."

We were feeling our way toward reconciliation—an arduous and pleasant process.

"Are you sure Jim planted the stolen goods?"

"Oh, absolutely." She steered the hack away from the station. "You should have seen him when the police came to make the search. He was bursting with enjoyment."

"I know the phenomenon," I said grimly.

"Like a man about to make love," she said. "Well, the way I imagine a man would look when he's about to make love."

"His tricks give him great pleasure," I agreed. "He doesn't mean any harm. But lately they've gotten out of hand. He'll probably pay the bail himself before the day is over, but we'd better not take a chance."

"I know they didn't take the diamond."

"What diamond?"

"The one's he's been trying to give me all summer. He tried again, after the time the Gypsies were chased off the Barry grounds."

"I see."

"So he must have taken the watches and rings from the other rooms in the Drake and hid them in their wagon too."

"He's capable of it, it's sort of the second twist that he likes in his jokes. Did the police bother you when you tried to pay the bail?"

We were on the gravel road now. The speedometer said we were going forty miles an hour.

"They were not at all nice." She kept her eyes sternly on the road. "I told them that they'd better be careful or they would have some very important Chicago politicians after their jobs. That scared them a little bit and they let me leave their ugly old jail."

"Democrats or Republicans?" I asked with a chuckle.

"Both," she said seriously and then chuckled too.

She had used my father's name—boldly and unabashedly I was sure.

"I'm sorry about last Sunday," she continued briskly. "I

acted terribly. I don't know what happened to me. . . . Yes, I do too. I wanted you to be perfect and was so disappointed that you weren't perfect. So I proved how imperfect I am. I hope you will forgive me."

"You beat me to it again, April Mae Cronin. I was about to apologize for making a fool out of myself. I don't normally lose my temper from one end of the year to the other. Being in love does strange things to a man's personality."

"A woman's too."

I glanced at her. She was smiling broadly. So I smiled too.

We sped down Highway 50 toward Kenosha, rushing through Twin Lakes as though it were not there.

Beyond the golf course, she slammed on the brakes. The car rocked like it had hit a brick wall.

"Vangie! Look what he did to their cute little wagon!"

The yellow and green cart had been overturned, the fabric torn, the contents scattered. The two ponies were grazing on the other side of the road.

We climbed out of the hack to examine the damage. Their dishes were broken, their few pathetic clothes torn and tied into knots, their cheap jewelry thrown on the ground and trampled. A plaster statue of the Madonna and Child had been deliberately smashed against the side of the wagon.

"How horrible!" Tears were streaming down April's lovely face.

I put my arm around her. "Dad gave me some money. I'll give it to them. It'll pay for the repairs."

"Your father is a wonderful man."

"For a Republican."

"And West Side Irish!"

Laughter quickly chased away the tears.

I whistled for the ponies, attempting to demonstrate my skill with horses.

They picked up their ears, but didn't move. Apparently,

my whistle wasn't in Romany. I whistled again. Grudgingly they ambled across the road and permitted me to tether them to the tree and April to pet them admiringly.

"He did it, didn't he?" she said when we were back on Highway 50.

"It's the sort of trick he would play. He doesn't mean—"

"I know *that*, but he does harm just the same. What if those two women were assaulted last night?"

"I'm sure they weren't, not after my father's phone call."

"That's not Jim's doing, poor man." She was sympathetic to him again. April's capacity to be angry at the unfortunate was severely limited.

"He'll probably try to give them money before the day is over, more than they need. That's his way."

"I think he wanted to . . . well, to make love with both of them and they refused. After I wouldn't take his ring."

It was the sort of thing Jim would try to do.

"You turned him down cold?"

"I tried to be clear. All summer long, I've tried to. He doesn't seem to understand that I like him, but I don't love him. He doesn't hear what I say."

"Were you tempted to say yes? I'm sorry, that's none of my business."

"It is too your business." She swerved around a slow bus. "I liked him and I felt sorry for him and I thought maybe I could help him and no one had ever asked me before. And this week . . . well, I thought you'd never forgive me for the way I acted last Sunday. But when he asked me again yesterday, I knew I could never be his wife."

"Uh-huh."

We were entering the outskirts of Kenosha, pleasant enough little neighborhoods. The town itself was a lake port turning into a small industrial city. It somehow managed to look shabby even in prosperous times.

"He was so pleased with himself for something he had accomplished on Saturday. One of his business deals, you know. Do you think he's involved with bootleggers?"

"Maybe."

"He tried to become affectionate . . . not the way you do. Just the opposite, like I was a thing to be played with . . . almost a prostitute. So I pushed him out of my room and screamed at him to go away. He did finally."

Poor Jim. He had blown his best chance. It was as inevitable as one of the Greek tragedies the Jesuits at St. Ignatius College had made us read. Except Jim was not the tragic-hero type.

Which didn't mean his agony wasn't any less painful.

I had done my part, but it hadn't been enough. Could I have done more? How had I failed him?

"Do you think he did these terrible things to the Gypsies because he was angry at me?"

"Don't blame yourself, April. Jim's behavior doesn't fit ordinary explanations."

The redbrick Gothic courthouse and jail in Kenosha looked like it had been built right after the Civil War and had never been remodeled or even painted. It smelled of rot and human excrement.

The deputy in charge on Labor Day was a man not much older than me with a rapidly developing potbelly. He wore a Sam Browne belt, riding trousers, puttees, and a massive colt revolver.

"You're the politican's kid from Chicago?" He sneered at me.

"Captain John O'Malley." I promoted myself and tried to sound like an efficient cavalry officer.

I heard April draw in her breath at my fib.

"Captain?

"106th Cavalry."

He was impressed, as I knew he would be.

"You see action, sir?"

"A little."

"I missed it completely. Never got out of Georgia."

"It was no picnic, I can tell you that."

"But I bet you wouldn't trade it for anything, sir?"

"That's right, Deputy. Now, can we arrange this matter quickly? I've requisitioned my vehicle for an hour."

"You bet, Captain, sir."

April drew her breath in sharply again.

I handed the deputy her fifty dollars bail. He gave us some forms to sign.

"You're not likely to see this money again, sir." He counted it carefully. "They'll leave the jurisdiction before the sun is down."

I slipped him ten dollars from the roll Dad had given me. "I think that's probably the best outcome for all concerned, Deputy."

"Yes, sir." He winked at our little conspiracy. "Thank you, sir. I understand, sir. Now, sir, if you don't mind, I'll bring the . . ."—he glanced nervously at April—"the prisoners."

"Carry on, Deputy."

"Vangie," my love whispered, "you're terrible!"

"All right," I whispered back, "I anticipated my promotion a little. But everything else was true. Collapsing on the parade ground was certainly action and it certainly wasn't a picnic. And I wouldn't trade it for anything, because when I came out of my fever I had a dream of a beautiful brown-eyed woman that I knew I'd meet someday."

"Really?" She grabbed my arm. "How romantic!"

Oh yes, it was all of that, God knows.

"Shush! Here comes the deputy with his prisoners."

He read them a warning about what would happen to them if they violated their bail bond. They listened dully, as if such warnings had been read before.

Then they walked out into the September sunlight with us, timid and cautious, not knowing, as Romany never know, what would happen to them next.

"Now." April took charge. "We're going to drive you back to your wagon. Some terrible people have damaged it, but we're going to give you some money to repair it. We've tied up your ponies so they won't run off, though the poor dears showed no sign of running. It would probably be a good idea if you cross the border to Illinois by tomorrow morning. All right?"

The two women, fear still in their eyes, hardly knew what to say.

"Thank you, kind lady," the older finally said, bowing low. "You are very good."

"This young man will tell you that's not true. Anyway, we'd better leave here while we still can. Vangie . . ."

I held out to the older woman the roll of bills Dad had given me. "We're very sorry about the harm you've suffered because of one of our friends. This might help you to repair some of the harm."

The woman looked at the roll and at me, afraid to touch it, afraid that we were buying her and the girl for some evil purpose.

"It's a gift," I said awkwardly. "Nothing more."

"Please don't be afraid of us," April added. "We won't hurt you."

The woman glanced at the other Gypsy and then gingerly accepted our gift. She continued to watch us as if she expected something terrible to happen. Then she sighed deeply.

"I can only say thank you."

"That's all you have to say," April said briskly. "Now we really must leave."

We stopped at their camp on the way back. Both women wailed at what had been done to their cart. We helped them turn it over on its wheels and waited while the woman pronounced a "holy blessing" over us in Romany.

"Did you make enough sketches?" April asked when we waved good-bye to them.

"You should have been watching the road instead of peering at my work."

"I think they're beautiful."

"The women or my drawings?"

"Both."

Mrs. Kennelly sent me back to my room at the priests' house. I put on my trunks, threw a towel around my shoulders, and walked to the pier. April was waiting for me in her red swimsuit with the gold belt. I sat next to her and put my arm around her waist.

"Are we friends again, April Mae Anne Cronin?"

"I hope so." She snuggled close to me.

Then Jim arrived. April and I separated from one another self-consciously. I'm sure he didn't notice our embrace.

He felt compelled to tell me in great detail and much laughter about his wonderful joke on the Gypsies.

We listened without comment and then excused ourselves. We wanted to swim before the storm clouds marching across the sky from the west drove us away.

We swam far out into the lake together and, treading water, kissed each other passionately.

"*Well,*" my love sighed. "Now we know you can kiss in the middle of a lake."

"Kiss effectively."

"Definitely."

We swam back. Jim had disappeared.

"We must be nice to him one more day," April begged me.

"One more day. Then we see each other without him as chaperone."

"Can you stay the night? I can. We could take the morning train—"

"And watch the bonfire that ends the summer?"

"Wouldn't that be fun!"

"I'll call my parents. They like you already, though I

can't imagine why. My boss won't mind if I'm a bit late tomorrow morning."

"I'll call my parents too."

"And we'll sit on the pergola after the bonfire."

Pause.

"I'd love that, Vangie."

It was not to happen. I would die again several hours before the bonfire.

She wrapped a towel around her shoulders—no beach pajamas required now—and we walked back to the Drake.

There was no one on the porch. So I stole another kiss, the most passionate yet. My hands roamed her body, soothing, caressing, demanding.

"Vangie," she begged.

I stopped.

She took a very deep breath. "That was very nice."

"A little too much?"

She grinned. "Just enough. Now go dress for lunch."

"Yes, ma'am."

The wedding, I decided on the way back to the priests' house, would be in early January or after Easter at the latest.

Jim was waiting for us at the lunch table, decked out in black-and-white checkered finery.

He insisted that I drive with him to a "friend's place" where he would get some "swell whiskey" for the bonfire.

I wanted to spend more time with April, but I had promised both her and myself that I would be nice to Jim for one last time.

The rain clouds loomed above us as we lurched along the road to the golf course. The smell of rain was already in the air, deep, earthy, pungent.

The two Romany women were about to leave their campsite when we drove by. The ponies were hitched to the hastily patched wagon.

Jim passed them and then stopped the Duesy.

"Hey, they're out already. I was going to bail them out

tomorrow. Well, I'd better give them something."

He jumped out of the car, strode over to the two Romany, said something and then laughed at his own joke. He pulled several bills out of his pocket and thrust them into the older woman's blouse, patted her rump and walked away from them, beaming happily.

The two of them watched him, their expressions revealing implacable hatred.

"Well, that's that," he sighed with satisfaction. "No harm done, huh? Hey, isn't that older one a nice piece of ass? Would you like her? I think I might be able to arrange it."

"No, thanks, Jim."

I'd argued with him for the last time.

We turned off the main road and down a narrow dirt road through several miles of untilled farm fields, crossed a river on an old wooden bridge, and made another turn.

I was completely lost. I had no idea what the river was. Perhaps it was merely one of the broad creeks that creep along the shore of Lake Michigan, a few miles inland, and then suddenly, as though they have taken a deep breath, turn and rush for the lake.

"Say, I've got some swell news." He turned to another enthusiasm as we swerved down a dirt road that was no more than two ruts in a field. We careened toward an ancient farmhouse in front of which was a buggy that may have expired when Grover Cleveland was president.

"What's the swell news?" I asked wearily.

"Well, I've talked to April. Yesterday, before you came up. She's just about agreed to marry me. After Easter probably, though it depends on what Momma says. Isn't that swell?"

"Are you sure, Jim?"

"Well, you know how women are. She just about said yes. I felt her up a little. She really liked it. We'll probably tell Momma at the end of the week."

When, I wondered, would it end?

Three men waited for us on the porch of the old house, grim, dark, bearded men in straw hats and overalls.

Just as we pulled up, the rains came, sudden and heavy. We were soaked instantly.

The men motioned us into the house. I noted with considerable unease that two Springfield rifles, clean and well oiled by the looks of them, were stacked inside the door.

The room was dark—one window that probably hadn't been cleaned since the Grant administration—and bare: a couple of rough chairs, a single wooden table. The room smelled of wood fires and whiskey.

Both of us were served two tumblers of what was certainly presentable bourbon. Jim babbled cheerfully. Our hosts said hardly a word.

When they did speak, it was in guttural whispers and with a strange accent I could not place.

Then when the drinking ceremony was over, they presented us with two milk bottles of the whiskey covered with paper caps and sealed with rubber bands.

Jim reached into his wallet for money.

They waved it away.

"See how generous my friends are?" he crowed. "Didn't I tell you they were great friends?"

He neglected to thank them, an omission of which the old Jim would never have been guilty.

They did not offer to assist us in putting the cover on the Duesy. We were soaked again.

The rain did not daunt Jim's good spirits. His friends had proven him right. The whiskey was really "swell." The drinks were taking effect. He began to sing, off-key, "One Alone" from *The Desert Song*.

I twisted uneasily in the seat next to him. Jim was drunk. He was driving too fast for a now muddy road. The rain was so thick I could see only a few feet in front of the car. And now hail was beating against the canvas top.

"Watch out, Jim," I yelled as a flash of lightning crackled in the sky ahead of us.

"I'm fine," he shouted above the roar of the thunder.

"The wooden bridge," I screamed as we hit the slippery planks.

"I can't brake!" Jim wailed.

The car seemed to sprout wings and fly through the air. A dark, raging current of water leaped up to meet us. There was a terrible wrenching crash. I was flung through space, cartwheeling back toward the water.

The river hit me a wet angry blow.

Everything turned black.

I thought, as I had on the parade ground, that I had yet to love.

The blackness became deeper. I searched for laughing brown eyes again. This time they weren't there.

Or maybe they were.

Then there was nothing at all.

❧ 31 ❧

The brown eyes were definitely amused.

I forced my own eyes to flicker open again.

My dream woman and my mother were standing at the end of my bed, arm in arm, smiling at me. Dad was on the other side of April, grinning cheerfully.

I closed my eyes in self-defense.

"We know you're awake, Vangie dear," April chortled. "You can't fool us. You're not that sick."

I gave up and opened my eyes.

"You're all right, son." Dad was trying to be sensible. "You're in St. Mary's Hospital in Kenosha. You had a bad bump on your head and a few bruised ribs and some nasty scratches, but the doctor says you'll be able to come home in a couple of days."

"And that sweet Mr. Hurley said you could take the next ten days off." April beamed at me.

"And your father and I think April is adorable."

"She plays a nice harp," I tried to say.

They all laughed at my raspy voice.

"Jim?"

"Not a scratch." Dad frowned. "That kind always lands on its feet."

"His mother took him home in tears," April continued. "Poor boy, he was so unhappy about his ruined car."

"The brakes had been damaged. Deliberately. He blames the Gypsies, but they've disappeared, lucky women. And it's unlikely they would know how to sabotage a car."

"Bootleggers," I said. "His friends."

"I thought as much." Dad nodded grimly.

"We're going back to Chicago, dear," Mom purred over me. "Your father has his usual Thursday meeting tomorrow."

"Thursday!"

"Today's Wednesday."

"What happened to Tuesday?"

"You slept right through it, Vangie." April giggled like a silly little girl.

"Dr. Cronin, who is such a nice man, says you'll be fine, but he's letting April stay over at Barry till you're ready to come home. He thinks she'll keep you out of trouble with the nuns."

"Such a nice man." I returned blissfully to sleep.

The next day, when April came to visit me, I was wide awake. My body was a solid mass of hurts, particularly my ribs and my head. But I was well enough to melt when my rhapsody in blue waltzed into the room.

"Are you being good, Vangie?"

"Only one nun bawled me out and I received Communion this morning."

"I'll agree to pose for your picture of the girl and the harp"—she was brisk and efficient—"on one condition."

"I think I'm dreaming this conversation," I said, truthfully enough. "But what is the one condition?"

"That you agree to marry me."

I gulped. "I was about to ask you, April."

"I beat you again. Is it a deal?"

"Sure it's a deal. The painting after the wedding, I suppose?"

"If you want"—she colored slightly—"but wouldn't it be more fun before the wedding?"

"It sure would."

Then she began to kiss me, paying no attention at all to my aches and pains.

I didn't pay any attention to them either.

So, we were married, at Thanksgiving as it turned out. April stole the show at the Black Horse Ball. Her parents liked me as much as my parents liked her.

Jim and Clarice were both in the wedding party. Jim never quite forgave me for marrying April. Clarice went back to Europe.

Both sets of parents suffered hard times at the end of their lives. But my parents lived to see the first three of their grandchildren—Jane Marie born in 1926, Charles Cronin (a pint-sized redhead) born in 1928, Margaret Mary born in 1931. And her parents, we always felt, liked our kids more than the other grandchildren.

For April and me there would be difficult times too, more difficult than we could have imagined; and our marriage, like all marriages, has had its rhythms, its ups and downs, but even in the lowest moments we have never stopped loving each other.

And, more important, we have never stopped being in love.

No man could ever stop being in love with April.

Our friends speculate as to which child is more like her.

Some say it is effervescent Jane, our cheerful firstborn. Others say it is Peg, our intense and tender violinist. Still others think it is Michael, our devout priest-to-be.

But April and I know they are wrong. The one most like her is Chuck, our contentious, difficult, frustrated account-ant, the self-professed white sheep of the crazy O'Malley clan, whose words you'll probably read after mine because I'm convinced my memoir will only be a prelude to the one he will write someday.

He is the one most like his mother, a passionate roman-tic just like her.

Charles's Love Story

1949

❧ 32 ❧

I read the manuscript twice. I wept after the first reading and sobbed after the second.

Dear God, I prayed, what a lucky guy I am to have those two as parents. No wonder all the O'Malleys are crazy!

I actually fell on my knees and repeated the praise, though God and I were not exactly on speaking terms because I was holding him responsible for Notre Dame.

Images, emotions, regrets, hopes, expectations, caroused around my head. I was as excited as I had been when we rounded up the black market gang outside of Bamberg, but then I understood the nature of the excitement. Now I realized that it would take much of my lifetime to sort out the meanings in Dad's memoir.

I wanted a wife like April Cronin.

Come to think of it, I had always wanted a wife like her.

I jumped off my bed and rushed down to the heated room in the cellar where Dad's paintings had been stored. I knew that I had seen a painting he called *Romany Women* when I was much younger. Though it was three o'clock in the morning, I had to see it.

As with everything in the life of the crazy O'Malleys, the storeroom was in chaos—half a hundred paintings propped up against the walls, piled on the floors, stacked in unstable heaps, covered with dust, the room illumined by a single forty-watt bulb. I suppose I should have been surprised that there was a storeroom, except that Dad treasured his paintings even if he didn't take very good care of them. Poor man, I thought as I searched through them, he's a great architect who wanted to be a great painter. Some of these are pretty good, but not quite good enough.

Some demon murmured folly about a photographer who wanted to be an accountant. You won a prize, the demon insisted.

And look what that got me, I said, dismissing the demon.

I found *Romany Women* under a mound of awful watercolors. As I had suspected it might be, it was the best thing Dad had ever painted, absolutely brilliant. The frame was broken, the stretcher loose, and the canvas was covered with dust. Fortunately it had not been torn. Gingerly I removed it from the mound and placed it delicately against the door. Compulsive neatness freak that I am, I tried to order the mound above it. And thus found the three nudes.

They were quite good too. Two of them were respectable and decently erotic, ingenious filmy protections in some but not all strategic places. The third was, what shall I say, candid, but reverently candid. The model was quite breathtaking. Who was she?

Mom!

The Girl with the Harp!

Embarrassed and guilty, I quickly turned them over. So, the legend was true!

I grinned complacently. Yeah, I was a lucky guy all right. No wonder I saw things differently from Father Pius. Too bad I couldn't have hung one of them in my room at the Golden Dome!

I hauled *Romany Women* upstairs to the breakfast nook, hunted for a pencil and paper by the phone, didn't find anything, and returned to my eagle's nest to write out in my precise script, "If you guys ever expect me to sleep here again, you'll hang this masterpiece in the most prominent place in the house. Charles C. O'Malley."

I then slept peacefully.

I caught them the next morning as they were eating their usual leisurely breakfast over the papers, a custom that had survived from the less hurried days over on Menard Avenue.

"I want a girl, just like the girl, that married dear old Dad," I announced, imitating Donald O'Connor, the song and dance man of the day, as I bounced into the room.

I kissed Mom fervently. "Woman, you'd try the patience of a saint," I informed her. "April Mae *June* Cronin indeed! You were nothing but a troublemaker! And that's all you are now too!"

I kissed her again.

"Well, dear," she said mildly. "You've always known *that*, haven't you?"

"Dad"—I clapped him on his shoulder—"you never had a chance, not from the first day."

"He always knew *that*," Mom said, now flushing brightly.

"You liked the story?" Dad asked, still anxious.

"Great, great story! Now I understand why all the O'Malleys are crazy, with only one exception!"

"You understood more about Mr. Clancy?" Mom said, frowning.

"What a jerk. Why did poor Clarice ever marry him? No wonder she fell down the stairs . . . I gotta run. Registration day at the University."

"You see why poor Rosie is the way she is, dear?"

"Rosemarie? Oh, she'll be all right. I wouldn't worry too much about her. She found herself a family."

Neither of them replied. I had the feeling I had missed something. No time for it now.

"You will hang that gorgeous painting, won't you?"

"If you want us to, Chuck," my father, greatly pleased, replied. "We certainly will."

"By the way," I said as I left the breakfast nook, "I think one of those nudes should be hung somewhere too. *The Girl with the Harp.*"

I didn't look back. I thought, however, that I heard laughter. Or at least sniggers.

Later that day I noted that the University (as everyone in Hyde Park called it in the blithe assumption that there was no other) differed in two obvious respects from Notre Dame.

It was outstandingly ugly even in a beautiful Indian summer.

The natives all looked strange.

The former phenomenon resulted from the fact that, as my father warned me, "Ralph Adams Cram's pseudo-Gothic does not a Cambridge make."

The latter resulted from the even more disturbing fact that few of the inhabitants were Irish Catholics, the only group that to my eyes did not look strange.

I didn't think I'd like it here. Not at all. Wouldn't it be better to seek out O'Hanlon and O'Halloran, Certified Public Accountants, and work till the next semester began? Then I could enroll in Loyola or DePaul or even the Pier.

(The University of Illinois at Chicago was then located at Navy Pier, a far more attractive setting than the present concrete monstrosity west of the Loop.)

I also discovered a similarity between this pagan institution and the Catholic school on the banks of the south bend of the St. Joseph River: bureaucratic underlings did not know what to do on registration day with a student that didn't fit recognizable patterns.

I submitted credits (carefully saved from summer school), filled out forms, answered easy questions on tests. Every time I asked a question I was told that someone else would have to answer.

I was shunted from Ida Noyes Hall to the blockhouse

Administration Building and back three times before I found an office in the upper reaches of the latter (an unsuccessful attempt to break with Cram's Gothic) where I was told by the young woman at the desk in the outer office that I had perhaps come to the right place but I would have to wait at least an hour.

I waited three hours. I managed to court all the available varieties of self-pity and despair during that time.

All right, I was free from Notre Dame. My dishonorable discharge had given me freedom.

But now what was I supposed to do?

Finally, I was shown into the office of the assistant registrar, who seemed to specialize in my kind of cases.

She looked over my transcripts with apparent interest. "Oh my," she said in a rich East Coast voice. "What a lot of school you've had!"

"Yes, ma'am."

"And you've performed very well in our tests; you've obviously worked hard in your courses and done a lot of reading on your own."

"Yes, ma'am."

"Well"—she peered at me over her glasses—"we will certainly admit you. And I see no problem about classifying you as a third-year student. Incidentally, that is the term we use here. There are no such things as juniors or seniors. Or even sophomores or freshmen. And, while we're at it, I should tell you that we call our professors 'Mister' not 'Doctor' or 'Professor.' "

"How democratic."

She grinned back at me. "You'll have to take some core courses this quarter and next quarter. Then I see no reason why you should not be able to graduate next year, assuming, as I think we might, that you do well in your courses."

It was the Hutchins era at the University and standards were more flexible than they would be later. But the University has always been freer of ritual requirements than most colleges, believing that if it made a decision it was obviously the right one.

"Are you sure, ma'am?" I was dazed.

"Quite certain." She smiled. "Welcome to the University, Mr. O'Malley."

"Thank you, ma'am."

I rode down the elevator and walked out into the late afternoon sunlight of the Quadrangle. According to the crumpled map I had studied all day, Swift Hall, the Divinity School, was on my right, the Physical Sciences on my left. Ugly still, but they seemed to want me. Ugly but warm. What the hell, Notre Dame had only been ugly to me.

I put the map in the pocket of my khaki Ike jacket. The wind had changed from southwest to northeast. It would be cold tonight, blanket weather. Winter was creeping down from the polar regions.

Somehow that thought exhilarated rather than depressed me.

I fumbled in my pocket for a dime.

I would walk back to the public phones in the lobby of the Ad Building.

It was time to phone Rosemarie. Did Dad's memoir move me to make that call?

I don't know. Maybe. Probably. Anyway, I told myself I wanted to thank her for helping me to win the prize and tell her that we were schoolmates again.

Maybe I should invite her to have supper with me.

❧ 33 ❧

I resolved that at the fourth ring I would disown the call and hang up. Halfway into the ring, I moved my finger toward the hook, ready to click it off.

"Rosemarie Clancy." The tone was crisp, efficient, a chief nurse maybe or a novice mistress in a progressive religious order.

My palms were sweaty, my heart was pounding swiftly. I was like a kid calling for his first date.

Well, maybe that's what I was. I almost hung up.

"Rosemarie *Helen* Clancy?"

"Certainly . . ." A touch of asperity in her musical voice. "Who is this? . . . Chucky?" Fear replaced asperity. "Is something wrong? Who's sick?"

"Me . . . maybe." I shifted the phone from my right to my left hand. "I thought maybe I could take you to supper tonight. I don't know this neighborhood very well. You'll have to choose the restaurant—"

"What?" She now sounded like I had announced the conversion of the pope to Mormonism. "You're inviting me on a *date?*"

"Uh . . . well, I thought we could celebrate my prize—"

"Our prize," she said promptly, contentious even when being invited to dinner.

"Precisely," I said, regaining some of my confidence. "So you're entitled to at least one dinner."

"You're not angry that we entered the picture?"

"I should be, but I'm not."

"Uh-huh. So I'm being invited to one inexpensive dinner?"

The brat was laughing at me.

"Your adjective."

"*Well*, there's a nice Chinese place around the corner on Fifty-seventh Street. . . . Do you like Chinese food?"

"Never had any."

"Willing to take a risk?"

"Two in one day?" It was my turn to laugh, somewhat sheepishly.

"Let me see . . . it's four-thirty. I can be ready by six. Is that all right? Not too early?"

"I'm hungry already."

"You're *always* hungry, Chucky Ducky." Now she was teasing me. "See you at six. Does Peg know you're calling me?"

"No. And don't tell her."

She laughed again, an impish, to-hell-with-you laugh.

I was certain as I left the public phone booth in the lobby of the University Administration Building that she was already on the phone to my sister.

Still, given the fun she could have had at my expense, I had been let off easily.

I walked out into the glory of Indian summer. I was very well aware that my decision to phone Rosemarie was impulsive and dangerous. I had been driven to it, one mean-spirited corner of my brain told me, by the need for womanly comfort in an unpleasant turning point in my life.

I was hurt, lonesome, and bewildered. I needed solace; so, as Christopher would have said, I was seeking warmth at Rosemarie's breasts—figuratively, I hasten to add.

Why had she not rejected my invitation, an insult surely to suggest a date at the last minute?

Probably because, damn her, she perceived that it would be much more fun to bait me about my bad manners.

I slouched through Hyde Park, killing the hour and a half, angry at her and angry at myself. I considered forgetting the whole business, but I feared the wrath of Peg, the most loyal and loving of sisters save when she had to choose between her friend Rosie and me.

Today Hyde Park, saved by the University and urban renewal from racial resegregation, looks picturesque. In October of 1949, it seemed only old and depressing, despite the colors of Indian summer and the pungent, poignant smell of burning leaves.

The immediate postwar era was coming to an end, though we didn't realize it then. The Russians had exploded their first atomic bomb; Communists in East Germany and China were establishing governments. What we would later call the Cold War was under way. The X-1 had soared to sixty-three-thousand feet, and Jackie Robinson, the first black player in the major leagues, would win the MVP award although his Dodgers would lose the World Series to the Yankees. Leon Hart of Notre Dame would win the Heisman trophy. The last encampment of the Grand Army of the Republic was attended by six of the sixteen surviving Civil War soldiers.

And I had a date with Rosemarie Clancy.

Promptly at six, I pushed the doorbell in the vestibule of her apartment building at Fifty-seventh and Kenwood.

"Yes?" Still brisk and efficient.

"I'm on time."

"Remarkable. I'm ready."

"Even more remarkable."

A moment later I heard a crashing noise on the stairs; Rosemarie was graceful, but not quiet, like a hundred does rushing through a forest—when she wasn't a timber wolf.

She flung open the door, eyes dancing with mischief.

"Oh, good," she exclaimed. "I was afraid you'd overdress for the Chinese place."

I was wearing a sweatshirt and Army fatigues.

"I could comb my hair."

"Waste of time." She grabbed my arm and shoved me out of the vestibule. "Come on, I thought you were hungry. I know I am."

I obeyed her without protest because I was dazzled by her good looks. I had known her most of my life, yet I was not immune from a deep gasp for breath every time I saw her.

She was dressed simply, doubtless expecting that I would not be ready for an elegant restaurant—dark blue skirt, light blue blouse, no discernible makeup, long hair braided behind her head, low shoes so that her five feet five inches did not threaten my five feet seven and three-quarter inches—an efficient, dedicated undergraduate at, by its own admission, the world's greatest university (just as the *Chicago Tribune* in those days claimed to be the World's Greatest Newspaper, whence the letters WGN for its radio station.)

She looked like a serious student, but one whose beauty would cause people to stop in the street and stare, a rare enough phenomenon in Hyde Park.

I was so troubled by the events of my twenty-first birthday and so bemused by her wide shoulders, swelling breasts, narrow waist, and flowing hips that I almost kissed her there in the vestibule of the three flat. That would have been the end of everything.

Rosemarie bounced and danced beside me as I slouched down Fifty-seventh Street.

"Someone really has to do something about your clothes, Chucky. You're not half bad-looking, you know. If you'd dress right and stand up straight, you might amount to something yet."

"You want me to look like an accountant as well as studying to be one?"

She clapped her hands and howled at that. "An accountant who won a prize from *Life*."

"For a picture of a kid with bare shoulders who might not have had anything on beneath the cropping."

"But who in fact had a swimsuit on because the photographer was scared."

"Of her strong right arm, known to devastate tennis balls and fresh young men."

"Depends on the man," she said primly. "Anyway, congratulations on the prize. It's a great achievement."

"Thank you." I felt myself blushing. "I'm still going to be an accountant."

"Chucky, you can be anything you want."

More unrestrained laughter. She was as scared of this date as I was.

That thought almost undid me again. Rosemarie was a person like me, what I would later learn should properly be called a "thou," an other who could feel the same anxiety and pain I felt.

Bad business.

"So how come you're not in a dorm?" I demanded. "I thought freshmen, oops, first-year students, had to live in dorms."

She flicked an eyebrow at my correct use of the University of Chicago terminology. "I live at home," she said brightly. "At 1101 North Menard Avenue."

"That's what the University thinks?"

"It's also the truth." Her eyes flared and her skin, always prone to blush, turned pink. "I just happen to have a *pied-à-terre* here that I use sometimes. That's all. *Pied-à-terre* means—"

"I know what it means. . . . So your own apartment and your own car and you're going on eighteen."

"Not bad, huh?" She grinned. "I know, I'm a spoiled rich brat—"

"No you're not." I dug my hands deeper into my pockets. "I don't believe that anymore. I suppose I never did."

"Chucky, you astonish me."

"Well." I was sure I was blushing more than she was. "I wouldn't quite—"

"Your twenty-first birthday worked wonders. You should have one every year. Happy birthday, by the way. You don't look a day over fifteen."

"And you don't look a day under twenty-five." ·

"Thank you." She bowed ceremoniously.

"How is your father?"

"He's all right." Her face was guarded, neutral. "Same as ever. Part of growing up, I guess, is understanding that you can't change your parents or even help them all that much."

How had he and his alcoholic wife produced such a striking and vital daughter?

"He doesn't mind your living out here?"

"He doesn't have any choice . . . anyway, I can take care of myself." Then, decisively changing the subject, "Hey, is this your first date?"

She shoved me into a store that from the outside looked like it might be an opium den. It was not much more prepossessing inside, a few bare tables, some wooden chairs, the smell of exotic food, a timeless Asian woman behind the cash register.

" 'Aro, Rosie," said the woman, smiling broadly. "Cute boy."

"Her son." I bowed. "Can't you see the family resemblance?"

"Ar Irish rook arike." The woman bowed back.

"Don't make fun of her." Rosemarie grabbed my arm fiercely as we were led to the table and whispered in my ear. "Orientals have trouble with the *L.* What she said was—"

"I know what she said," I grumbled.

Naturally, Rosemarie had already made friends with the woman of the house. She probably knew every shopkeeper on Fifty-seventh Street. Everyone liked Rosemarie—when she was sober.

I considered the lovely young woman who sat across from me, brimming with happy devilment. I didn't know much about such matters, but it seemed a reasonable bet that her beauty was durable. She would always be attractive. Unless, like her mother, she set about destroying her attractiveness. Unless, like her mother, she would kill herself with an accident in a drunken stupor before she was forty.

"So?" she demanded, her appetizing lips curving up in an impish smile.

"So what?"

"You didn't answer my question: is this your first date?"

"Well." I pondered the issue. "There was my senior prom . . ."

She dismissed it with an abrupt wave of her hand. "You were shanghaied."

"You ought to know about that."

Could I call my nights with Trudi in Bamberg when I was a member of the Constabulary in the Army of Occupation dates? We would not discuss that issue. And Nan Wynne, the cute WAC lieutenant I had kind of dated in Bamberg.

"There's Cordelia . . . I don't know whether—"

"Definitely not." She waved her hand again. "Cordelia would *never* say that she was dating you. Whatever happened to her, anyway?"

Her sapphire eyes turned shrewd. She was trying to solve a problem over which she and Margaret Mary, a.k.a. Peg, had pondered long and hard last summer.

"Promise you will tell Peg?"

"That I *will* tell her?" Rosemarie paused in mid-flight.

"I can't have you two worrying about that all year."

"Brat." She slapped my hand playfully. "Well, what *did* happen?"

She suspended the conversation long enough to give her friend from behind the cash register a detailed order of what she wanted and what I wanted.

It saved me the trouble of making my own decisions. Or of even reading the menu.

"And?" She returned to her cross-examination about Cordelia.

"She didn't think romance was consistent with her ambition to be a concert pianist. Felt we were getting too serious. I guess I agreed."

"She dumped you?"

"You could call it that."

"How did you feel?"

"Hurt for a couple of days. Then relieved."

"Not brokenhearted?"

"No."

She was silent a moment with thoughts of her own. "Is she any good?"

"As a pianist? To tell the truth, no, she isn't. I mean she hits all the right notes and her training is the best her father's money could pay for and she works hard; but, alas, practice and teachers and dedication are no substitute for real talent, of which, by comparison, my sister the fiddler has lots."

"Poor kid." Rosemarie's sympathy was genuine. "Did you tell her?"

"No."

"Why not?" Her exquisite forehead furrowed into a dangerous frown.

"I don't think she would have believed me. Who am I, just because ours is a musical family, to make such judgments? And I thought it would be cruel to destroy her illusion. Maybe she needs it now. Maybe it won't do her any harm."

"We all need our illusions." Rosemarie nodded solemnly.

"I guess."

"Just like your illusion that you're going to be a stuffy old accountant. . . . Anyway, have you seen her this semester?"

Like an Irish country woman about to buy a new farm, Rosemarie Helen Clancy was getting the whole lay of the land. Careful, little one, a single date does not a romance make.

Especially with someone who certainly will not marry until 1954. If then.

"Yeah, I saw her a few days ago at the office of *Compact,* her magazine, you know."

"And?"

"And she didn't ask me to work for the magazine. I think I'm just one more Notre Dame boy now."

"Stupid." Rosemarie seemed angry, more at Cordelia than at me.

"What about Christopher?"

"What about him?" She tapped her finger impatiently on a knife.

"You can't ask about my romances and expect me not to ask about yours."

"It's different." She abandoned the knife.

"How?"

"I'm me and you're you, that's how."

"Hmm . . ."

"Anyway," she sighed. "He *is* a very nice boy. I don't know how he puts up with you as a friend."

"I don't either."

"You be *quiet,* while I explain. I think he was getting pretty serious about me and I had to warn him it wasn't a very good idea."

"Why not?"

" 'Cause I'd drive him crazy, that's why not. He really is a very quiet and serious boy."

Not quite what Christopher had told me.

"North Side German."

"Something . . . Which reminds me, Notre Dame boy, why aren't you there today? Is the Feast of the Holy Rosary a holiday or something?"

"Feast of the Holy Rosary?"

"Right. October seventh. Anniversary of the Battle of Lepanto at which John of Austria, a year older than you are, routed the whole Turkish fleet and saved Europe. Chesterton wrote a poem about it . . . "Dim drums throbbing on a hill half heard where only on a nameless throne a crownless prince has stirred" . . . which doesn't explain why you're not at Notre Dame."

"Because I'm here in Hyde Park taking you to dinner at this sumptuous Oriental restaurant for my first fully certified date."

"Something *is* wrong, Chucky." Her eyes were soft with compassion, the compassion I had wanted and that now embarrassed me. "What is it?"

"I was thrown out. On my birthday."

Well, I would take any pity I could get.

"Why?" She dropped the spoon with which she'd been approaching her pale yellow soup—egg drop if I remember rightly.

"For drinking."

"But you don't drink!"

"I was framed. . . . My rector didn't like me. He'd been trying to get me for months. So finally he had to make up the evidence. I was told to be on the five o'clock South Shore." I would not tell her that the photo of her had angered my hall rector. No point in burdening her with that knowledge.

"Bastards!" She pounded the table, spilling some of our soup. Her wonderful face was dark red in anger. "They have no right . . . where are you going to school . . . out here?"

"I guess we're schoolmates again, Rosemarie. They accepted me this afternoon. The good April wanted to make sure that I told you so you could take care of me."

She didn't laugh. Her eyes filled with tears.

I took her hand. She enclosed it in her two hands.

"I'm so sorry, Chuck. I know how much Notre Dame

meant to you. Since you were a little boy you wanted to go there. It's not fair."

I tell you, sympathy from a pretty woman you can't beat.

"They seem to want me here," I said with a pretense of manliness.

"All those lonely months in Germany you dreamed of the Golden Dome." Tears were falling down her cheeks now. Her grip on my unprotesting hand tightened. "They have no right at all to do what they did. They're a disgrace to God and the church. As bad as nuns."

"It's over." I tried to sound like I had been healed of all my resentment. "Maybe a good thing too. Like Mom said, I never was really happy there."

That theory was dismissed with yet another abrupt hand wave. Her hand quickly returned to join its partner enfolding mine. "How do you get out here? On the El?" Then she grinned broadly and her face lit up—an unfailing sign that she had thought of something outrageous, something that she ought never to say and was about to say it anyway. "*Well,* I hope you don't think"—she doubled up, hands to her face to stop the laughter—"that you're going to be *my* roommate!"

I joined in the laughter and discovered that in our shared amusement all my hurt and confusion had been swept away.

So that's what Christopher meant by consolation at the breast?

"The idea had not occurred to me"—I struggled for a straight face—"but I don't think I could afford the rent."

"Mind you"—she held up a warning finger—"if you're caught in a blizzard and agree to be locked up in the parlor, I *might*—"

"An attractive offer. Free?"

"Nothing is ever free, Chucky Ducky. Now eat your egg drop soup. It's good for you."

"Yes, ma'am."

"Charles Cronin O'Malley, are you holding my hand?"

Patently I was.

"Absolutely not."

"Well, it's my right hand, so I can eat . . . You're becoming dangerous, Chucky. You invite me out for your first date and then you hold my hand."

"I'd never do that."

"And you certainly won't put your arm around me when we walk home or kiss me good night either."

"What absurd ideas!"

"I'm glad to hear it. . . . Now eat your egg drop soup."

"I have something else to tell you."

"Hmm . . ." she said, swallowing a spoonful of the delicious soup. "I can tell that it isn't good."

She squeezed my hand reassuringly.

"I had your picture tacked to the wall in my room at the Dome—"

"Hey!" She pounded the table. "I've at last made it as a pinup!"

Then her exuberance withered and her grin faded into a dangerous frown.

"You mean they threw you out because of the picture?"

"Not exactly . . . Father Pius was gunning for me because of the picture. He tore one copy up, so I made a sixteen-by-twenty and tacked it on the wall. . . . So you were really a tackup!"

"Tacky." She permitted a tiny smile to suspend her rage temporarily.

"I'm sure that's why he planted the beer in my room."

"We'll get even, Chucky. We'll get even."

"It would be a waste of our time to worry about that," I said piously.

"I suppose you're right."

"I didn't belong there."

"You think you belong here?"

"As long as you're around, I do."

"How sweet!" she exclaimed, her anger dismissed.

My sister Peg claims that I have a quick mind and a quicker tongue. She says that I get in trouble because my tongue races ahead of my mind. That had often been true in Bamberg. It was still true. My compliment had exploded spontaneously off my lips. Now I was in trouble. Yet, it was worth the risk to see the radiance of her smile.

And at such a trivial compliment!

"My body is not dirty, Chuck, is it?"

Now she was sad again. And fragile.

"Not that I've ever noticed," I said with an approving glance at her.

She grinned again. "They're wrong, aren't they!"

For an answer I sang "Younger than Springtime."

She joined in the chorus. Everyone in the restaurant joined the second chorus.

"Not a bad act!" she said exultantly. "Maybe we could go on the road. . . . Tour all the Chinese restaurants. Now eat your egg foo young before it gets cold."

"Yes, ma'am."

I put my arm around her waist as soon as we left the restaurant. She responded in kind.

"Well," she said, feigning a sigh of relief, "I'm certainly happy we're not walking back to my apartment embracing one another."

"That would be vulgar."

"Exactly. And it would be even more vulgar to sing as we do it."

"The natives would think we're crazy."

"Shouldn't let the Irish Catholics in because first thing you know the whole neighborhood will go to pieces."

"Right."

I began to sing "Younger than Springtime" again. We worked our way through *South Pacific* on the way home. To her home, that is. The natives smiled. Even Hyde Park locals had to smile at Rosemarie.

When she was washing "that man right outa my hair," she pretended to scrub my wire-brush red head.

"Careful," I said, "you'll cut your fingers."

"Just filing my nails."

In the lobby of her apartment building, she sighed. "At least I don't have to worry about fighting off a kiss at the end of this date."

"Certainly not," I said, drawing her close.

My kiss was sweet and gentle and tender—and the most satisfying kiss thus far in my life.

Rosemarie sagged against me, her head on my shoulder.

"Oh, Chuck," she gasped. "What a wonderful kiss. You're the one entitled to consolation after what they've done to you. Instead you console me."

Was that what I'd done?

"I didn't kiss you," I insisted as we clung to each other.

"I know that," she giggled. "So you won't kiss me again the same way."

"I'd be afraid to," I said, repeating the kiss, this time even more tenderly.

"Thank you, Chuck," she said, slowly slipping out of the embrace, tears streaming down her cheeks.

Why was she crying? Better not ask.

"Good night, Rosemarie," I said. "Great date for the first time. You won't hear from me again in a day or two about going to the movies."

"I wouldn't expect to," she sniffed.

"Great, so I won't be talking to you."

"And I won't tell Peg anything about our first date."

"Naturally not."

I kissed her forehead and departed that lobby as quickly as I could.

With a song in my heart!

"Younger than Springtime," of course.

I hummed it over and over again on the ride home on the Illinois Central and the Lake Street El. I would have to avoid Peg when I got into our house. No, that wouldn't be necessary. The good Margaret Mary would pretend to know nothing, lest she disturb the delicate fabric of our initial relationship.

I was, unaccountably, a very happy young man.

❧ 34 ❧

"This Princeton isn't a bad place," Jim Rizzo assured me. "There's some former gyrenes like me and they're good guys even if they are kind of stuffy."

We were in the Magic Pub, Jim, Monica, and I. It was the fifteenth of October, 1949, a date I have always remembered very easily and not because the Communist armies had captured Canton, as we used to call it.

"Funny thing," Jim went on expansively, "I take to this law stuff. For some crazy reason I seem to be real good at it. Some of my professors actually treat me with respect, even if they do think I'm a greasy little wop from Chicago."

Monica slapped his arm.

"I've told you, James, that I don't ever want to hear you use that word."

"Even though it's true," I added. "Actually I prefer the phrase 'cutthroat Sicilian.'"

In high good humor we all laughed. Jimmy and Monica were to be married on Thanksgiving weekend. He had found an apartment for them in Princeton and a job for her in a Catholic school. They would go on their honeymoon over Christmas and then settle in for the two and a half remaining years of law school. The only shadow in their lives was that Big Tom had forbidden Monica's family from having any part in the ceremony. So it would be a small wedding, much to the dismay of his family, which loved big weddings.

There was also continuing good news about Tim Boylan. He was now taking some courses at the Pier and seemed to have settled down, most of the time anyway. He and Jenny seemed to be falling in love.

All was right in the world.

They insisted on taking me home because of the thunderstorm. I can't remember why we dropped Monica off at her Austin Boulevard apartment first. If I were engaged to such a delightful woman, I would get rid of the red-haired punk first.

Or maybe I was a chaperone.

Anyway, we turned left at the Judson Baptist Church and on to Potomac and entered Oak Park.

"I am one very lucky guy," Jimmy told me. "There were three or four times I thought I wouldn't live another hour. Now I'm going to Princeton and a wonderful woman is willing to take a chance on spending her life with me. I don't deserve it, but that's not going to stop me."

Before I could answer, the end of the world happened. We were crossing Taylor Street, the second street in Oak Park. Jim was driving slowly because of the rain. A sizzling flash of lightning illumined the intersection. A car plowed into us at high speed. Jimmy's battered twelve-year-old car spun around and tipped over. I flew through the air and landed on the parkway to the accompaniment of an ominous roll of thunder. There was another burst of lightning and more thunder, this time almost instantly after the burst. The Ruskies are closing in on us, I thought. All we need is Wagnerian music. I reached for my weapon. No, I wasn't in Bamberg anymore. I was in Oak Park, not a notoriously dangerous place. A third flash of lightning revealed that the car that hit us had disappeared.

Then I smelled leaking gasoline. That could be danger-

ous. I'd better get my corporal out of the car. Or was Trudi
still in it?

Despite my confusion and my flight through space, I
was able to walk, somewhat unsteadily, to the ruined car.
It wasn't my Bamberg Buick. It was an old jalopy. Surprisingly my corporal was Jimmy Rizzo. No, I wasn't in
the marines. What was a marine captain doing in my car?

The smell of leaking gas was strong. I'd better hurry
before the fire came. I pulled on the driver's side door. It
wouldn't move. I uttered some curses of which the good
April would not have approved and yanked again. The
door fell off and I fell on the street.

A voice in the back of my skull warned me to hurry;
the car was about to blow.

Jimmy was unconscious. In retrospect the sound advice
would have been not to move lest I complicate his injuries.
I pulled him out of the car and across the slick pavement
on which water and gasoline were mixing, onto the parkway, and over the sidewalk. I made it to the lawn and
indeed up to the bushes. Then the car exploded in a dirty
orange fireball that knocked me off my feet.

The Oak Park fire department and police arrived about
a half century later. They found me lying on the lawn
gasping for breath, next to a very unconscious Jimmy
Rizzo.

"Who are you, kid?" a cop asked me.

"Cronin, Charles C. Staff Sergeant, First Constabulary
Regiment . . ."

I rattled off the first numbers of my serial number and
then lost the rest of it.

"You're not in the service any longer, kid. You're in
Oak Park. . . . You really a sergeant?"

I struggled to my feet.

"They always ask that. . . . How's my driver? . . . No,
Captain Rizzo . . . is that my blood?"

Your Legion of Merit winner almost fainted.

I told the police what happened. Someone had rammed

us and driven off. Hit and run. I was thrown free and landed on the parkway. I smelled gasoline and pulled him out of the car. Then it exploded.

"You saved his life," the cop said.

"How is he?" I asked again.

"Unconscious. His breathing is shallow. I'm no doctor, but I think he's probably got a concussion. I think he'll be all right."

"He was talking about the four times in the Marines he thought he was going to die when they hit us."

"I was a marine too. We'll take good care of him, Sarge. We'd better take you down to West Suburban too, just to look you over."

"I'm fine."

My legs wobbled under me. The ex-marine steadied me.

"They'll just look you over. . . . Did you get a good look at the car, maybe catch its license number?"

"It was night and pouring rain. It might have been red."

"That's not much to go on. We'll see what we can find out."

In fact, it was a red Ford, late model and, while I had not seen its license number, I knew what it was. Instinctively I kept that information to myself. For the present.

At West Suburban Hospital, a relic in those days of the Edwardian era, I was examined at considerable length and pronounced in "good" condition with cuts and abrasions. They put me in a bed and gave me a sedative so I could get a good night's sleep.

"Mr. Rizzo," I was informed, "is in satisfactory condition with a fractured collarbone and a concussion. He has regained consciousness but is still very confused. You both were very lucky."

"Angels," I replied. "Legions of them."

At some later point, the O'Malley clan arrived en masse, the womenfolk looking pale and distraught, Dad angry.

"You're not the only one who flies out of cars," I said to him.

Rosemarie's face, tearstained and drawn, came into focus.

"There is a serious possibility," I said, resisting an impulse to touch her hand, "that I will survive and live a reasonably normal life. However, I will need constant care and affection and must be humored at all times."

Though I was a patient in a hospital and had barely escaped death, they laughed at me.

At that point, according to eyewitnesses, I fell asleep. There was considerable concern among the O'Malleys that I had slipped into a coma. It took a resident, two interns, and several nurses to reassure them.

A priest brought me Communion the next morning. The resident told me that I would be released in the afternoon.

I stole up to the next floor to visit Jimmy.

The room was filled with noisy Sicilians lamenting the accident and celebrating his recovery.

"Well, Captain, sir," I said as I worked my way through the crowd. "That was a close one. That 88 had our range."

His left arm was in a sling. There were some minor bandages on his face and neck. Otherwise he looked fine, but a little confused. Monica clung to his free hand with grim determination.

"The Japanese didn't use 88s, Sarge," he said with a grin. "The medics say you saved my life."

"I don't think, sir, that the captain's lady would look good in black."

They all laughed. It wasn't really that funny, but I guess they needed laughter.

Monica hugged me fiercely.

"Chuck, I owe everything to you!"

"Only an invitation to the wedding, ma'am."

"Thank you, Sarge." Jimmy removed his hand from Monica's grasp to shake mine. It was not exactly a firm grasp. Monica promptly recaptured it.

"I think the woman looks good in black," he added,

"especially if it's lace, but I guess I'll have to wait to find
out."

More nervous laughter from the Sicilian contingent and
a modest blush from Monica.

I backed away to make room for worried aunts, cousins,
and sisters. Mrs. Rizzo, a handsome woman with a touch
of gray in her hair, was sitting on a chair fingering her
Rosary beads.

"I'm Salvatore Damico," a tall, saturnine man with
deadly brown eyes informed me.

"Hey, Uncle Sal," I said, shaking his hand.

"I want you to know, Sergeant, that Jimmy is family. I
value his happiness. He wants to go to Princeton, I say
fine, Jimmy, go to Princeton. He wants to marry a beautiful
Irish girl, I say, fine, Jimmy, you have great taste. If someone saves Jimmy's life, I say, hey, Sergeant, I owe you.
Anytime you need a favor there's a marker there to pick
up."

For those who don't understand the rhetoric of this particular subculture, that's high praise indeed. Maybe someday I'd need to pick up a marker.

"I appreciate that, Uncle Sal," I said. "I'll keep it in
mind."

That's also the appropriate response.

"And, I tell you this, I swear on my mother's grave that
if I find out who did this to you and my nephew, he'll
wish he'd never been born."

There was silence in the room for a moment. A jihad
had been proclaimed.

I filed that fact in my memory.

I knew who had tried to injure us, perhaps to kill us.
The question now was what to do with that knowledge.

My parents came over in the afternoon to bring me
home. I was treated as if I were a fragile newborn who
had just been removed from an incubator. Naturally I reveled in my new status. Take it whenever you can get it.

I was installed in a couch in the music room. Mozart

was put on the phonograph to soothe me. Peg brought me a huge dish of chocolate ice cream. I was lapping it up with little attention to table manners when Rosemarie drifted in, solemn and sympathetic, but also determined.

"Red Ford, Chuck?"

"What else?"

"License number?"

"It was 405–216."

"You saw it?"

"I was flying through space, so I didn't see it. But no one but you and I know I didn't see it."

She nodded solemnly.

"What are we going to do about it?"

I almost changed "we" to "I." Then I thought better of it.

"Intimidate Big Tom."

"You think he actually tried to kill you?"

"Maybe not actually kill. Maybe just send a message."

"Loud message, Chuck."

"Very loud."

"How do we intimidate him?"

Patently we were both crazy kids. But I'd been down similar roads in Bamberg. And, however different, Rosemarie was Jim Clancy's daughter.

"With my own ears I heard my good friend Sal the Pal swear on his mother's grave that when he finds out who tried to do us in, the aforementioned party would wish he'd never been born."

She shivered.

"We're not going to do that, are we?"

"Certainly not. We may need only to threaten."

Thereupon the two of us outlined a plan. It was madness, but if I do say so myself, brilliant madness. Rosemarie and I were a dangerous team, a nice irony if one considers the story I had read about our ancestors.

❧ 35 ❧

"What do you two want to see me about?" Big Tom stood at his desk in his sumptuous office in the West Side Bank Building at Harlem and First Avenue in Melrose Park, a glitzy postwar product that my father did not design and of which he would be acutely ashamed if someone had assigned responsibility to him.

Rosemarie responded, taking charge at the beginning.

"We told the woman who did not want to let us in that we wanted to see you about a red postwar Ford, license number 405–216."

"What about it?"

Big Tom glowered at us, his face red beneath carefully groomed (and probably dyed) wavy silver hair, a hurricane ready to sweep away two trivial sand spits.

"We have reason to believe that it was driven by two off-duty Chicago policemen who attempted to kill your daughter's fiancé on Saturday night and that these policemen were your employees."

Rosemarie was mimicking Mr. District Attorney, a radio series character of the day.

"Prove it," he sneered.

"We also have here photographs of the same car and the policemen watching a softball game at which your daughter and her fiancé were present."

I laid out the first set of pictures.

"Moreover," Rosemarie continued, "we have witnesses who will testify that these men began to follow your daughter when she moved out of your home because of your opposition to her marriage."

"That marriage will never occur."

"If your hired killers had been successful the night before last"—I pointed an accusatory finger at him—"the marriage would never have occurred. And I might be dead too."

"I would not have mourned for either of you," he laughed. "The world would be better off without you. But you won't be able to prove those charges."

"We may not have to." Rosemarie laid the second set of pictures on his huge and perfectly empty oak desk.

"These are photographs of the same policemen assaulting me in front of my home in Oak Park the day after I took the photos in our previous exhibit. You'll note that the red Ford is clearly visible in the picture because we used color film. So too are the faces of the two policemen. Finally, the last photograph is an enlargement that shows the license plate on the car. You will note its number."

"None of this has any implication for me. You two little brats get out of my office."

However, he made no attempt to throw us out.

"Providentially, I made a report to the Oak Park police about the, ah, visit on that morning. They'll have a record. When I tell them that I can identify the car that crashed into us the other night, they will remember the incident. Your cop friends will be in real trouble. They might want to name their employer to get off easier than they otherwise would."

Some of the color faded from his face.

"Cops protect one another. If these outrageous charges are made, the Chicago cops will provide alibis for their own."

"I'm sure they will. However, the Oak Park police are notorious for their incorruptibility."

"It might not make any difference for you." Rosemarie took up our scenario, as we closed in.

"What do you mean?"

A muscle under one of his eyes was beginning to twitch.

"I mean," I went on, "with my own ears I heard a certain Salvatore Damico, also known as Sal the Pal, say that he had sworn on his mother's grave that when he finds out who tried to kill his beloved nephew, that person would wish he'd never been born."

"I don't believe you."

"It's your risk," Rosemarie said coldly.

She was, beyond all doubt and all my doubt, quite a woman.

"Have no doubt, Mr. Sullivan," I said, "that unless you satisfy us, we will move on this matter today. We will not inform Mr. Damico. We will not have to. He will find out. By tomorrow evening you might well wish you'd never been born."

He sat down in the vast chair behind his desk.

"What do you want?"

"Four things," Rosemarie replied, her voice as cold as the Arctic tundra. "The first is you leave us and Mr. Rizzo alone. You stop interfering with your daughter's marriage to Mr. Rizzo. You refrain from all punitive actions against them for the rest of your life."

"And the final thing we want, Mr. Sullivan"—I delivered the coup de grâce—"is that you write out in your own hand and sign this confession."

I laid it on his desk.

It read:

"I, Thomas Francis Sullivan, do hereby confess that I authorized two off-duty Chicago policemen who were in my employ to do serious bodily harm to my daughter's fiancé, James Rizzo, on the night of October 15, 1948. I further confess that I understood clearly that Mr. Rizzo's death might occur as a result of this bodily harm."

"I won't do it," he shouted.

"Fine," I said. "You can keep the pictures. Incidentally, all our evidence is in a safe place and safe hands, so it won't help you one bit if you try to harm us."

"Indeed," Rosemarie continued. "One of our associates has been authorized to call Mr. Damico at eleven o'clock this morning unless he hears from us that he should not place the call. Before making the call, he will unseal an envelope that outlines our evidence against you."

"He" clearly was Margaret Mary O'Malley.

He opened a drawer in his desk and removed a blank sheet of paper.

"On your personal letterhead," I said lightly.

He stared balefully at me and hesitated.

Then, shrugging slightly, he put aside the blank sheet and removed a letterhead from another drawer. He carefully copied our neatly typed document.

I picked up our original and his copy from the desk, glanced over them, and nodded.

"Thank you very much, Mr. Sullivan. You might want to consider the fact that if our morals were like yours, Sal the Pal would already be working you over."

"See you at the wedding," Rosemarie said cheerfully as we left his office.

Before I closed the door, I glanced back. Big Tom Sullivan had shrunk. He was slumped over his desk, head in hands, a beaten man.

That night Monica called me to say that there was really good news. Her father had come to the hospital, shaken hands with James, had a nice conversation with both of them, and said that he had no objections to the marriage. I called Rosemarie in Hyde Park and told her the good news.

"Well," she said, "he was a good loser."

"I don't think so," I replied. "He knows how to lose and put a good face on it."

❧ 36 ❧

L'affaire Sullivan was an isolated incident, albeit a fascinating one in my courtship of Rosemarie Helen Clancy, if it can be called a courtship. I told myself it wasn't a courtship. She never said it was. My quixotic and erratic quest was against my better judgment. To pursue it nonetheless was to risk everything I thought I stood for. She was not the kind of sober, sensible woman I told myself I wanted to marry. She would not wait till 1954. I knew about her drinking problem. I knew about her parents. I remembered her sobbing in St. Ursula's Church that night so long ago. It made no sense at all. I thought about her ugly, evil father.

He was the same rival Dad had to fight, wasn't he? Couldn't I rout him if I wanted to?

The drinking problem scared me. What would I do with a drunken wife?

Then why "date" her even if the dates were in places like Chinese restaurants in Hyde Park?

Because she enchanted me with her beauty and her intelligence and her laughter and her embarrassingly obvious love for me, because she was irresistible, because I longed for a woman. And perhaps because I had always loved her.

In a way it was my father's courtship all over again.

Different woman, but same enemy. A much more powerful enemy this time around.

I didn't think about that then—not as far as I can remember. However, even today I remember vividly the compliant firmness of her body and the sweet warmth of her lips.

Like our first tender embrace on Fifty-seventh Street was yesterday.

It did not take me long to figure out how the University worked. Its very distinguished faculty was bored by most students and affronted by the pushy ones who asked stupid questions. Professors valued wit and originality. Whatever else may be said of Charles Cronin O'Malley, he was long on both.

I turned in my assigned paper in a medieval history class at the end of the second week of the quarter.

"What's this?" the tall, austere professor with silver hair asked suspiciously.

"My term paper, sir."

"It's not due till the end of the quarter!"

I reached for the paper.

"No, I'll keep it," he said sternly. "You realize that I will probably give it a failing grade. No one could possibly finish a respectable paper on a medieval city in this period of time."

"I have an obsessive need for closure, sir."

He examined my face carefully as he tried to figure out whether I was pulling his leg—which of course I was.

"Well, we'll see about that, Mr. . . . ah, O'Malley."

"Yes, sir, Irish Catholic Democrat from the West Side of Chicago."

"Indeed."

Rosemarie, who had somehow managed to get in the same class, was staring at me anxiously from the doorway.

"You're out of your mind, Chucky Ducky," she protested in the dark and dingy corridor of the 1155 Eas

Fifty-ninth Street Building, a place where the Holy Inquisition might have held court.

"Wait and see," I said, whistling "Younger than Springtime."

At the beginning of the next class, the professor announced solemnly that he'd like to see, ah, Mr. O'Malley after class. He didn't have to look around for me because, as in all classes, I sat in the front row. It was easier to take on a professor from there.

He held the paper in his hand. A small *A* was printed on top of it.

"You were in Bamberg during the war, Mr. O'Malley?"

"After it, sir. For eighteen months. In the Constabulary. First Constabulary Regiment."

"Very few young men your age would have asborbed so much of that city in such a brief period of time. . . . By the way, how old are you?"

"I only look sixteen, sir. I achieved my citizenship a couple of weeks ago."

"The photographs are especially good," he said with a faint hint of a smile. "You could have an excellent career as a photographer."

"Thank you, sir. I plan to be an accountant."

He actually laughed as though he didn't expect that outcome. He was being careful because he wasn't sure what odd manner of person he had encountered.

"We actually had two very bright graduate students here before the war. Husband and wife. I suppose they were swallowed up in the war."

"The Richters, sir. Kurt and Brigitta?"

"Yes, as a matter of fact. Are they still alive?"

"Yes, indeed they are, sir. Doktor Richter was captured during the Battle of Kursk, the largest tank battle in history, sir, as I'm sure you know. Miraculously he survived and has returned to Bamberg. He is now teaching again at the university. It is rumored that he may be the next rector here. Frau Doktor Richter is the chief translator at our headquarters and is finishing her book on the second day of the Battle of Gettysburg. They both are active in Herr Reichkanzler Konrad Adenauer's party."

I removed a picture of the Richters from my wallet.

"They have three children now, sir."

I didn't tell him that the youngest was named Karl Krönin Richter.

"Amazing! My colleagues will be delighted to know. I'm sure we can write him at the university there. . . . Ah, is this young woman with you, Charles?"

Rosemarie was standing a couple of inches behind my right shoulder, ready to do battle if I should be threatened.

"Never seen her before in my life, sir."

"Would you mind repeating for Chuck what you said about his photography, sir?" she said with her most demure smile.

"What . . . ? Oh, yes. He should certainly pursue it as a career. He is very, very good. In fact, there is an interesting exhibition at the Art Institute just now on postwar photography . . ."

"Well, that's a sure A," she said to me in the corridor. "You own that man. And he'll tell everyone about you. You'll be a legend in the first quarter. I'm sure you're pulling something like that in every class."

"The Richters," I said modestly, "were a lucky break."

"You ought to be ashamed of yourself, Chucky Ducky," she said with considerable admiration.

"A little guy like me has to survive in this strange environment."

"You could have survived that way at Notre Dame if you wanted to."

"They wouldn't have cared about Bamberg and they would have rejected the pictures. They would have given me a D."

"C minus," she replied. "Come on, let's get lunch. I'm starved."

❦ 37 ❦

"You're a fraud, Charles Cronin O'Malley, a fraud, a phony, and a faker."

"I cheat besides."

My teacher and opponent that weekend before Halloween in 1949 leaned against the back of the bench in Skelton Park, an official place for nighttime beer drinking in my generation—despite the vigilance of the Oak Park Police Department. She was breathing heavily, her wondrous breasts moving up and down in delightful spasms. Her sweat-soaked white tennis blouse and skirt clung to her in a most appealing outline. Only a boor could win a set from such a vision, especially a boor in Army fatigues.

"You pretend to be a terrible athlete and actually you're not bad at all," she continued to pant.

"I'm not as good as you are."

"Of *course* you're not. Still, when I'm finished with your lessons, you should be able to beat me about a third of the time."

Rosemarie didn't like to lose. Neither did I, for that matter, but I had had lots of practice at losing and she very little. Or so I thought then.

"More like a fifth."

"Regardless." She shrugged her comely shoulders and

for good measure nudged my stomach with her tennis racket.

Indian summer had continued into late October. Rosemarie was staying at our house for the weekend. She had cajoled me into a tennis match at the park down the street. Peg, who under ordinary circumstances could have been expected to join us, pleaded that she had to practice the violin, a sure sign that they had been conspiring.

I knew the agenda—first we teach Chucky to play tennis, then we make him accept a car so he won't have to ride that horrid El train back and forth to school, then we dress him up properly so he looks right.

Then?

I didn't want to consider the next item on the agenda. But I knew that Peg and Rosemarie could count on the enthusiastic support of my sister Jane, her husband Ted, my brother Mike, and my parents in executing the whole agenda.

I was the moth skirting the candle, the lemming hesitating on the edge of the cliff.

"You're falling in love, Charles," Christopher told me on the telephone the day after our first date.

"Certainly not," I replied uneasily.

"Awfully close to it."

"A mild infatuation," I pleaded.

Christopher remained silent.

"Are you still there?" I felt my face twist into a suspicious frown.

"I don't want you to be angry at me."

"When has that ever happened?"

"You're right. Still . . ."

"Let's have it."

"God has thrown the two of you together . . . and don't say it: with a considerable assist from the University of Notre Dame."

"All right. So?"

"So if you hang around her, you'll end up marrying

her—probably sooner rather than later. She's beautiful; she's available; and the male mind at our age figures that a girl in hand is worth two in the thicket."

"You've said that before."

"I know I have." He was so calm, so rational, so much a Scholastic philosopher. A lay Saint Thomas without the Dominican robes. "You're not immune from the ordinary human drives, Charles."

"I'm well aware of that, Christopher; but as I've told you often when we've discussed the subject of the ravishing Rosemarie, I know her too well. She drinks too much, she's the daughter of a monster and a drunk. She's a bad risk . . . doomed probably."

"When your blood gets hotter, you will hardly notice those problems."

"You're warning me that if I don't get out now, it might be too late, say next week?" I laughed as I said it, knowing how ridiculous such a suggestion was.

"Say next Christmas." He didn't laugh.

"Not a chance. I can control my passions."

"I'm warning you because I think I should, but I'm not sure I want you to control your passions."

"You want me to marry her, don't you, Christopher?"

"Yes, I do. I think it would be a good match."

"Why does that matter to you?"

"Because I love you both." His response was prompt, blunt, and utterly unsentimental. North Side German.

"I understand that." A lump rose in my throat. Sentimental West Side Irish. I didn't understand it at all. "And I appreciate it, but I'm not courting Rosemarie and I'm not going to marry her."

"We'll see, Charles," he laughed easily. "We'll see. Frankly, I envy you."

"Why should she want to marry me?" I changed tack. "She's only eighteen. She could have her choice of almost anyone. Why me?"

"I suppose she thinks she loves you."

"Is in love with me?"

"That too. But, Charles, face it, she loves you. The poor kid has always loved you."

"Why?"

He seemed to think that question was hilarious. "If you can't answer that, Charles, I'm sure I can't answer it for you."

So, my lay father confessor was no help.

After our dinner at the Chinese restaurant, I tried to be virtuous and avoid Rosemarie. "See you around the campus," I said cautiously, after our two modest kisses.

"If I don't see you, I'll see you." She grinned mischievously, threw open the door, and rushed up the stairs like a herd of zebra fleeing a leopard.

That was Rosemarie: don't walk, run.

And that, I told myself, was that. Clean, neat, definitive. No passionate kissing, no tears, no promises.

To be able to avoid someone at a small university with a relatively compact campus (especially in those days) requires that you be alert so that you can see that person. Thus to avoid Rosemarie, I had to be on the lookout for her.

Right?

Surprisingly I didn't find her for several days, so there was no opportunity or occasion to avoid her. You'd think that she'd stand out in a student body where good-looking young women were so scarce one might suspect they were going out of fashion.

Especially good-looking young Celts.

Nonetheless, despite my considerable efforts to spot her so I could avoid her, four days went by without any opportunity to put my virtue to the test.

Then I saw her in the reading room of William Rainey Harper Memorial Library, a locale as cozy as Union Station and as quiet as a mausoleum. She was sitting at a desk in the far corner of the room, a stack of books at her left arm, a notebook in front of her, head bowed over the notebook, pencil poised, ready to write. (I have good eyes, at least when I'm looking for women to avoid.)

While I watched she began to write in the notebook.

I failed the test to my virtue. Totally and completely. I walked over to the table and sat down across from her. She continued to scribble feverishly. The books were closed, so she was recording thoughts, not taking notes. Her face was intent, serious, dedicated. And, to be honest, a little frightening.

Today she was wearing a brown skirt and a beige blouse; her hair was still tied behind her head. All business.

And so radiant that she illuminated the whole drab, dour William Rainey Harper reading room.

Sensing finally that someone was at the table with her, she glanced up at me, warning me, whoever I might be, that an interruption would not be welcome.

Then she smiled and the rest of the reading room, the rest of the world in fact, disappeared.

"Chucky," she whispered. "What are you doing here?"

"Admiring your diligence."

"Silly." She reddened. "Wait till I'm finished and we can walk up to Jimmy's for a hamburger."

"Okay."

Thus for my virtue.

We established a pattern. I would arrive in the reading room at eleven-thirty, sit across from her and study quietly till noon, and then we would walk over to Jimmy's for a hamburger and a beer (in those days eighteen-year-old women were "legal" while men had to wait till they were twenty-one, a law that only made sense if you agreed with Rosemarie and Peg that women were superior to men and in better control of their vices).

Jimmy's was a bar on Fifty-fifth Street at which the University intellectuals and the working class met in a strange juxtaposition. It made the intellectuals feel tough. don't know what, if anything, it did to the truck drivers.

They were, it seemed to me, a rough, foulmouthed crowd. Most of them eyed Rosemarie appreciatively whenever we walked in, but no one made a crack about her. You don't mess, I guess, with a grand duchess.

The hamburgers were good.

Then depending on what day of the week it was, I would walk with her back to her apartment and return alone to the reading room or ride the Fifty-fifth Street bus over to the El and down to the chambers of O'Hanlon and O'Halloran. On Wednesdays we both went back to the reading room because we had an afternoon class.

I wasn't courting her, however. Not at all.

I did not refuse, however, to be bathed by and absorbed in her smile whenever she looked up and saw me across the table in the dark, intimidating reading room.

You say that I was already hopelessly in love with Rosemarie Helen Clancy and lacked the honesty and the integrity to admit it to myself?

You say that I used the excuse of her background and her problems to cover up the fact that I was terrified of her?

I was making a fool out of myself, I won't deny it. I was your typical immature late-adolescent male caught in the tug of the energies that keep our species in existence while he still pretends to himself that he is in control of himself and his energies.

Indeed, all my behavior since my honorable discharge over a year before had been immature. The last mature thing I did was to drive Trudi and her mother and sister from Bamberg to Stuttgart one jump ahead of the cop who wanted to turn them over to the Russians. I won't hide behind the pretext that I was merely a late-adolescent male trying to escape the tender trap. I added to the stereotype a special twist of dishonesty and perversity.

I had even stopped going to church on Sunday in protest against my treatment at Notre Dame, as if God and Monsignor Mugsy and Saint Ursula were to blame for my hall rector.

Mom and Dad never said a word about my refusal to get up on Sunday morning.

I could imagine her saying, "It's just a stage the poor dear is going through."

The trouble was that she was right and I knew it even then.

I did not understand then and I still don't understand what Rosemarie could have seen in that obnoxious little squirt.

So as Halloween approached and Indian summer persisted, as my Yankees beat the Dodgers, Jackie Robinson, the first black player in baseball, was elected National League player of the year (which led to a celebration at the O'Malley supper table), Rosemarie and I went forth on weekends to Skelton Park (pronounced by generations of kids as "skeleton" park because, as it was alleged, skeletons appeared there at night) for my compulsory tennis lessons.

Weekends at the crazy O'Malleys' were usually chaotic. I had hoped when we left behind our tiny Depression apartment in the ten hundred block on North Menard for a big home on Fair Oaks Avenue in Oak Park my parents would finally put their lives in order. But the confusion, mental and physical, merely multiplied to fill up the available space.

I'm not sure how we earned our label "the crazy O'Malleys." Possibly it arose from our inability to find things or to come on time or to keep our home in order or to sustain grudges or to live within our means when the means were meager indeed. However, the title fit; everyone else in the family was proud of it.

Need I say I was offended by it? I was not crazy. I kept accurate records and files, I was never late, my quarters were always impeccably neat, I did not forget offenses, and I budgeted my finances carefully and conservatively.

Moreover, I vowed I would not permit my camera to become the equivalent of Dad's paintbrush and Mom's harp—essentially distractions from the serious business of keeping the architect business running smoothly.

"Chucky Ducky," Peg told me on one of those autumn weekends in 1949, her eyes glowing with admiration. "You're the craziest O'Malley of them all."

My life since then would prove Peg an uncannily accurate prophet. I can't quite figure out how it all happened.

There was trouble in the house of the crazy O'Malleys on those October weekends in 1949. Michael seemed more withdrawn and reflective than ever. Dad and Mom were under great strain to complete the construction of the new St. Ursula's Church, our parish church. Dad had won prizes for the design, but the contractors who were supposed to be building it were both incompetent and arrogant since the president of the company was a nephew of the late cardinal. Jane and Peg had romantic difficulties.

I had found Peg in the music room of our sprawling house about nine o'clock on that Saturday morning. Dressed in brown slacks and a blue Notre Dame sweatshirt, she was studying the score of a Brahms sonata.

"Isn't my alma mater playing the hated Trojans today?" I removed a stack of harp music from one of the chairs in the room and seated myself on it.

"You mean Leon Hart's team?" She grinned as she picked up her violin.

"And Vince Antonelli's?"

"Who's he?" She wrinkled her pert nose. "Can't say I've ever heard of him."

"Oh?"

"He thinks we broke up." She adjusted the violin under her chin.

"But you haven't?"

"We'll break up only when I agree we've broken up." She sighed and rested the violin on her lap. "And I haven't said that yet. You're playing tennis with Rosie today?"

"I'll do what I'm told. But you and Vince—"

"I hear"—her eyes flared—"that you give him the same advice Chris Kurtz gives you."

"It applies to him, not to me."

"He's a dear boy." She sighed again. "And I don't propose to let him get away. But this social inferiority stuff would try the patience of a saint."

"He'll call up by tomorrow night and apologize?"

"Presumably."

"And you want me to stay out of it?"

"Oh, no, Chucky." She poked my ribs with her bow. "Keep preaching what you don't practice. It suits me fine."

That morning, however, Peg seemed a bit more disturbed than she was prepared to admit. I resolved that I'd warn Vince that people do fall out of love, especially when they grow weary of the same false song being sung over and over again.

"Too good for the Antonellis and not good enough for the McCormacks? Kind of ironic, isn't it?"

Peg laid aside her bow, put the violin on the table, and folded her hands on her lap.

"Big difference. Vince's stuff is a bore but it's minor. If he doesn't drop it, we won't get married. Jane and Ted are already married. Doctor is trying to dictate her choice of an obstetrician."

"And?"

"Ted is arguing that Doctor is right."

"The jerk better make up his mind."

"Remember how we put Doctor down at the wedding?"

"Great fun. It was all your doing."

"Chucky Ducky, you were the ringleader."

Not true, but you learn not to argue.

As we recalled our put-on of "Doctor" at the wedding reception, I studied my sister's animated face in the glow of the autumn morning sun through the French windows of our music room, head tilted, hand under chin. I saw the perfect moment for a shot. But, not having my camera, I did not take the photo. Indeed there was no film in any of my cameras. I had not taken a single shot since I won the prize. I would not permit a silly hobby to seduce me away from my serious career.

A critic once wrote of my work, "It is in no sense a negative comment to say that O'Malley may be the best snapshot photographer in the world." Later enemies transformed the comment to say that I was only a snapshot taker. Basically the remark is correct. I can do the usual technical things with camera, film, and developing chemicals that anyone can do. But what makes me different from a lot of photographers is that I have an instinct for exactly when to push the shutter button. No, let me be more precise: I sniff the crucial second coming even before it appears.

Edward Weston said it took him years of looking at light, texture, and form before he "saw." I was lucky; I "saw" even before I ever picked up a camera. I often see, as I did the lovely lines and planes of Peg's face that Indian summer morning, even though I don't have a camera. I guess you can say that I became a photographer against all my better judgments because my "second sight" forced me to take pictures.

There were some humans involved too.

Sometimes the "sniffing" works better than others. Perhaps I remember that Saturday morning so clearly today because the "smell" of shape and light and texture was so acute that day.

Or maybe only because it was the first time I ever won a tennis set from Rosemarie.

Our laughter about routing Doctor that Saturday before Halloween was interrupted by the appearance of a young woman in tennis garb carrying a tray with cornflakes and bananas in one hand and a coffeepot in the other.

"Breakfast time, children; what's so funny?"

"Doctor!" we said together.

"Bad man." Rosemarie was not amused. "Bad man."

She then dragged me off to the courts at Skelton Park, bordered that pre-Halloween day by oak and maple trees glowing in orange and gold. Rosemarie was a natural athlete. She picked up a tennis racket and held it without any reflection in just the right grip. She swung a golf club with an easy, unselfconscious swing. Her muscles were solid and her grace and balance was effortless. Rosemarie was a winner who did not like to lose. I was a loser who did not like to lose.

(Some of the muscle development was the result of jujitsu—as we called it then—training from a Japanese American veteran of the Italian campaign called respectfully "revered master." Peg and Rosemarie must have been among the very first American women to take the martial arts seriously.)

She was, moreover, a good teacher, even when her pupil was doomed from birth to be forever clumsy. He did not, be it noted for posterity, object to lessons from a young woman, especially a very pretty young woman who found more than one occasion in which it was necessary to put her arm around him in order to facilitate her instructions.

Then he had the ill grace to win a set, partly because of luck, partly because his teacher was weary from having won three already that morning, and partly because he wasn't completely clumsy.

Rosemarie was not amused.

"I'm sure that last serve was in." She tossed a maroon sweater around her shoulders. "I think you cheat."

"Would I cheat?" I sat next to her on the bench.

She considered me suspiciously. "I suppose not. Anyway, I won't be a bad loser. You played real good."

"Very well too."

"Shut up." She shoved my arm, none too gently, with her racket, now securely protected in its press (where I put it immediately after the last point).

"Yes, teacher."

"You are definitely a fraud . . . admit it, you did try to

score the touchdown in the last game with Carmel. You weren't just running away from their linemen, were you?"

"Uh, I just wanted to escape them when Vince's blocked pass tumbled into my hands."

"I know that's the public story, but I don't believe it. I think you deliberately won that game and that you enjoy being a hero and that you enjoy even more pretending that you're not a hero."

"Me?"

"You . . ." The racket poked me again. "And when you fished me out of the lake after the prom, you told everyone that the water wasn't deep and I wouldn't have drowned anyway."

"It-wasn't deep."

"I could have drowned in a bathtub that day."

"You were pretty heavy then. Baby fat, I guess. It would have been hard to pull you out of a bathtub."

"Beast!"

"Me?"

"You." No poke this time. Instead she wiped the sweat off her forehead and slipped her sweater on. "Put on your Ike jacket. I don't want you to catch cold."

"Yes, mother."

"Is there something wrong with my knees, Chucky? Why are you staring at them that way?"

I felt my face become warm. "Pretty knees, nice architecture, right fabric, good light. If I crop the shot here"—I traced a pattern above and below her crossed knees—"I could do a pretty good abstract design."

"Really?" She considered her knees with interest. "Anyone's knees?"

"No, *your* knees. They're the only ones here."

"But you don't have your camera." She transferred her gaze to me. "Do you just go around seeing shots?"

I nodded. "Even before I owned a camera. I guess that's why I started taking pictures."

"Really?"

"Really." I took her hand and dragged her to the other side of the court. "Now isn't that maple gorgeous, every shade of red and gold and orange?"

"Uh-huh."

"Now, come over this way; duck down here, next to this bench, and kind of squint through the frame my hands make. See what I mean?"

"Oh, Chucky, it's so gorgeous that it's scary. You see things that way all the time?"

"Sometimes more than others, especially on days when I beat stuck-up girls at tennis."

"Chucky the accountant," she sighed. "All right, have it your way. Come on, let's walk home. Tell you what." She unbuttoned her sweater and began the task again, this time taking care that each button went into the proper button-hole. "I have an accounting job for you."

"Oh?"

"Take charge of your parents' records. They don't have any idea how much money they're making or losing or whether they're broke or wealthy."

"I thought Mrs. McAteer was keeping their books."

"Mrs. McAteer is one of the best bookkeepers of the late eighteenth century. Moreover, she's senile."

"Mom won't want to hurt her feelings."

I didn't like Rosemarie's idea. What if I found that they were broke or hopelessly in debt? Or owed the government money? Well, better me than the IRS.

"You can soft-soap her like you do every other woman. Make her think she's teaching you how to do accounts, just like"—her eyes lit up with mischief—"you make me think I'm teaching you how to use your backhand."

"Who me?"

"*You.*" Her racket resumed its assault on my defenseless ribs.

A battered old black 1942 Ford was parked on Fair Oaks Avenue in front of our house.

"Gosh." Rosemarie pointed at it in disgust. "I'm surprised they let a car like that on the streets here in Oak Park."

"Not overnight."

The available family was gathered in the music room, the usual assembly point. Michael was at school, Quigley having class on Saturday in those years to protect seminarians from association with the laity. Mom and Dad, Peg, and Jane and Ted were waiting for us.

"We thought you'd like some nice apple cider, dears." Mom peered at us over her glasses. "Before the ceremony."

"What ceremony?"

Ted had his arms around Jane's expanding waist, he proud, she content, both of them dizzily in love with one another. How could Doctor fight that?

Or maybe the question was, could that finally beat Doctor?

"Just a little ceremony. Now drink your cider first and eat a doughnut."

"One, Chucky," Peg insisted.

"As many as he wants, dear."

"That means every doughnut in the world." Rosemarie drained her cider glass. "I'm ready. Let's start the ceremony."

"I've written a little poem." Dad cleared his throat.

There were a few boos: Dad's doggerel demanded boos. In their absence he would have been disappointed.

"Hush." Mom began to pluck at her harp.

> We come to honor Chucky this Octoberfest
> Of our second-born children surely the best
> Kinky redhead, camera hero, always filled
> with zest
> At present signs the last one to leave our
> family nest.

Peg and Rosie applauded; Mom increased the beat on her harp. Poor Ted was trying unsuccessfully to control his laughter.

Each day he journeys to Moscow Tech
Through storm and rain and snow by heck
And comes home again at night a wreck
So long an El ride, a pain in the neck.

We all groaned. Dad beamed contentedly. Moscow Tech
was what the Chicago Irish called the University in the
totally mistaken assumption that it was a radical institution.

We know you're too poor to afford a motor car
Chuck, caught in the Depression you still are,
Though inflation is the worse threat by far
And you our prize-winning camera star.

"What's this leading to?" I demanded.
Peg and Rosemarie cackled derisively.

It is not our intent to mock or tease
We want your daily ride to have more ease
Since you'll only take a bag of fleas
Chuck, here for your battered Ford, the keys.

Mom, joined quickly by Peg and Rosemarie, sang "My
Merry Oldsmobile," an inaccurate but in their mind an appropriate song. Then they turned to "Some Enchanted Evening." There was hugging and kissing and congratulations.

I had been mouse-trapped. Like it or not, I was stuck
with a car. I had no choice but to accept it graciously.
Well, graciously for me.

"Gee, I was expecting a Cadillac. Or maybe a Benz."

Boos from the assembly.

"But I'll make a deal with you: Mom and Dad, I'll accept this Halloween treat on the condition that you let me
get some practice for my accounting career by working on
your books."

Rosemarie beamed and nodded her head in approval.

Sometimes, Chucky Ducky, you show a few signs of intelligence.

Mom frowned. "I don't know, Chucky dear. We don't want to hurt Mrs. McAteer's feelings."

"Mrs. McAteer is one of the most accomplished book-keepers who ever retired from Sears. I'll just explain to her that I want her to teach me accounting the way Rosemarie teaches me tennis."

The latter worthy blushed and rolled her eyes in feigned dismay.

So, it was arranged. Just the way Rosemarie Helen Clancy wanted it to be arranged.

That night after supper the family was wasting time as it usually did over a bottle of port—a special bottle opened to commemorate Chucky's "new" Ford. I drank apple cider. Unfermented apple cider.

The phone rang. Since no one else even heard it, I slipped off into the living room to answer it (that was in the days when even a big house had only one phone).

"Crazy O'Malley residence, least crazy speaking."

"Chuck . . ."

Vince, naturally.

"So you slaughtered the evil Trojans."

"Sure did." He didn't seem too happy about it.

"You're an idiot, Vince." I continued my practice of offering him the same advice that Christopher gave me—appropriate in Vince's case but not in mine. "You're never going to find a better girl or one who loves you so much. If I were her, I'd tell you to creep back into your hole in the ground with all the other Neapolitans who are ashamed of their heritage."

"I know," he said humbly. "I've been acting like a jerk."

" 'A damn fool' would be a better expression. I don't know why she puts up with you."

I was laying it on thick, but what the hell. It was fun to be dishing out advice.

"I don't know why either . . . I don't suppose she wants to talk to me."

"I don't think she should want to talk to you, Vince. But I suppose she will. Don't go away; we're having one of our affluent Irish orgies and I may have to drag her away from it."

I ambled back into the dining room. Peg caught my eye as soon as I came in the door. So, she had heard the phone too.

"The Neapolitan." I jerked my head in the direction of the phone.

Peg thundered by me like she was running for the finish line at Arlington Park.

" 'Bout time, the big jerk," Rosemarie murmured.

"Hush dear." Mom raised a finger to her lips. "Men are that way."

In bed that night I did not wonder if the car and my assignment to straighten out the crazy O'Malley family accounts were Rosemarie's ideas.

Obviously they were.

❧ 38 ❧

"Cordelia," I said urbanely, "this is Rosemarie Clancy . . . Rosemarie, this is Cordelia Lennon, a friend of mine from the Golden Dome."

My date smiled genially and extended her hand.

"I'm very happy to meet you, Cordelia," she said cordially. "I'm interested in what a musician like yourself thinks of the soprano."

We held all the cards. I had caught Cordelia off guard in the lobby of the Chicago Opera House.

"Cordelia, great to see you again! How are things going at *Compact*?"

Her usual savoir-faire deserted her.

"Chuck . . ."

Her date was someone named Chad who went to Northwestern Law School, at least half a foot taller than me. He seemed utterly bored at the prospect of wasting time with shanty Irish from the West Side of Chicago, even if one of them was totally gorgeous in a black cocktail gown with thin straps.

Trying to recover her poise, Cordelia stumbled again. She ignored both our questions.

"It was so unfair what they did to you at Farley Hall, Chuck. So terribly unfair . . . Are you in school?"

Christopher had not told her. Good for him.

Rosemarie had made me dress up for *La Traviata,* gray double-breasted suit, white shirt, conservative tie. I would have been thoroughly presentable if she had been able to do something with my hair.

"Third-year student at the University."

"He's only been there a month, Cordelia," Rosemarie said, one woman conspiring with another, "and already he talks like a native. He means the University of Chicago."

"You go there too, uh . . ."

"Rosemarie. I know Chuck from grammar school, however. I apologize for not being able to do something about his hair tonight. But that's a difficult task, as I'm sure you know."

I wasn't sure whether my date—who really wasn't a date—was trying to embarrass my former date or to charm her. Maybe a bit of both. Poor Cordelia was not in the same league as this black Irish witch.

"I went to Harvard," Chad informed us.

"Why doesn't that surprise me?" Rosemarie said, beating me to the punch. "But I do want to know, Cordelia, what you think of the soprano?"

Cordelia realized that she was not in the house of the Borgias and that she could relax.

"Lovely, in the lower registers, I think."

"And very smooth when she dodges the high notes. Still, she's a wonderful actress, isn't she?"

"Oh yes, Rosemarie. Very tragic."

"It's a tragedy all right. . . . Yet also very Catholic. Forgiveness and salvation for everyone."

"I had never thought of it that way, Rosemarie. You're right, however. That's a very perceptive observation."

The two young women had decided that they liked each other, cautiously and guardedly perhaps, but still they were not about to let me interfere with a possible friendship.

"I wonder if you could write your observations about the opera in an article for our little magazine . . ."

"How many words?"

"Twelve hundred?"

"Sure . . . And"—nudging me with her elbow—"you can use my name. . . . Chuck will give me the address."

"Splendidly done," I whispered to her as we walked in for the second act. "How did you know I had written an article for *Compact*?"

She stopped humming the "Drinking Song."

"Vince sent a copy to Peg. . . . I feel sorry for poor Cordelia. The guy is a creep. She still loves you."

"Does she?"

"Totally. Too late. She can't have you."

"You were certainly friendly."

"Someday she might need a friend in the real world."

She resumed her humming.

As the curtain slipped up, she stopped humming and took my hand firmly in hers.

"No whispering."

I hadn't whispered during the first act, but I could not now defend myself without violating her rule.

I had listened to opera records at home all my life. *La Traviata* at the Chicago Opera, soon to die a painful death, was the first one I had attended. It was wonderful, especially with my gorgeous date. I'd be back.

So long as she continued to pay for the ticket.

Our dating, as I have related, had begun with a movie in Hyde Park, then one at the Lake in Oak Park on a weekend. Always accompanied by suppers at inexpensive restaurants—which she chose but for which I paid. Then it escalated to a string quartet and the opera for both of which she paid. I thought I should argue with her and then realized it would be a waste of time. Next week we would drop into Orchestra Hall for a Friday matinee and then eat supper at Rickets on Chicago Avenue.

She was gradually civilizing Chucky Ducky.

Since we weren't really dating, much less courting, I did not have to worry about the possibility of a serious emotional involvement. My family pretended they knew nothing about our relationship. I pretended to myself that it was not serious.

You can't beat denial for dealing with a problem.

Besides, I was having a wonderful time. I looked forward to seeing her every day in the library and even more to our nondates.

Chucky Ducky in love? Nonsense! We were just friends who enjoyed each other's company. Nothing else.

As she drove us home to Oak Park that night (as usual she was staying at a spare bedroom in our house that was now officially known as "Rosie's room"), she spoke again about Cordelia.

"Are you awake, Chuck?"

"I think so."

"Just barely . . . About Cordelia?"

"Yes?"

"She was deeply involved with you, wasn't she?"

"She dumped me."

"I understand. But it was very hard for her, wasn't it?"

"I think so."

"You could have changed her mind, couldn't you?"

I hesitated.

"Maybe."

"You didn't try?"

"No."

"Why not?"

I squirmed in the seat of her Studebaker. She stopped for the traffic light at Washington Avenue and Laramie.

"I figured it wouldn't be fair to her."

Silence.

"Were you in love with her?"

"I thought I was."

"You got over it very quickly, though, didn't you?"

"Yes. . . . How does the court rule?"

"Not guilty."

That was the end of that.

❧ 39 ❧

In early November Rosemarie knew all the regulars at Jimmy's by their first names. Also their wives' names. And their children's names. And their birthdays.

On their birthdays, she brought them small presents—scarves, gloves, ties, socks.

If she were running for office she would have carried Jimmy's precinct unanimously.

Our routine was to enter through the door on Fifty-fifth Street, pass the bar, order our hamburgers or chili at the end of the bar, and then go into the adjoining room and sit at one of the battered card tables and eat our food and drink our beer or Coke—one beer only for Rosemarie and that every other day.

The week before Thanksgiving, the good news at the crazy O'Malleys' was that Vince and Peg were firmly reconciled. The bad news was that Ted and Jane would not spend Thanksgiving with us. Doctor demanded their whole day. Mom thought it would be nice because then they could split Christmas between Evanston where Doctor lived and Oak Park.

I've always had an irrational hatred for Evanston, perhaps because Northwestern was there, perhaps because it was Republican, but mostly because I thought Evanstonians looked down on Chicago.

"Not as much as Oak Parkers did," Dad would reply.

"That was before we Catholics moved in and took over," I would insist.

"That's not the way to deal with Doctor," Rosemarie had contended. "He's just like my father. Give him an inch and he'll take a mile."

On weekends, Rosemarie always dutifully checked in at the house on Menard Avenue, spoke with the ancient Kerry woman who was housekeeper, and then almost always adjourned to her home away from home at our house. It had become so much a part of everyone's routine that no one questioned it or wondered about Rosemarie's attitude toward her father.

"She loves him, poor man," Mom observed. "But it's hard to live in the same house with him."

Two weeks before Thanksgiving I had promised Rosemarie a report on my work with the family account books. We therefore had an agenda for our chili lunch at Jimmy's. The agenda did not, however, prevent Rosemarie from taking time to present "Wally" with his birthday present— two pairs of "Christmas socks" in red and green which were so loud that they would have smashed a mirror if there were one behind the bar.

The other regulars applauded enthusiastically.

"Some girl you got there, kid," a certain Freddy informed me.

"You're right," I agreed. "Only I don't got her."

Freddy shook his head, whether in disbelief or sympathy I could not tell.

There were two big guys—tall and fat—at the end of the bar who had not been there before. They leered at Rosemarie and murmured something lewd. She froze them as was her wont when someone crossed the line between what she deemed appropriate and inappropriate freshness.

When Rosemarie froze you, you were really frozen.

The bigger of the two guys—an ugly fellow with a vast

handlebar mustache and an enormous potbelly—muttered ominously into his beer mug.

I turned to mutter back at him—an instinctive and ridiculous male barroom response.

Rosemarie firmly seized my arm and propelled me into the other room.

"Act your age, Chucky," she hissed.

"Yes, ma'am."

The second room at Jimmy's smelled of human sweat, stale beer, and the sawdust that covered the floor. A few rays of autumn sunlight managed to find their way through the thick cigarette smoke and dirty shopfront window next to which we always tried to sit. Just as the blue-collar types dominated the bar, University types dominated the second room. The latter, feeling tough and masculine in Jimmy's, managed to make only a little less noise than the working class.

"Now then." She arranged her chili dish and her beer at a table near the window. "What has Charles Cronin O'Malley, would-be CPA, found out about his family?" Her eyes narrowed anxiously. "Are they living above their means?"

The American economy was beginning to falter in the first serious postwar recession. Inflation was worrying everyone although income had far outstripped it. The Chinese Nationalists were retreating to Formosa. The L.A. Rams, quarterbacked by Jane Russell's husband Bob Waterfield, were dominating the NFL. Army had beat Navy 38–0. Louis Armstrong was playing in Paris. The critics were raving about the new Bogart film *The Treasure of the Sierra Madre,* and Tracy and Hepburn, lovers in real life though none of us Catholics knew it then, were back together in the film *Adam's Rib.* The war was forgotten but not the Depression, as I was to learn in the next few weeks.

"Not only are they not living above their means." I sunk my teeth into one of Jimmy's succulent hamburgers (I always ordered two). "They probably could not do so if they wanted to. Rosemarie, they have more money than they think they have, more money than they know what to do with, more money than it's probably good for them to have. Despite Doctor, these have been good years to be an architect."

Rosemarie exhaled contentedly. "I thought that might be possible."

"Which is why you put an A1 accountant on the job. Moreover, if they used their time and their resources properly, they would have even more money and be able to take vacations at Grand Beach and in some sunny clime in the winter—instead of hanging around the offices worrying that they don't have enough cash to make ends meet."

"Really?"

"Really. And to address myself to another of your concerns as the fairy godmother to the crazy O'Malleys—"

"I am *not*," she snapped furiously.

"Whether you are or not we can debate on another occasion." I dismissed her quibble with the sort of hand wave with which she often favored my irrelevancies. "The fact is that they could easily provide Ted and Jane with an 'allowance' that would exceed Doctor's."

"Better call it a loan." She wiped a small trace of chili from the corner of her mouth. "That's what adults do."

"Regardless. Now there are some reforms that are necessary."

"Such as?" From her dark blue skirt (which matched her sweater, the latter garment leaving little question about the perfection of her breasts) there appeared a notebook.

"One. They have to hire a draftsman. It's a waste of resources for someone as talented as Dad to spend his time inking plans. Second. They must hire a secretary to see to the correspondence, the bill-paying, and the filing of plans. Third. They should take in some bright kid from IIT, as they call Armour Tech now, to act as an apprentice.

Fourth. They should consider forming a partnership with said kid or some other young genius within the next year. Fifth. They should have me glance over Mrs. McAteer's shoulder once a month. I have figured out how to deal with her and make her love it."

"As to the last"—Rosemarie sipped her beer—"I don't doubt it in the least. But if you take away from your mother her task of searching for lost blueprints, what will there be left for her to do?"

"That at which she's best. She can be Mom—which is to say she can answer the phone, make appointments, smile at people, and take care of everyone. We'll call it office manager."

Rosemarie nodded sagely. "I think we can sell it all, Chuck, if we put it the right way. And what a relief it will be for them to know they don't have to worry anymore. . . . You really are good at this accounting stuff, aren't you?"

"I told you I was."

"Bet you never win a national prize at it." She winked.

"That is irrelevant." I felt my face turn hot as it often did when Rosemarie scored on one of her verbal thrusts, as she did with alarming frequency.

"Well, you can tell them how to reorganize the firm; they'll find the recommendations coming from an odd source. You're the one who is sure the Depression will be back; yet you'll advise them to act like it isn't."

I had yet to tell Rosemarie that I now knew enough to be quite certain the Depression would not return, not for a long time, and that the present recession was meaningless.

"I'm not going to tell them. You are. This was all your idea."

"I will *not*." She shoved aside her chili plate. "You're their child. I'm not."

"Come on, Rosemarie." I sat back in my chair. It teetered dangerously. "Don't give me that. You're the favored child in the family."

"Don't you dare say that!" She pounded the table. "Are you jealous or something?"

"Me?" Rarely did I have the advantage in our verbal sparring. "Why should I be? I'm the favorite second child. But you're the favorite of everyone. None of the rest of us mind."

"That's not true!" Her gorgeous face contorted into an ugly frown. "I'm not even a member of your family! You're looking for a fight."

"Guilty conscience? You meddle in our family problems like you were a member. Not that any of us mind because you always help. But why argue about it?"

I wanted to drop the whole debate now. I had no idea how you cope with a woman as bright as Rosemarie when she becomes irrationally angry.

"We'll argue about it"—she pounded the table again, harder this time—"because it's a damn lie!"

Some of the other people in the room began to glance at us. We had gone over the approved noise level.

"Cut it out, Rosemarie," I said, trying to sound disgusted. "You're acting like a spoiled brat again."

She sat up straight, to her full five feet five inches, eyes blazing, face pale, nostrils quivering—the Celtic woman warrior ready for battle. "I am—"

"Being ridiculous."

A smile began to twitch at the corner of her lips. It turned into a sheepish grin. She lowered her eyes.

"—an absolute goof. I'm sorry, Chucky." She glanced up again. "I guess I'm the most loved because I'm the most lovable, right?"

"I won't fight that." I relaxed. I'd won a battle with the wench. "But I might say that as an Irish matriarch-in-training, you need more love."

"Irish matriarch-in-training?" Thunderheads began to assemble again. "What do you mean by that?"

"Someone who runs things like the good April."

"I really would be happy if I were like her," she sighed. "But she'd never lose her temper the way I just did. Anyway, I do need more love, I guess." She touched the tips of my fingers with hers. "I'm sorry, Chucky. I thought I had the bitch inside me under better control."

"She sure is pretty when she appears."

"Silly." She shoved my fingers away like I had touched hers. "Well, what about if you and Peg and I tell them your report? Is that a good compromise?"

"Better than I expected. I'll do the talking and you do the persuading."

She laughed happily, the angry bitch now effectively banished. Scary character—that angry bitch. But I had shut her up. Not bad. I'd have to brag about my accomplishment to Christopher when I saw him the Friday after Thanksgiving.

"Come on"—she stood up—"I have to finish a paper this afternoon. The trouble with the quarter system is that it's the end of term before you know it. I suppose you're up to date on all your assignments."

"All papers turned in," I said modestly.

"You make me mad." She gathered her brown cloth coat over her arm and glanced back at me to assure me that the bitch was still in her box. "Not really."

We entered the bar, which was more crowded, noisier, and more foul-smelling than usual. Rosemarie elbowed her way through the crush at the near end of the bar and passed the two strangers who had made the snide remarks when we had entered a half hour before.

Everything happened so quickly that it was only afterward that I figured out what had happened—and understood that once again I had fallen on my face.

Someone unintentionally jostled Rosemarie. Accidentally she brushed against the big guy with the handlebar mustache. His eyes glazed from too much of the drink, he groped for her breast, almost automatically. She pushed him aside. His red face wrenched in anger and he grabbed again. This time he captured his prize and squeezed it brutally. His friend seized Rosemarie around the hips and dragged her to the bar between them.

All of this took less time to happen than to describe. Remember that the regulars at Jimmy's adored Rosemarie. Our two friends were already in deep trouble.

Some manic Celtic berserker ignored the presence of allies and Rosemarie's training in martial arts. No one messes with his girl, right?

This berserker snatched the two beer mugs from the bar and hurled the contents into the faces of the two molesters. Then I banged the jaw of the one who had seized Rosemarie's breast. He seemed startled by the sudden pain, so I hit him again, and he slipped slowly to the floor.

Then I turned to the second man, ready to clobber him too. By then my help was not needed. I saw the final motions of a response Rosemarie had learned from the "revered master."

The guy was sailing backward, feet off the ground, arms flailing, a cry of terror on his lips. He crashed against a table, rolled off it and tumbled to the floor.

I glanced at Rosemarie, expecting that she would be crying. But her face was hard and grim. She held her hands, outside edge forward, at forty-five-degree angles, ready to continue the fight.

Dear God, what have we done?

A maelstrom of bodies swirled around us. The two men were hauled to their feet, threatened with terrible fates if they ever came into the bar again or even if they were seen in the neighborhood, and, on wobbly legs, forcefully ejected into the chill November sunlight.

"Geez, kid," Freddy said to me, awe in his voice. "That's some girl you got there."

"I don't got her, Freddy."

"She threw the guy like he was a little kid . . . really

something. You're really something too. That other guy didn't know what hit him."

"I hope he wasn't badly hurt."

"Boy, you two are really some team. I wouldn't fool with her, kid, not if I were you."

"I have no intention, Freddy, of fooling with her."

Rosemarie was ice-cool, collected, in perfect possession of herself—just as I presumed the "revered master" had prescribed under such circumstances. She thanked her allies for their support, picked her coat up off the floor, slipped into it (with my ineffectual help), wished Wally a happy birthday, and with the aplomb of a queen empress, strolled out the door.

Followed by her jester, who was trembling like the proverbial bowl of jelly.

We crossed Woodlawn in silence. In the shelter of the shopfront at the stoplight, Rosemarie leaned against the wall and sagged.

"First time that ever happened?"

She nodded. "Like that anyway. Men make passes at pretty girls. Crude men make crude passes. They'd tell you I wanted it . . . blame it all on me. Maybe they'd be right."

"Huh?"

"I wear a tight sweater, I come into a tough bar, I joke with the men, I push my way through the crowd . . . what kind of woman does that make me?"

"I don't understand, Rosemarie . . . I mean you had as much right to be there as they did. Wally and Freddy and the gang all respect you. Pretty breasts don't make a woman a whore."

"Don't they?"

"They certainly do not. The dirt is in their minds, not in your body."

"Sweet Chucky Ducky." She patted my cheek. "You always say the right thing."

Mind you, I had my full share of lascivious thoughts about her bosom.

"The revered master would be proud of you."

"I must tell Peg," she smiled wanly, "that it really does work. . . . Now, would you walk home with me? I want to take a little nap and get to work on my paper about Plato."

We walked the three blocks to her apartment quietly. I began to realize what a fool I had made out of myself.

"I'm sorry, Rosemarie," I said at the door to her building. "I made a real fool out of myself."

"Whatever are you talking about, Chucky? You were a hero again."

"Like I always am. You didn't need me charging in like that. You were quite capable of taking care of those galoots yourself. Freddy and Wally and the guys would have protected you. I probably made things worse."

"Oh, Chucky Ducky." She grabbed my arm. "You were so funny. If the revered master hadn't taught us to concentrate at times like that I would have died laughing at you. Beer in their eyes! How wonderful!"

I laughed too, despite myself. "Yeah, I suppose it was pretty funny. But I was unnecessary. You don't need me to take care of you."

She patted my arm and released it. "Even if I didn't need you, it was nice to have you there. It's so good to know that someone will take care of you. Thank you, Chuck, thank you very much. Now I must have my little nap."

She bolted through the door and left me standing there, under the grim clouds that were scudding in from the prairies. How had I come to be cast in the "taking care" role?

It had been a dumb scene, but, as Freddy had said, we were a pretty dangerous team.

Rosemarie was not in the library on Tuesday.

That night a kid who was in my econ class had phoned me. "O'Malley? I knew you lived in Oak Park. Hey, that lovely woman you study with in Harper? Well, I was in Knight's bar until a few minutes ago. She's drinking a lot.

Shouting and arguing with people. That's not safe for a woman in that bar, know what I mean?"

"Thanks, Howard, I'll be right out."

There were no expressways in Chicago, so the ride from Oak Park to Hyde Park required forty-five minutes.

Rosemarie was behind the bar, her clothes disheveled, sound asleep and smelling like a brewery.

"I didn't know what to do with her," the soft-spoken bartender told me. "A guy said he was going to call her boyfriend, a tough little redhead, he said. That you?"

"My twin brother."

He paused and then laughed. "She's a real looker. You shouldn't let her come in this place alone."

"Ever try to argue with an Irish woman?"

He laughed again.

I woke her up, found her coat, pushed her arms into it, and dragged her back to her apartment. It was a disorderly mess—dresses, shoes, lingerie, books, notebooks tossed around. I helped her to remove her dress, dumped her into bed, and pulled the blanket over her.

"Chucky, you're an asshole," she murmured as I turned out the lights.

"At least you know who it was that took off your dress."

"A real asshole." Her voice was slurred. "Why didn't you leave me in the bar?"

"That's a very good question."

When she thanked me the next morning, she was properly contrite. I'm sure she didn't remember the use of language that was strictly forbidden in the O'Malley house.

"I'm glad I was there," I had said fervently. If I hadn't found her in the bar on Fifty-fifth, she might have been there all night or collapsed in the snow on the way home. Rosemarie needed a keeper all right, only it shouldn't be me.

"You didn't take my slip off this time." She nudged my arm.

It was the first reference she had ever made to the incident at Lake Geneva.

"Dress and shoes seemed to be enough for the occasion. Mind you, I thought you might do well with a nice warm bath!"

"You're wonderful, Chucky." She squeezed my arm this time. "Simply wonderful."

"Why, Rosemarie?"

"Why do I do things like that?"

"Yes."

"I'm not sure. I become discouraged and I don't care ... but I won't do it again. I promise."

I didn't quite believe her, but I didn't know what to say.

At our Thanksgiving dinner she was nervous and quiet—her eyes ringed in dark shadows. Had she drunk herself into oblivion again?

Moreover, our after-dinner, over-the-port confrontation with Mom and Dad was a failure, mostly because Rosemarie listened silently while I carried the ball and Peg tried to run interference for me.

They were delighted to learn that they were not running short of money as they had feared; but they didn't want to reorganize the office.

"There isn't enough room for all those people," Dad said. "Mind you, Chuck, we appreciate the analysis. At least there's one sound business head in the family."

"You could expand into the library for the time being and then build an addition in back in the spring. You *are* an architect and the house does need something in back to match the music room on the other side."

"That's true, but we'd have to get a zoning permit."

"Just like you did for the music room," Peg commented.

"It's such a *change*, dear." Mom shook her head unhappily. "All those strangers in our house."

"Two more," I said. "And they'd be in the office wing. You'd have as much privacy as before."

"I don't know; what do you think, Vangie?"

"Well, it makes economic sense." He gestured at my neat books. "As Chuck has proven. Maybe we can think about it in the summertime when we find out whether this recession is going to get worse. I'd hate to have to cut back after expanding."

"This really isn't the time to think about a change." Mom shook her head. "Is it, dear?"

Peg signaled me to lay off, wise advice.

"Well, so long as you think about it." I abandoned ship quietly. "There's no need for immediate action. You've been doing fine for almost five years this way. I only wish you could find more time to enjoy your success."

"We'll certainly think about it," Dad agreed, glad that the troubling discussion was over.

"And we're very grateful for you help, Chucky," Mom chimed in. "You're *so* smart about these money things."

"He takes pretty good pictures too," Rosemarie said glumly.

"They're superstitious," Peg whispered to me later. "Afraid that if they try something new fate will take it away from them again."

"I guess . . . Hey, what's the matter with Rosemarie?"

"She's down on herself again." Peg shrugged as though it were a minor matter. "By the way, she tells me that you are sensational in barroom brawls."

"And without help from any revered master either."

Christopher and I went to the first screening of *The Treasure of the Sierra Madre* on Friday morning, not early enough to escape half the adolescents in the city—none of whom were capable of understanding the subtle ironies of the B. Traven/John Huston classic.

At lunch at Berghoff's, over two sauerkraut sandwiches, we debated the question of who Traven really was. I held out for the theory that he was in fact Jack London, who had only pretended to die.

There was no response to such an argument—erroneous as it now turns out—other than some literary similarities, but I found it sufficiently bizarre to be amusing and to twist Christopher's logical, reasonable Teutonic mind.

"So how is your love affair with the Clancy child progressing?" he asked, raising an eyebrow.

"It is not a love affair, Christopher," I insisted. "It is rather a modest friendship, remarkably free of passion."

"Oh?"

"We enjoy each other's company. We study together and occasionally eat together and on very rare occasion attend some cultural work together. Nothing more."

"You don't expect me to believe that, do you?"

"It's true. We hold hands on occasion or extend our arms around each other. Our kisses at the end of an excursion, I could hardly call it a date, are very gentle."

"Not nearly as satisfying as your exchanges with Cordelia or Trudi?"

I figured I'd better tell the truth.

"Far more so."

"Aha!" he said triumphantly. "And you are very gentle and tender with her because you figure that's all she's ready for right now!"

"I don't want to hurt her," I pleaded.

"So speaks a man who is really in love," he insisted.

Then I told him about the bar brawl and Rosemarie's retreat from the world for two days.

"You didn't call her that night?" he asked.

"Well, I didn't think about that."

"Or the next day?"

"Uh, no."

"You didn't go over to her apartment to see if she was sick?"

"I guess not."

"Charles, even if you don't love her, wasn't that pretty thoughtless?"

"I didn't want to embarrass her, know what I mean?"

"It would have given you an opportunity to clear the air about her drinking."

"I don't want to clear the air," I said stubbornly. "If she wants to become a fall-down drunk like her mother, that's her problem not mine."

Christopher shook his head. "Sometimes I don't understand you, Charles, I really don't."

"Sometimes I don't understand myself either."

I should either expel Rosemarie from my life or assume some responsibility for our friendship. Christopher was right. Why had I not thought of calling her? Why was I so triumphant at the possibility that she had gone on another binge?

I should stay away from Harper library till the end of the quarter—only two more weeks.

Monday morning, bright and early, I was at our table waiting for her to appear.

When she came she was radiant and cheerful, bright summer sunlight in the midst of the winter's first major snowstorm.

❧ 40 ❧

We all went to the Rizzo-Sullivan wedding. It was the first time I had been in church since I was ejected from the Golden Dome. I ostentatiously refused to go to Communion.

Rosemarie was displeased.

"They'll think you and I are doing something sinful," she whispered.

"I should be so fortunate!"

"Shame on you."

I realized that my anger at the Catholic Church could not go on much longer. I would never make a good Mediterranean anticlerical.

The Irish are not very good at that sort of thing.

The wedding was a massive celebration, much to the delight of Jim's numerous family. Sal the Pal appeared in full three-piece navy blue pin-striped glory—complete, would you believe, with spats.

Monsignor Mugsy and Father Raven held their own over the murmuring congregation but only just barely.

"I hear," Rosemarie said, as she drove us out to Butterfield, "that Big Tom has done a complete turnaround. He thinks Jimmy is a wonderful guy."

We were in her car because she informed me that it was

"unthinkable" that they would let my car into the club's parking lot.

"Who did you hear that from?"

"Father Raven, whom else?"

I almost corrected her and then, after a quick review of the appropriate grammar, realized that as always she was right.

"He appreciates the irony of that change?"

"Naturally. He doesn't understand what happened, however."

"I wouldn't believe the bastard."

"Father Raven does."

That made it official.

"He wants us to be gracious and forgiving. I said I would but that I wasn't sure about you."

"Forgive him! He almost killed me!"

"Father Raven says that forgiveness is the essence of Jesus's message. He forgives us everything and so we're supposed to forgive everyone, just like Our Father says."

"You win," I said. The Lord knew well how much forgiveness I needed.

In the receiving line we were hugged and kissed by the bride and groom, both of whom insisted that we were responsible for the happy day.

They didn't know the half of it.

Big Tom shook hands warmly.

"You know, you guys were right. He is a hell of a fine guy!"

"You don't mind a dark-skinned grandchild?"

"A healthy grandchild will be all that matters."

"You'll get a bill for our services," I said.

"Don't worry," he said with a broad smile. "I'll take care of that eventually. I owe you . . . And I mean that positively."

"He didn't even ask that we tear up the letter."

"He knew we wouldn't."

In the midst of all that joy, there was sadness, heartrending sadness.

When Rosemarie drifted away with Peg for the women's room, I wandered around the vast club. In one of the small rooms, I encountered Jenny Collins. She was slumped in a chair, head and shoulders bowed. She looked like a little girl S'ter had banned from school for misbehaving.

"Where's Tim?" I asked stupidly.

She looked up. Her eyes were dry, her face twisted in anguish.

"I'm so glad to see you, Chuck . . . Tim's gone."

"Gone!"

She handed me a handwritten note on lined paper.

"Jenny, I'm leaving. I'll never come back. Forgive me. Don't wait for me. Tim."

Trembling, I sat down on the chair next to her.

"What happened, Jenny?"

"I don't know. Nothing. Everything. We had begun to love each other, I mean seriously love each other. We didn't make any plans exactly. I didn't want to push him. He was the one who talked confidently about our future. Then we got the invitations to this wedding. He seemed delighted to be my date. . . . Then I got this note in a plain envelope."

"The jerk!" I said angrily.

"Don't blame him, Chuck. He tried."

Was I to blame anyone?

"I'm sure he did. Did you talk to Dr. Berman?"

"He couldn't tell me much for ethical reasons. He only said that it was as much a surprise to him as it was to me."

"I'm so sorry, Jenny."

"Thank you, Chuck. I'll be all right. I'm the resilient type."

"I don't doubt that, Jen. One tough Irish woman."

She smiled sadly:

"My question is whether I should wait for him. What do you think?"

It didn't take me long to think about that question.

"A month or two, Jenny. No more. I'd take him at his word."

She nodded. "So would I."

I told Rosemarie only after we had left Butterfield.

I had expected her to be angry, but she was not.

"High-risk prospect, Chuck," she said softly. "Poor guy."

"Poor Jenny."

"She knew the risk she was taking. . . . It's just like the risk you're taking with me."

She would have surprised me no more if she had stuck a knife into my stomach.

"I'm no risk-taker, Rosemarie."

"The hell you're not."

❧ 41 ❧

I was indeed a risk-taker, more than I realized.

I look at a picture of Jim Clancy from an article in the business section of the *Daily News* at the end of that year. Clancy's investments in hotels in Las Vegas are described. The names of his colleagues have a suspicious First Ward look to them. The Outfit. Clancy argues that gambling is not wrong. Rather it is entertainment. And provides a tax base for "worthy projects." The picture makes him look like an Outfit killer, a gross little man who might hide in an alley waiting for a target to walk by. The eyes are the eyes of a psychopath, devoid of emotion or conscience.

But perhaps I exaggerate. Who looks good in one of these? And do I read too much of what I would later learn and of subsequent events into this picture? He is not a nice man. That does not mean that all his life he has been a man who enjoys giving pain, does it?

I put the picture back into the envelope. I still hate him. God forgive me for it. He's been dead all these years. And he probably wasn't to blame for most of what he did. He is nothing more than a short funny little man with a bald head.

He *is* funny until you examine his face. Then your heart skips a beat at what you see.

Hunger, raw, ungovernable hunger.

And hatred.

~ 42 ~

We broke up the week before Christmas.

It was a warm December day, temperature in the fifties. The snow was melting, the streets gloriously slushy, as if spring were just around the corner. One could pretend that the worst of winter was over. I suggested to Rosemarie, who had settled in her room in our house, that we walk over to Pedersen's Ice Cream Parlor on Chicago Avenue near Harlem to celebrate our first quarter at the University.

"You just want to rub it in that you got four A's and I got a B."

"Yep."

"They give you A's," she said, "because you have a reputation in the whole university for taking on faculty and getting away with it. They think you're a genius."

"Better that than they think I'm shanty Irish punk."

I had taken on a faculty member who had made fun of Catholicism and won the whole class to my side. He ended up liking me. Hence my fourth A. It was General Meade and Coach Smith all over again.

So, we drank a toast in the best malts in Chicago Land as the *Tribune* presumed to label much of the Midwest, to our future at the University.

Rosemarie seemed preoccupied. I had learned not to

press her about her problems unless she gave a hint that she wanted me to.

I had two malts. My reputation would have suffered if I settled for anything less. She let me pick up the tab, which should have been a warning that something serious was about to happen. On the way out of Pedersen's we encountered my St. Ursula classmates Leo Kelly and Jane Devlin, who I had heard were now a summer item up at Lake Geneva. Leo was a quiet kid who had left the seminary after three years and was now at Loyola University. Jane was a vivacious woman whose dark blue eyes sparkled with mischief. She was a taller and a somewhat more voluptuous version of my companion.

"Back from Germany, Chucky?" Jane began. "I hear you prevented World War Three while you were there."

"A couple of times," I said modestly.

"You haven't changed a bit," she went on. "Has he, Rosie?"

"More impossible than ever."

"Two malts today?"

"Naturally."

"Are you in school?" Leo asked.

"Not really. Rosemarie and I are both students at the University."

"Notre Dame?"

"Chicago!"

"Wow! Do you like it?"

"He faked his way into four A's this quarter."

"Same old Chucky," they said in chorus.

"You're at Loyola, Leo?" I asked.

"I graduate this year. Then four years in the Marines. You were lucky to get off with two years."

It would be much less than four years for poor Leo, who would disappear in Korea.

"He had a great time," Rosemarie informed them. "Ran he whole Constabulary Regiment over there. Even the generals asked him for advice."

They all laughed again.

Actually, generals *had* asked me for advice.

"I heard," Leo continued, "that you won a medal over there and not just a theater ribbon. Legion of Merit?"

"What's that?" Rosemarie demanded. "You never told me."

"I never told anyone, except Dad. Somehow Janey found out and told Monica who told Jimmy, but it's still a secret."

"What did you get it for?"

"Won't tell."

"Leo?" She turned to him for an explanation.

"For extraordinary service in a position of grave responsibility."

"Chucky!" the two women exclaimed. "You didn't?"

"It was all a mistake, like winning that football game."

"You have to tell us what you did," Rosemarie warned me.

I'd better tell her.

"I helped break up a black market."

"Was it dangerous?" Jane asked, wide-eyed.

"I banged up my knee, but they wouldn't give me a Purple Heart."

"How did you do that?" Rosemarie insisted.

"I was attacked by a parked car."

More laughter.

We promised each other that we would get together in the spring, before Leo went off to the Marines.

"Marines!" Rosemarie exclaimed as we walked back to the O'Malley manse. "That could be dangerous."

"He could be attacked by a parked car too."

"Silly!" She slapped my arm.

"I'd say they're in love."

"No doubt about it."

We never did get together at the lake. Leo was already on his way to Korea.

Rosemarie became silent as we sloshed through the

melting snow. The sky was clouding over again and there was a chill in the air.

"I have four things to say," she informed me.

"All right."

"First, I am sorry that I let you and Peg down on Thanksgiving when you were arguing with the good April and Uncle John. I'll make up for it."

"Okay."

"Second, you have to forgive Notre Dame and even Father Pius. You only pretend to be a hater, Chuck. But you're too sweet even to pretend. Okay?"

Now the woman was preaching to me. Women do that.

"Okay," I said doubtfully, knowing that I'd have to think about it.

"Well, at least think about it. Third, I wish you'd go back to your camera. You're going to a great photographer someday. You won't be able to escape it. You are too good and you like it too much. You'll never be an accountant, not for long anyway. I don't want to argue about it. I'm just stating a fact."

"Okay."

"Okay, what?"

"Maybe you're right. I don't think so, but maybe you are."

She sighed. She had said that she didn't want to argue about it, but of course she did. Actually, she was wrong. Or so I told myself then.

"Finally"—she took a deep breath—"I think we should stop dating."

"Why?"

"There's a chemistry between us, Chuck. When we were kids it made us fight. Now it makes us like each other. We're a good team. We make each other laugh and we know how to make other people laugh, like Leo and Jane. Sometimes we help people out like Jimmy and Monica."

"That's bad?"

"There's a sexual component to the chemistry. We play it very low-key. But it's there."

"A touch of it," I admitted.

"But mostly we really like each other, we enjoy each other's company, we have fun together. We're good dates for each other. You make me laugh all the time."

"This is bad?"

She nodded.

"Chuck, we pretend that we're not dating, that we're not really serious. The truth is that we're very close to courting."

"Huh?"

We crossed Augusta Boulevard. The north wind was blowing in our faces. We both shivered.

"Like Vince and Peg, without his social-class hang-ups."

"Shouldn't it be hangs-up?"

"Don't distract me. I'm serious."

"I can see that."

"You may be ready for courtship, Chuck. I'm not. I'm too young and I have too many things I have to resolve."

Like drinking too much.

"If you want to break up," I said slowly, "it's your call."

Twice in six months. I was on my way to being a perennial loser. Both times because women thought they were too young.

"It's not breaking up, Chucky darling. I'll still be around a lot, both here at home and out in Hyde Park. We can go out occasionally if you want. Or if I get an opera ticket. It's just that I don't think we should go out as steadily as we have been."

"Okay."

"Are you angry at me?"

"Rosemarie, how could I possibly be angry at you?"

"I realize that I must sound a lot like Cordelia."

"It's totally different."

Suddenly it was totally different. When Cordelia dumped me, I felt relieved almost at once. Now I didn't feel relieved at all. I didn't want to lose Rosemarie. I had worried about her drinking. I had halfheartedly searched for an excuse to escape from what might be a trap. Now there was a valid excuse. I didn't want to escape.

"How?" she demanded.

"I don't know. I'll have to think about it."

"It's not that I don't love you, Chuck. . . . I suppose that sounds like Cordelia."

"It doesn't."

"Sure you're not angry?"

"Why should I be angry if you're doing something that you think you have to do?"

"You're so quiet."

"I'm surprised. I have to think about it for a while. Even after I think about it, I won't be angry."

"You are really sweet, Chuck my love."

She kissed my cheek.

"She solved your problem for you, didn't she?" Christopher asked me the next day at Berghoff's as he systematically disposed of a dish of sauerkraut.

"Yep. I don't have to worry anymore about falling in love with a drunk."

"You don't sound too happy about it."

"Nope."

"Why not? Don't like a losing streak?"

"Nope."

"You're beginning to think maybe she's worth the risk?"

"Maybe."

"Think you can save her?"

"She has to save herself."

"Without any help?"

"Nope."

"Think you can get her back?"

"Maybe."

"What makes you think that?"

"She looks like her heart is breaking."

"Oh," he said softly.

Then after a moment's silence, he added, "And that gets to you?"

"Yep."

"Breaks your heart."

"Could be."

"What are you going to do?"

"I can't violate her wishes to cool it, can I?"

"Can't you?"

"I don't know."

"I guess I'm no help," Christopher sighed.

"Yes you are, Chris. You make me think."

The problem was that I did not know how to begin to think about my Rosemarie problem.

Father John Raven was not much help either.

"Do you want her, Chuck?" he asked me when I stopped by St. Ursula's rectory.

"Yes . . . No . . . I don't know."

"I have no doubt that if you want her and play your cards shrewdly enough, you can get her."

"And the drinking?"

"That has to stop, Chuck. Do you think she'd stop it for you?"

"I don't know. . . . Can she stop?"

"With your help, perhaps."

"That's not much."

"What more can I say?"

"Dad quotes Grandma O'Malley that you shouldn't marry anyone to save them, but only because it would be intolerable to live without them."

"Sound advice."

"If I can't live without her, then I should pursue her and hope and pray that we can beat the booze and her evil old man together?"

"That's one possibility."

"Big 'if.' "

"It sure is, Chuck. And a very big risk."

A foolish risk, I told myself as I trudged home in the falling snow.

It hurts more to lose her than to lose Cordelia.

But maybe it's the best outcome for both of us. Again.

❧ 43 ❧

Christmas 1949 at the crazy O'Malleys' was a mess. Even the picture of the Romany women over the fireplace didn't cheer us up. No one said anything about *The Girl with the Harp* in the library. We pretended it wasn't there.

For much of the day it was the first unhappy family Christmas I ever experienced. What's the point in being crazy unless you can celebrate it? Midnight mass in the old St. Ursula—the gym in which Rosemarie had toppled off the ladder on top of me at the May crowning when she was in eighth grade—was depressing because the new church had been scheduled to open for Christmas. It wasn't Dad's fault, but he was shame-faced when people asked him if the church would ever be finished.

"Next Christmas for sure." He would try to smile.

"Blame the contractor, not him," I would snarl at the offending parishioner.

"Hush, dear," Mom would say. "Wasn't the choir wonderful?"

Neither Peg nor I had the courage to drive home the sword: if they had reorganized the firm a year ago, they would have known that the contractor was too busy making money on a suburban development to fulfill his contractual commitments to St. Ursula.

But Mom and Dad both knew what we were thinking.

It was time that I reestablish diplomatic relations with God. In previous conversations, the Deity had not bothered to reply to me. On that particular night, He seemed ready to engage in a long conversation, though it was merely my imagination making up the responses. Maybe.

"Good evening," I began during the carol singing.

"It's morning, Christmas morning."

"I understand."

"It's nice to see you back."

"You noticed?"

"Oh yes . . . I notice everything, as you well know."

"I know."

"Rosie was right, you know."

"Rosemarie."

"I call her Rosie, okay?"

"You're the boss."

"I know."

"What was Rosie right about?"

"About hate . . . That could be a bad habit if you don't stop it now."

"I can't hate Notre Dame or Father Pius any more?"

"Nope."

"I gotta forgive them?"

"If you expect me to forgive you."

"That won't be easy."

"I didn't say it would. . . . Also, she was right about your camera. Or cameras."

Well, He didn't rub it in and say that a woman had given me each of them.

"I can't be an accountant?"

"I didn't say that. I said that she was right when she said that you have to start using them again. You know that without my having to tell you."

"I guess so."

"Okay."

"Was she right about breaking up?"

"It's about time you got to that."

"Well, was she?"

"Nope."

"Nope?"

"Nope . . . I want Rosie."

"Should God want a woman?"

"God wants everyone. I need help usually. It's your help I need with Rosie. We both love her desperately, I more than you."

"Ah."

"She's the best hint of what I'm like you'll ever encounter. You must not let her get away."

"Okay."

"That's not enough."

"I'll do whatever I can."

"That'll be enough. For the present."

"Can I receive Communion tonight?"

"Sure, why not?"

"I turned my back on you."

"You tried, but you really didn't. No one can turn their back on me."

"Won't it be a sacrilege?"

"Am I a Dominican religion teacher?"

"I hope not."

"Okay."

"Why do you sound so much like me?"

"Because I have to work with your imagination."

"You also sound a lot like Rosie."

"That's because she's always in your imagination."

Then He signed off.

"Thanks for getting me out of that place," I shouted (mentally) after Him.

I made it all up? God did sound a lot like me when I'm in a certain mood. Or like Rosie when she's in a certain mood. Excuse me, Rosemarie. Maybe I was just being honest with myself.

Anyway, I did receive Communion. When I told John Raven about our dialogue later, he laughed. "It was God all right, Chucky, even if He was talking through your imagination."

"I know that."

Then as now Catholicism messes up a lot of opportunities provided by its tradition, but midnight mass is so powerful a narrative symbol that even the most vigorously incompetent clergy can't mess it up.

It has everything—the crib scene, evergreen trees, poinsettias, carols, maybe snow on the ground, young people home from college (even in 1949), engagement rings, joyous greetings after mass. I suspect that maybe half of the Catholic tradition gets passed on at Christmas and half of that at midnight mass.

Later I would try to make up to God by doing my book *Midnight Mass,* which turned out to my publisher's surprise if not to mine to be a coffee table best-seller.

For symbol and for photographs you can't beat renewal.

Dear God, how much we needed renewal that Christmas of 1949. And how ingenious Your response was to our needs.

I was still sulking over my expulsion. And not touching my cameras.

Michael was more silent than ever. Vocation problems, I thought. Who is the girl?

Jane and Ted would not be with us at all during Christmas Day. Doctor had threatened to cut off the allowance completely if Ted left the family home at all. He said he didn't much care what Jane did because she had nothing to add to the McCormack family celebration.

Except the first grandchild, who I suspected would always be considered inferior because he had O'Malley genes in him. Or her.

Peg had not heard from Vince, the stupid son of a bitch, for two weeks and resolutely refused to discuss the matter with anyone, especially me.

Rosemarie was at mass with her father and his aged housekeeper, looking terribly unhappy.

Christmas in Bamberg had been better.

And I wondered about Trudi and worried about her and Magda and Erika.

It was not my fault she had disappeared. I had tried my best to find her.

But maybe I had been as dumb with her as Christopher said I had been with Rosemarie after the fight at Jimmy's.

We sang the carols in the music room after mass with less than our usual vigor and then gratefully escaped to our beds. I was sure that Peg's pillow would be wet with tears.

The stupid Neapolitan son of a bitch. I ought to teach him a thing or two. Trifle with my sister's affections, will he?

First, however, I would seek lessons from the revered master.

That was my pious Christmas thought as I fell asleep.

No, I think there was one other: that was the prudent caution that even with the help of the revered master I would be no match for Vince.

When I woke up in mid-morning the family was still listless and frustrated. Snow glittered on the lawn. The Christmas tree in the parlor glowed cheerfully. The candle in the window—an old Irish custom, Mom had insisted—welcomed the lonely traveler. Presents were heaped in front of the "second" tree (the one that really counted) in the music room. But our hearts were heavy.

Not so heavy that I didn't eat a breakfast fit for two people and down a quart of eggnog—unfortified by rum, I hasten to add.

"Sometimes I think the Christmases were better in the old apartment on Menard Avenue." Mom permitted herself a rare display of gloom.

"Maybe you're right," Dad agreed.

"Kids grow up," I philosophized between gulps of eggnog, "they have problems."

"Well, at least you don't, Chucky dear." Mom hugged me. "You're as steady as Gibraltar."

"He eats more," Dad laughed.

Good old steady Chucky Ducky.

"I thought Jim Clancy looked terrible at mass last night," Mom continued. "I don't see how he stands to live the way he does."

"Rosemarie looked a bit tired too," Dad agreed. "But even tired she's still gorgeous, isn't she, Chuck?"

"I didn't notice," I lied.

"Poor dear child." Mom shook her head pensively. "She's so loyal to the poor man."

Rosemarie was definitely the favorite child.

In early afternoon we adjourned to the music room for our annual festival of carols—at least Mom and Dad and I did. Michael had gone for a walk and Peg "wasn't feeling well, poor dear."

The Neapolitan sickness.

We tried "O Holy Night" and "Le Cantique du Noël"; the results were not impressive.

"It's hard to have a festival"—Mom caressed the strings of her harp—"with only three people."

Then the ghost of Christmas present arrived in the person of Rosemarie Helen Clancy, bearing a huge collection of carefully wrapped presents and enough Christmas cheer for the whole of Oak Park. Her face was flushed from the cold, her eyes sparkled with winter diamonds, her green knit dress with red trim would have made a corpse smile, her vibrant energy brought craziness back to the O'Malley clan.

Not a moment too soon.

"Stay away from the mistletoe, Chucky! I really have the Christmas spirit today!"

"I accept the warning."

I wasn't very worried. Rosemarie would kiss me only when I started the process; and that I had no intention of doing.

I would, however, as a compromise join my whiskey tenor (as I called it) with her soprano in the carol festival.

We shook the rafters. Peg recovered from her headache and joined us as the alto. Michael came in from his walk, paused at the door of the music room, saw Rosemarie's signal to come in, and added his bass to Dad's.

The crazy O'Malleys were operational again.

Then the miracles started to happen.

Ted and Jane appeared, stars in both their eyes.

"Put two extra plates on the table, April." He embraced Mom. "We're both hungry."

"We have lots, dear; and you two are eating for three."

"You sound wonderful," Jane enthused. "We could hear you on the street."

Game and set to the O'Malleys. Love–one against Doctor.

Vince was the next to join with a big present and a passionately tender kiss for Peg.

A kiss in which there was so much pain and so much sorrow and so much love that it could break your heart.

Even my fairly hardened heart.

Rosemarie started us on "Vincent the red-faced reindeer," a spontaneous parody of "Rudolph," who made his appearance that year.

"Well," said Vince, delighted as he always was when we poked mild fun at him, "he was a reindeer you could count on at the last minute."

Peg was radiantly lovely again. And my heart ached for the two of them and for love.

At supper Mom announced that "Rosemarie has found us the cutest little young man from IIT who's going to come work with us after the first of the year. And a very lovely secretary too."

Rosemarie, huh?

"He went to Leo High School," Dad chuckled. "Grew up in St. Sabina's. The South Side triumphs again."

"Naturally, dear," Mom agreed, as though doubt on that proposition was unthinkable.

At the exchange of presents after dinner, Rosemarie handed me a package that contained no surprises—elegant tennis whites and twelve rolls of Kodachrome 64.

"And I won't ever be seen again on the tennis courts with you unless you're properly dressed." Her eyes twinkled with mischief.

"What if he puts on weight?" Peg teased me.

"Chucky doesn't put on weight." Jane hugged me—for the fifth time since she and Ted had appeared.

"If he eats that second fruitcake, he might start."

"Could I get someone else"—I struggled out of my chair—"some eggnog? You can't attack a second fruitcake without eggnog."

She's behind the whole thing, I decided. She found the two kids for the office. Mom and Dad couldn't resist them. She encouraged Ted to resist Doctor. She chewed hell out of poor Vince. Matriarch-in-the-making, all right, and she's only eighteen.

And she does it so gently that only a cynic like me knows what's going on.

When all the visible presents had been distributed, there was a moment of relative peace while everyone in the music room basked in the joy of Christmas recaptured.

"I think there's something missing." I left the room. "Don't go away, anyone."

"I wonder what it is?" Jane said.

"A surprise!" Peg looked baffled. "What's happening to Chucky? He's becoming a romantic."

"Fat chance." Michael had actually opened his mouth.

I returned with a box.

"Wrapped as a present!" Jane crowed. "He really has changed!"

All my other presents had been wrapped too. I suspect that the women in my family had guessed whom this was for.

"Marshall Field's wraps presents," I grumbled. "Uh, Rosemarie, Spirit of Christmas present, I don't expect you to wear this tomorrow, but next summer it should stop traffic at Grand Beach and Skelton Park."

"For me!" She was astonished. "Oh, Chucky, how wonderful!"

She almost kissed me. She would have if I hadn't ducked back. She clawed at the wrappings and the box.

"*Oh!*" all the women in the room exclaimed in unison. "Isn't it cute!"

"That's one word for it!" Dad chortled appreciatively.

It was the sexiest tennis frock available in 1949—white with maroon trim (of course), low back, plunging neckline, the shortest of sleeves, and a skirt that foreshadowed the mini.

Beyond all right reason there was an instant demand that she put it on, a demand to which she succumbed. She bounded out of the room like a charging rhino. I quickly loaded the Kodak she had given me before I had left for Germany. She bounded back in—barefoot and devastating in my present.

I will admit I gulped. I fired away with the camera. She gave me a thumbs-up signal.

Everyone else applauded.

Rosemarie glanced around at the crazy O'Malleys and then, unaccountably, began to cry.

I found myself holding her in my arms on the love seat in the corner of music room. The rest of the family struck up "Adeste Fidelis," not necessarily appropriate for the moment. Through her tears, Rosemarie joined us.

She saves Christmas for the rest of us and then breaks down over what was after all a very minor present.

She is unbearably beautiful in it, isn't she?

And she feels like she belongs in my arms, doesn't she?

I would have to maneuver her in the direction of the mistletoe when she dried her tears.

Maybe Christopher and Father Raven and God were

right. Maybe I ought not to let her get away. Maybe some-how I could beat the drinking bouts. Maybe she *was* the closest thing to God I'd meet in all my life.

"Rosemarie," I whispered as she clung to me, "I have responses to your four points from earlier in the week."

"Oh?" She raised an eyebrow.

"They are yes, yes, yes, and no."

Note

Some will think my description of the University of Notre Dame during the postwar world is excessively harsh. However, I have vetted it with contemporaries who attended the Golden Dome during those years. Although they have fond memories for the school, they acknowledge that my description is essentially accurate. Obviously the university has undergone several transformations in the last half-century.

The English Jesuit is based on Father Martin D'Arcy, the author of a Catholic classic in that era, *The Mind and Heart of Love,* which he summarizes at the dinner with Chuck and Cordelia.